THE LONELY HEARTS BOOK CLUB

LUCY GILMORE

sourcebooks
casablanca

Published by Sourcebooks Casablanca, an imprint of Sourcebooks
P.O. Box 4410, Naperville, Illinois 60567-4410
(630) 961-3900
sourcebooks.com

Cataloging-in-Publication data is on file with the Library of Congress.

Printed and bound in the United States of America.
LSC 10 9 8 7 6 5 4 3 2

This one's for Mary. Arthur and Sloane belong
as much to you as they do to me.

"All things great are wound up with all things little."

—ANNE OF GREEN GABLES

SLOANE

1

THE DAY I MET ARTHUR MCLACHLAN was perfectly ordinary.

I woke up at my usual hour. I ate my usual bowl of oatmeal while hunched over the last few pages of my library copy of *Parable of the Sower*. I can't remember what I wore, but I'm pretty sure it was both machine washable and designed for comfort.

Everything in my closet was machine washable and designed for comfort, but not by choice. Rule number one of being a librarian: You'll leave work every day looking like you waged battle with a league of ancient scribes. Adapt early and adapt often, or your dry-cleaning bills will bury you.

When Arthur first came barreling into my life, I was in the Fiction section restocking a bunch of titles someone had moved for the sake of internet kudos. There was a new TikTok trend going around where people descended on bookstores and public libraries in order to write out sentences using titles. If you ignored the part where *I* was the one who had to put everything back where it belonged, it was kind of clever.

Looking for Alaska Where the Sidewalk Ends
We Were Liars Under the Never Sky
Are You Anybody? I Am No One

I was still chuckling over that last one when I heard the sound of an annoyed cough behind me.

"Young lady, you are blocking the way to Roman History."

Years of practice had me immediately stepping back, an apology on my lips. As I pushed my cart aside, I noticed the man was elderly, his wire glasses perched on the end of his nose and his tweed jacket sporting a pair of suede elbow patches. He walked with the aid of a gold-tipped cane that looked as though it might conceal a sword stick inside.

"Do you want me to look up a specific title for you?" I asked, since he had some way to go to reach the nonfiction shelves. "Anything by Tom Holland is good, but I find I prefer to get my history from Mary Beard. Her approach is wonderfully emotional."

He snorted. "Typical sentimental claptrap."

I blinked at him, wondering what I could have said to cause offense. "I'm…sorry?"

He tapped his cane sharply. "Emotion doesn't belong in history. Emotion belongs in maudlin childhood literature. You should know that, *Pollyanna*."

I was taken aback but not dismayed by the belligerence in his tone. Strange though it seemed, we had actual library rules about patrons like this. Soothe and disarm, that was the order of the day. Leave them in a better frame of mind than when they arrived. And never, under any circumstances, engage.

"You don't have to read anything you don't want to," I said with a careful smile. "But my name isn't Pollyanna. It's Sloane."

Instead of accepting my peace offering, Arthur tilted his head and appraised me. Something about the intelligent gray eyes behind his rims caught my attention.

"You know what I meant," he said, stabbing a finger at my cart. Sure enough, a copy of Eleanor Porter's beloved childhood tale sat on the top. One of the teens had had the audacity to pair it with John Grisham's *A Time to Kill*.

I held both books up with a laugh. "Don't blame me," I said. "It's *A Time to Kill Pollyanna*."

He looked pained.

"It's a joke," I explained. "Kids trying to make sentences out of book titles. Some of them are actually pretty good. Maybe I should try my hand at it next time I run into a patron." In an attempt to defuse the tension, I said the first title that came to mind. "*Pollyanna* is *Pleased to Meet You.*"

"Those kids are a plague on the public library system," he said, glaring. "And so, I'm starting to think, are you."

I had no response for this. Well, to be fair, I *had* one, but I knew better than to voice it aloud. One of my greatest skills in this world— some might say it was my only skill—was how good I was at being inoffensive. The trick was to look bland, act blander, and voice no opinions whatsoever. The looking bland part I had down pat, my frizzy brown hair and lightly freckled skin blending into the background so easily that I sometimes felt like a potted ficus. The acting part was easy, too. I could go for days at a time without opening my mouth to say anything but "Yes, of course" and "No, you're right," and no one seemed to think there was anything odd about it.

The opinions part was harder, but working in a public space like the Coeur d'Alene library had taught me the value of tact.

"Well?" he demanded. "Don't you have anything else to say?"

I shrugged, wishing—not for the first time—that I was more like my sister Emily. She'd have known *exactly* how to wrap a grouchy old man like this around her finger. I don't know if it was all the doctors she grew up around or just her natural charm, but she'd had a way of making even the meanest grumps do her bidding. Before she'd gotten too sick to roam the neighborhood with me, we used to visit an ice cream shop a few blocks away from our house. No matter how many fingerprints we left on the glass or how exasperated the shopkeeper got with all our requests for free samples, she always walked out of there with at least one extra scoop.

What would Emily do?

"We could probably incorporate some Roman history, if it helps," I said, thinking of the towering ice cream cones Emily used to carry home with her. She'd never been able to eat the whole thing, but that hadn't been the point. It had been the *triumph* of it she'd enjoyed. In all the years since I'd lost her, I hadn't triumphed over anything.

Or anyone. Not even myself.

Before I could think better of it, I reached for a copy of Toni Morrison's *Beloved* and held it up. "How about *Beloved Pagans and Christians*? You have to admit it's catchy."

I could have almost sworn that Arthur's nostrils flared to twice their size. "So that's how you want to play this, huh?"

I wasn't sure I wanted to play much of *anything*, but I was already in too deep at that point. There was no ice cream at the end of this particular rainbow, but I couldn't help feeling that Emily would have been proud of me all the same.

"*The Roman Triumph Of Mice and Men*?" I suggested, thinking up Roman history titles as quickly as I could. Inspiration struck, and I snapped my fingers. "Oh! I know. *I, Claudius, Journey to the End of the Night*. These are good. I should probably write them down."

Something almost like respect was starting to spark in Arthur's eyes. "You seem to know an awful lot about books on ancient Rome," he said grudgingly. "Why? Are you planning to stab someone in the back?"

This time, I didn't hesitate over my reply. "Only if he deserves it."

A sound somewhere between a bark and a laugh escaped him. "Is that your way of telling me that Caesar got what was coming to him? Is that what it says in your precious Mary Beard?"

"Not exactly," I was forced to admit.

If this conversation kept going along these lines, I was going to have to admit a lot more: namely, that I wasn't nearly as conversant with Roman history as I was letting on. As far as librarians went, I was more of a jill-of-all-trades than a deep scholar. I knew lots of random book titles and could recite the first line from almost every classic piece of literature, but I could only talk intelligently on a subject for about three minutes before my storehouse of knowledge petered out.

"Ha!" he practically shouted. "That's what I thought. You don't know anything about Caesar that isn't written in the back-cover copy somewhere."

This was the point where I should have bowed gracefully out of the conversation. I'd already broken all the rules about not antagonizing the patrons, disorganized my own library cart, and said unthinkable things to a man who was old enough to be my grandfather.

For the first time in my life, however, I didn't bow out. Strangely enough, it didn't even occur to me to try.

"That's not true," I said as I pushed the copy of *Pollyanna* back on the shelf where it belonged. "I just think that anyone who had as many enemies as Caesar did should've been more careful. If he didn't see that knife coming, that's on him. My only enemy is the copier by the south window, and even I know better than to believe it when it says the toner levels are totally fine."

That was when it happened. I wasn't a good enough writer to describe it, but it was as if Arthur decided, right then and there, that I was an adversary worth having.

"I've forgotten more about Roman history than you'll ever know," he said, pointing his cane at me.

"That's probably true," I admitted.

"And I've already read every word Mary Beard has ever written."

"That's...impressive," I said.

He didn't appear to find my return to meekness to his taste. With suddenly narrowed eyes, he added, "And when I want book recommendations from a second-rate Pollyanna who wouldn't know a good book if it landed in her lap, I'll ask for it."

This barb stung more than he realized. Finding pleasure in reading—*losing* myself in a story—was the one thing I did know.

"*The Art of Racing in the Rain*," I said.

He blinked and took a step back, as if even the title of such—what had he called it? *sentimental claptrap?*—had the power to harm him. "What did you just say to me?"

I wore a smile that was only partially faked. He couldn't have been more outraged if I'd told him we were holding a book-burning party down by the lake that made our little city famous.

"If you're looking for a book recommendation, I think you should pick up *The Art of Racing in the Rain*. It's what I suggest to all our regular patrons. I know it has a reputation for being sad, but—"

The spark in his eyes grew almost martial. "Not now. Not ever. Not if it was the only book left in the world. If I want to immerse myself in someone else's pointlessly self-indulgent drivel, I'd give in and listen to podcasts."

I kept my mouth shut. It just so happened that I loved that book. I loved podcasts, too, though that was mostly because I never cared for sitting alone in a silent apartment. There are these really fun ones of people reading classic books in a flat monotone to help you go to sleep. You haven't known true peace until you've drifted off to Proust read aloud in B-flat.

Arthur took himself off after that, muttering under his breath about Roman conquests and literary abominations and librarians who should know when to keep their uninformed opinions to themselves.

And all I could do was smile after him, feeling like I'd eaten a *dozen* scoops of ice cream.

"I can't believe you just tackled Arthur McLachlan and lived to tell the tale," a deep, rich voice said from behind me. I turned to find Mateo, my fellow librarian, watching me with a detached look of awe.

I'd always liked Mateo. Everyone did. His voice made him seem like he should be seven feet tall, but he was as slight of build and limb as I was. Add to that a boy-band swoop of inky-black hair and a willingness to laugh at everything—including himself—and it was impossible *not* to enjoy his company.

"You know who that guy is, right?" Mateo asked.

"No," I said, my brow furrowed as I watched the gold-tipped cane and elbow patches disappear into the German Philosophy section. "Should I? I've never seen him here before."

"That's because he comes first thing in the morning and only lets Octavia help him. He says everyone else here drains his brain cells by proximity." Mateo clucked his tongue. "You never open, so you've never seen him reduce the staff to terrified goo. We usually have to keep a mop handy."

I thought about that spark in the old man's eyes that only intensified when I started to push back, and shook my head. "He's not that bad. A little curmudgeonly, maybe, but—"

"Yeah, right," Mateo interrupted. "Mark Twain was a curmudgeon. Ebenezer Scrooge is a curmudgeon. Arthur McLachlan is Satan's grandfather. One time, he even managed to eke a tear or two out of Octavia. He's that bad."

"Really?"

This was a more sinister warning than Mateo realized. Of all of us on staff at the Coeur d'Alene Public Library, Octavia was the best—and the fiercest. Mateo found himself here because this was as far from working in a hospital as he could physically get, and I was here because reading was my only real life skill, but Octavia was hard-core. She'd been a librarian for more years than I'd been on this earth, and I was pretty sure she had the Dewey decimal system memorized. As in *all* of it.

You know that thing when people come into a library and ask for a blue book with weird writing on the cover? She always knew the exact book they were talking about. Without fail. Someday, I was going to grow up and *be* her.

"Take it from me, Sloane," Mateo said. He eyed me up and down, sympathy in every sweep of that gaze. "If you want to keep this job, you'll stay far away from him. He'll tear you to pieces…and worse, he'll enjoy every second of it."

———

Mateo's words turned out to be truer than he knew.

Not the part about me keeping my job—my post as a librarian meant everything to me—but about Arthur's single-handed determination to reduce *me* to a puddle of goo. For the next few weeks, he waged a campaign that Caesar himself would have been proud to call his own.

"Good morning, Sloane," he said the day after our first meeting. I was so surprised to see him again—and in that same elbow-patched tweed jacket—that I almost dropped all five pounds of the *Cryptonomicon* I was shelving. "Any more painfully obvious historians you'd like to suggest I read today?"

Mateo squeaked and hid himself behind the nearest computer kiosk, but I wasn't about to let Arthur win so easily. Especially since I had the Neal Stephenson to protect me.

"No, but they just put out a new list of Reese Witherspoon's summer book club picks. I'd be happy to put a hold on anything that catches your fancy."

Arthur's eyes goggled so hard that I was afraid he might have popped a blood vessel. "Never say those words to me again, young lady."

"What?" I returned brightly. My second-rate Pollyanna charm was on high, but only because I felt sure he'd be disappointed in anything less. "Reese Witherspoon? Or book club? I hope it's not the latter. I've always wanted to start a reading group for the library, but I've never been able to convince Octavia to allocate the resources."

"Good for her. I knew there was a reason I liked that woman."

I tilted my head and pretended to consider him. "If I grabbed you a volunteer application, do you think you might like to help me get one going? We could meet over cups of hot cocoa and explore John Green's backlist together."

"Balderdash!"

From then on, Arthur showed up to the library every day at the same time. Ten thirty on the dot, an exact half hour after I clocked in for the day. The precision of it wasn't lost on me—or on Mateo, who always scurried away the moment he caught sight of his nemesis.

"I talked to that boss of yours, by the way," Arthur said as he thumped past me, his cane making pointed jabs at the blue-carpeted floor. "I warned her that if you try to start a book club, I'll write a letter to the mayor and have this whole place shut down. I can, you know."

"For shame, Mr. McLachlan," I said. I set down the pile of recycled paper I'd been sorting through and smiled sweetly at him. "Banning books from the public? What's next? Shutting down food pantries? Painting the rainbows out of the sky?"

"Harrumph!"

By the time two months had passed, Arthur McLachlan had all but lost his power over me. When Mateo saw him coming, he still ran for cover—or, in this particular instance, ducked behind me—but not me. I was made of sterner stuff...and more to the point, I actually *liked* him.

"If you sacrifice me to that old goat, so help me, I'll be out of commission for the rest of the day," Mateo warned on this particular day. He clutched at me with his hot, ink-stained hands. They were likely to leave marks on my favorite yellow skirt, but that wasn't anything new.

"I'm pretty sure goats are historically the ones who get sacrificed."

"You know what I mean," he said. "I don't know how you can stand the way he talks to you. You usually cry every time Octavia calls you to her office. Sometimes more than once."

That was true, but only because Octavia rarely had anything good to tell me. Today's meeting had been a rough one in particular, and my eyes were still stinging with the tears I'd only just managed to keep in check.

"I can't explain it," I said—and I couldn't. Not in a way that Mateo would understand, anyway. I barely understood it myself. All I knew was that I'd come to enjoy these little scuffles with Arthur McLachlan. His tongue was sharp and his tone acid, but he never cut any deeper than I could handle. And he always seemed happy to see me, even if nothing would prevail upon him to let it show.

"It's another beautiful day, don't you think?" I called to him as soon as Mateo maneuvered an exit strategy. "The sun is shining, the spines of all your favorite depressing German philosophy books are uncracked, and there are half a dozen librarians hiding from you in dark corners."

"Not today, Sloane," Arthur said. His head was down as he moved past me, an unfamiliar shuffle in his step.

I paused in the middle of the aisle, my hand poised over the copy of *A Little Princess* I'd planned to slip into his stack of books when he wasn't looking. I'd spent most of last week coming up with a plan diabolical enough to take our strange friendship to the next level, and this had seemed like the best approach.

"What's wrong?" I asked. "Is something the matter?"

"I just want to browse the library in peace today, if that's all right with you," he snapped, genuine anger in his voice for once. "I don't need you following me around like a lost child, questioning my every move."

"I didn't mean to… That is, I'm not…" My voice trailed off as a hot, pricking sensation rushed to the surface of my skin. This was the point where I'd normally tuck tail and run, but something made me stand my ground. It might have been my confusion at the sudden one-eighty in Arthur's personality, but I suspect it had more to do with the expression on his face. Instead of looking outraged or amused, like he usually did, he looked…*bleak*.

"I'm sorry if you're not having a good day," I said. Then, because I couldn't seem to leave it alone, I added, "If it helps, mine hasn't been too great, either."

My confession seemed to revive him. "Why? What's the matter with you?" He turned and peered critically at me over the top of his wire-rimmed glasses. "What happened?"

"Nothing catastrophic," I said, recalling my meeting with Octavia with a wince. "There was an opening on the library acquisition board and I didn't get it, that's all. My boss told me about it just a few minutes ago."

He narrowed one eye and looked me over, a frown curling his upper lip. "Why didn't you get it?"

I offered him a shrug in lieu of a reply. The truth—that Octavia thought I was too sentimental for the post—wasn't something a man like Arthur McLachlan would understand. Everything on his personal reading list revolved around the themes of deep dark gloom. Heavy philosophical tomes, war biographies, the occasional bloodcurdling thriller… Unless a book reinforced everything that was awful about humanity, he wasn't interested.

"You might as well tell me what you did," he grumbled, leaning heavily on his cane. I suspected it wasn't good for him to spend too much time standing, but I knew better than to help him to a chair.

"What is it? You dog-eared all the westerns? Mispronounced a word during story time?"

I couldn't help laughing at these mock atrocities. "How dare you, Mr. McLachlan," I teased. "What kind of a person do you think I am?"

That playful essay into camaraderie was a mistake. In this mood, with his brow darkening and a cloud starting to form over his head, Arthur seemed every bit as scary as Mateo had originally painted him to be.

"Well?" he asked. "What's wrong with you?"

I splayed my hands in a last-ditch effort to keep things light. "How long do you have?"

To my surprise, he barked out a short, sharp laugh. At least I *thought* it was a laugh. There was a phlegmy undertone to it that didn't sound great. "Let me guess," he said. "They're looking for someone less naive."

I blinked, taken aback by the accuracy of his remark. Octavia hadn't used the word *naive*, but she'd come perilously near it.

"I'm not naive," I said, my protest sounding feeble even to my own ears. "I know things. I read things." In the back of my mind, I knew I wasn't saying this to Arthur McLachlan so much as to the world at large, but it didn't matter. He believed me as much as they did.

"Ha!" He turned and started picking his way toward the back of the library. "Reading about life isn't the same as living it. The things you know about the real world would fit in the tip of this cane."

"That's not true," I protested to his retreating back. And it wasn't—it really wasn't. I might not have crossed off all the items on my bucket list, but I was only twenty-seven. I had a college degree. I was gainfully employed and engaged to be married. Those things might not have signified much to a cantankerous old grump, but they meant something to me.

They *mattered*.

He paused long enough to turn back to me. "When was the last time you cared about something so much you couldn't eat?" he demanded. "Or sleep? When have you ever felt the fire of life burn so bright that it hurts? When did you ever bother to *fight* for something you loved?"

When I didn't answer right away, Arthur snorted. "That's what I thought. You may as well leave me be. I'm not your pet or your library mascot, and I'm *definitely* not your friend."

All the air seemed to leave my lungs at once.

"I see you for what you are," he added. "It's written on you as clearly as the words on a page."

I shouldn't have asked. No good ever came from standing in front of someone and asking for the truth, especially when a person like me was doing the asking.

I did it anyway.

"And what am I?"

"An echo with nothing and no one to call her own," Arthur announced without preamble. Clearly, this was a subject he'd given some thought to. "A friendly facade. An empty smile. A scared little girl without an opinion of your own, latching on to other people's bigger and brighter lives because you're not willing to fully live your own."

It was difficult to say which one of us was more shocked when he was done. His face had gone gray, his shoulders shaking in a way that seemed to zap him of all his strength. I felt sure I looked the same.

"Arthur," I gasped.

"Don't—" he began, but I had no way of knowing what he wanted. *Don't start crying? Don't take me at my word? Don't expect to ever see me in this library again?* Before the words could be uttered, Mateo had an arm around my shoulders and was guiding me to safety, leaving Arthur to stand there, glowering at nothing, until he turned and stomped away.

"I warned you what would happen," Mateo said as he led me away.

"His kind is always the same—only happy when everyone around him is miserable. My mom is like that. Yours, too, now that I think about it."

"Your mom is the nicest woman on the planet," I said, but there was no point. Especially since Mateo was determined to see me safely tucked away behind the reference desk, out of harm's—and Arthur's—way. "And I'm not upset about Arthur. Not really. It's been a long day, that's all."

"Sloane, you've been here less than an hour."

"Fine. It's been a long week."

"It's literally Monday."

I heaved a sigh and let myself sink to the decrepit swivel chair saved for whichever unfortunate librarian was posted at this desk. I didn't know why all the worst furniture found its way to the Reference section, but it did. In the age of digital dictionaries and Wikipedia, people just didn't respect research like they used to.

"This is about the library acquisition seat, isn't it?" Mateo prodded. "Your meeting with Octavia this morning? That's what's really bothering you?"

If news traveled fast in a small town, it went at lightning speed inside a public library. "You heard about that?"

His wry smile was all the answer I needed. "If it means that much to you, I'll turn it down," he said. "Lincoln was planning on taking me out to celebrate tonight, but—"

"Wait." I blinked up at Mateo through annoyingly damp eyes. "You got the job?"

Mateo beamed and nodded, his whole body lighting up.

"Can you believe it? *Me.* Octavia says I have a good eye for what's inside people's hearts."

If that was even a little bit true, he'd have realized how much his words were causing *my* heart to seize and give up right then and there. I'd been vying for that job for years, putting in the hours and biding my time until a spot finally opened up. A seat on the acquisition board wasn't just an opportunity to help select which books the library would buy and shelve, though that was how most people saw it. For me, it represented a way to shape the community, to dig deep and have a real impact on people's lives. *The protector of wisdom. The good fairy of literature.* I got goose bumps just thinking about it.

If I was being perfectly honest, it was also a way to prove I was more than just an echo, but I wasn't going to admit that out loud. Not while Arthur McLachlan was still somewhere inside this building.

"Mateo, that's fantastic!" I wiped my eyes and threw my arms around his neck. Like me, he smelled of printer toner and antibacterial hand wash. "You should have told me straightaway. Congratulations."

From the way he started to vibrate all over, I could tell he was pleased. "You mean it? I was a little afraid to tell you, but it was going to get out eventually. You should come celebrate with me and Lincoln tonight. He's always happy to see you."

Mateo spoke nothing more than the truth. His boyfriend, Lincoln, *was* always happy to see me, but that was because he was always happy to see everyone. He was a chainsaw artist, which meant he spent most of his days in his shop transforming logs into decorative woodland creatures—and he had the good-natured humor to match.

"Thanks, but I have a dinner thing with Brett's family after work," I said. "His sisters will be there. *All* his sisters."

Relief rendered Mateo even more sympathetic than before. "No wonder you let that grouchy old man get to you. The last time you had dinner with your in-laws-to-be, you were prostrate for three days." He grinned and handed me a stack of magazines that needed to be processed before they were tossed out. "Your problem, Sloane, is that you only seem to attract people with personalities that are stronger than yours."

His words, though well-meaning, still hit hard. I could almost picture Arthur sitting on his shoulder and prodding the words out of him with his cane.

"Do I?" I managed, faking a smile. I was good at that. I'd certainly had enough practice.

Mateo winked. "Then again, I have yet to meet anyone who doesn't make you run screaming for the hills. You might just have to start getting used to it."

2

—

B ELIEVE IT OR NOT, I WAS engaged to be married to a doctor. Technically, he was a chiropractor, but I'd learned early on in our relationship that to introduce him as anything but Dr. Marcowitz would end in a battle royal.

Since one of my primary life goals was to avoid battles of all kinds—especially royal ones—I was quick to adapt. He might not have been a medical doctor, but he had a doctorate degree, and that was more than enough for him. Brett was really good at things like that. No one treated him with anything but respect for the simple reason that he refused to accept less.

"Brett says he's going to be late." His mother, a round woman with round cheeks, a round helmet of steely hair, and a will almost as strong as his, hung up the phone with a sigh. "You'll have to get used to this sort of thing, Sloane, if you're going to be a doctor's wife."

I ignored the undercurrent of this remark—if, if, *if*—and smiled. "I'm sure his patients appreciate his dedication. What's keeping him?"

She blinked at me, her eyes making a mockery of round shapes everywhere. It was as if she'd been stamped out of an elementary school textbook.

The rectangle was a rectangle. The square was a square. Francine Marcowitz was a circle. These were the things we knew to be true.

"What's wrong is that my son is the best chiropractor within a three-hundred-mile radius."

See? *Radius.* She even talked in circles. It was uncanny.

"He's in high demand these days. At this rate, we'll be lucky to see him at the wedding." She laughed as though she'd just made a grand joke. Jabbing her elbow—the only part of her that didn't fit the spherical mold that shaped her—into her husband's side, she added, "Wouldn't that be something, Stan? A runaway groom? Have you ever heard of such a thing?"

Stan hadn't, of course. Whenever his wife and daughters gathered under one roof for any appreciable amount of time, he didn't hear anything. If he hadn't been a real estate attorney, he'd have made an amazing diplomat.

"Leave the poor girl alone," he muttered with an apologetic grimace at me. "Can't you see you're embarrassing her?"

"It's fine," I was quick to say—and it wasn't a lie. Not really. Any embarrassment I might have felt was smothered under the ebullience of affection that poured through these doors every time I opened them. "I'm proud of Brett for having his priorities straight. We'll have a nice, cozy dinner without him."

That one *was* a lie. Although the two-story colonial home had all the markings of coziness, the people who filled it were anything but. Brett's three sisters were…not round. They were tall, like him. They were confident, like him. They also had a weird, unrelenting regard for me that I couldn't quite work out.

Like him.

"*There* you are, Sloane, and looking so delicious I could eat you up." The oldest of his sisters, another always-call-me-doctor dentist named Tabitha, breezed through the door and took my face between her hands. "Where do you find clothes like these? Librarians 'R' Us?"

Since I hadn't yet had time to change out of the ink-stained yellow skirt, this remark wasn't unwarranted.

"Hi, Tabitha," I replied as Brett's two other sisters entered the living room in her wake. The Marcowitzes were fans of a formal cocktail hour before dinner, which meant we'd squeeze together drinking gin and tonics until there was so much liquid in my stomach I wouldn't be able to eat. I nodded at them both. "Hey, Rachel. Hey, Rosalie."

"I'm Rosalie," the one on the right said. She nodded at the woman next to her. "You can always tell Rachel by her split ends."

Rachel, who was twenty-two and the spitting image of Rosalie, the elder by ten months, stuck out her tongue. Even though I'd seen the baby pictures and could confirm that these two weren't technically twins, I found it impossible to tell them apart. They both had beautiful gray wide-set eyes, lips like a cupid's bow, and gleaming mahogany hair that I was almost positive had never seen a split end.

Like I said, there was an unmistakable family resemblance. Brett was equally attractive. Sometimes I looked at him and wondered how such a beautiful human being wanted anything to do with me.

"You're just jealous because my hair grows two times as fast as yours." Rachel flung herself onto the couch next to me and twined her fingers through mine. "I have good news, Sloane. I talked to my friends from the team, and they're in."

I blinked at her. Trying to balance my gin and tonic while my free hand was being squeezed in her rugby-playing grip was difficult, but I knew better than to pull free. In a game of tug-of-war with my limbs, the Marcowitz sisters would win every time.

"They're in what?" I asked.

"Oh, good!" Tabitha didn't bother to acknowledge my question. "With the three of us and Cousin Dora, that'll make, what, eight?"

"If Brett ends up with two best men, like he's threatening, we'll need one more, but we can work on that. Didn't you say you had a friend in mind, Sloane? Someone at the library who might do in a pinch?"

Understanding hit me almost as hard as the gin on my empty stomach. "Oh. You're talking about my bridesmaids."

"We can buy an extra dress now and have it tailored as we get closer to October. That won't be a problem, will it, Mom?" Rosalie was the one to ask this question. Of all the Marcowitzes, she was the one who terrified me the most. She was only twenty-three and already ran three separate hotel franchises. I felt pretty sure she wouldn't stop until she ran them all.

"I don't see why not. Have it added to the order. In for a penny, in for a pound."

Stan's brow lowered. "A pound of flesh, you mean. *Mine.*"

"Don't be such a cheapskate." Francine swatted her husband on the arm. "It's your only son's wedding. If we want the numbers to be even, we have to do it this way. You know Brett has a large social circle."

I tried not to look as uncomfortable as this conversation made me feel. When Brett first proposed, I'd imagined a quiet beachside ceremony. Unobtrusive and simple, over with as quickly as possible. The idea of me standing in front of a huge church in a puffy white gown—*me*, of all people—was preposterous. Public speaking had never been my forte. Neither had puffy gowns, not even when I was five years old and could pull off the look. In my childhood photos, I was the kid in *Little House on the Prairie* cosplay.

Unfortunately, Brett's social circle *was* large. There were far too many people who cared about him—myself included—for some shabby ceremony on the sand.

"This is really nice of you guys, but—"

"But nothing." Rachel finally released my fingers. It took a second for the blood to get flowing again, but when it did, it came with a vengeance. "You're family now, Sloane. It's the least we can do."

"Hear, hear!" cried Tabitha.

"I'll drink to that," said Rosalie.

"Once the license is signed, there's no going back," came the murmur of Francine's low voice.

After an outburst like that, I didn't have the heart to tell them that not only was Mateo more of a work acquaintance than a friend, but he wasn't likely to sign on for wearing one of the bridesmaid dresses. Their dismay when I'd confessed that I was without *one* close friend to fill the role of bridesmaid, let alone eight, was matched only by their kindness in offering to fill the ranks for me.

I defied anyone to find better prospective in-laws than these people. Honestly. A few crushed hand bones were a small price to pay for this level of acceptance without question.

"I'm sure I can find someone before the wedding," I said, my voice only slightly wobbly. Since we had a good four months before I was set to officially join the Marcowitz clan, I didn't despair of making good on the promise.

After all, making friends was something regular people did all the time. They joined sports leagues and had chance encounters at coffee shops. They commiserated in line at the DMV and got squished together in the back seat of an Uber Pool.

I didn't mind that I was approaching the end of my third decade and didn't have a Diana Barry or Charlotte Lucas to call my own. I really didn't. I had her once, but then I lost her.

Once upon a time had always been good enough for me.

3

THE DIFFERENCE BETWEEN THE WARM, IF overwhelming, welcome I received at the Marcowitz house and the reception at my
own ancestral home a few days later was like something out of a twisted
fairy tale.

In this case, "ancestral" was an exaggeration. My parents had only
lived in their condo for a few years, having sold off everything they
could carry—and quite a few things they couldn't—to purchase a lakeside two-bedroom with access to a rooftop terrace and a twenty-four-
hour gym. To the best of my knowledge, they'd never once set foot on
the terrace, and I wasn't convinced that the gym actually existed, but
once they made a decision, they stuck to it.

"Oh, good. You're here. Will you please tell your father that I need
him to call a plumber to look at the garbage disposal?" My mom swung
open the door and wandered away, her feet shaking the floor with every
step. Even though she wasn't a large woman, basically an older and
slightly faded version of me, she walked as though she carried the entire
weight of the world on her shoulders.

"And can you tell your mother that I'm not a phone service? If she
wants a plumber, she can call one herself." Belatedly, my dad planted a
kiss on my forehead. His round black glasses slipped down his nose and
stayed there. "Hey, pumpkin. You look tired."

"Honestly, James. You can't tell a woman that."

"If that woman is my daughter, I can tell her anything I want."

"How would you like it if she breezed through the door and mentioned that your hair plugs are starting to fall out?"

"They're not falling out. Nature is healing. It's all part of the process."

A thump from the back wall indicated that the couple from next door wasn't enjoying this argument any more than I was. I usually avoided participating in my parents' fights by taking the coward's way out—namely, by not visiting unless it was an emergency or one of them had plans to be out.

This situation didn't technically qualify as an emergency, but after my dinner with the Marcowitzes, it was close enough to count.

"Do you still have that box of my college stuff?" I asked before either could pick up the threads again. "I remember where you kept it at the old house, but I wasn't sure if you tossed it out or put it in storage when you moved."

"College stuff?" My mom turned back, her heavy tread retracing her steps from before. Since the day my parents started living here, there had been three different owners in the condo directly underneath theirs. At this point, it could only be rented out as an Airbnb. The listing had it down as "haunted" so the people staying there were charmed instead of appalled by all the shouting and pictures randomly shaking off the walls. "What do you want that for? You're not thinking about going back for *another* degree, are you? Oh God. Did Brett break it off? I told you it wouldn't last, James. Remember? I said there was no way a man like that—"

I drew a deep breath and dug my nails into my palms, reminding myself that my mother's remarks were only a slightly more caustic version of Francine Marcowitz's—and that I'd said the same thing to my own reflection more times past counting.

"I was hoping to find the contact info for a few of my old

roommates, that's all," I said in as bright a tone as I could muster. "I'm short on bridesmaids. I didn't have any luck finding them on Facebook, but I might be able to track them down the old-fashioned way."

"Short on bridesmaids?" my mom echoed just as my dad said, "If we still have any of that junk, it'll be down in storage."

"Sloane, please tell your father that your cherished childhood memories aren't *junk*."

"Sloane, please tell your mother that if she has something to say, she can say it to my face."

That was all my parents needed to set themselves off again. Snagging the storage key that hung by the door, I slipped away, my relief heavily outweighing my guilt. That might sound callous, but there was no use in my sticking around to bear the brunt of their resentment for each other. I'd learned that lesson the hard way.

Till death do us part had a much more ominous ring when you'd witnessed it in action for as long as I had. Most people—*normal* people—would have filed for divorce a long time ago, but we Parkers had never been good at living alone. Like animals boarding the ark, we spent our lives moving in pairs. Grandma and Grandpa. Mom and Dad. Sloane and Emily.

And then just Sloane.

It wouldn't have been so bad if I'd had a piece of my parents to ease the sting of my solitary state, but I didn't. No part of them—their arguments or affection, their concern or their curiosity—was mine to hold. They were too wrapped up in each other to care about me. It was touching, in a way, these two people who lived and breathed and fought together, who every day enacted their own broken version of a happy ending.

See, that was the thing they never told you about happily ever after. Sometimes, there was no happy. Other times, there was no forever. Only the *after* remained. I knew that better than anyone. The *after* was what I'd been living for the majority of my life, and it wasn't even close to the fairy-tale promise I was fed as a kid. Literature was full of lies like that.

Tennyson's "'Tis better to have loved and lost than never to have loved at all"? *False.*

Dostoyevsky's "The darker the night, the brighter the stars"? *Nope.*

Even J. K. Rowling didn't manage to get it right. "Those we love never truly leave us, Harry. There are things that death cannot touch." *Not even close, J.K. You're wrong about so many things.*

It was why I felt so determined to hunt down a spare bridesmaid even if it killed me—which, if the shattering of a vase from behind the door was any indication, it very well might.

"I *will* marry Dr. Brett Marcowitz," I said aloud, the words giving me the strength I needed to make it down the hallway to press the elevator button for the basement. "Ours *will* be the perfect wedding. We *will* live in quiet, peaceful accord every day of our lives."

And if a certain grouchy someone with wire-rimmed glasses, a gold-tipped cane, and a hole where his heart should be thought that made me naive, so be it. Other people could have their big and bright lives.

I could make do with much less.

———

I barely managed to get my key in the special basement access slot before the elevator started moving down, called by someone on the floor below. As soon as I gave the key a quick click to the right, the doors slid back open and I was joined by a tall, broad-shouldered man who made my parents look like the Cleavers. He radiated simmering annoyance in a way that had my back up and my instincts on high alert.

"Five," he said as the doors closed us in. Scowling, he added, "I can't take this another minute."

"Oh, um, I already turned the key."

"What key?"

I held up the offending item. "The one that takes us on a straight shot to the basement."

"What?" He whirled and started pushing elevator buttons at random, but none of them lit up. "Can't you make it stop?"

I shook my head and pressed against the wall of the elevator, my hands behind my back. Something about my posture—meek, small, and only trying to make myself smaller—forced the man to take a deep breath and wipe the scowl from his face.

"Sorry. I didn't mean to scare you," he said as he scrubbed a hand over his jaw, which bore just enough scruff to make a scratching sound. "It's the people who live in the condo above where I'm staying. I've never heard so much noise in my life. I was heading up to ask them to stop."

Even with the milder expression, there was something about the man that made me hesitate to expand my presence. He was around my age and dressed in a rough, understated way, but I could tell right away that he was the kind of person who couldn't enter a room without changing it.

Mateo was like that. The Marcowitzes, too. It was one of those attributes that fascinated and repelled me in equal measures. Under no circumstances did I want to attract that kind of attention, but I couldn't help wondering what it must be like. To be so present in the world, so much a part of it, that it had no choice but to shift and make room for you. I was the sort who slid in like a lizard darting into the water, determined not to make a ripple.

This man, with his heavy brow and his dark brown hair worn too long, a nose that looked as if it had been broken more than once, made ripples.

"It won't do you any good," I managed as the elevator lurched to a halt on the bottom floor. The doors opened to allow a blast of damp, musty air that smelled like what it was—the haze of unwanted belongings. "They won't stop. The noise, I mean. You're talking about 512, right?"

The man's hand shot out and held the elevator doors open above my head. He glanced down at me, a look of scrutiny sparking his deep-set brown eyes. Something about that spark felt familiar, but I couldn't pinpoint why. "You know them?"

"Everyone in this building knows them," I said. It wasn't a lie, so my conscience allowed it to slide. "Why do you think your Airbnb was so cheap?"

"*Ghosts*," he muttered and released the doors.

My heart thumped in unexpected alarm when he stepped out and followed me into the basement. I wasn't sure why he was sticking around to chat, but I'd read enough thrillers that my imagination—overactive on the best of days—immediately came up with a pretty convincing story-line. There were several good hiding places down here, and the man didn't seem notice when I slipped my key between my fingers with the pointy side poking out, but I still didn't like my odds.

"You don't believe in ghosts?" I asked, since it seemed like the most logical response.

He laughed, a short, barking sound that was almost as familiar as that flash in his eyes. "Of course not. What I *do* believe is that people who live in a communal building should at least try to keep it down. I think they're throwing plates now."

That didn't surprise me. My parents had never physically hurt each other, but they enjoyed the act of destruction too much to give up on the threat of it. It was why I didn't like loud noises. Or thunder. Or being trapped in a basement with a man who looked like an act of destruction was just another day on the books for him, too.

"They'll stop eventually," I promised.

"That's what they all say."

Since the man showed no signs of leaving me to my business, I started backing slowly away. My heel thumped against an empty box, and I faltered.

That was when he noticed me—I mean, *really* noticed me—for the first time. A little nervous and a lot shy, a key pointing outward from my fist. He took one look at me and uttered a low curse that would have done Arthur McLachlan proud.

It was on the tip of my tongue to apologize, but he didn't stick around long enough for me to form the words. With an abruptness that left me dizzy, he turned on his heel and returned to the elevator. It swallowed him in one quick bite, leaving me all alone and with far more adrenaline than I knew what to do with.

"O-kay then," I said, relieved and feeling *silly* for being relieved, hoping the sound of my own voice would inject some normalcy into the scene. It didn't, but I'd never been one to give up a lost cause. "I'd say that went well."

I hesitated, half expecting a reply, but there was no sound down here. It was just me and my echoing footsteps. Me and the rattling of the storage cage door swinging open. Me and the thump of the dusty boxes that contained everything I used to be.

It didn't take long to find what I was looking for. My parents may have had a messy relationship, but they were scrupulously tidy when it came to every other aspect of their lives. My own apartment was a disaster of dirty laundry, dishes, and far more knickknacks than any person under the age of eighty should own. Brett hated it, and had mentioned on more than one occasion that my hoarding couldn't continue after our marriage, but I didn't know how to explain to him that I *needed* the upheaval of mess all around me.

That upheaval meant I was living. Not *well*, obviously, and not in any way that would spark envy among home renovation enthusiasts, but enough so that some evidence of my existence remained. Even the smallest, most insignificant Roman housewife got to leave her shards of pottery behind.

The box of my college belongings was smaller than I remembered and composed primarily of old, battered textbooks and sweatshirts emblazoned with the University of Washington logo. Back in those days, I'd lived on a diet of my dorm room, my headphones, and all the dead-white-guy classics I could stomach. I'd partied with the likes of Sylvia Plath and dressed myself in Miss Havisham's splendor. I *had* hung out with a few real, living friends, which was why I was so happy to discover my old address book wedged in the bottom of the box, but I'd have been lying if I said I'd spent half as much time with them as I had the inhabitants of East Egg.

That was when I spotted it.

At first, I thought the flash of purple was a trick of the overhead fluorescent lights, but my fist closed around the brooch before I knew what I was doing. The gleaming bronze setting and rich amethyst-colored stone made it seem like it should be a heavy, burdensome thing, but I knew for a fact that the bronze was just twelve layers of metallic Sharpie over plastic and the stone a paste gem that was starting to cloud with age.

"Hey, Emily," I said as I sank to my knees and stared at the brooch.

Like my large, intimidating friend from the elevator, I didn't believe in ghosts. I'd tried—I really had. I'd booked myself overnight stays in several haunted hotels, walked through every single graveyard in Coeur d'Alene well past midnight, and even attended a séance that ended up being a sales pitch for a set of pots and pans that promised to "last your entire lifetime...and beyond." None of them had brought me any closer to the afterlife—or to the person I most wanted to see there.

Still. That didn't stop me from trying to reach out. It was like I said—when it came to lost causes, Saint Jude and I were in a neck-and-neck race to see who would end up on top.

"I thought Mom and Dad threw this old thing away years ago." I turned the brooch over to find that the clasp still worked, albeit with a slight bend to the pin. I lifted it to the fluttering collar of my floral blouse and stabbed it through. The silk would never be the same after that, and even the small weight of that plastic setting tugged at my neckline, but I didn't care.

"'A perfectly elegant brooch,'" I said, fingering the edges with a smile. "'What I used to think diamonds were like. Long ago, before I had ever seen a diamond.'"

As I quoted the words aloud, I could feel myself slipping into the light British accent that both Emily and I used to adopt whenever we'd enacted a scene from *Anne of Green Gables*. I wasn't sure where we got the idea, except that somewhere in our youthful brains we'd decided that all events that had taken place before the 1950s were somehow British in origin.

We'd loved this stupid old brooch. In fact, we'd loved the entire Prince Edward Island community—nosy neighbors, closed-minded old ladies, and all.

"You'll see, Sloane," Emily had said late at night when we'd been hiding under the covers with a book and a flashlight, our eyes bleary from lack of sleep. It had been against the doctor's orders, but some childhood rites of passage never wavered, even when you were living with a ticking time bomb in your chest. "Someday, we'll get out of here and find a place just like Green Gables. A place where—*THUMP*—everyone takes care of—*CRASH*—everyone else and no one—*HOW COULD YOU*—gets mad."

I'd believed her, then. It had been easy enough to do, our feet warm from the pockets of air, the dog-eared pages of the library book bearing witness to how many times we'd checked it out. With Emily's arms around me and her broken heartbeat keeping time with mine, nothing in the world was as terrible as it seemed. But then daytime came—and with it, reality. Emily had always been good at ignoring the signs of emotional upheaval that lay scattered all over the living room floor the next morning. I was...not.

I left the brooch pinned to my blouse, allowing it to knock gently against my sternum as I packed the rest of the things inside the box and returned it to its rightful place. The sensation wasn't the same as my sister's gentle, erratic heartbeat lulling me to sleep, but it was close.

As close as I'd been able to get in this lifetime, anyway.

With the address book tucked firmly under one arm, I locked up the storage bin and headed back toward the elevator. Now that I had a concrete plan of action, I felt better about my chances of landing a bridesmaid. People loved weddings—or at least they loved the *idea* of them, which amounted to the same thing. Someone from my collegiate days was sure to crave the romance of—

"Don't scream."

The address book fell from my armpit as I jumped back from the elevator, the scream trapped in my throat per the large man's command. I'd always been exceptional at following directions; I was basically a kidnapper's dream come true.

"It's not what you think. I'm not here to hurt you." He leapt to his feet with his hands up. It was meant to be a soothing gesture, but that only counted when the person doing it didn't have fists the size of small hams.

"Have you been sitting in there the whole time?" I asked. My voice only sounded hysterical on the downbeat, so that was something. "On the elevator floor?"

"I think I need your key to get out of here," he said by way of answer. "I pushed all the buttons. Even the emergency ones. The elevator won't move."

When I didn't do more than stand there, my mouth at half cock, he swallowed and took a step back.

"You don't have to ride up with me. I just need you to use your key so I can get one of these…blasted buttons to work."

He said the word *blasted* as if it tasted foreign on his tongue. That was when I noticed his posture. It was that of a man prepared to flee at the first sound of a harsh word—not because he feared me, but because he was trying desperately to ensure that *I* didn't fear *him*.

"Blasted?" I echoed.

"Gosh-darned? Son of a biscuit?" A tinge of red touched his cheeks. "I'm sorry. I'm not very good at this. What can I do to convince you I'm not a murderer?"

I didn't tell him that he'd already done it, mostly because talking with strangers wasn't something I excelled at. Especially not strangers who would rather lock themselves inside an elevator than scare an unwitting librarian with sentiment where her common sense should be.

"You should've said something," I said as I brushed gently past him into the awaiting elevator. "I've been down here for twenty minutes."

"Twenty-five, by my count." Instead of joining me, he reached down and scooped up my address book. Holding it out, he added, "I would've looked for a stairwell, but I didn't want you to think I was lurking around the basement."

I accepted the address book and tilted my head in a gesture for him to join me. He did, but with an exaggerated step that carried him to the opposite side of the elevator, where he hunched himself into the corner. I noticed him noticing my brooch, but neither one of us mentioned it.

"Which floor?" I asked politely as I turned the key. When he didn't answer right away, I pressed the button for the fourth floor, which would take him back to his Airbnb. "I don't recommend you confront the people in 512. It won't end the way you're hoping."

"I wasn't going to *confront* them," he said, but with another of those tinges of red, this one creeping up toward his ears. I thought, but didn't say, that the next time he wanted to make a woman feel less like he was going to murder her and hide her body inside a storage bin, all he needed to do was blush like that. "I was going to ask them politely to stop."

"That won't end the way you want it to, either." The elevator lurched as it reached its destination. "They're not bad people. They just…"

I let my voice trail off, uncertain of what I want to say. Actually, that was a lie. I knew *exactly* what I wanted to say. The words had been building up inside me for decades. Two decades, in fact, twenty long years in which I'd been forced to bear their emotions all by myself.

"They're unhappy. Miserable. So wrapped up in their mutual antipathy that they don't take any notice of the world around them." I smiled and held the door open, gesturing for the man to step out. Only the knowledge that he was a temporary guest—that after a visit like this one, he wasn't likely to book a return stay—kept my mouth moving. "You could spend a lifetime trying to break through to them, but it wouldn't make any difference. You don't matter. You never have, and you never will."

"That's…weirdly specific."

There was no chance to explain myself further. The doors were already starting to close. "I'll talk to them for you, but if you want my advice, you're better off staying at a hotel," I said.

And as far from this place as possible.

4

—

I DIDN'T NOTICE THE TIME UNTIL OCTAVIA poked me on the shoulder with a pencil and ordered me to take a lunch break.

"Go. Eat. Breathe some fresh air." She drew the pencil down the line of my white blouse. White was always a risk, but this particular top was my favorite, floaty and ethereal even after several hours of hard wear. It looked quite nice with the amethyst brooch I'd pinned to the lapel. Ever since my essay into the condo's basement, I hadn't been able to take it off. I hadn't gotten up the nerve to contact any of my old college friends, either, but that part went without saying.

"You know what?" Octavia continued. "You should bring me back something with chocolate in it. Preferably of the cake variety."

I glanced up from the printer I was trying to unjam. "You want cake? What time is it?"

"Half past twelve and well past time for you to eat lunch." Octavia's face lit up in a grin. "Oooh, you should go to that bakery across the street. Here—I'll get my purse."

I stood still as she bustled away, hearing rather than seeing her go. Octavia was a woman of textures, most of which came from the layers of clothing that crackled as she walked. I'd suffered many an electric shock from touching her without first grounding myself.

"Twelve thirty…" I echoed blankly. "Twelve thirty."

It wasn't until I looked up at the clock that the importance of the time sank in.

"Where's Mr. McLachlan?" My glance skimmed the entire top floor of the library, no chair left untouched. "Why isn't he here yet?"

I wasn't sure why I felt such a quick spasm of alarm. Considering how cruel he'd been to me the last time we spoke, I'd been dreading our next meeting. Mateo thought I should pointedly ignore him, but I wasn't sure I could. Did you ignore the car barreling down the road to run you over? Did you ignore the bear growling at you from across the forest floor?

Of course not. If you knew what was good for you, you tucked and rolled.

"All I have is a fifty." Octavia flapped the bill at me, heedless of how conspicuous it was to throw large bills around a public library. "You might as well pick up a whole cake. We can put it in the break room to boost morale."

What she meant, but was too tactful to say, was that it could sit in the break room to boost *my* morale. I'd always been partial to eating my feelings.

"Did you see Mr. McLachlan come in today? Or at all this week?" I asked, refusing to take the bill. If I was going to eat an entire pity cake, I'd buy it with my own money. I did have some standards. "I was busy with that virtual author meet and greet this morning and didn't notice. And I was doing the new software training every day before that, so I wouldn't have noticed if he was here or not."

"Huh." Octavia stopped and dropped her hand, her rustling coming to an abrupt end. The curve of her bright fuchsia smile flattened. She almost always offset her rich, dark skin with lipsticks that I wouldn't even dare to look at, let alone buy. "Now that you mention it, I haven't seen him for several days. That's odd."

"I hope this isn't about our confrontation," I said, once again glancing around the library to see if I missed anything. An abandoned jacket thrown over a chair, for example, or a cane lying mysteriously in a corner. I'd been on a cozy-mystery kick lately, so I knew better than anyone what had to have happened when a cane was found abandoned. That was an undeniable murder clue. "Do you think I hurt his feelings? Did I scare him away for good?"

From the way Octavia's lips quivered, it was obvious that Mateo had given her the full rundown on our battle—and that popular opinion said I wasn't the one who'd emerged victorious.

"Let's not jump to conclusions, shall we?" she suggested. "He probably took a few days off to go shopping or went on vacation. I'm sure he'll be back soon."

I shook my head, unable to accept these excuses. Arthur McLachlan wore the same elbow-patched jacket every day, regardless of the weather, and his shoes always bore the fresh polish of a man who intended to make them last for decades. Shopping was the last thing he spent his time on. And as for vacation...well. All I had was a gut feeling, but that gut feeling said Arthur wasn't a man who enjoyed sunshine and tropical drinks on the sand.

"Sloane, no. I absolutely forbid it."

I blinked, startled to find Octavia glaring at me with the full force of her thirty years of library experience—and with a few more years of life experience thrown in for good measure.

"What are you talking about? I didn't say anything."

"It's against library policy. It's against *my* policy. Go buy us a cake and then get to work setting up the ornithology display." She shoved the bill into my front pocket. "I'll even let you pick which books to face out."

This was a much bigger concession than it sounded like. Choosing which books to put title-side-out was a treat she didn't extend very often. Not to me, anyway.

"But I wasn't going to do anything," I protested.

"Get me an iced latte with the change, please," she said by way of answer. She glanced over her shoulder and added, "Extra ice."

As she walked away, the crinkle of her shirt and the swish of her nylons trailing off into the distance, I realized she was right. I *was* going to say something, and I *was* going to do something, and no number of iced lattes was going to stop me.

Waiting only until her attention was distracted by someone's screeched warning that the bathroom was flooding—again—I dashed behind the checkout counter and logged into the nearest computer. I didn't need her to remind me of the rules and regulations or to point out that some lines weren't meant to be crossed.

Of all the lines Octavia had drawn—and there were quite a few—patron privacy was the one she'd put down in permanent ink. Especially when it came to a man like Arthur McLachlan, who eschewed every offer of help and turned up his nose at every smile. According to her, libraries were the final bastions of the civilized world, the one place left in society where you could spend time but not money. People came here to learn, yes, but they also came to hide. Our job was to let them.

What she didn't realize, however, was that the ritual Arthur and I had begun over two months ago had been forged in steel and carried out like a genuine military campaign. Ever since our first clash, Arthur had never failed to appear at his usual time, ready for battle. For him to miss not just *one* day but several...

I remembered, then. The phlegmy cough I hadn't quite trusted. The shuffle in his step. That new and different look on his face—that look of terrible, bleak nothing.

I knew that nothing. I'd *felt* that nothing. On particularly rough days, birthdays and anniversaries, those cold mornings when I awoke from Emily-fueled dreams to find my sister just as gone as always, that nothing came back all over again.

I *knew* I should leave Arthur alone. I felt *sure* there was a perfectly good explanation for his absence.

His address popped up on the screen before I could second-guess myself.

"I'm only going to peek in on him," I said aloud as I jotted the address down on a slip of paper. "Just to make sure he's all right. What Octavia doesn't know won't hurt her."

"Oh yes, it will. And it'll hurt you a heck of a lot more."

I turned to find Octavia standing with a plunger in her hand and a look of stern foreboding on her face. How she snuck up on me, when every step she took was like the warning rattle of a snake, was beyond me.

Thrusting the plunger at me, she gave a single curt nod. "That's it. No chocolate cake for you. Sloane, you *know* the rules."

I gulped as I accepted the plunger. "Yes, but—"

"Yes but nothing. For once in your life, please keep your focus—and your emotion—where it belongs. Both stalls are in need of your attention, which is more than I can say for a man who won't appreciate you barging into his private home on a whim."

"You want me to save my emotions for a plugged toilet?"

She didn't find this amusing, but her expression wasn't unkind. If anything it was *too* kind. *I understand you*, that expression said. *I know all your weaknesses, and that's no mean feat given how many of them there are.*

"Considering the state of the bathroom when I left it, yes," she said and gestured for me to go. "Both you—and the plumbing—need the workout."

———

"You haven't touched your dinner."

Brett picked up a roll from the basket in the center of the table and lavishly buttered it. Placing it on the edge of my plate, he nodded encouragingly for me to eat. I brought the roll to my mouth, but small nibbles were all I could manage.

"Sorry." I dropped the sourdough with a sigh. "I'm not hungry."

"That's it. Get my kit. Call the ambulance. Put the morgue on hold. This is the end as we know it. Sloane Parker is passing on carbs."

I managed a small smile, but it was a weak attempt, even for me.

"Look, Sloane. I've already apologized for missing dinner with my family. I know it was last-minute, and you hate being left alone with them, but—"

I slipped my hand over his and shook my head. "That's not it. They were great. Really."

"Were they badgering you again about your bridesmaids? I told them to stop pushing, but you know how my mother is."

"Loving? Supportive? Invested in your life's happiness?" My smile was a little less forced that time. Francine Marcowitz was a force to be reckoned with, but I'd have taken a dozen of her over my own mother any day. "I promise it has nothing to do with your family."

"Then what is it?" He eyed me narrowly. "Why do you look like someone just burned your favorite book?"

I gasped in mock outrage, but Brett wasn't fooled.

"It's that library thing, isn't it?" he prodded. "The promotion you weren't qualified for?"

His words hit me hard, but they were irrefutable, so I went ahead and absorbed them. I'd only been to Brett's chiropractic office as a visitor rather than a patient, but I imagined this was the same way he got to the bottom of everyone's ills. Relentless kindness tinged around the edges with condescension.

"What would you do if a patient missed an appointment?" I asked. Before he could answer the obvious way—by asking his receptionist to reschedule—I added, "I'm not talking about any patient. I mean one who's getting on in years. Who doesn't have anyone living at home. Who might have gotten sick or fallen down the stairs, and doesn't even have a cat to send for help."

"Cats wouldn't be any use in that sort of situation," he said, regarding me through serious eyes. "You might be able to affix some sort of message to its collar, but there's no relying on them to carry it to the right place. And that's assuming they can even get outside, which—"

A laugh escaped before I could stop it. Brett sat back, looking affronted, and stabbed at his chicken parmesan.

"I don't see what's so funny. You asked."

"I know. I'm sorry." As a peace offering, I shoved half the roll in my mouth. "I just meant that he's not likely to have any pets to care for. I doubt he's loved a living thing a day in his life. But if you were worried about his safety, what would you do? Wait and see what happens? Call the police? Drive by his house once or twice to see if there are signs of life inside?"

I held my breath over that last one, waiting to hear Brett's advice. He had a handy way of reducing the biggest problems to straightforward solutions, even if they were usually chiropractic in nature.

"That depends," Brett said carefully. "When was his last spinal alignment?"

It was too much. Choking on my mouthful of bread, I laughed so hard that the entire table shook. Our glasses of wine—Chianti, slightly chilled—rattled until I started to feel light-headed. Brett took one look at me and yanked my glass to his side of the table.

"Honestly, Sloane. How many of these have you had?"

"I'm sorry," I said again. "It's not the wine, I promise. I'm just really worried about a patron from work. It's making me giddy."

Brett heaved a sigh of long-suffering—and of understanding. That second one was important to note. With the exception of my sister—and possibly Arthur McLachlan—no one had ever understood me as well as this man. I didn't have a single flaw that he hadn't pulled out, examined, and preapproved as acceptable in his future life partner. "We'd better get the check, then."

"Wait. What?" My eyes flew up to meet his.

"I know you, my love. Better than you know yourself. You aren't going to get any sleep tonight until you drive by his house and see for sure that all is well."

———

When we drove by Arthur McLachlan's house, it was to find that all was well.

His neighborhood wasn't what I'd expected. As much as I hated making assumptions about people based on their appearance, his neatly pressed slacks and leather cross-bag denoted a man of impeccable standards. I'd always pictured him living on one of those neat, tidy streets where everyone's house was made of the same red brick and no one was allowed to have a garden gnome taller than eight and a half inches.

The road we pulled onto was paved, but just barely, several deeply rutted pits indicating that no one with any influence in local government had lived here in quite some time. A few yards boasted colorful flower beds, but just as many were covered with the nodding heads of blowsy dandelions.

"See, Sloane?" Brett pulled his car, a Tesla so quiet that a kitten purred louder than it did, to a halt in front of the house. "Everything looks fine."

"What are you doing?" Even though the windows were tinted and dusk had started to fall, I ducked my head so that no passerby would be able to identify me. I wasn't sure if it was Octavia's wrath or Arthur's I feared more, but the quake was in my heart either way. "You can't stop directly in front of the house you're staking out. Haven't you read *any* spy books?"

Brett chuckled but didn't move the car. "There's nothing illegal about parking on a city street. We have every right to be here."

That may have been true according to the laws of north Idaho, but it didn't make me feel any better about being caught idling in the street. I didn't argue with him, however. One thing all librarians excelled at was time management. Getting Brett to accept that there were *some* places it was better not to be the center of attention would take more time than I had to give.

From my crouched vantage point, I couldn't make out as many of the details as I'd have liked, but the lights appeared to be on inside the clapboard house, and I could see a shadow of someone moving around inside.

"Happy now?" Brett asked. "You can't ask for better proof of life than that."

He was right. Light and movement and what sounded an awful lot like Doris Day emanating from the front room were all signs that Arthur McLachlan was inside, living his best life. In fact, it was one of the most welcoming houses on the whole block, which was what really alarmed me. Nothing about that man had ever been welcoming before.

The Body Snatchers. The Stepford Wives. The Host.

I'd read the books. I knew what was happening. Body hijacking was a real problem in the literary world.

"Something's not right," I said, reaching for my seat belt. "I'm going in."

"Sloane, don't—" Brett began, but there was no chance for him to finish. No sooner had I gotten myself unbuckled than a loud knock on my window scared a scream out of me.

I twisted to find myself facing a strange woman wearing a smile so wide it practically touched her ears on either side. It wasn't an unattractive smile—and she wasn't an unattractive woman—but something about the way she gestured for me to roll down the window put me on my guard.

"Hey-ho!" she called as soon as I cracked the window. "Are you lost?"

"Lost?" I echoed.

"Oh, are you an Uber? I'm sorry. It's just that we don't get many cars like this on our street."

Something about the woman's overt friendliness caused me to relax my guard. Well, that and the fact that Brett was seated next to me. He was neither as large nor as intimidating as the man from the elevator, but I trusted him to keep me safe.

"It's a Tesla," he informed her unnecessarily. "Model S."

I took another moment to breathe deeply and examine the woman. She was older than I'd first thought, with a good fifteen or twenty years on me, but it was obvious she'd rather not draw attention to that fact. Her too-blond-to-be-real hair was piled in a messy bun on top of her head, her body swathed from head to toe in expensive athletic gear that didn't look as though it had been put to use anytime recently.

"My ex is always talking about getting one of these, but I doubt he'll pull the trigger. Metaphorically, I mean. He doesn't actually shoot people." She took her lower lip between her teeth. Laughing nervously, she added, "Well, he did that one time, but it was an accident. He was playing a bachelor party."

Both Brett and I blinked bewilderedly at the woman, but she didn't seem to notice. Thrusting her head further into the car, she swept the interior with an appraiser's eye.

"So does this mean you aren't Uber?"

"No, we're not," I said, fighting the urge to cast Brett an accusing glance. *This* was why you didn't park directly in front of the house you were staking. For a man with all the answers, Brett was sometimes wholly lacking in questions.

"Oh! Then you must be friends of Arthur's." Her voice dropped to a conspiratorial whisper. "The poor lamb. You should have seen how many ambulances they had out for him. Three. Well, two and a fire truck. They had to restrain him to get him on the stretcher, and the racket he made while they did... Hoo boy. You never heard anything like it. Have you come to check on him?"

"Yes," I said, just as Brett set his jaw with a firm "No."

The playful tones of Doris Day were suddenly masked by a loud and angry male shout. All three of us turned toward the house. A crash and a thump were followed almost immediately by the shattering of glass.

Not even Brett could sit still after that. His chivalry was of the order that waited until it was *certain* of disaster before he swooped in. Once it kicked in, however, he was a force to be reckoned with. One time, I watched him plunge into a freezing-cold river to save a teenager floating helplessly by. He could have avoided a lot of trouble if he'd allowed me to call for help the second I'd spotted that speck bobbing along the rapid current, but he hadn't wanted to intrude on what might have been a pleasure cruise down the Spokane River in February.

The newspapers had heralded him as a local hero for months after that. Witnesses called it a superhuman feat. The teen's family found it nothing short of a miracle.

No one had asked me for a quote.

Switching off the car, Brett prepared to leap to the rescue. He'd have been halfway across the street, too, only the woman called out to stop him before he got the door open. "No. Wait. I wouldn't just yet."

She seemed more curious than alarmed, so as was the case that day at the river, I forced myself to sit still and watch as events unfolded.

Unfolded was a mild term for what happened next. Unfolding implied intent and caution, an effort to keep things intact. I should have known better than to assume anything Arthur McLachlan did would happen so mildly.

The front door swung open. A youngish woman in pink scrubs appeared in the doorway, her whole body braced as if for war.

"When I *want* someone to rearrange my modernist literature collection, I'll ask them to," Arthur's voice sounded from inside. "Or better yet, I'll throw the books in a pile out back and burn them. After the way you mishandled them, that's what I'll have to do anyway."

The woman wasn't about to take this lying down. "They're a *fire hazard*, you miserable old crow. I could lose my job if I leave them there."

"Congratulations. You just lost your job anyway."

The door slammed shut, the windows rattling as though the whole house shared Arthur's rage.

"Oh dear," the woman at the car window murmured. "She's the second one today."

"The second what?" Brett asked.

I was no expert, but I had the answer ready. "Nurse," I said. I looked to the woman for confirmation. "That's what she is, right? A nurse hired to take care of him?"

She nodded. "The first nurse was so upset that his brother had to come pick him up. Some of the things he said to poor Mr. McLachlan… I have a teenage daughter, and I didn't know what half the words meant. That's when you know it's bad."

"Sloane, don't." Brett put out a hand to prevent me from stepping out of the car. "He won't thank you for it."

"How do you know what I'm going to do?" I demanded. That marked the second time this had happened to me today—someone anticipating my thoughts before they managed to settle in my brain— and I wasn't sure how I felt about it. I was as much a creature of habit as the next neurotic overthinker, but I liked to think there were some surprises in me yet.

"Because it's the same thing you always do," he said. He rolled his eyes toward the woman and smiled in a way that was meant to charm and reassure in equal proportions. "She can't help herself. She thinks everyone can be fixed with some tea and a nice chat about literary analysis."

"I wasn't going to make him tea," I protested. "And I stopped trying to talk to Arthur about anything literary weeks ago. He always manages to bring everything back to Schopenhauer."

Both the woman and Brett blinked at me, so I didn't bother explaining. The bleakness of German realism was a conversation we'd have to save for another day.

"Will they send over another nurse?" I asked instead, trying not to sound as anxious as I felt. Medical professionals always brought out that feeling in me. No matter how much time passed, I couldn't see a pair of scrubs without reverting back to a helpless little girl unable to do anything but hold her sister's hand while the needle went in. "To replace that one?"

"Of course," Brett said.

"They don't have any other choice," the woman said over the top of him. She lowered her voice and added, "The only way they let him out of the hospital in the first place was by making him sign up for in-home care."

It was obvious from Brett's look of relief that this was the clincher to an argument neither of us was willing to have.

"Did you want me to let him know you two stopped by?" the woman asked. She cast a quick, anxious glance at the house and gulped. "I'm sure I can pop in later, when his temper has cooled a little..."

I shook my head, but not before taking her hand in my own and pressing it warmly. "Thank you, but no. I'll come by another time to check on him."

The woman returned the pressure so intensely that I feared my fingers might crack. "You do that, hon. He's lucky to have a friend like you looking out for him. That's what you are, right? Not a... grandchild?"

If I'd have been sitting in the car by myself, I might have lied. A grandchild had much more of a right to be here than an overly intrusive stranger from the library, and the last thing I wanted was for this woman to think I was deranged.

But Brett was faultlessly truthful, which meant I was, too—yet another reason why aligning my life with his was such a good idea. He kept me levelheaded and honest, prevented me from barging into houses in the twilight to make a nuisance of myself.

"I'm more of an acquaintance," I said. "Arthur McLachlan doesn't strike me as the sort of man to have friends."

The woman curled her lips, understanding in every line of that smile. "You can sure say that again."

5

___

WAITED ONLY UNTIL BRETT'S CAR WAS out of sight of my apartment before changing my clothes.

Now that I'd enjoyed one unsuccessful attempt at espionage, I didn't intend to make the same mistakes a second time. I layered a black T-shirt over a pair of capri-length black slacks—the only ones I owned—hoping that my tall black socks would make up for the lack of inches at the hem. A dark-gray sweater that I made myself (and thus boasted several large holes in the knit) and a black beret completed the ensemble.

The end result wasn't as dashing as I'd hoped, but black was the one color I didn't own much of. I always felt like an impostor when I wore it, a stranger in my own skin. People who wore black were important. Thoughtful. *Worldly.*

As Octavia and Arthur McLachlan would have been sure to point out, I was none of those things.

Fortunately, my car was a lot more nondescript than Brett's. It was a dark-blue Kia, and not one of the nicer kinds. No one would think to look twice at it—something I was banking on as I shoved a few granola bars in my purse and headed out into the night.

I wasn't sure what compelled me to return to Arthur's street, my car creeping along with the lights off until I reached a house a few doors down from his, but I suspected it had to do with the promise

I'd made that nice lady. If I was the closest thing to a friend Arthur McLachlan had, then he needed all the help he could get.

Brett would have been the first to say that I was being ridiculous. And Octavia…well. She'd probably fire me on the spot—and with good reason. What I was doing right now technically qualified as stalking.

I didn't regret my decision. All the lights in Arthur's house were off—a likely outcome of it being well past ten o'clock, but also a cause for minor concern. I didn't see a nurse's vehicle parked anywhere. Chances were they'd send a new one in the morning, but it seemed like a good idea to stick around until one got here. I didn't want him to spend the whole night alone.

If I were to take a microscope or one of Brett's digital X-rays to my motivations in coming over here, I knew I wouldn't like what I found. There was little enough I could do for Arthur from this distance. I wasn't his relative or even a close friend, and as had been pointed out to me ad nauseam, he was the last man on earth who'd appreciate a ministering angel at his door.

"Good thing I don't plan on ministering, then," I muttered as I settled in with a thermos of coffee and a book to keep me company.

All I was going to do was keep watch. For two months, Arthur had been the timepiece to my day—a thing I'd looked forward to and anticipated, a thing I'd *enjoyed*. That might not seem like much to most people, but I knew better.

Sometimes, the only thing you could give a person was a companion to lie under the covers with them and read late into the night.

For now, it would have to be enough.

———

"Here. I brought you a breakfast sandwich."

The sound of a woman's voice at my window startled a scream out of me. It also sent my book—a small-town cozy mystery with recipes at the end of every chapter—to the floor of my car, where the half-empty thermos had already spilled across the mat.

"Oh dear. You were sleeping, weren't you?"

Dazed, I swiped at the drool sliding down the side of my face and blinked up through the window. I'd cracked it a little after midnight in hopes that the fresh, bracing air would clear my head, but that plan had obviously failed. Instead of keeping a vigilant watch on my quarry, I'd fallen into a deep, dreamless sleep that appeared to have left a kink in my neck.

"Sorry. I'm an early riser, so I don't always pay attention to the hour." The woman from yesterday—once again dressed as though she was about to head to an upscale yoga studio—smiled at me. "I'm a night owl too, so I noticed how late it was when you got here. I have a sausage biscuit or a vegan avocado smash. There's nothing gluten-free in the house, but I can always run to the market if you're celiac or anything like that. Are you?"

My bemusement upon awakening in a strange place under a strange woman's watchful eye didn't abate. "Am I celiac?" I echoed blankly.

"It's hard to keep track these days, isn't it?" She waved the two paper-wrapped sandwiches at me. "Well? What'll it be? I can eat whichever one you don't want."

The wafting scent of breakfast meat under my nose worked wonders in bringing clarity. "Um, the sausage sounds great."

"Oh good." Instead of handing me the sandwich, she bustled around to the passenger side door and let herself in. "I was hoping you'd be a carnivore. Bacon is a gift from the gods, and we should treat it with the respect it deserves." She raised her sandwich to mine and touched them together in what I recognized as a toast. "Cheers. I'm Maisey, by the way. Maisey Phillips. I didn't catch your name yesterday—or of that gorgeous hunk of man you were with. Is he your boyfriend?"

I delayed my response by taking a bite of the breakfast sandwich, which was every bit as delicious as it smelled. The meat was hot and salty, the homemade biscuit pulled straight from the oven. Since the clock on my dashboard flashed the time as seven twenty-two, I guessed Maisey had been up well before the sun.

"It's good, right?" She sighed happily. "I was going to take one to the other guy keeping an eye on Arthur's place, but he didn't show up today. I hope he's all right. It can't be easy, being forced to watch your loved one suffer from across the street."

There was so much to unpack about this statement that I almost choked.

"There's someone else watching the house?" I asked.

"Oh yeah. He's been coming and going all week. For a while there, I thought he was some kind of security guard for the staffing company. To protect the nurses." She rolled her shoulder in a half shrug. "They never did send another one after you left, by the way. I think they gave up."

The breakfast sandwich joined my book and the coffee on the floor of the car.

"Wait. Mr. McLachlan's in there all alone? *Still?*"

She cast a nervous glance at the front porch. "Um, yes? Unless that other guy finally got up the nerve to go in. I haven't seen anyone pull up."

I was out of the car before I knew it. My black clothes were rumpled with sleep, and I didn't even want to guess as to the state of my hair, but I was carried along by a power that was well outside of my control.

Images of Arthur McLachlan flashed through my mind, each one more alarming than the last. Passed out on his bed, his legs hanging over the edge. Crumpled in a heap at the foot of the stairs, his cane well out of reach. Crawling slowly toward the door, desperate for someone to come to his aid before it was too late.

That last one accounted for why I climbed up the steps and pulled open the door without knocking. I'd always been useless in emergencies for this very reason; instead of keeping a cool distance and appraising the situation for what it was, I let my imagination—and yes, okay, my *emotion*—run wild. In this instance, it ran right into Arthur McLachlan's house without regard for how intrusive I was being.

The moment I swung open the door, it was to find myself facing a toppling heap of books that went flying across the parquet entryway. I had no doubt that if I were to scoop a few of them up, they'd have revealed themselves to be the modernist fire hazard that had caused the last nurse's flight from this house.

"Mr. McLachlan?" I called, tentative at first. "Mr. McLachlan, are you in here?"

When I didn't get an answer except for the ticking of an ancient timepiece that sat mounted, askew, above the fireplace, I became more frantic.

"Mr. McLachlan... Arthur. Arthur, please say something. I don't know where—"

I cut myself off as I ran into yet another stack of books. The huge, dusty tomes were stacked near the foot of the stairs. As they went flying, I realized that several of them were acting *as* the stairs themselves. The bottom step had long since been eaten away by termites or mildew or both, leaving a scraggy hole plugged by—what else?—Arthur's old standby, Schopenhauer.

"Seriously?" I said as I kick the books into a more seemly pile. My sympathies, which had been roused in Arthur's favor, were starting to strongly lean toward the nurse. "What happens if someone has to come down these steps at night?"

That was when I heard it. At first, I thought it was the groaning of a house falling apart under the weight of its extensive and poorly organized library, but it took a decidedly human turn. A human *and* irritated turn.

"Arthur?" I called again, peeking my head around a corner.

A low, muttered curse that I knew all too well greeted my ears. It was the curse of an incredibly erudite man. I'd have recognized it anywhere.

"I'm coming in," I said to the oak-paneled door that seemed to be the source of the noise. There was no handle, just a metal panel where the knob should have been, so I pushed my way through. "I hope you're decent."

Technically speaking, Arthur McLachlan *was* decent—and by that I meant all his requisite body parts were covered. To anyone with a brain in her head and a heart in her chest, however, he was a wreck. A bloodstained, blood-spattered wreck who looked as though the first strong breeze would send him toppling over.

"You poor thing." I rushed forward. In the library, Arthur McLachlan had always seemed like a solid man, his frame carried along not so much by strength but by decades of practice and an ironclad will. Inside this pink-wallpapered kitchen, one hand clutching the sink and his knees starting to buckle underneath him, I felt as though I towered over him. "Let's get you into a chair. Is there someone I can call? A nurse? A friend? 911?"

That last suggestion imbued Arthur with the strength he'd been hitherto lacking. With a withering stare, he straightened to a standing position and waved a hand at me.

It was a mistake for a lot of reasons, not the least of which was the fact that the waving hand was the source of all that blood. And I, already deemed useless in emergencies, felt myself starting to falter.

"I don't need an ambulance, you fool. Or a chair. What I want is—"

"Pressure, some antibiotic, and probably a stitch or two. But superglue will work in a pinch. You'd be surprised how many of my daughter's childhood wounds I sealed up that way." The sound of Maisey's bright, unfaltering voice from the doorway brought so much relief that *my* knees were the ones in danger of buckling. "Why don't you help Arthur to the table, and I'll go grab my first aid kit."

"If I wanted your help, I'd ask for it," Arthur muttered, but I noticed he didn't eschew the offer of a first aid kit. Seizing the opportunity, I pulled out a chair and gently guided him down into it, careful to keep my eyes averted from the wound on his finger. A quick glance at a cutting board on the counter, where a few jagged slices of apples and a knife looked like a horror movie gone right, was enough to set the scene. The way he lurched as he lowered himself to the chair told the rest.

"Hold tight," Maisey said as she handed me a wad of paper towels. "I'll be right back."

The door swung to a close somewhere behind me, but I didn't take my eyes from Arthur's face as I stanched the bleeding. He looked... unwell. I was no medical expert, but the library staff was required to get a CPR certification every year. His heavy, rattling breathing and the way his eyes didn't quite fix on anything weren't good signs.

"Typical," Arthur muttered as I continued applying pressure to his wound. "I can't go one day without running into you. Everywhere I turn, you're right there, trying to get me to read a romance novel."

"Um, it's been a few more days than that," I said, really starting to worry. If he was losing track of time on top of everything else, then he was in a much worse state than I'd imagined. "And when have I ever suggested a romance novel to you?"

His head started to droop.

Since I had no idea how long it was going to take Maisey to track down her superglue—or if that was even going to save this man from passing out in my arms—I did the only thing I could think of to revive him.

"Of course, it wouldn't kill you to pick up something with a love story in it. *Wuthering Heights*, maybe, or anything by Nicholas Sparks. People love Nicholas Sparks."

His harrumph of outrage started to restore the color to his face, so I kept going.

"Me? Now, I prefer my romance to have a true happily ever after. Give me Nora Roberts and Beverly Jenkins or give me death. I think you'd like Jenkins. She's got a real flair for love scenes."

"Now, see here." Arthur's head snapped up, his eyes glittering as they struggled to focus on mine. "I don't need you to tell me about *romance*."

"Is this where you remind me that my life has no value outside of the library? That my naivete and—what was it?—Pollyanna outlook make it impossible for me to understand how the real world works?"

"I never said that."

"For all you know, I'm a romance author on the side." I did my best to maintain a calm facade. Arthur was coming around now, I felt sure of it. In this man, the spittle starting to collect in the corners of his mouth was as sure a sign of life as any. "Maybe I write erotica. Maybe it wins awards."

"Don't you dare talk to me about erotica, young lady."

"Why? Does it hurt your maidenly principles?"

His snort was half outrage, half triumph. "Please. My generation grew up on the likes of Henry Miller and the Marquis de Sade. You don't know erotica until you've read—"

"Feeling better already?" Maisey's entrance interrupted Arthur before he got to the good part—which was a shame, because I was genuinely interested in his thoughts on the father of sadism. Then again, that first aid kit under Maisey's arm was a welcome sight. "That's good, because you aren't going to like this next part. Why don't you hold his good hand, honey, and I'll see to this wound?"

I didn't hold Arthur's good hand, for the primary reason that he yanked it far away from me and shoved it behind his back.

"It's the blasted medication they have me on," he said as Maisey snapped open the kit and got to work. Neither Arthur nor I dared to watch. "It makes everything in the house spin."

"What medication is that?" I asked in what I hope was a casually disinterested voice.

He chuffed out an indignant breath. "Some stupid diuretic. It doesn't matter. Like I told those nurses they keep sending over, I'll be fine in a few days. If I've made it this long without tying myself to a hospital bed, I'll last a few more years. Arthur McLachlan doesn't go down easily."

I believed him. No one could accuse this man of being *easy.*

His next words proved it. "Make sure you don't glue my fingers together, you silly woman. I know where you live."

This was such a nonsensical and weirdly endearing thing to say that I couldn't help smiling. I also noticed that the fight was starting to ebb out of him, leaving him looking even smaller and more drained than before.

"It's not ideal, but it should hold," Maisey said as she finished wrapping a bandage around his finger. "Do you want us to help you to bed or—?"

"What I want is to be left alone," Arthur grumbled, but without much enthusiasm. "Don't let the door hit you on the way out."

Maisey's eyes met mine over the top of Arthur's head. There was a look of such warm understanding in them—of camaraderie—that I couldn't help flushing.

"I'll make sure Mr. McLachlan gets settled," I said. "I'm sure he just needs a little time to compose himself."

I suspected that what Mr. McLachlan really needed was professional medical assistance and enough sedatives to keep him unconscious until next month, but I wasn't about to say as much out loud.

"Right-o. I'll catch you on the flip side. Toodles!"

Each of Maisey's cheerful farewells was met by me with a smile and by Arthur McLachlan with increasing ire. And a good thing, too, because that ire was the only thing that got him to his feet as I led him back to the living room.

There was a hospital bed set up in one corner, but I could tell from its crisp sheets that it wasn't the place where Arthur chose to rest his weary head. The couch, a sagging beige-ish heap with several books scattered over the top, looked a much more likely resting place. I gently propelled him toward it.

"Right," I said as he lowered himself into a reclining position and propped his head against the back. I resisted the urge to pull a crocheted blanket over him, but just barely. "A snack and some tea, I think, and then your medication. You said something about a diuretic?"

He opened one eye and leveled it on me. There was so much power in that stare that I could only be grateful he didn't have the energy for both eyes.

"I don't need a nurse."

"Of course not."

"I can take care of myself."

"Obviously."

His next words were lost under a coughing fit that sounded as hacking as it did painful. "That tea sounds nice," he admitted as soon as it ended. His voice was so weak that I had to strain to hear him.

Without a word, I took myself off to the kitchen to prepare the promised tea. I also took it upon myself to clean up the carnage wrought by Arthur's attempt at breakfast. I couldn't bring myself to scrub the blood from the cutting board, but I did put it in the sink to soak and tossed out the bloodied apples that had been the cause of all this in the first place. A quick peek in his fridge revealed a meager offering of half-withered fruit and a carton of eggs with a questionable expiration date. I also found some bread in the freezer, which even my culinary skills could turn into impromptu toast.

As I waited for the kettle to heat and the bread to toast, I did a quick Google search on my phone to discover what condition might require a diuretic medication. The results weren't ideal. Kidney stones, hypertension, an excessive and dangerous amount of fluid in the lungs…that last one had several symptoms that matched Arthur's, and I didn't like the sound of any of them.

Trouble with breathing. Sensations of vertigo. Heart failure. A complete breakdown of the pulmonary system. WebMD was happy to supply me with any number of worst-case scenarios, most of which were accompanied by optimistic advertisements for male enhancement pills.

The toast popped up, almost scaring me out of my wits. I yelped, but Arthur was either too far away to hear or accustomed to women screaming helplessly in his kitchen. I plunked a bag of chamomile into the hot water and arranged neat triangles of toast onto a plate before carrying them back to the living room.

He didn't look happy to see me.

"You shouldn't have come here," he accused as I set the breakfast things down on the coffee table. I handed him the cup of tea, wincing when his hands shook so hard they caused the hot liquid to slosh everywhere.

"I know."

"I could have you arrested for breaking and entering."

"I know."

"This tea isn't the right temperature. Herbal should always be brewed at a full boil."

"I know."

I could tell that my monosyllabic responses were irritating him, but I was afraid that my voice might crack if I said too much. He was so overwhelmingly exhausted that it hurt to look at him.

I sat down on the chair opposite the couch and clutched my hands between my knees, waiting until he'd taken a sip of the tea and a bite of toast before I spoke.

"It would mean a lot to me if you'd let me stay," I said, holding his gaze steady. "I know I have no right to ask it of you, and I understand if you want me to go away, but I'd like to keep you company. Just for a little while. Just until I know you're settled."

His own gaze wavered before mine. "I suppose you think I owe you this."

It took me a moment to register his meaning. "Because of those terrible things you said to me at the library?"

As the sensations of that day came rushing back, I felt a thick, cloying feeling settle in the back of my throat. I could breathe, but speech was impossible. Luckily, it didn't matter, because Arthur sighed and set his tea down. He passed his hand over his eyes.

"You'd be right," he said. "Blast you."

I took that as permission to stay in place—a thing I did so quietly and so long that it wasn't until I heard the gentle sounds of his snoring that I realize he'd fallen asleep.

"That settles it," I murmured as I gave in and slipped the blanket over his knees. I had no idea how long he was likely to nap, but I had a few hours until my shift started.

Besides, there was plenty to keep me occupied until he woke up. Arthur's personal library might have been in desperate need of someone to organize it, but there was no shortage of books to choose from—including the Marquis de Sade.

As I settled in to read the trials and tribulations of various maidens unfortunate enough to have been born in the eighteenth century, I couldn't help but relax. If it weren't for the grouchy old man I was terrified would stop breathing in his sleep, a quiet morning with a good book was as close to paradise as I'd probably ever get.

6

"OHMIGOD, SLOANE. YOU'RE HERE. YOU'RE ALIVE."

The second I walked through the door to the library, Mateo fell on my neck like an albatross.

"Do you have *any* idea what you've put us through?" he demanded as he dragged me inside. Despite my new Mateo scarf, the cold, overly conditioned air caused goose bumps to break out over my skin. "No—don't answer that. Don't answer anything until you've secured legal counsel. Octavia's furious."

"I know I'm late, but—"

"*There* she is." Octavia turned to face me from behind the checkout counter. Furious or not, her expression was inscrutable. The expression of the woman next to her, however, was as easy to read as, well, a book.

"Sloane, you had us worried sick!" Rachel Marcowitz took one look at me and instantly burst into tears. "Brett stopped by your apartment this morning, but you weren't there. So we called and called, but there was no answer. And then…"

She cast a wild look around the library, where I noticed no fewer than half a dozen of my fellow employees had gathered as though attending a funeral. Even Ian from IT was here, and he almost never came up from the basement for air.

"Mateo, please call the police and notify them that we've found our missing person," Octavia said in a tone so dangerously flat that it made my goose bumps stand out even more. "Pull the flyers from the printer and make sure they end up in recycling."

"Police?" I echoed, bewildered. "Flyers? Guys, it's not even noon. I'm only like an hour late."

"We thought you were dead," Rachel said. "Or kidnapped, at the very least. Didn't you get our calls?"

I winced as I remembered that I'd turned my ringer off so as not wake Arthur from his nap. The sleep had done little to improve either his color or his mood, but I was still glad he'd gotten it. And so, I think, was he.

"No, I didn't check my phone. I knew I was running late, so I just jumped in my car and got here as fast as I could. Sorry."

As if just noticing me for the first time, Mateo narrowed his eyes and cast a sweeping glance over my attire. "Why are you dressed for a heist at a yarn store?"

Rachel's sob transformed itself into a snort. She covered it by taking her lower lip between her teeth and stepping slowly away. "I'd better let Brett know he can call off the search party. Mom's going to be so disappointed. She hasn't had a chance to pull out the church tree in ages."

"Octavia, I don't understand," I said, since my boss was the *one* person who shouldn't have overreacted to my late arrival. Mateo once forgot three shifts in a row after he got concussed from a flying puck at a hockey game, and all anyone said was that it was a good thing his skull was so thick. "I know I should've called, and I apologize for showing up late like this, but—"

"Where were you?" Octavia asked.

I blinked, unprepared for this sudden attack. Surely her relief at finding me alive should have lasted a *few* more minutes. "Um. I overslept?"

"Incorrect. Your internal alarm clock goes off a half hour before your real alarm. Try again."

She was right. No matter what time I set my alarm for, I always woke up an annoying thirty minutes before it started to chime. I liked to think it was because I was in tune with nature and the cyclicality of the sun, but it was mostly my anxiety refusing to let me lower my guard by so much as an inch.

"I had a doctor's appointment," I said, thinking fast. "They put me on a diuretic."

My mention of an actual medication made Octavia do a double take. "What for?"

"Kidney stones," I lied. I'd always known my Google searching skills would come in handy someday. I'd just never realized for *what*.

As this response was also accurate—and quick—enough for Octavia to question herself, I pressed my luck. "I have no idea why Brett is in such a tizzy over this. I told him I had an appointment this morning, but he must have forgotten. You know how men get…in one ear, out the other."

"But Sloane, Brett swears you didn't have an appointment." Rachel returned to the conversation before I could think to hip check her out of the way. "He was afraid you went back to that crabby old man's house and got yourself murdered."

In that moment, I discovered another of literature's great lies. A person's life didn't flash before their eyes in the moments before death; it did it right *now*. Caught in a lie and trapped on all sides, I saw everyone staring expectantly at me for an explanation that fit. Unfortunately, there was nothing I could say and no lie powerful enough to free me from this snare, and my brain knew it.

"Well. Um. Yeah." I sighed. "Oops."

"Don't you dare say 'oops' at me like you just dropped a stack of overdue books," Octavia said. "I mean it, Sloane. I'm too angry with you for deflection."

"I'm not deflecting," I protested. "I'm trying to come up with a believable lie."

Octavia didn't find this amusing. "There's no point. I won't believe you anyway. Did you go to Mr. McLachlan's house this morning?"

Several pairs of expectant eyes turned my way. I tried to swallow, but my mouth had gone completely dry. "Yes?"

"After I expressly told you not to?"

"Yes?"

"And did you go inside his house? Does he know you tracked him down?" I knew, before she even finished, what she was really asking: *Can he file a complaint against the library and put both our jobs in jeopardy?*

"Is it too late to plead the Fifth?"

"That's it. Out."

At first, I thought Octavia was ordering *me* out, and that I was about to be forcibly removed from the best place on earth, but she turned her stare onto the rest of the assembled crowd instead. Pangs of proximal discomfort hit me from all sides.

"I'm sorry," I said, though I had no idea who I was apologizing to—or, if I was being honest, what I was apologizing for. If given a chance to do this morning over, I'd still park myself in Arthur McLachlan's living room and make sure he finished every bite of his cold toast and every sip of his even colder tea. "Please don't make me leave. Not like this."

"Oh, stop acting like I'm about to walk you off a plank," Octavia muttered. It might have been hope rearing its feathery head, but I thought I detected a note of humor in her voice. "I looked it up when you left work last night. It's only a suspension."

"Wait. You looked it up? *Last night?*"

"Of course I did. Do you think I was born yesterday? I knew you were going to stop by that dratted old man's house before you did." She heaved a sigh that felt as weary as my soul. "I'd rather you adopted some common sense for once in your life, but you can't change a leopard's spots."

"This feels like a personal attack."

"That's because it is." She jerked her head toward her office, which was part of a row of one-room cubicles along the far wall. "Come on. I had some free time, so I figured I'd get a head start on the suspension paperwork."

"This feels *a lot* like a personal attack."

Octavia looked at me in a way that was decidedly maternal. At least, it was what I always assumed maternal looks were supposed to be—a sort of exasperated affection that neither time nor poor decision-making could mar. My own mom had lost every expression except annoyance a long time ago. "We're looking at two weeks unpaid leave, but you can use your vacation days if you have any left. It's not ideal, and we'll have to get in some temp help to cover your shifts while you're off, but I don't have to fire you. *This* time."

"Two weeks?" I cried. "But that's—"

"Nothing compared to what'll happen if I catch you at this kind of thing again."

My shoulders slumped as I followed her toward the wall of offices, my feet moving like leaden weights. Prisoners heading toward death row had more dignity, but I couldn't help myself. This job was the one thing I was good at.

"Take this time to relax," Octavia said as though offering me a treat of no mean order. "Catch up on your reading. Plan your wedding. I don't care what you do, as long as you leave poor Mr. McLachlan out of it."

I paused on the threshold to her office, my hand clutching the doorframe. "Wait. What?"

She fell to her chair with a whoosh and a rustle before slipping her readers onto the end of her nose. "You heard me. If and when he starts coming back to the library, I want you to steer clear of him. Got it? Mateo can handle all his inquiries from here on out. Or one of the gals from processing. I don't care, as long as you minimize contact."

"Octavia, I can't just *abandon* him."

She peered up at me over the top of her glasses. Her look was a lot less maternal this time around. "You can, and you will. It's non-negotiable, Sloane."

I shook my head, even though it pained me to see the inflexible tightening of Octavia's jaw. One of my favorite things about her was how soft a person she was—of shape and of sentiment—and I hated to be the undoing of that.

Still. I did it.

"I promised him I'd be back as soon as my shift's over," I said, fixating on a patch of exposed brickwork a few inches above Octavia's head. It was a trick I'd learned a few years ago at a confidence-boosting seminar. The guy who'd run it said the most important thing when confronting someone was to look them straight in the eyes and say what was in your heart.

After six grueling hours of practice and more discomfort than I cared to remember, he'd decided I was better off picking a point at random and confronting that instead.

"He's all alone in that house, and he refuses to let any of the nurses back in," I continued, addressing the brick. "There's a pushy woman across the street who *might* be able to get a foot and a sausage biscuit through the door, but I wouldn't put any money on it. I promised him takeout from Sichuan Palace for dinner."

Octavia didn't speak for a full sixty seconds.

"I know it sounds as if I'm overstepping his personal boundaries, but it's not like that. He has *nobody*, Octavia. Not a single living soul who cares whether he lives or dies. If I don't help him, who will?"

I thought about that other car Maisey claimed to have seen parked outside Arthur's house. There was a chance that whoever was in it cared enough about Arthur to extend an offer of help, but there was no guarantee. Not in this world, and not with that man.

"You have people who care about you, Sloane," she said, so quietly that I had to risk getting closer to make sure I heard correctly.

"I know I do," I said. "That's the point. Arthur's the one who's alone."

"You aren't alone."

"I *know*. Are you even listening to me?" Frustration went a long way in helping me with that whole confrontation thing. I wasn't quite looking her in the eyes yet, but I had her forehead on lockdown. "He's got something called a pulmonary edema—that's when a dangerous amount of water gets in the lungs—and his medication makes him too dizzy and disoriented to take care of himself. He needs someone to—"

"Sloane." Octavia shot to her feet so suddenly that I was left staring at her belt buckle. "You are *not* Arthur McLachlan. I want to hear you say it."

Wrinkling my nose, I tried to keep the tingling behind my eyes at bay, but it was a struggle. Especially once Octavia's meaning hit me at full speed.

"I'm not Arthur McLachlan," I said. "I have people who care about me. I'm not alone."

They were lies, of course. That was why the tingling was winning—and why I wouldn't back down even as the tears began to fall.

Octavia meant well, I knew. What she wanted me to admit was that I was a young woman at the start of her career and the start of her life, the whole world unfurling before her feet. When I walked out that door, it would be to join my fiancé and his generous family, to fall into the cradle of their collective warmth for however long I needed to get back on my feet again. I wasn't a crotchety old man who threw people out of my house—and no matter how dire my life got, I never would be.

Except I was.

Okay, so the throwing people out of my house part didn't fit, and I liked to think I was prickly rather than crotchety, but Arthur was the only one who saw me for what I really was. In fact, he'd summed it up so well that I didn't dare improve on his words.

An echo with nothing and no one to call her own. A friendly facade. An empty smile.

And there it was. The truth in a tiny, impenetrable nutshell, a secret buried so deep inside my heart that I'd thought it would be safe there forever.

I didn't love Brett Marcowitz, and I didn't love his family. I didn't love my parents. I'd never loved any of my old college roommates, and the friends I had now were more like work acquaintances than kindred spirits. Since the day my sister Emily died, her life snuffed short by a hole in her heart that no number of surgeries could fix, I hadn't loved anyone who didn't exist between the covers of a book. At this point, I wasn't even sure I knew *how*.

"I have to go, Octavia," I said, dashing the back of my hand against my cheeks and straightening my posture. "He's counting on me. If that means you have to fire me, then so be it."

Octavia threw up her hands. The gesture was meant to convey a feeling of playful frustration, but I knew better. She'd reached the end of her patience. "It's not an empty threat," Olivia warned. "I *will* fire you if you disobey my orders. I'm not about to lose my own job over this."

"And I wouldn't want you to," I said. "But it's not like I have a choice in the matter."

"Of course you have a choice. Everyone has a choice."

I shook my head. The thing I couldn't make Octavia understand was that my fate and Arthur's had somehow become tangled, and the knot was impossible to undo. Since the day he'd walked into this library, refusing all my book suggestions and overtures of friendship, I'd known that he meant something—that he meant something to *me*.

If Octavia had any idea how bleak and empty my life had been for all these years, how desperately I'd wanted to feel that human connection again, she'd know. I could no more walk away from Arthur McLachlan than I could my own sister.

She must have gotten an accurate read on my silence because she flattened her lips in a frown. "So that's it? You're walking out? Just like that?"

"I am," I agreed, my voice tight, my chest tighter. "I'm really going to miss you guys."

I wished I could say that I made a smooth exit after that, with my head held high and an air of cool imperturbability wrapped around me, but I didn't. I cried and packed a small box of my belongings. I accidentally stole a copy of Amanda Gorman's latest book of poetry, which I'd been saving at the bottom of my lunch bag for a rainy day. I also discovered, too late, that I'd left my car keys on Octavia's desk.

In the end, I decided to take the bus and come back for my car another time. Some trials weren't meant to be borne in the broad daylight.

Slinking back to the only home I'd ever known with my tail between my legs was one of them.

MAISEY

7

YOU KNOW HOW IT'S POSSIBLE TO just look at some people and tell everything about them?

Take the mailman, for example. Not the regular one—the one who was always on the phone when he slid the mail through the slot, too busy chatting with his girlfriend to notice what he was delivering. I meant the other one. The guy who filled in sometimes. The one who left greasy fingerprints all over my Victoria's Secret catalogs.

Him I knew. *Him* I'd dated.

Metaphorically speaking, of course. A man who didn't even *try* to hide that he was spending his lunch break oozing mayonnaise onto the Dream Angels collection was the same no matter where you found him. In a back alley. Creeping outside a club. Peeking into your mail slot in hopes of catching you vacuuming in the nude, and all because you read an article about how airing out your vagina could reduce the incidence of UTIs.

One time. I'd done it one time, and up until I'd noticed those wet blue eyes peeping up at me, I'd been feeling pretty good about it, too.

Anyway. It was a talent of mine. A sixth sense of sorts. All it took was one glance, and I could tell if a person was going to be friend or foe.

That sweet curly-haired girl with the purple brooch who sat

outside Arthur McLachlan's house all night? Who barged into his house without warning and even convinced that horrible old man to let me bandage his finger?

She was going to be a friend. I just knew it.

"That guy was here again." I bounced out my front door to where she was struggling to get several takeout bags out of a city bus. It was the same bus my Bella used to take coming home after her shifts at Paul Bunyan's, but that wasn't why I was watching it.

At least, it wasn't the *only* reason.

The girl looked like she'd had a heck of a day, poor thing, still in last night's clothes and with red-rimmed eyes, her brooch hanging heavily at her throat. I didn't ask about any of it. I recognized a heart-break when it stood in front of me.

"What guy?" she asked as I lifted one of the takeout bags and waved to the bus driver with my free hand. Magda had always been great about letting me know when Bella didn't get on the bus at her usual time, so I was careful to stay friendly. Moms had to stick together, you know?

"The one who watched Arthur before you did," I said. Since the girl seemed to be struggling with the second takeout bag, I grabbed that one, too. I'd put a casserole to warm in the oven in case she came back hungry, but I could always reheat it for tomorrow. Whatever was in these bags smelled heavenly. "I offered him some snacks, but he doesn't seem to like my cooking as much as you do. Do you have forks and stuff, or do you want me to grab some?"

"Oh. Um. I'm not sure." She blinked at me through those red-rimmed eyes, looking so much like a lost puppy that I had half a mind to call up that gorgeous man in the Tesla and demand he come collect her.

Only half a mind, though. That one had foe vibes all over him. The car practically reeked of them.

"If this food is for Arthur, we'd better take forks." I nudged her toward my front door with my knee. "From the little I saw of his kitchen this morning, you couldn't pay me to eat off of anything in there. I'll get my first aid kit, too, in case he needs a dressing change."

The girl's face fell. "Uh-oh. Does that mean he didn't get a replacement nurse?"

"Nope. I mentioned it to the other guy, hoping he might be able to call someone, but all he did was stare at me before driving off at full speed." I set the food down on my table and started gathering everything I thought the girl would need if she planned on spending the evening with Arthur McLachlan.

Plates. Forks. Napkins. Steel-plated armor and a defensive weapon.

Ha-ha. I was kidding about those last two. Mostly.

"Red wine, do you think?" My hand hovered over the IKEA wine rack mounted on the wall. My house was so tiny that almost everything I owned was stored vertically. "Or something stronger? I have a bottle of Grey Goose in the freezer for emergencies, but..."

She wrinkled her nose. "I don't think he's supposed to drink with his medication."

"Of course. I should've thought of that." Since I had no idea what medication Arthur was taking, or even what had caused that fleet of ambulances to come by the other night, I added, "And, uh, what's wrong with him, exactly?"

To my surprise, the girl laughed. It took a second for me to realize that she was inviting me to join her—which was a good thing, because her laugh was one of the infectious kinds. Light and soft, but so *real* you just knew she'd never hurt anyone with it.

"Medically, the best I've been able to come up with is a pulmonary edema. As for the rest of him?" She shrugged. "Loneliness, probably."

I nodded, struggling to find a response that struck the right balance of wisdom and sympathy. For all her fragile, skittish air, this girl didn't lack intelligence. Arthur McLachlan didn't either, which was probably why he was willing to let her into his house. Before he retired, he used to be an English professor at the college.

I, unfortunately, had never been accused of being too smart. Too inquisitive? Yes. Too pushy? Obviously. Too much?

Always.

"I've lived on this street for almost a decade, and I've never seen a visitor at his house," I said. I knew how this made me sound—a sad, slightly crazed woman who spied on her neighbors—but this spade had never been anything but. "Not once, not even during the holidays. I've tried reaching out, but..."

"He doesn't reach back?" she guessed.

"People aren't meant to live alone the way he does." I tried not to look as self-conscious as I felt. If this girl looked too closely at her current surroundings, she'd notice the telltale signs: the one coaster on the table, the single hand-washed mug sitting ready for tomorrow morning's coffee. "The neighborhood used to pitch in—shoveling his sidewalk in winter, checking in when the power goes out, that sort of thing—but he doesn't like it when we meddle."

"No," she agreed. "He wouldn't."

I was dying to ask more about her relationship with Arthur, but she glanced doubtfully at the door. "I'd better get these soup dumplings over to him before they get cold." She made no move toward the exit, so I hoisted the bags and did it for her.

"Then we'd better get going," I said. "Hunger isn't going to improve a man like that one."

A startled laugh escaped her. "Does it improve any of them?" She hesitated before extending a hand toward me. "I'm Sloane, by the way. Sloane Parker. I don't think I introduced myself earlier."

I took her hand and shook it. Her palm felt warm and clammy against mine, but I didn't mind. If I knew Arthur McLachlan—and I did—a warm and clammy reception was a heck of a lot better than the one we were likely to receive across the street.

"I didn't manage to get a picture of the guy, but I got his license plate, the make and model of his car, and a few shots of his tire tread after he sped away."

I pulled out my phone and flipped past my selfies until I found what I was looking for. Arthur McLachlan harrumphed and refused to touch the phone, but I could tell he was secretly impressed. Either that, or he was afraid we might leave if he pushed us too far. When Sloane came in through the door bearing takeout and a determined smile, I could've sworn he looked almost *glad* to see us.

"Oh dear. Should I ask?" Sloane scrolled through the pictures in question. She shook her head and handed the phone back to me. "I don't recognize the car, but I trust you. You seem to know a lot about what goes on around here."

I tried not to look as ashamed as I felt. The tire tread photos might have been taking things a little too far, but I'd already been out there with the phone. And they always seemed to come in handy on *CSI*.

"It's not as bad as you think," I said. "I'm a single woman living alone in a town where sixty percent of the population owns a gun. I like to make sure I cover all my bases."

"Oh." Sloane blinked at me. "This morning, I thought you said you have a teenage daughter."

"I do," I said and closed my mouth. Anyone who knew me would have found this hard to believe—*Maisey Phillips closed her mouth?*— but there were some things I didn't care to talk about. My relationship with Bella was one of them.

"I don't see why you're going to all this cursed trouble," Arthur said as he struggled to his feet. I could see how much Sloane wanted to get up and help him—I felt the same way—but we stayed in place.

The fact that we were sitting inside Arthur McLachlan's house was strange enough. That we'd dined with him was even stranger. That he'd offered to make us coffee and invited us to stick around for a bit?

There was no way we were upsetting *that* apple cart. The poor man was obviously in a much worse state than he wanted to let on.

"I don't need a couple of babysitters, and I don't need some nosy neighborhood watch photographing every deliveryman who shows up on the street. I'm *fine*."

Sloane and I shared a look that was full of meaning. We waited only until Arthur disappeared behind the swinging kitchen door before pouncing on each other.

"There's no way we can leave him alone tonight," Sloane hissed. "Did you notice his face when we came in? I've never seen anyone that relieved before."

"I wish I could stay, but I've got an early shift tomorrow," I apologized with a wince. "I could always call in sick, but—"

Sloane shook her head, sending her crop of curls bouncing. The longer I sat here with her, the more jealous I was of her hair—how it grew and expanded with her every movement. My own hair was thin and lanky, and only getting worse with age. All I could do was pile it on my head and hope no one noticed how little of it there was left.

"Please don't do that," she said. "One of us losing our job over this thing is bad enough."

"Wait. You lost your job?" Suddenly, those red-rimmed eyes and last night's clothes looked a lot less like a love affair gone wrong. "Because you stayed with Arthur this morning?"

She nodded and brushed at her right eye in a way that indicated long practice. To an untrained observer, she might have been tucking a wayward curl behind her ear, but I knew better. That was someone who'd taught herself a long time ago how to cry so no one would see.

"Well, that's the stupidest thing I've ever heard. What'll that place do without you?"

She was so startled by this that she forgot to brush away the tear from her other eye. "How do you know where I work?"

"I don't," I admitted. "But that doesn't mean they aren't lucky to have you. I bet you're the best art therapy instructor—"

"Um, I'm not an art therapy instructor."

"Elementary school teacher?"

"Getting warmer."

I snapped my fingers. "Oh, I've got it! Librarian."

She laughed. The sound went a long way to lift my spirits. And hers, probably. "That's not half bad, actually," she said. "Can you do that for everyone?"

"Just about," I admitted. Like my ability to distinguish friend from foe, I was excellent at ferreting out problems with relationships, careers, and anything else that might be leveraged for personal gain.

Which, yes, sounded terrible. It *was* terrible. But everyone had to make a living.

"Is that where you met Arthur?" I asked. "At the library?"

"Yeah. I, uh, well…" Her voice trailed off and she looked toward the kitchen door. "We're not allowed to use the library system to look up the personal details of our patrons. But when Arthur didn't show up for a few days, I started to worry and did it anyway. My boss had no choice but to fire me."

"Good for you, honey."

She stared in surprise, but there was no chance for her to ask what I meant. Arthur came struggling through the kitchen door carrying a tea tray.

"Let me get that for you." Sloane sprang to her feet and, after only a minor tussle, managed to wrest the tray from Arthur's determined grip. It said a lot about her that she only spilled half the coffee while she did it. For all her fragility, she had some serious steel where this man was concerned.

"I'm not dead yet," Arthur grumbled. "I can carry a pot of coffee through my own living room."

"And *I* looked up the side effects of your medication," Sloane countered. "You shouldn't be carrying anything, let alone scalding beverages."

"Oho, so you're a doctor as well as a librarian?"

"I can read a label. It doesn't require a medical degree to know you should be taking things easy." She set the tray aside and started clearing a spot for Arthur. "Now sit down and stay there. I don't want to have to tie you to this sofa."

"You and what army?" he countered, but he sat down—and without any physical restraints needed.

A sudden burst of inspiration struck me. They do that sometimes, not like a bolt of lightning, but like a baseball bat to the head.

"Well, that settles it," I said.

"Settles what?" they both asked. The fact that they glanced at me with the same tilt to their heads, the same surprise widening their eyes, confirmed my decision. Two more perfect people for each other had never existed.

"Sloane is going to be your new nurse." Before either of them could protest—a thing I *knew* was coming from the way they both opened their mouths to speak at the same time—I did the one thing I was best at. Talking.

"You probably haven't heard yet, but you got Sloane fired from the library today," I told Arthur. Sloane tried shooting me a warning glance but I pretended not to see her. "She doesn't have a job anymore, and there's no one to blame for it but you."

"That's not quite how it—" Sloane began, but I was ready for her.

"And Arthur has thrown a temper tantrum with every single person who's been inside this house for the past week. If I hadn't walked in next to you, he'd have probably thrown that vase at my head."

"That vase is an heirloom. I'd have thrown the coatrack."

Sloane's lips twitched as she struggled to suppress a laugh. I saw my advantage and pressed it.

"See what I mean? *Someone* needs to be here to make sure Mr. McLachlan takes his medication on time and doesn't hurt himself at meals. And Sloane can't pay her bills without some means of financial support. It's the perfect solution. You owe it to each other."

I didn't actually know if any of this was true. That young man in the Tesla looked as though he could pick up the tab for several of Sloane's bills, and Arthur McLachlan could have woken up tomorrow morning in perfect health, but telling people what they wanted to hear was my superpower.

Arthur was the first to speak. "The last thing I need is some dewy-eyed dreamer trying to tell me how to run my household."

I winced at the harsh words, but Sloane seemed to grow a little taller under them. "And the last thing *I* need is to play nursemaid to a bitter old man who doesn't know how to say thank you."

For a moment, I feared I'd lost them. They glared at each other in a way that seemed to kindle the air, both of them ready to run at the first sign of fire. But then Arthur did it again.

"Of course, if you wanted to stay and catalog my books, then you might actually be of use to me," he said.

"You want me to catalog your books? Really?" Sloane cast a quick, eager look around the living room, where books of all shapes and sizes practically spilled from the seams. My ex used to do that with vinyl records. Half of them were for bands no one had ever heard of, but he'd hoarded those dratted things like they were pieces of eight.

Considering what they won him in the end, he wasn't wrong.

"You're a librarian, aren't you?" Arthur demanded. "What else are you going to do all day? Read me fairy tales?"

Sloane shot me a helpless look, but I busied myself pouring coffee and biting down on the tip of my tongue. The last thing these two needed was the benefit of my advice. It was *good* advice, and it was killing me not to offer it, but some situations called for restraint.

"You do seem to have an awful lot of books lying haphazardly about," Sloane said. "I'm assuming upstairs is more of the same?"

"Is that a hint to go poking around the rest of my house?"

"If I'm going to handle your personal library, I'll have to do *some* poking. Since you've already started dividing out a Modernist section, we'll have to figure out what kind of taxonomy you'd prefer. Genre and surname might work in a smaller personal library, but with something of this size, we're looking at more niche classifications." She picked up a book from the top of a stack and started rifling through it. I didn't understand half of what she'd just said, but Arthur seemed impressed.

"I can't stay here *all* the time," she said, once again looking to me for assistance. I offered an encouraging nod, so she continued. "But maybe for tonight, I can sleep over so we can go over a few things. Then I can come back for regular shifts throughout the week…"

I handed her a cup of coffee before preparing one for Arthur. He took one look at the white cream swirling in the center and sneered at me. "You *would* put cream in it," he said, as if two-thirds of the population didn't drink their coffee that way. Then he ignored me to focus on Sloane. "I'm not paying you a penny above minimum wage, mind. And I know exactly which books are the most valuable, so if you try to run off with one…"

Instead of being insulted by this—an emotion she would be fully justified to feel—Sloane laughed. "I wouldn't dare, Mr. McLachlan. The librarian code of honor forbids it."

I knew it was a done deal when that cranky old toad set his coffee down and fixed his hard gray eyes on the younger woman. He was susceptible to that sweet laugh of hers, too. I just knew it.

"Call me Arthur," he said, and so gruffly we had to lean in to hear the words. "If you're going to be lurking all over my house, rifling through my personal belongings, I won't have you Mr. McLachlaning me this and Mr. McLachlaning me that."

Sloane flashed such a bright, happy smile that *I* had to pretend to push a lock of hair behind my ear. Satisfied that I'd done my good deed for the day, I got up from the couch.

"Wait—are you going?" Sloane asked, but she'd already started shuffling the books at her feet into two different piles.

"I'll check in on you two after work tomorrow," I promised, thinking of that casserole. If I took a long lunch, I could probably eke out enough time to bake a huckleberry pie to accompany it. "I'm sure you have plenty to talk about without me."

I headed out before either of them could pretend to protest. If there was one thing I'd learned in this lifetime, it was that it's much better to be the one doing the leaving. Even when the party was still going, when there was nothing waiting for you at home but a dark house and a sink full of dirty dishes, it was important to never overstay your welcome.

Otherwise, there was a good chance you wouldn't be invited back.

8

___

For the last time, Mr. Davidson, I'm *not* going to tell you what I'm wearing. If that's the kind of phone call you want to make, there are plenty of other numbers I can give you."

With a sigh, I adjusted my headset and risked a quick peek at the clock above my desk. It was shaped like a cat, the minutes ticking by in a burst of colorful yarn dangling from his paws. Not for the first time, I reminded myself to get something less ornate. The cat was cute, but no matter how hard I stared, I could never tell if his paw was on the four or the five.

"Fine," the voice on the other end of the line grumbled. "But it's a fair question. I'm not paying for relationship advice from some random housewife in yoga pants."

His words didn't sting nearly as much as he wanted them to. I knew *way* too much about this man's personal life to let his judgments weigh too heavily. Even if I was random and—yes—clad in yoga pants.

"Your fixation on appearances is what got you into this mess in the first place, Mr. Davidson," I said. I put a little extra husk in my voice just in case. At $3.99 a minute, it was getting harder and harder to keep clients on the line. "What a woman wears is much less important than what she has to offer in her heart, remember?"

"Yeah, yeah. I remember." Mr. Davidson paused. "Does this mean my date tonight is going to go well? You see it?"

I could almost swear the cat's paws started moving in reverse.

"I see opportunity and excitement," I said with complete honesty. "This date is a clean slate, a chance to be your best self in front of someone new." Less honest, I added, "You stand on the horizon of great change. What path you take to get there is entirely up to you."

"A clean slate," he echoed. "A new horizon. That's right."

I bit back a sigh. There was nothing new about the horizons Mr. Davidson faced. He'd been a regular of mine for over two years, and nothing I said seemed to get through to him. No matter how many times I told him to pick up a hobby, a volunteer job, *anything* to make himself more interesting and attractive to the opposite sex, he always ended up in the same place.

On the phone with a 1-800 psychic, begging for a change we both knew would never come.

"I think this might be the one," he said, a tinge of optimism rendering his voice almost boyish. We were forbidden from looking up our clients or peeking at their social media accounts, but I always did it anyway. Mr. Davidson was a sprightly fifty-three, an insurance salesman with a bad haircut and a heavy face that was as far from *boyish* as a man could get. "Thanks, Maisey. You've been a real help this time."

He couldn't see me nod, but I did it anyway. As a parting gift—and because my timer indicated that he'd racked up a bill of over $150 on this phone call—I said, "By the way, I'm wearing what I always wear when I look into the mysteries of the universe. Kitten heels and a full ball gown. The spirits demand nothing less."

And then I hung up before my laughter overtook me.

Since the paw *was* on the five instead of the four, I had barely time to dash to the oven and pull out my pie before it started to burn. The crust was bitterly dark, the juices seeping out in a way that rendered my leaf pattern all but invisible, but it smelled good enough to eat.

Or so I hoped. It was my only real passport into Arthur McLachlan's house, so I had to make it count. I'd been watching that poor man and his black hole of solitude for so long that I'd become emotionally invested in the outcome. There was no way I was missing it now that Sloane had entered the picture.

I slid the pie into a box alongside yesterday's casserole and headed out the door.

"Knock-knock!" My hands were full, so I had to shout my way into the house. "I come bearing gifts. *Heavy* ones."

"Oh, thank goodness." Sloane's face appeared in the doorway. "I was hoping you'd be here soon. Are you sure you don't mind giving up your evening for this?"

"I always have time for friends," I said.

Not surprisingly, Sloane reared back at my use of that word—*friends*—but she was too nice to say anything. I wasn't as clueless as I seemed; I *knew* it took more than a few chance meetings on the street to build a friendship, but there was a lot more of Mr. Davidson in me than met the eye. Optimism always had a way of creeping in.

"What's he done this time?" I asked as I shifted the box from one hip to another. Sloane's nose twitched as soon as the scent of the pie hit her, so I figured I was good for an hour's entry, at least. "If it involves bodily injury or a scrubbing pad, you can count on me. *Books*, however…"

Sloane shook her head in warning as I stepped into the house. It looked much the same as it did yesterday, full of dust and clutter, but a warbling tenor from the back added a cheerful air.

"Is that Arthur?" I asked. "Singing? A *show tune*?"

"You." Arthur burst through the kitchen door with his customary frown. There was a hitch in both his step and his breath, but he didn't let them slow him down. "The busybody from across the street. You have to save me."

Since the singing was still going on, I could only assume there was another person in the kitchen. And since Arthur was about to throw himself on my chest, I guessed it wasn't a person he liked very much.

"How good are you at getting rid of unwanted guests?" he demanded. Without waiting for an answer, he laughed. "Who am I kidding? All we have to do is start you talking, and anyone in their right mind will run screaming for the hills. Quick, Sloane... What are that fool's least favorite topics of conversation?"

Once again, he took it upon himself to answer. He pointed at me. "Tell him the plot to your favorite soap opera. That'll do the trick."

Since soap operas were *literal* experts when it came to telling a compelling story that kept people coming back for more, I didn't let his insults get me down. Arthur McLachlan was a man who wouldn't know a good amnesia backstory if it bit him on the a—

He took one glance at the box under my arm and grunted. "And hide that food. Whatever you've got in there smells delicious. It'll only make him want to stay."

The box was lifted from my hands, and I found myself being pushed through to the kitchen. Sloane uttered a faint protest, but as soon as I stepped onto the cracked linoleum floor, I saw my mission as clearly as the newly cleaned windows along the back wall.

"Tesla Model S!" I called brightly. "I didn't notice your car outside."

The man who'd accompanied Sloane the first night whirled at the sound of my voice, the Gershwin song dying on his well-molded lips. From the way his sleeves were pushed up to his elbows and the air reeked of vinegar, it was obvious he'd been at his window-cleaning task for some time.

"Oh," he said, blinking at me. "It's you."

I was ready for this reaction. In my forty-four years on this planet, I'd never been the sort of woman who lit up a room when she walked into it. I'd been cute enough in my twenties, partly because I'd jumped headfirst into the lifestyle and wardrobe of a post-hardcore groupie, but mostly because *everyone* was cute in their twenties. It just took a couple decades of hard living and suddenly sagging skin to realize it.

"You're the lady who got Sloane into this mess in the first place," the man continued flatly. "The one who made her sign up to be that old man's caregiver."

"That's me," I said without letting the smile from my lips. "And *you're* cleaning those windows wrong. Paper towels leave streaks. What you want is a wad of newspaper."

"I know how to clean a window, thanks."

I shrugged. "Just trying to help. You want a hand?"

He eyed me suspiciously but held out a spray bottle. "Have you come to relieve Sloane's shift for the night? This arrangement seems highly irregular—actually, this whole *situation* does. In my medical practice, we'd never approach a care plan so haphazardly."

"You're a doctor. Because *of course* you are," I said, more to myself than to the man. The expensive haircut, the car, the fact that he was wearing surgical gloves to apply a mild vinegar solution to glass—it was written all over him. "Let me guess. Dermatology? No. Radiology?"

I tapped my teeth and called upon the powers of the universe—or, in this case, the fact that he was off from work before six o'clock and looked incredibly well rested for a member of the medical profession. With a snap of my fingers, I had it. "You're a chiropractor, aren't you?"

"Sloane told you, didn't she?"

With that, my decision was made. Even if it killed me—even if I had to recall a decade's worth of soap operas until I found the slowest, most ridiculous story line—I was getting this man out of Arthur's house. He could have at least *pretended* to be impressed by my clairvoyance.

"I knew a chiropractor once," I said as I sprayed the vinegar solution onto the nearest window and swiped. It was just like I said—streaks. No matter how hard you tried, paper towels always left residue behind. "He had three wives, but none of them knew the others existed. No kids, thank goodness, but his second wife wanted them really badly. After a while, she got so desperate she started to stuff her shirts with pillows to make it look like she was pregnant. And a good thing, too, because she got shot in a bank robbery gone wrong, and those pillows saved her life. Should we open these windows to let in a little air, do you think?"

A snort of laughter caused me to turn around. Arthur stood a few feet back, his body curved over his cane like a comma. "Leave them closed," he said. "I like the smell of vinegar."

This felt a little *too* obvious to me, but Sloane's doctor only grimaced. He obviously wasn't an easy man to dislodge.

Unfortunately for him, neither was I.

"The woman had to have emergency surgery, but they managed to save her life just in time," I continued. "Only the blood donor they used had a rare condition that causes instant and spontaneous pregnancy."

Sloane's doctor coughed indignantly. "That's not a thing."

"Oh, it's a thing," Arthur interrupted without missing a beat. "My late wife had it. We had to be very careful with her diet, or who knows how many kids we would've ended up with."

"You're making that up. Both of you."

"It's a form of porphyria, I believe," Arthur continued. He rolled a knowing eye toward me and explained, "Many literary sources link porphyria with the earliest tales of vampirism. Browning, in particular, heavily influenced the concept."

I nodded as though I understood what he was talking about. The only literary vampires I knew were the ones from the Twilight series—which, to be fair, heavily influenced a conception of my own. There was a reason my daughter was named Bella.

"I don't see what vampires have to do with anything," the doctor said irritably.

"No," I agreed. "That story line didn't come until a few years later. I think the writers got lazy."

That comment was the poor man's final straw. He goggled first at me and then at Arthur, realization washing over him like a solution of vinegar water. "Are you two talking about a *story*? From a book?"

"It's actually from *Flames of the World*," I said, rolling my shoulder in apology. "I don't read nearly as much as I should."

I had no idea what would have happened if Sloane hadn't chosen that moment to join us in the kitchen. The doctor took one look at her and immediately started heading for the nearest exit.

"Sloane, love, we should get going," he said as he expertly snapped the gloves from his fingers and tossed them into the garbage. "My parents are expecting us at seven. My mom said something about inviting Cousin Dora so you two could have a chance to meet."

A pained expression flashed across Sloane's face, so quick that you had to be watching to see it.

But I was watching—always watching, a forever spectator with my face pressed against the glass. And so, it seemed, was Arthur. In a burst of drama that would have given *Flames of the World* a run for its money, Arthur fell into a fit of coughing so draining that even Sloane's doctor was moved to help.

"It's fine," Arthur said between deep, noisy draws of air. "I'll be okay on my own for the rest of the night. I wouldn't want to keep you from Cousin Dora."

"You should be on oxygen," the doctor said. His brow puckered, the sudden harshness of his features doing much to explain what Sloane saw in this man—beyond his money and good looks, I mean. That was the face of a Man Who Got Things Done, a man who could be counted on to do the work even when he'd rather be doing literally anything else.

FEMA workers had that face. Roofers had it. Fathers of multiples had it.

"You should also be propped up in bed. Sloane, you didn't let him lie flat when he went to sleep last night, did you?"

"Um. Yes?" Sloane winced. "I didn't know that was bad."

The doctor heaved a sigh. "Right. Because you're not a nurse. Or even a nurse's aide. I *told* you."

Sloane cast an accusing look at Arthur. "I'm sorry. I wasn't given instructions about how to position him."

"Oho, so now it's my fault I'm going to die?"

"A little, yeah." She turned to Arthur with her hands on her hips. "How am I supposed to know these things if you don't tell me?"

"You could ask this fancy young gentleman of yours. He seems to have plenty of opinions on what's best for everyone."

"That fancy young gentleman is a *doctor*. Remember those? The people who saved your life? Who warned you not to leave the hospital for this exact reason?"

The fancy young gentleman watched this interaction with a growing frown. "Sloane, what are you doing? You can't yell at your patient."

"I'm not *yelling* at him," she yelled. She flushed and added, "And he's not my patient. Not really. I'm here to catalog his books, remember?"

"I remember," the doctor said, and in such a quiet voice that I had to strain to hear him. "What should I tell my mom about tonight?"

Sloane sighed, so I grabbed Arthur by the arm and hoisted him to his feet. He was a lot heavier than he looked, his frailty offset by his determination not to be moved until he was good and ready, but I managed to get him up.

"We'll just, ah, give you two a few minutes." I nudged Arthur toward the next room. The old grouch obviously wanted to stay and hear what the verdict was about Cousin Dora, but we could always press a glass against the wall from the next room. Honestly, had no one ever taught him how to eavesdrop?

"Sloane, if this is about money, you know I'm happy to—" I heard the doctor say as we pushed through the door.

"It's not that. At least, not *only* that—" came Sloane's quick response.

I managed to get Arthur to the living room before he threw off my arm. All that fake coughing must have done a number on his lungs, because his breathing grew labored as he fell to his well-worn couch.

"How long has he been here?" I asked, taking the chair opposite. Neat piles of books sat in an arc around it, so I could only assume this had become Sloane's base of operations.

"Only about an hour, but it feels like a lifetime. He left work early to check on Sloane. *To keep an eye on things*, he said. Some people just don't know when they're not wanted."

His pointed stare wasn't necessary; I was able to pick up on the subtext just fine. I was also not getting up from my seat that easily. One should never underestimate the staying power of a woman who had literally nowhere else to be.

"You weren't half-bad in there, by the way," he said with such a begrudging air that I had to fight a smile. Just in case I got the wrong idea, he narrowed his eyes and added, "You still talk too much."

"I know."

"And I didn't invite you into my home."

"I know that, too."

"If it weren't for Sloane, I'd have you forcibly removed."

"That's fair."

He harrumphed, obviously unhappy to find that I wasn't going to rise to his bait. I *wanted* to, but I'd always been able to see things with painful clarity.

I talked too much. I wasn't invited. And if people like Sloane Parker didn't take pity on me, I never would be.

"Why do you have so many copies of this one book?"

A few hours later, with my casserole eaten and Sloane's doctor long gone, I sat cross-legged on the floor of Arthur's living room, holding a battered paperback of something called *The Remains of the Day*. Dust bunnies marched by at every blast of air, and Sloane's organizational system seemed to consist mostly of taking books down from the shelf and lining them up in disordered stacks, but my stomach was too full of huckleberry pie for me to move.

"Put that down," Arthur snapped. "I need those."

"You need five copies of the same book?" I turned it over and skimmed the description. A book about a butler in post-WWII England sounded about as dry as you could get. I didn't know who this Kazuo Ishiguro was, but he could have used a few more vampires to liven things up. "What are you going to do with them all?"

"Sloane, please take that away from her before she ruins it."

Sloane pulled her attention away from her contemplation of a leather-bound volume that looked to weigh as much as she did. "Take what away?" As soon as she saw what I held, she tsked and shook her head. "Don't be such a scrooge, Arthur. Let her have it. I was planning on tossing the extras anyway."

"You wouldn't dare throw a perfectly good book away."

She laughed. "Okay, I was planning on taking them to a used book store or sticking them in some of the Little Free Libraries around town, but you know what I mean. There's no need to be so dramatic."

"Dramatic? *Me?* I'm not the one who brought that overbearing white knight of a man into a stranger's home—"

"It's okay," I was quick to interrupt. I didn't *think* Sloane was likely to fold under Arthur's sharp tongue, but I wasn't taking any risks. "I don't really want the book."

I could hardly be blamed for my caution. Sloane had come out of that kitchen earlier looking like a rag doll that had been tossed about in the wind. And her boyfriend—who it turned out was actually her fiancé—hadn't looked much better. I never did manage to get a glass to the wall, but from the way he'd walked out of here, all rigid and cold, I was guessing their conversation hadn't gone the way he'd wanted it to.

Which was no surprise, really. That wasn't the sort of man who was used to being stood up to. And unless I was very much mistaken, Sloane wasn't a woman used to doing much standing.

"What do you mean, you don't want the book? Have you read it?" Arthur demanded.

"Well, no."

"Then take it. Take two. I think it might help."

"Help with what?" I asked.

He waved a hand in my general direction, treating my dusty black yoga pants and rapidly withering topknot as personal insults.

"Don't do it," Sloane warned. "I once asked him what he thought of me, and it didn't end well. He was ruthless."

I was agog to hear what sort of things Arthur McLachlan could say about a sweet, inoffensive slip of a girl who'd done so much for him, but no one bothered to enlighten me.

"I meant every word," he told her, a mulish set to his jaw. "Especially now that I've met your young man."

For the first time, Sloane seemed to feel the sting of his insults. "I beg your pardon? What does Brett have to do with any of this?"

"You know *exactly* what he has to do with it. Good God, girl. You can't really mean to marry that walking, talking block of a man."

"He seemed nice," I offered, but I might as well have been invisible for all the attention anyone paid me.

"Why shouldn't I marry him? He's kind. He's generous. He came over here and cleaned your kitchen for you, not to mention taking your blood pressure and oxygen levels. What more could you ask out of a person?"

I knew the answer to that question. People like Arthur McLachlan didn't call the psychic hotline very often—for reasons I hardly needed to explain—but we got them sometimes. Usually when they were desperate for someone to argue with, their need for human contact so strong that they'd pay four bucks a minute just to have someone to yell at. They didn't call us any names we hadn't heard a hundred times before, the same things we said to ourselves in the mirror every single morning, but they usually had a lot to say.

"You know what? I think I *will* take this book." I fluttered through the pages. Several passages had been highlighted in yellow, but I passed them in a blur. "I don't know much about World War Two—or about butlers—but I'm always happy to learn more."

As I'd hoped, Arthur turned his emotional energy toward me instead of Sloane. "It's not about either of those things, you clodpole."

"But it says here—"

"They're *literary devices*," he said, emphasizing the words with so much force that it set him off coughing again. Instead of coming to his aid, Sloane turned to me, interest arching her brows.

"Do you really want to read it?" she asked. "That one's been on my TBR list for years, but I keep putting it off. My boss likes it when we're on top of what's new and hot in the book world, so the older ones tend to fall through the cracks."

I had almost no interest in the book, especially now that I knew there were literary devices lurking about, but that didn't stop me from seizing opportunity with both greedy hands.

"Do you want to read it together?" I asked, trying not to sound as nervous as I felt. I imagined this was what people proposing marriage had to deal with. "As a...book club?"

"Ha! This should be good."

Sloane and I both ignored Arthur. "Are you serious?" Sloane asked. "I can't think of anything I'd enjoy more. One of my pet projects at the library was to try and get a club up and running, but the timing and budget never aligned. I'd love to have someone to read the book with. I haven't had a good, deep literary discussion in ages."

The paperback in my hands suddenly started to feel awfully heavy. It wasn't a long book, not compared to some of the ones sitting around Arthur's living room, but a glance at one of the highlighted quotes had me rethinking my offer.

"'Perhaps it is indeed time I began to look at this whole matter of bantering more enthusiastically,'" I read aloud, wrinkling my nose. "'After all, when one thinks about it, it is not such a foolish thing to indulge in—particularly if it is the case that in bantering lies the key to human warmth.'"

"Give me that." Arthur dashed out his hand and snatched the book away so quickly that it left a paper cut behind. "You can't have that one."

"Oh, for Pete's sake," Sloane said. "You don't need all five copies. You're just being mean."

"I don't want all five copies. I only want this one." He held it to his chest, his grip so tight that the bulbous blue veins stood out on his hands. "She can have the rest, but this one is mine."

At this, I kind of wanted the super-important highlighted one, but I knew when to pick my battles.

"Does this mean you'll join us?" I asked.

"Please say you will, Arthur." Sloane added her entreaty to mine. "I know how you feel about book clubs, but I'd love a chance to hear your thoughts on something that doesn't end in gloom and despair."

He narrowed one speculative eye. "I thought you said you'd never read it."

"I haven't."

"Then how do you know it doesn't end in gloom and despair?"

She shrugged. "If you'd rather we pick something else, I could always go to the library and snag some copies of *The Art of Racing in the Rain*."

"Please don't do that," I was quick to say.

"Ha! I knew you'd come in handy." Arthur puffed his chest out at me, something almost like approval in the hard glint of his eyes. "See? Even the frumpy housewife doesn't want to read that sentimental garbage."

"It's not that," I explained. "It's just that when I saw the movie last year, I cried so hard I burst a blood vessel in my eye. I still get a little heartbroken every time I think about it."

I had no idea what I said to set them off, but from Sloane's shout of laughter and Arthur's of outrage, I felt sure it was the right thing.

9

_

"NO ONE TOLD ME THIS BOOK would be so sad."

Our inaugural meeting of the Racing in the Rain Book Club—a name Arthur violently opposed and that Sloane and I were only allowed to use in secret—took place two short days later. I hadn't been able to get too far in my reading yet, what with balancing my work shifts and the frenzy of cooking I'd been doing to keep those two fed, but the book was a lot more interesting than I'd expected it to be. I said as much as soon as we sat down in Arthur's living room.

"I got to that part about bantering," I explained when Arthur released a grunt. "The section you have highlighted in your copy of the book."

"It's not what you think," he said, but with such a shifty movement of his eyes that I knew he was lying. "This is the copy I used back when I taught the book to my students. Several of the passages have been annotated for their literary importance."

"You taught *The Remains of the Day*?" Sloane asked, her chin propped on her hand. Despite the progress she'd made with Arthur's personal library, we were still surrounded by towers of books. At least the coffee table was cleared enough to enjoy the fruit and cheese plate I'd brought over. "What class?"

"Unreliable narration," he said shortly. He cast a look toward me that I felt certain had a deeper meaning. "That's when the person telling the story isn't to be trusted. It's up to you, the reader, to decide how much of what they say is the truth and how much is self-delusion."

"That's why it's so sad," I insisted. I might not have known the right terminology, but I was familiar with self-delusion. It was literally how I paid my bills; no one called the psychic hotline because they had a clear picture of what was going on in their lives. "The narrator—Stevens—*is* unreliable, but how could he know that? No one ever sat him down and told him what's really going on."

Arthur grunted. "Telling an unreliable narrator that he's unreliable isn't a thing."

"I don't see why not. People can't learn from their mistakes if they don't know what their mistakes are. If I were writing a book, that's the first thing I'd do."

"Oh my God."

I recognized his outburst as a cue to stop talking, but I was on a roll. "All the poor guy wants is to make a friend. That's why he's trying to learn how to banter, even though it's not something he likes. Or something he's good at. He has to do *something* to connect with people."

Sloane swiveled her head to look at me, her expression not unlike that of an inquisitive bird. "You're enjoying this book, aren't you?"

"It's not the sort of thing I'd pick up in line at the grocery store, but I can see why it won all those awards," I admitted with an uncomfortable shrug. "Connecting with people is kind of my job."

"You have a job?" Arthur demanded.

"Of course she has a job." Sloane was quick to leap to my defense. "How else would she make a living? Do you think she's getting by on a secret trust fund or something?"

"Stranger things have happened."

I couldn't help laughing. "If I had a trust fund, I'd be living somewhere a lot more glamorous than this. Bali, maybe. Or Venice. Boise, at the very least." I scooted closer to Arthur and gestured for his hand. "Here. Give me your palm, and I'll show you."

He yanked his hands out of my reach so fast that I was pretty sure he pulled a muscle. "The devil I will. What do you want it for?"

"So I can see your future. Or as close to it as I can get on such a short acquaintance. It's not that big of a deal. You might even enjoy it. People pay me a lot of money for this."

"How *much* money?" Arthur asked, one eye appraising me while the other narrowed in disbelief. "I've never met a real charlatan before."

"Arthur! You can't call Maisey that."

"By definition, it's what she is. You heard her. She tells people lies, and then charges them for the privilege. How is that anything else?"

"I don't *lie*," I protested. "I talk to someone long enough to figure out what they're most worried about, and then I help them through it. It's no different than therapy, except I don't have a degree."

"Or qualifications?" Arthur suggested.

My cheeks started to flame, but Sloane swiveled her head to look at me. "You mean you just tell people things they already know?" she asked. "Like a fortune cookie?"

I shifted uncomfortably in my seat. "Well, it's not *exactly* like a fortune cookie. What I do is more personalized than that."

"So…it's like a BuzzFeed quiz?"

"Yes."

"Okay. Then you can read my palm." Sloane turned to me with her palm outstretched. "I took a quiz this morning that told me my dream career is travel agent. And that the Disney character I'm most like is the pig from *Moana*. Those can't possibly be true."

"Sloane, you aren't really going to let her read your future," Arthur said in a tone that was less like a question than a plea. "You're a woman of education. Of *wisdom*."

I didn't need him to say the rest: *unlike Maisey Phillips.*

"Education, yes," Sloane admitted with a wrinkle of her nose. "Wisdom, no. I've never had much of that. My sister did, though. I was the sensibility to her sense, the Marianne to her Elinor."

Arthur released a sound somewhere between a snort and a cough. "That's not anything to boast of, girl. Austen wrote Marianne out to be a fool. A sappy, melodramatic fool who's only redeemed in the end by having the romance literally bled out of her."

"I know." Sloane sighed. "It's always been a source of great shame to me."

Once again, I felt myself getting abandoned in the shallow end of the pool—only this time, Sloane robbed the sting of it by bestowing a sunny smile on me. "Go ahead, if you please. I bet you're really good at this. You have a way of making people feel comfortable."

My eyes swam as I ducked my head and made a quick survey of Sloane's palm. As before, her hand felt clammy to the touch. It could have just been her natural state of being, but it also could have been a sign that she was prone to panic attacks.

Bella got those, so I understood. When she'd been little, we used to blow them away with paper bags and silly songs, but those stopped being effective around the same time I had.

"You aren't going to read my love line or anything, are you?" Sloane asked as I continued examining her hand. "Because I'm not sure how much I want you peering into that."

"Not if you wouldn't like it. But if you want to know about work or your past lives or even which scratch tickets to buy, feel free to ask." I paused. "Well, that last one can be a bit dicey. I've never actually predicted any lottery winnings, but I know which ones are the most fun. I like the ones where you get to play a crossword puzzle while you try to win."

She laughed softly. "Thanks, but I don't need any of that."

I could feel Arthur watching me closely, taking notes on my

technique and storing up insults to throw at me later. It was strange to be doing this in person rather than over the phone, but the principles were the same: be chatty and open, lower your client's guard, and get them to tell you all the things they'd never willingly put into words.

Then pounce.

I wasn't sure when I'd first discovered this gift in myself, but it was something anyone could do, as long as they were willing to play the part. I wasn't bitter about it—I really wasn't—even though it sounded that way. I used to read tarot cards, back when all this had been a hobby instead of a career, and the one that had always popped up in my own readings, no matter how many times I shuffled the deck, was the fool.

Immature and inexperienced, full of innocence, a blank slate.

At first it had hurt, this idea that I'd never be more than the butt of other people's jokes, but people underestimate fools. When they're in a fool's company, they feel safe. They stop trying so hard.

"I guess I wouldn't mind knowing a little more about my love life," Sloane admitted. "If you've already seen something, that is. We might as well not waste it."

See? I hadn't even done anything yet, and I was already well on my way to answers. Not all was well with Sloane's engagement—that much I knew for sure. She hadn't mentioned Brett a single time since he'd been over here cleaning windows. Like me and my silence where Bella was concerned, it was the nothing that said the most.

"I was almost married once," I said. I could feel Sloane's start of surprise, but I wasn't ready to let go of her hand yet. The process was just getting started. "He was the lead singer in a rock band. You wouldn't have *believed* the abs on this guy. We're talking all six cans, lined up in two perfect columns. He used to wear these tiny leather pants—I tried putting them on once and I couldn't even get them over my knees, they were that tight. He used to have to peel them off like wet skin. But in, like, a sexy way."

"This can't be happening to me," Arthur moaned.

"That's amazing," Sloane breathed. "Why didn't you go through with it?"

I rolled my shoulder in a shrug. "The usual reasons. Rock star impregnates groupie. Groupie manages to rope him into about six months of cohabitation before things go south. It's a pretty boring story, when all's said and done. I could name you three other girls who went through the exact same thing."

"What does *any* of this have to do with palm reading?" Arthur asked. "I think you should demand your money back, Sloane."

"Before things have a chance to develop? Absolutely not." Sloane settled more comfortably in front of me. "That's who you had your daughter with, right? The one you mentioned before?"

I nodded. "About a year ago, she decided she'd rather live with him." The cool parent, the one who owned every record known to mankind, the one who didn't spend all day chatting with strangers about their love lives. "He's got this great new wife who's done a lot to steady him. He even teaches music lessons down at the Guitar Shoppe now. I get custody one weekend a month."

"Oh. That's not very much." Her face fell. "I'm sorry."

I ducked my head again, grateful for the distraction of her hand to keep me busy. "The point I'm trying to make is that your story isn't like mine. You started with stability instead of the other way around."

"This is just nonsense. Every word of it. I thought we were here to discuss literature."

"This *is* literature," Sloane insisted. "It's the story of my life."

"Your life isn't—"

"I know. It isn't worth the paper it's printed on. But it's the only one I have, so I'm keeping it." She nodded at me to continue. "You think Brett is stable? That's good to hear. I like stable things."

"No, you don't. You're just afraid of what happens when the stability goes away."

"Wait." Sloane tried to snatch her hand back. "What are you talking about? That's not on my palm."

She was right—it wasn't. But it *was* in the way she showed up here every day, determined to help an old man who'd done nothing to deserve it. It was in the way she'd quietly and gently removed her fiancé from this house, unwilling to let him upset the delicate balance she'd managed to reach. It was in the way she always looked a little bit startled when someone was nice to her, as if it could be taken away at any moment.

This wasn't a girl who liked chaos. This was a girl who did everything she could to keep things on an even keel.

"You and your fiancé will be very happy together, that much I see for sure. But he's not your great passion."

"Arthur, you wretch." Sloane managed to yank her hand free and turned toward the couch, where Arthur smacked his lips with something like satisfaction. "You put her up to this, didn't you? You told her what to say."

He put his hands up in a gesture of surrender. "Acquit me, my dear. I'd have chosen a more reliable tool for the job."

I was pretty sure that was an insult, but I didn't dwell on it—partly because I felt smug at having hit the nail on the head, and partly because I realized I'd just had my first literary breakthrough.

"You're a lot like Stevens." I returned my attention to the dog-eared paperback in front of me. Arthur had actually groaned when he saw what I'd done to the pages, but since he'd taken a highlighter to his own copy, I didn't see what right he had to judge mine. "He wanted stability so much that he spent his whole life serving a man who never appreciated it. Or who appreciated him."

"Maisey!" Sloane protested, but it was no use.

"I was right," I insisted. "It *is* a sad book."

"Well, I'll be damned." Arthur put his hands down and looked at me with a new light in his eyes. "The housewife might not be as bad at this as I feared."

10

—

QUICK, BELLA. I NEED YOU TO run outside and accost a strange man."

I dashed down the hallway and stopped outside my daughter's door, where a not-so-invisible line separated her room from the rest of the house. The piece of masking tape she'd put across the threshold was so dirty it was practically black, but I knew better than to touch it.

Or to cross over it.

"Ohmigod, Maisey. You can't ask a teenager to do that. Don't you know anything about how the world works?"

I stiffened at the sound of that *Maisey*. She only called me by my first name to get under my skin, but that didn't make it hurt any less.

"I meant that you need to run outside and accost a strange man under my careful supervision," I corrected myself. "I just need you to pop out and lower his defenses. If he sees me coming, he'll drive off before we get anywhere."

The look my daughter leveled on me was full of meaning in the way only a sixteen-year-old could manage. *You're an idiot*, that look said. *I can't believe you gave birth to me. Maybe that man drives off because he wants nothing to do with you.*

That might have sounded like a mouthful for a pair of brown eyes ringed with so much eyeliner that I had to buy new pillowcases every time she stayed over, but you had to trust me on this one. They were very talkative eyes.

"Please, Bella?" I put my hands up in a pleading gesture. It was the same one she'd used when she was a little girl and wanted an extra spoonful of powdered sugar on her French toast; the same one she'd pulled out when she'd first begged me not to fight the petition for custody changes. "I know it sounds weird, but it's not for me. It's for some friends of mine."

That got Bella's attention. She even pulled out one of her earpods. The tinny, echoing sound of a K-pop band filled the air. "What friends?"

She didn't ask this question in a cruel way. At least, I didn't *think* it was meant to be cruel. The one weekend a month she spent with me wasn't enough for us to keep up-to-date on each other's social lives, so she might have been genuinely curious. To be fair, *I* kept pretty close tabs on *her*, thanks to her TikTok account and an Instagram feed that seemed to be mostly pictures of her attempts at the perfect cat's-eye, but there wasn't a lot of reciprocation. My last post only got two likes, and one of them had been from a bot trying to sell me life insurance.

"You don't know them," I said, sounding more defensive than I cared for. "They're new."

"Ew. Did you find them on an app or something?"

"Not exactly." I cast a quick look over my shoulder, fearful that Arthur's stalker would drive away before I had a chance to send Bella out for information. "Look, will you do it or not? I already got a picture of his license plate, so if he kidnaps you, it should be easy to track you down again."

"Mom!"

I was so happy to hear that word from her lips that I forgot everything else. "See, Bella? You *do* know how to say it."

She unfolded herself from the bed with the long limbs and easy grace of a teenager who knew herself to hold all the cards. "If I do this, will you let me spend the night at Hilary's like I wanted to?"

I gripped the doorway so tightly that I could hear the cheap wood starting to splinter. *I won't say it. I'll stay strong. I'll wear this smile if it kills me.*

"Is that the coworker who picks up every free shift she can get, or the one who always forgets to fill the napkin dispenser?"

My smile was starting to crack around the edges, but Bella was too surprised by my question to notice.

"How do you know about my work friends?" she demanded.

I slid my free hand behind my back and crossed my fingers. I promised myself a long time ago that I'd never lie to Bella, but life had a way of crushing the best of intentions. "Oh, you know. Your father must have mentioned them."

"She's the napkin one," she said, eyeing me suspiciously. "Does that mean I can go? I like going to her house. She's the oldest of four, so there's always a lot to do there. It's not so...empty."

As soon as that word—*empty*—touched her lips, we both knew the answer to her question. But only one of us realized the cost.

"Of course you can go, honey. If it's what you really want."

"Yes!" She pulled out the other earpod and started texting excitedly on her phone. With only half her attention on me, she asked, "What do I need to go do to this guy first? Just say hi?"

To be honest, my heart wasn't really in the game anymore. I still wanted to know what that man had to do with Arthur, but Bella had sucked all the fun out of it. For a second there, I'd thought it might be something we could do together, one of those unlikely bonding experiences that other moms and daughters seemed to share.

But Bella was already zipping up her overnight bag, grabbing a phone cord and her toothbrush—her two primary signs of life inside this house.

"You don't have to do anything." I handed her a twenty and some bus fare from my purse. I knew from long experience that she wouldn't accept a ride to her friend's house. She wouldn't want anyone catching a glimpse of me in the car. "Will I see you tomorrow, or do you plan to go straight to your dad's afterward?"

"I'll just go straight home," she said as she brushed a distracted kiss on my cheek. Thankfully, she didn't notice my wince or the way my whole body recoiled at that word.

Home, with her rock star father and new stepmom.

Home, the place where she felt most comfortable.

Home, anywhere but with me.

"Thanks, Maisey!" she called as she ducked out the door and dashed down the street toward the bus stop. "You're the best. See you next month!"

I watched her go with a smile and a wave, both of which stayed in place long after she disappeared from view. Anyone looking out the window at me would think I'd lost it, but no one ever looked out the window at me, so it was okay.

Only this time, it turned out I *was* being watched. No sooner did I blink than I spotted him: the guy in the car, the watchful stranger, the man who'd turned away every delicious treat I'd offered him. He glanced away as soon as he realized I'd noticed him noticing me, but it was too late. Before I even knew what I was doing, I crossed the lawn to where he'd parked—and without a single baked good in hand, which proved how upset I was.

"Did you enjoy the show?" I demanded, placing my hand on top of the window so he couldn't roll it up. He also couldn't speed off without dragging me down the street, so he had no choice but to face me. "Have you seen enough, or did you want me to call her back so we can do it all over again? I should warn you—she won't come. Not for a million dollars. Not if I was the last person on the planet."

"Look, lady, I don't know what you want." He tried the window button, but it was no match for me. "I don't want anything to eat, I'm not here for a friendly chat, and I *definitely* wasn't watching your daughter run away from you like a bat out of hell."

That last one was the final straw. Sliding my hand over the top of the glass, I popped the lock and yanked the door open.

"Hey! You can't just climb in here—"

"Go ahead and call the cops," I said as I plopped myself in the passenger seat and planted myself as deep as I could go. "I'm sure they'd be *very* interested in how many hours you've spent stalking a helpless, dying old man."

"He's *dying*?"

The guy turned to me then, his face drained of all color, the fight slipping right on out with it. That's when I noticed the resemblance.

I wasn't sure which part of him reminded me of Arthur McLachlan. In fact, I wasn't sure that any specific part of him was the same. His nose was too big and too crooked, as if he'd been in a bar fight or two in his time. His eyes were a dark, glittering brown instead of gray, his jaw squarer, his build more like a linebacker than an academic.

But the resemblance was there all the same.

"No…no. Of course he's not dying." I reached over and gripped his hand, surprised at how chilly his skin was, as if his blood had literally run cold. "I only said that to get a reaction out of you."

"Jesus, lady. It worked." He yanked his hand back, leaving that icy impression of stone behind. He didn't, as I feared, immediately kick me out of the car. With a sideways glance at Arthur's house, he asked, "He's okay, though? Not…sick?"

Since I was almost a hundred percent certain this guy was related to Arthur in some way, I pushed aside my qualms. "Well, he's not doing *great*. His breathing is almost all the way under control now, except for at night. And I think he's gained some strength, but every little task seems to zap his energy—"

"You have to get me in there."

I blinked, startled by his force. "Into…his house? Have you tried knocking?"

To my surprise, he laughed. Like Sloane's unusually warm trill, there was something disarming about it. "Of course I haven't tried knocking. How desperate do you think I am?" He caught a glimpse of himself in the rearview mirror and grimaced. "Never mind. Don't answer that."

"You're his grandson?"

He swiveled his head to stare at me. "How do you know that?"

"I didn't know he had kids," I said by way of answer. There was no sign of it inside his house—no family portraits lining the walls, no strip of masking tape marking a boundary that could never be crossed.

"He doesn't. Not anymore." The guy slumped in his seat, his hands beating a nervous pattern on the steering wheel. "You've been going over there, right? Taking him meals? Making sure he's not passed out on the floor?"

"I do my best, but Sloane's the one doing most of the heavy lifting."

"Sloane? Who the devil is Sloane?"

The way he asked this question was so much like Arthur at his surliest that I had to fight a smile. "His temporary caregiver—but don't call her a 'caregiver' in your grandfather's hearing unless you want to start playing baseball with his furniture. Technically, she's only there to catalog his books." I couldn't help a feeling of pride from puffing through me for this next part. "She's also in our book club. We're meeting tonight, if you're interested."

He couldn't have been less interested if I'd offered him a plate at an invisible buffet. "I'll pass, thanks. My grandfather and I don't read the same type of books."

Which was one possible explanation for why he'd sat out in this car for so long, but I doubted it. "He and I don't read the same type, either," I admitted. "But the one for our book club isn't all bad. It's about this butler who's obsessed with his job."

The guy's expression of disgust said everything I felt upon first popping the cover.

"Here." He scrambled around until he pulled a wallet from his back pocket. "Since you've been feeding him and everything, I'd like to pay you back—"

"No way." I scooted so far back that my head thumped against the ceiling, my hands behind my back to keep him from pressing a fistful of bills into them. "You don't owe me anything. I'm happy to help out."

The guy didn't look as though he believed me.

"I'm serious," I said—and I was. "I like him."

"Yeah, right. No one likes him. He makes damn sure of that." As soon as the curse word slipped out, the man winced and apologized. "Sorry. I didn't mean for it to come out like that."

He sounded so genuinely sorry that I couldn't help softening.

"Can I tell you something?" I said. "Something I've never told anyone?"

"I wish you wouldn't."

"Your grandfather is the only person I know who doesn't pretend to feel anything except what's in his heart. Do you know how many times he's ordered me out from under his roof?"

"I'm guessing about the same number of times I've asked you not to bring me breakfast sandwiches?"

I grinned. "More. *Way* more. And he means it—that's the thing. I could be murdered and tossed into the lake, never to be seen or heard from again, and he wouldn't notice."

The guy eyed me askance. He looked about five seconds away from going full Arthur McLachlan on me again, but at least he wasn't trying to shove money at me anymore. "What does this have to do with my grandfather's heart?"

"Because everyone else is the exact opposite," I explained.

I wasn't sure *why* I was telling this guy any of this, but it felt good to get it off my chest. I suspected it was that book starting to get to me. The more that butler went on and on about bantering and dignity and how much his boss *wasn't* a Nazi even though we could all tell he totally was, the more I felt the urge to unburden my heart in the same way.

Well, except for the Nazi part.

"Everyone's always saying the same things to me. 'The invitation's in the mail, Maisey.' 'We should totally get coffee sometime, Maisey.'" I sighed and pushed my hair out of my face. Bella convinced me to try wearing it down today so I'd look less like a peeled onion, but that had only made it worse. My hair was all scraggly wisps and wayward strands I kept mistaking for spiders. "Only the invitation is *never* in the mail. And no matter how many times I call, no one ever has time for coffee."

The guy's brow wrinkled for a moment, but he didn't run screaming from the car, so that counted for something. "You like my grandpa because he doesn't promise to send you invitations to things?"

"Your grandfather has called me every horrible, true thing he can think of—and several things that aren't true but are still horrible."

Last night, for example, he'd called me a teratoma of hair and teeth. The night before that, it had been a witless Wife of Bath. I had to google both those things once I got home, but it didn't take long for me to realize they weren't meant as compliments.

"That doesn't sound very nice," the man said.

"It's not," I admitted. "But no matter what he says or how many times he says it, he always opens the door when I knock. I bet if you come knock with me, he'll let you in, too."

The guy was silent for a moment, and I was afraid I'd scared him away. If he'd spent the better part of two weeks sitting out here, trying to muster up the courage to go inside his grandfather's house, he needed encouragement, not a depressing picture of what lurked on the other side of that door.

But I meant what I'd said. Arthur McLachlan was sharp-witted and sharp-tongued, and there was a good chance he'd shred his grandson to pieces before he managed to get a foot in the door, but if he was willing to accept a middle-aged nobody whose own daughter couldn't stand the sight of her, I felt sure he wouldn't throw this poor young man out.

That was $3.99 worth of worldly wisdom right there.

"Yeah. Okay. Thanks."

I so rarely won any arguments that it took me a moment to realize what he was saying. "You want to go see him?" I asked. "Right now?"

He hunched his shoulder in a half shrug. For the first time, I realized how large a man he was, how careful he'd been not to make himself seem overpowering inside this tiny space we shared. "If you're not busy, I mean. I don't want to be a bother."

"Of course I'm not busy. You saw what happened earlier."

"That was your daughter?"

I nodded, not trusting myself to speak, but feeling somehow that this young man understood. Especially once he slid out of the car without asking any questions.

"By the way," I added, heading up the sidewalk to the house, "if your grandfather throws the coatrack, you should probably duck, but the vase is an heirloom."

He blinked at me, perplexed.

"That one you'll want to catch."

11

―――――

I T'S ABOUT TIME YOU GOT HERE."

I stepped through Arthur's front door to find him sitting on the bottom step of his staircase, the fractured boards trapping him like a broken picture frame.

"Don't just stand there gawping, woman. Can't you see I need help?"

I stood there gawping for a few seconds longer, at which point Arthur grunted in irritation.

"Where's Sloane?" he demanded as he struggled to get to his feet. "She moved all my stair books. How the hell am I supposed to get around without my stair books?"

I was pushed ruthlessly aside by the young man as he made his way into the house. This wasn't how I'd have planned the first meeting of grandfather and grandson, but one of the things I always told my clients was that we could only choose which path to take to our destination. What happened along the way was entirely up to chance.

In this case, *chance* was Arthur McLachlan being lifted bodily into the arms of a young man I felt about eighty percent sure was a construction worker of some kind. Either that or a firefighter. I wasn't yet ready to mystify him by announcing his vocation in front of an audience, but I was getting close.

"Are you hurt?" he asked. He carried his grandfather toward the living room as though he were lifting a kitten rather than a fully grown man. "Is anything broken?"

"Greg? What do you think you're doing here?" Instead of waiting for an answer, Arthur struggled to free an arm so he could point an accusing finger. "Did that meddlesome woman let you in here?"

In case it wasn't obvious, *that meddlesome woman* was me, and he flung the words like he was about to tie me to a stake and light me on fire. Which, I was sorry to say, was a threat I got far more often than you'd think possible in this day and age. When my psychic advice went wrong, or—as was usually the case—because it was spot-on, people had a way of jumping straight onto the witch train.

I was about to open my mouth to defend myself when I caught sight of Greg's face. What I saw there—guilt and desperation and an all-encompassing panic wrapped up in one—flooded me with a bravery I didn't know I had.

"Yes, Arthur. It was me." I put my hands on my hips and did my best imitation of a woman who was about to demand to see the store manager. "He didn't want to come in, but I told him it was a matter of life or death, and that I'd report him to the authorities for elder abuse if he didn't do as he was told."

"Who are you calling an *elder*?" Arthur asked. Not content with flinging his bad temper at me, he turned to his grandson and added, "Put me down, you fool. There's no need to act like a circus strongman. I was stuck in a stair, not buried six feet deep."

I had to fight a laugh as Greg dumped his burden onto the couch, depositing the old man into a cloud of pillows that left him even more annoyed than before.

"Is that better?" Greg asked, watching as a few puffs of goose feathers flew up from the cushions.

Since Arthur could hardly complain about his grandson doing exactly as he was bid, the only response we got was a series of low muttered curses. They did the trick, though, giving animation and energy to an old man who looked as though he desperately needed them.

"Forty-five minutes," he said when he finished with his tirade. "That's how long I was in that blasted stair. Where's Sloane? Did she put you up to this?"

Once again, I saw my way with painful clarity. Some women were born to be great leaders. Some were meant to inspire greatness in others.

And some, like me, worked best as scapegoats.

"Sloane has nothing to do with this, so don't take your bad temper out on her. Or Greg. Or the stair. It was *my* idea, and I stand by it." Instinct warned me to make myself scarce, but Greg cast another of those pleading looks at me, so I settled myself on the nearest chair instead. There was a good chance I was about to be called a witch again—with or without a slight adjustment to the spelling—but if history had taught me one thing, it was that no good would come of trying to make myself the hero of this particular story.

Or of any story, really. Even my own.

"Why don't you thank your grandson for coming all this way instead of yelling at him for helping out?" I suggested as I made myself comfortable. This next part would be good. "Go ahead. I'll wait."

"I'm not thanking him. I didn't invite him."

"No, you didn't," Greg agreed, and in a tone that matched Arthur's for bullheadedness. "And you didn't call, either. I had to hear about your fall from the hospital."

"Ha! That shows what you know. I didn't fall."

Greg cast a pointed look at the stair, which looked even more battered now than it did before.

"I meant the *first* time," Arthur grumbled. "And what right does the hospital have to tell you anything? You're not listed as my next of kin."

"They were desperate to find a family member—*any* family member. Apparently, that's what happens when a man has to be restrained for fear he's going to pull out his oxygen tube and kill himself."

Arthur set his jaw. "What else was I supposed to do? They were going to let me die in there. Hooked up to a machine. Tied to the bed. Without a single—"

He cut himself off so suddenly that I knew exactly what he refused to say. *Without a single person there to witness it. Without a single person to hold my hand and watch me go.*

It was a fear I shared so deeply that I couldn't find any words to fill the stark, sudden silence of the living room. Which was for the best, really, because a temper like Arthur's had to be vented somewhere. Better for it to fall on the silence than on his grandson.

"Is this what you wanted?" Arthur demanded of me. "Do you feel better now that you've witnessed the happy reunion?"

"A little bit," I admitted. "Should I pop into the kitchen and make us something to eat? I feel like we could use something to eat."

"*No.*" Both men practically shouted the word. Interpreting this as an invitation to stay rather than a commentary on my cooking, I submitted.

"You're not staying here," Arthur said to Greg, with a mulish look about the lines of his mouth. "You'll only be in the way. Sloane is turning my guest room into the nonfiction section."

Greg's mouth grew equally hard, both of them chiseled as if from stone. It was starting to feel like Mount Rushmore in here, only instead of presidents it was two angry men who happened to be related to each other. "You prefer books to the company of your own grandson?"

"Infinitely."

"Fine. Whatever. I'm sure I can extend the stay at my Airbnb. No one else will touch the place." Greg's face twisted in what looked almost like a smile. "It has ghosts."

As a psychic—even one with a phone headset attached to her face—I was always interested in things that went bump in the night, but there was no chance for me to follow up. As soon as I opened my mouth, the front door swung open. Sloane's voice hailed us along with one of her light laughs.

"I know we were only supposed to read up to chapter five, but I couldn't put the book down last night," she called by way of greeting. "I finished it in the wee hours. I can't wait to hear what you thought of—"

She stopped as soon as she spotted Greg, her eyes wide.

"You," she said. "You cornered me in the basement."

"You," he said at almost the exact same time. "You trapped me in an elevator."

I had no idea what any of these things meant, but I easily recognized the flush that sprang to both of their cheeks.

"I don't... I'm not..." Sloane turned to me, her color still heightened. It was a nice look on her, like the bloom on a rose. I hadn't yet found an opening to tell her so, but I always thought Sloane looked her nicest when she was animated—usually because she was in the middle of taking Arthur down a peg or two—but this embarrassed surprise was nice, too. "What's going on?"

"I see you've already met Greg, Arthur's grandson," I said, stepping cheerfully into the breach. "Greg, this is Sloane Parker, the woman I was telling you about."

"Wait. *She's* my grandfather's caretaker?"

I bit back a sigh. Of course he'd have to say the *one* word I told him not to.

Arthur struggled to get into an upright position. "Of course she's not my caretaker, you dolt. What am I, a baby? A seedling? An ancient manuscript in need of climate control?"

That last one sounded pretty accurate to me, but I'd once again become the least important person in the room.

"No, you're a stubborn old man who'd rather spend hours buried under a pile of books than admit he needs help," Greg retorted.

"You're right. I would," Arthur said with a sniff. "Books are more reliable than you'll ever be."

"All the books in the world won't save you from yourself. You need an exorcism for that."

As I watched the argument progress along its predictable lines, I stepped back until I was out of the line of fire. I expected Sloane to range herself with me, but she didn't. Instead of shrinking under all the anger in this room, so thick I could wear it like a sweater, she only seemed to grow taller.

"That's enough," she said in a sharp tone that made me realize what a great librarian she could be. "Arthur, if your grandson has come all this way to see you, the only thing you should be doing is thanking him. And as for you…" She turned to the younger man, faltering a little. But only a little. As if forcing herself to remember her self-appointed role, she said, "Yelling at your grandfather isn't going to help this situation. He's been through a lot. What he needs right now is peace and quiet, not someone who's going to cause a relapse every time he opens his mouth."

There she ran out of steam—or courage—or both. Not that it mattered. Her message had made it through loud and clear, causing Greg to stare at her like she'd just pierced a sword through his chest. His grandfather took one look at his expression and laughed like the devil himself had just delivered the punch line.

"See?" Arthur said, almost gleeful. "I told you I don't need you. I already have all the meddling outsiders I can handle."

"Don't you think we should go back to the living room?" Sloane asked as she shot an anxious glance at the kitchen door, her lower lip between her teeth. "It's awfully quiet. What if they're murdering each other in there?"

I continued layering lasagna noodles in the rectangular pan in front of me, the scent of garlic and roasted tomatoes filling the air. Cooking had always been a soothing activity for me. My love language, a therapist used to call it, and the reason we were fighting an obesity epidemic in America. We didn't last long, that therapist and me. She used to throw away the cookies I brought her when she thought I wasn't looking.

"I have a freezer in my basement that would easily fit Arthur's body," I said as I started tossing fistfuls of cheese into the pan. "But Greg's might need to be chopped up first. I have an electric carving knife that should do the trick. It cuts through my Thanksgiving turkey every year like butter."

It took Sloane a startled moment to recognize the joke. "Maisey, you can't kid about things like that! I'm emotionally vulnerable right now."

I knew that, which was why I was cooking up a storm and cracking jokes about the cold storage of dead bodies. "I'm sure they're behaving themselves. You made sure of that when you raked them both over the coals." I paused, smiling. I'd enjoyed few things lately as much as I did that little altercation in the living room. "Did you really trap Greg in an elevator? Who'd have thought a sweet thing like you would have the nerve."

I held out a bunch of oregano that I'd plucked from my herb garden and gestured for her to start chopping.

"It wasn't my fault," she said as she picked up a knife and started hacking away. She was going to bruise the crap out of those poor herbs, but I suspect she needed the outlet. "He scared me."

I snorted. "I think you have that backwards. From where I was standing, he looked *way* more afraid of you."

She glanced up at me, her knife poised in midair. "That's not true. No one has feared me a day in my life. Especially not a guy like that."

I didn't bother to reply to this. Sloane obviously wasn't ready for the full force of the Maisey Phillips psychic experience.

"Careful with that knife," I suggested instead. "The last thing we need is another superglue incident."

She gratefully accepted this way out. "What do you think happened to cause such a rift between them? I don't get along with my parents, but I'd *never* talk to them the way Greg does to Arthur."

"The only things that ever seem to cause that kind of drama in *Flames of the World* are money and betrayal, but I get the feeling it's not either of those things," I said.

"So what does that leave? A love affair gone wrong?"

"You might not be too far off the mark," I said. I doubted there was an affair involved, but love certainly came into play. "Don't forget that I've seen Greg sitting out there watching the house since the day Arthur came home. No matter which angle I saw him from, he always looked so…"

"Angry?" Sloane guessed. "Aggressive? Belligerent?"

I shook my head. "Lonely. Like he's never had a friend a day in his life."

She stopped and looked at me then, her expression hard to read. When she spoke, it was with a slight lilt to her normal speech. "'At the enchanted metropolitan twilight I felt a haunting loneliness sometimes, and felt it in others.'"

"That's pretty. Is it from our book?"

She shook her head. "No, it's from *The Great Gatsby*. I was pulling out copies for our Lost Generation section—we're putting it in Arthur's back hallway—and got sucked in. I did a few courses on Fitzgerald in college."

I nodded, my interest not all the way faked. Hearing Sloane

and Arthur talk about books was like listening to a song in another language. The message didn't always make it through, but that didn't mean I couldn't appreciate the melody.

"That passage was highlighted," she added.

That got the rest of my attention. "You mean like in the forbidden copy of *The Remains of the Day*? I still think we should try and heist it out of here one night. I bet Arthur only does that to the dirty parts."

Sloane laughed, but she tossed the suggestion aside. "Arthur came in before I could look too closely, but that quote in particular stood out. I had a high school teacher who made us do that. Not highlight the school copies, obviously, but keep a quote journal. When we came across anything that struck a chord or seemed important, we had to write it out by hand in these little notebooks he bought us. I probably still have mine somewhere."

"Please don't mention that to Arthur," I begged. "The last thing I need is for him to assign me homework on top of everything else."

I started pulling out the makings of a salad even though Arthur had very determinedly informed me yesterday that salads "are what food eats." If I didn't give him something to be angry about, there was a good chance he'd take it out on his grandson, and then where would we be?

No closer to figuring out the cause of their family drama than before, that was where. Call me inquisitive, call me meddlesome, call me—okay, *fine*—nosy, but that was one mystery I felt determined to solve.

"Do you think I should invite him to stay with me?" I asked as I started peeling carrots.

"What? Who?"

"Greg," I said, even though she already knew the answer. "If renting the condo below your parents is as awful as you say it is—"

She grimaced. "It is."

"And if Arthur isn't willing to house him here—"

She grimaced deeper. "He isn't."

I splayed my hands in a gesture of helplessness. "Then there you go. The poor guy obviously came a long way to visit his grandfather, and he just as obviously wants to make amends. The least I can do is put a roof over his head for a few days."

My decision made, I added the clincher.

"And who knows? He might even want to join our book club."

12

WHEN I TEXTED BELLA TO LET her know that a strange man would be sleeping in her bed for the foreseeable future, it took her two hours to reply.

gross

That was it. One word. One comment. She had no interest in who the strange man was or the likelihood of me being murdered under my own roof. Or even how a woman who almost never left the comfort and safety of her own street could have met a man—strange or otherwise.

I was about to ask how her friend was doing, if she needed me to bring an extra set of pajamas, if the bonds of motherhood meant *anything* to her, but Greg coughed before I managed the first emoji.

"I wouldn't, if I were you," he said.

My hand hovered over the phone. "How do you know what I'm doing?"

I knew the answer before he even opened his mouth. From where he stood, his massive form filling the doorway leading into my living room, he had a clear view of the half-empty bottle of wine that sat at my elbow. There was only one path leading away from there.

"You're either texting a date or your daughter," he said.

Since it seemed I was in the company of a fellow psychic, I handed him the phone. At seeing himself referred to as a "strange man," a light smile touched his lips.

I wished Arthur could see that smile. Or Sloane. No matter how many times I'd tried to draw him out, Greg had sat silently throughout dinner, not saying anything that hadn't included the words *please* and *salt*. He'd eaten a hefty chunk of the lasagna, though. That had to count for something.

"Wait until morning, and then ask her something unrelated," Greg suggested. "Something she has no choice but to answer, but that leaves me out of it. Like where she put an old board game you can't find or if she needs a notebook you found wedged under the mattress. The lack of follow-up will hook her."

His plan was a good one, but I wasn't sure I liked where this was headed. "Are you a professional pickup artist or something?"

He chuckled and tilted his head in a way I recognized as a question. Scooting over to make room for him on the couch, I patted the cushion. That was another thing I wished Arthur and Sloane could see—the quiet, unassuming politeness in him. Until I invited him to come closer, he planned to stay a respectful six feet back.

"Or something," he said as he sat. His weight dragged the cushions down. "I work with kids. You won't get anywhere with them by being sincere. Not at that age, anyway. They fight against anything that feels like real emotion."

Hmm. I pursed my lips and examined him out of the corner of my eye. It was starting to look like time to reconsider my original reading of this man; construction work and firefighting weren't exactly kid-friendly professions.

"What?" he asked. "Why are you looking at me like that?"

"Give me your hand."

He immediately yanked his arm so far out of my reach that I was reminded, once again, of how much he resembled his grandfather.

"Don't be such a baby." I pointed to the side of the living room where my desk and the cat clock were set up. "It's my thing. I read people's fortunes for a living. I tried to do your grandfather, but he reacted...strongly."

"That sounds about right. I've never known him to react any other way." Something like a smile touched his lips. "But there's no need to read my palm to get answers. I'll tell you anything you want to know."

I blinked, unsure how to handle this reaction. People *never* told me what I wanted to know. They lied and pretended they had appointments on the other side of town. They buried themselves in work, in books, in anything but honest-to-goodness human interaction. This man, in particular, had sped away from me several times already, his foot heavy on the gas as he shot away as fast as metal and gasoline could carry him.

"You'll tell me literally anything?" I asked.

A tinge of red touched his cheeks before creeping up to his ears. "Not *anything*, but stuff within reason. The stuff a psychic would know, anyway."

I decided to test him.

"What do you do for a living?"

"Officially? I code for a tech firm. But the kids I was talking about are part of an after-school boxing program I volunteer for. We do weight training, drills, that sort of thing."

This answer satisfied me on so many levels that I didn't hesitate to ask another. "How long would you have stayed out in that car, too afraid to tell your grandfather that you came all this way to see him?"

"Weeks, probably. Or months. I don't know. I packed up everything when I heard what had happened. I wanted to be here in case... well, you know. They made it sound pretty bad."

"Oh, wow." That one floored me a little. I couldn't think of anyone who would willingly drop everything and come running if I suddenly fell ill. Bella *might* come around to spending her one weekend a month with me instead of her friends, but I wouldn't put money on the likelihood. "But you're not close, right? You and Arthur?"

"You could say something like that." Greg's mouth set in a grim line. "My mom left the house the day she graduated high school, barely eighteen and pregnant with yours truly. I saw him a few times growing up, but he never tried to reach out to me, never wanted more than a cursory relationship. I'm here to try and fix that."

All of a sudden, I wasn't so sure about this brutal honesty approach. At least when I told people's fortunes, I could pretend to give them happy backstories…and outcomes. I doubted Arthur was going to give this man a happy *anything*.

"Why didn't you say any of this?" My question came a little more quietly this time. "To your grandfather, I mean? You barely spoke two words to him over dinner."

"Because he didn't ask."

I relaxed back against the cushions, suddenly feeling overwhelmed by this influx of information—offered without strings or emotion, and by the last person I'd expect it from. The feeling reminded me of the first time I ever took Bella to the ocean. Lake Coeur d'Alene was a gorgeous body of water, don't get me wrong, and the beach here was perfect for a day of swimming and sun, but there was no current. The lake water had a way of lapping lazily at the shore, tickling toes and offering a gentle playfellow. The ocean, though—that was something else. Bella had run up to the edge of the water, expecting her old friend, only to find herself pulled under by the freezing hand of a stranger.

Greg must have sensed some of my feelings, because his wry smile deepened. "I apologize if that's more than you wanted to know. I'd just rather tell you than have you try to nose out my history through other means. Sorry."

"Don't be," I said, though the words were distant—mechanical. "I'm not used to it, that's all."

He got to his feet and nodded down at my phone, a not unkind expression on his face. "Ask her about the board game, and then give it a few days before you try again. If it doesn't work, I promise to help you catch her interest in some other way."

"Like an after-school boxing program?" I made a face. "No offense, but she's not the type. She doesn't like to sweat."

He chuckled softly. "I'm sure I can come up with something that'll work. I might not be great at dealing with grandfathers, but surly teenagers I can do."

———

Greg's advice about Bella worked much better than I expected it to.

It wasn't as if she texted back immediately, or even the next day, but I was sitting over a plate of Lean Cuisine Alfredo on my lunch break a few days later when I heard my phone buzz.

> did you find my old Ouija board?? the one you said you couldn't find?

My eyes widened at the sight of that text, an unprecedented event under most circumstances, and downright suspicious when the last fifteen texts I'd gotten from her were one syllable long.

"What's wrong?" Greg asked from his side of the table. He was eating one of my famous hand-pressed ham paninis with cheese oozing out the sides.

"It's from Bella. She wants to know if I found the missing Ouija board. And before you laugh, it's the only game we own, so I had to pick that one. We're not a Monopoly sort of family."

A grin touched his lips, and he took another big bite of the sandwich. "Told you. Works every time."

"How should I respond?" For some strange reason, my hands were shaking. "Do I play it cool? Lie? I don't think you understand, she *never* reaches out to me. Not if she has literally any other option."

If he noticed the way my voice cut out toward the end, he didn't let it show.

"What's your goal?" he asked.

"My goal?" I blinked. The answer to that should have been fairly obvious: a relationship with my daughter. For her to spend one weekend under my roof without running away like it caused her physical pain. "I don't know…for her to answer, I guess. And to *keep* answering."

Even as oversimplified a response as this one was hard for me to get out, but Greg didn't seem to think less of me for it.

"Then make sure there's always an opening. Something she won't be able to put a lid on." He polished off the rest of the sandwich in three easy bites. "Kids are curious little bastards, even though they'd rather die than admit it. I once broke my tibia during a training session—bone sticking out of my leg, blood everywhere—and every last one of the kids ran out of the gym like they were on fire. But wouldn't you know it? The longer it took for the ambulance to get there, the more of them trickled back in, demanding to see, wanting to snap pics for Instagram. I kept them on the line for weeks after that, feeding them recovery shots every few days."

"Oh dear." Even though he spoke lightly, my every maternal feeling came rushing to the surface. "That sounds awful, Greg. I'm so sorry."

"I'm not." He pushed back from the table and, as if to prove his return to health, stretched vigorously. "The physical therapy was a bitch, and I can feel the break when there's a storm coming on, but I still have contact with some of those kids—adults now, I guess. We bonded, in a way. Pain will do that, even if you're the only one feeling it."

I toyed with my phone, my fingers moving over the buttons in an empty pattern. "I guess I could always tell her that I found the Ouija board, but that her great-aunt Portia wouldn't say anything about the missing money when I tried to reach out to her on it."

"That's…an interesting choice. *Is* there missing money? Or a great-aunt Portia?"

I laughed. "Portia was real enough, but I don't remember her having two pennies to rub together. I don't think she needed it. She was my father's favorite sister, one of those beautiful, charming, larger-than-life women who always had people trailing after her. I've never known anyone to hold a room spellbound the way she used to."

He nodded as though this made perfect sense. "Like you."

Before I could do more than blink at this startling piece of information, a reflexive spasm crossed his face.

"Speaking of pennies, I wish you'd let me pay you for the room." He nodded down at his empty plate. "*And* the food. It doesn't seem right, me taking advantage of your hospitality like this. Especially since you're already doing so much for my grandfather."

I started picking up our plates with so much force that my favorite IKEA pattern got a chip on one of the edges. "Don't be silly. It's the least I can do. Sloane is the one doing the actual work. She was only supposed to stop by his house a few times a week, but I think she slept over there again last night."

Greg's grimace was impossible to ignore. "She did. I put a mark on her tire to see if the car moved."

For the first time, I felt as though I had a rival in my quest for prying. "You're keeping tabs on her?"

A tinge of red touched his cheeks. "Of course not. I'm just afraid she's doing a lot more for my grandfather than she's letting on. I still don't really understand. Who the devil *is* she? And what does she want with him?"

"She's his librarian," I answered, not failing to note the heat in his voice. "And I think she's just being nice."

"No one is that nice. Except maybe serial killers." He paused. "Or gold diggers."

I swiveled my head to stare at Greg, certain I couldn't be hearing him right. "You think *Sloane* is a gold digger?"

His red color deepened until it reached the tips of his ears. "I didn't say that."

"A woman who owns a cardigan in every color of the rainbow?"

"You're putting words in my mouth."

"A woman who sat quietly and listened while your grandfather went over every detail of his JFK conspiracy theories?"

"Some of those CIA theories carry real weight."

"A woman who literally lost her job to make sure he wasn't left alone inside that house for one night longer than he had to be?"

Greg pounced eagerly on that one, a dog so desperate for a bone that the tiniest sliver satisfied him. "That's what I mean. Who does that? No one is that nice in real life—not unless they have an ulterior motive."

I couldn't help laughing. "Sloane won't hurt him." I hesitated before adding, "Or you."

He couldn't have reacted more strongly if I'd hit him over the head with a Ouija board. "I don't know what you're talking about."

He absolutely did, but I wasn't about to push my luck. Instead, I sent off a text to Bella, careful not to emit any of the details of Great-Aunt Portia's mythical fortune. That child never could resist a treasure hunt.

"If you're worried about Sloane's quality of care, then we'll just have to head over there to keep an eye on things." At his startled expression, I patted my hand on his shoulder. "Don't worry. I'll be with you every step of the way. As someone wise once told me, I might not be very good at handling teenagers, but irascible old men are something I can do."

13

—

W HAT DO YOU MEAN, HE HAS to have a registered nurse? He *had* a registered nurse. Four of them. He ran them all off."

No sooner had Greg and I made our way across the street than we found Sloane standing at the door talking to a woman in a suit. It was an official-looking suit, and she was an official-looking woman, but neither of those did much to make me feel better.

"I'm sorry, but it's not my call to make," the woman said. "When he left the hospital against medical advice, Adult Protective Services required us to—"

"Could you please keep your voice down?" Sloane stepped the rest of the way out of the house and closed the front door behind her. She was dustier than usual today, her hair swept up in a kerchief like she'd recently returned from picking apples in the countryside. The purple brooch she never went without held the scarf together at the back of her neck. "Arthur just dropped off to sleep, and that's only because I told him he had to either nap or listen to my favorite soap-making podcast."

The suit woman blinked bewilderedly at her.

"He hates podcasts," Sloane explained. "And anything that reeks of domesticity. He hates almost everything, including registered nurses and the people who come to force them on him."

"Now see here, young lady. If this is an attempt to scare me away before I meet with Mr. McLachlan…"

I coughed and nudged Greg with my foot. So far, he hadn't said a word about the events unfolding on his grandfather's doorstep.

"I'm not attempting anything except to save you from sharp-edged projectiles." Sloane didn't go so far as to nudge Greg, but she did turn a pair of beseeching eyes his way. "Help me, Greg. Tell her you're his family. Tell her you refuse to force unwanted medical care on your grandfather."

The woman perked up, her pen poised above her clipboard with a suddenly sprightly air. "Oh. Are you the next of kin?"

It took Greg a moment to respond, and when he did, he sounded more like he was grunting than speaking. "Yeah. Sure."

The woman handed him a piece of paper with a stamp across the top. "Then I'm giving you a week to find him proper home care, or we'll have no choice but to intervene." She turned to all three of us with a smile that was far too pleased with her day's work. "I'm sure this young lady means well, but he needs to have a professional caregiver on his rotation until he's restored to full health. For his safety as well as yours."

We stood back and watched as she trotted down the steps, waving a cheerful farewell as she slid into her understated blue sedan and drove away. It said a lot about our current state that none of us spoke until she rounded the corner and disappeared from view.

"Do you think she'd count a chiropractor as a professional caregiver?" I asked as soon as I felt it was safe enough to speak.

The grimace that passed reflexively over Sloane's face was all the answer I needed.

"Oh dear," I murmured. "He won't come back here, will he? After we ran him away last time?"

"Who?" Greg asked.

It was more animation than I'd seen out of him since we crossed the lawn, so I was quick to answer. "Sloane's fiancé. He stopped by to help one day, but Arthur and I may have conspired together to get rid of him."

"*May* have?" Sloane asked. "You guys recited the plot to a soap opera and tried to convince him it was real."

I bit back a laugh. "It was Arthur's idea, not mine. All I wanted was to help him wash windows."

Sloane looked as though she'd like to argue further, but she only heaved a sigh. "Don't worry. It's not as if it would matter. I doubt I could get Brett back here under any conditions. He's not…happy with the way I'm handling things."

I sensed an opportunity to poke further into the open wound of her relationship, but I didn't want to do it while Greg was watching.

"Does he at least know of any nurses we might be able to hire?" I persisted. I wanted to think that I was fighting solely on Arthur's behalf, but that would have been a lie. I was mostly terrified of what would happen if the book club disbanded before we found out what happened to that poor butler.

Not to mention what would happen the moment Sloane and Arthur and Greg moved on with their lives. They had no idea how much I *needed* this: someone to cook for, someone to care about. Someone who might, if I was tied to a hospital bed and knocking on death's door, be a little sad to see me go.

"Your fiancé must have access to a temp agency or know of nurses looking for extra income," I suggested. Even though I was hardly in a position to start handing out financial favors, I added, "If money's the issue, I could pitch in to help—"

"Absolutely not," Greg said, and with so much force that Sloane took a step back. He looked immediately regretful before hunching his shoulders to shrink them to half their usual size. In a more moderate tone, he added, "You're not paying for my grandfather's medical care, Maisey. You're already doing too much."

He cast a quick, furtive glance at Sloane before looking just as quickly away again. "You both are."

Sloane sighed. "Well, it's not as if it matters, because I doubt any of the nurses Brett knows would be of any use. They're used to working in a chiropractic office, not…"

"A battlefield?" I suggested.

Greg snorted. "More like the gates of hell."

"It doesn't matter what you call it." Sloane pointed a finger straight up. "We're forgetting the most important part."

"Are we talking about…God?" I asked doubtfully.

Sloane laughed and shook her head. That sound helped all of us feel less weird about standing around discussing the future of a man who wouldn't thank us for it. "Arthur. Even if we *could* find a nurse willing to sign off on his care, how would we get her through the door? He'd tear her to shreds within minutes."

That piece of reasoning was so shattering that no one could think of a reply—which in my case was saying a lot.

"She did say we have a week to figure it out," I said after a moment's pause. "We have time to consider our options."

Since there wasn't much we could do to fix this problem right now, we filed into the house, careful to keep our footsteps soft and our voices softer. Greg was the last to go through, pausing to hold the door.

I thought at first that he was just being polite, but his gaze was fixed on the back of Sloane's head. He stared at the brooch holding her scarf in place as if he was trying to work out a puzzle.

Like the book discussions I didn't always understand, that fixation wasn't something I could decipher on my own. It only reinforced a fear that was starting to grow stronger with each passing day: that although this strange trio didn't need me to keep the wheels of their lives turning, I wholeheartedly needed them.

And that was more terrifying than Arthur, Greg and, yes, Sloane combined.

"I've decided to invite my friend Mateo to join our book club."

Sloane made her announcement as soon as we'd finished with our latest book club meeting—which, I was sorry to say, mostly revolved around my recent discovery that *The Remains of the Day* had been turned into a movie starring Anthony Hopkins, and no one thought to tell me about it.

I loved movies. Especially older ones. Especially-*especially* older ones that might help me gain a deeper understanding of a book that flew over my head more often than not. This evening, we'd discussed how Stevens's obsession with dignity was an allegory for the driving forces of duty and obligation in the Nazis' rise to power.

And by discussed, I meant Sloane and Arthur yelled at each other while Greg and I sat back and watched. Allegories were above my pay grade.

Arthur snapped his book shut with a start. "What? Why? Who the devil is Mateo?"

"You know exactly who Mateo is. He works at the library."

Arthur's eyes narrowed with recognition, but he made us wait a full thirty seconds before he was willing to admit it. "The name *might* ring a bell."

Sloane rolled her eyes. "He's the well-dressed Filipino guy you send into hiding every time you walk in the door. I think he'll enjoy a chance to participate in our club. He's always saying he wants to expand his literary horizons."

Something about the way Sloane said this last bit, with the air of a speech that had been rehearsed inside her head, made me avoid saying what was on my lips: *Yes! Of course! The more of us there are, the harder the group will be to disband!*

"But we already have four people," Arthur protested. "And you all take up too much space as it is. All you ever seem to do is breathe and eat."

Since there was a backup oxygen tank behind the hospital bed in the corner, and I was the one supplying most of the food, I didn't see how this was a fair complaint, but Greg spoke up before I could say anything.

"I'm not here as part of the book club."

"You still breathe and eat," Arthur pointed out.

Greg grunted. "So do you."

"Not as much as you," Arthur retorted. "Anyone who lumbers and hulks around the way you do is using up more than his fair share."

As this was a singularly needless—and needlessly cruel—argument, Sloane held up her phone. "It doesn't matter because I already sent Mateo a text to invite him. He's so excited that I doubt we could keep him away now."

"Ha!" Arthur's laugh contained no mirth. "That shows what you know. We can make Greg kick him out. Otherwise, what's the point of having a lumbering, hulking—"

It was my turn to interrupt.

"Have we picked a book out for next time?" Mimicking Sloane's movements, I held up my copy of *The Remains of the Day*. "I only have about fifty pages left, so I'm hoping to get a jump start on the next one. Or at least to hunt down some SparkNotes before we get in too deep."

Sloane shook her head. "Not yet. I think we should let Mateo pick since he'll be new to the group."

"Oh my God." Arthur heaved an audible groan. "I've seen what he puts out on the shelves. Coffee-table books written by the ghostwriters of D-list celebrities. You might as well have us read cookbooks and be done with it."

Sloane sat back with a whoosh, unable to keep a triumphant smile from touching her lips.

"What?" Arthur demanded. "Why are you grinning at me like the Cheshire cat?"

"Because I was right. You *do* know who Mateo is."

———

"What's going on with your friend Mateo?" I asked as soon as I got Sloane alone. Cornering her in the bathroom was a risky move, since we'd left Arthur and Greg to square off over a coffee cake, but I was dying to know what she was up to. "Does he really want to join our book club?"

"I don't know," Sloane said, careful to avoid both my eyes and her own reflection in the mirror. "I haven't asked him yet. That bit about the text was a lie."

"Do you want me to do it? I can be very persuasive when I want to be. The trick is to ask at inconvenient times. You're much more likely to get a 'yes' out of people when they're late for work in the morning or waiting for their turn in line at the DMV."

Sloane laughed in that special way of hers, even though I wasn't *technically* making a joke. "Maisey, you're a treasure and a delight, but no. I should handle this one on my own. Mateo is terrified of Arthur. It's going to take every amount of bribery and charm I have to get him to agree."

"Um...are you sure we really want him, then?"

"Oh, we want him." She leaned forward confidentially. "Before becoming a librarian, Mateo worked as a nurse. A *registered* nurse."

"No way." I grabbed both of Sloane's hands and squeezed them much harder than the situation warranted, but what else could I do? I'd never felt so relieved in all my life. "Why didn't you mention this before?"

"Because I only just remembered." She winced. "To be honest, I try to avoid thinking too much about the library."

I clucked my tongue with ready sympathy. "You miss it?"

"So much it's a physical ache."

She sounded so forlorn that I was tempted to lock the bathroom door and demand more information. Even if we had the time, however, I didn't think I'd get much out of her. Greg might have been willing to sit next to me and tell his life story for no reason other than because I asked, but Sloane was a lot more closed off than that.

It was funny, when you thought about it. From the outside, Sloane looked about twenty times more approachable than Greg. She was a soft, sweet doll of a human being who seemed to be folded up in bubble wrap. But the more time I spent under this roof, the more I realized how much she and Arthur had in common.

They weren't easy people, the two of them. They were educated and well-read, smart in ways that I never would be, but neither of them had gone near bubble wrap a day in their lives. Those two were wrapped up in razor wire, I was sure of it. And for all my good intentions, I'd never get close without cutting myself to shreds first.

14

T HE SOUND OF BELLA'S VOICE WOKE me just after dawn.

At first, I thought I must be dreaming—one of those warm, liquid dreams that carried you along on a wave of happy memories—but when I heard a male voice grunt and shout, "What the hell?" I realized this was more than the workings of my subconscious mind.

"Mom! Mo-om! Moooo-ooooom!"

Stumbling out of bed, I paused just long enough to shove my arms through my favorite pink satin robe before dashing across the hall to the source. Even though I was still befuddled with sleep, it didn't take me long to figure out what I was looking at.

Bella, backed into a corner, her finger pointed at the half-naked and fully agitated man tangled up in her sheets. "There's a strange man in my bed!"

"Yes, love. If you'll remember, I texted you to tell you that a few weeks ago." I threw an arm around the trembling teen and steered her in the direction of retreat. With an apologetic wince for Greg, I added, "I *did* tell her, Greg. I'm so sorry—"

"It's fine," he said in a voice that sounded very far from fine. "It's my fault. Just give me a few minutes, and I'll get out of your hair."

"Absolutely not," I protested. "It's six o'clock in the morning. Go back to sleep."

As soon as I tactfully shut the door behind me, Bella pounced.

"Mom, what's going on? I didn't think you *really* had a man staying with you. I thought you made that up."

"Why would I make up a man?"

"I dunno…for the same reason all the other sad, middle-aged moms do?"

I had no idea which sad, middle-aged moms she was talking about, but it didn't matter. By the time we cleared the hallway, I realized she was fully dressed and that several suitcases stood by the front door.

"Bella!" I gasped, sensing my salvation in those suitcases. "Did you have a fight with your father? Have you come home to stay?"

"What?" She followed the line of my gaze and grimaced. "No. *God*, no. The exact opposite. Who is he?"

Since my heart was still coming down from that sudden euphoric flight, it took me a moment to follow her line of conversation.

"The man?" I asked. "Oh. His name's Greg. He's old Arthur McLachlan's grandson."

"Ew. You're sleeping with Arthur McLachlan's *grandson*? Isn't that, like, illegal?"

"He's a fully grown adult, and no, I'm not sleeping with him. I'm giving him a place to stay while Arthur recovers from his illness." As much as I had to say on this subject, I wasn't ready to give up on the suitcases. "I'm always happy to see you, and of course we'll find somewhere else to stash Greg for as long as you're staying, but what's going on? If it's not a fight with your father…"

Bella took a sudden interest in her cuticles. "Didn't he call you last night? He was supposed to call you."

I grabbed my phone where it was plugged into the wall and peeked at it. Sure enough, there were several missed calls and one saved message from my ex. "Oh. I must've forgotten to check my phone after book club."

"*You* forgot to check your phone?"

"Yes."

"You *forgot* to check your phone?"

"Um…yes?"

"You forgot to check your *phone?*"

"Bella, love. Emphasizing a different word isn't going to help me understand what's going on."

She resumed her interest in her nails. "I told you not to call me 'love.'" Then, "Maybe you'd better listen to the message."

The last thing I wanted to do was pull up a recording of the rich, sultry voice that once used to charm me right out of my pants—and all my common sense—but I wasn't likely to get a straight answer otherwise. Dropping to the table, I pressed the play button and did my best not to look as agitated as I felt.

Hey, Maisey. It's me. Cap. Bella's dad.

I had to fight the urge to roll my eyes. Cap had always been garbage at communication. He could sing straight from the heart, but I'd never been able to get anything else out of that organ.

Yeah, um, I don't know how to say this, so I'm just going to come out and say it. Penelope got a great job offer with some agency in LA. You know how hard it is to get your foot in the door for these things… They're starting her off with a small client list and letting her build it up from there. She's super stoked. She's—

I recognized the sound of his wife's voice in the background telling him to stop procrastinating and come out with it. Like I said—she was great, and even more to the point, she was great for him.

Okay, long story short. We found a place. It'll take a few weeks to pack up the house and get everything shipped, but the school district is top-notch. Bella already started the transfer paperwork, so she'll be ready come fall. Penelope thinks she'll really take to life down there. Sun, sand, opportunity… It'll be good for her. And us. And you, I think. Right? Right. Right.

He kept repeating that last word so many times that it started to twist inside my head. Right. Wrong. Right. Wrong.

Wrong. *Wrong.*

"Please don't say it, Maisey." Bella's voice was almost unrecognizable in its sudden, tense weariness. "I can't have this argument right now. There's too much to do getting everything ready. We're barely gonna have time to get things packed up for the movers as it is."

"I don't understand," I say, and I didn't—I really didn't. Cap wanted to move our daughter over a thousand miles away? And he hadn't thought to run it by me first? "When did this happen?"

Her eyes didn't quite meet mine. "It's been in the works for a while. We didn't want to say anything until we knew for sure. You know how you get."

I didn't understand that, either. How was the way I got different from literally every other mother on the planet when her child wanted nothing to do with her? Protective? Concerned? *Sad?*

"Okay," I said, reminding myself to breathe. It was funny how you could forget something like that. My whole life, my lungs had been doing just fine on their own—in and out, full and empty—but now they seemed as shell-shocked as the rest of me. "I'm sure there's some kind of legal action that should be taken, even with the amended custody arrangement. I'll need to talk to my lawyers, and—"

"Ohmigod. I knew it. I *knew* you were gonna be like this." The momentary lapse into weariness was gone; all that was left was the Bella I knew well. Angsty and irritated, a chip on her shoulder the exact same size as me. "For once in your life, Maisey, can you please act like a normal person? It's California, not the moon, and I *want* to go. I'm sixteen years old! I'm not some kid you can dress up and carry around like a doll anymore."

"I only meant that we need to update the arrangement—" I began, but it was no use. Bella had drawn the lines of battle between us. If I was being perfectly honest, she'd drawn them a long time ago, determined to place herself as far on the opposite side as she could get.

"I'm just here for my stuff, okay?" She pushed her hair out of her face. "Not to chat about old times. Not to gossip over a cup of coffee like some soccer mom you roped into friendship."

"But, Bella, I'm not—"

"I live with Dad and Penelope now. Real parents. *Normal* parents. The kind who don't need me to hold their hands at all hours of the night and day because they're too scared to be alone. The sooner you accept that and get a life of your own, the better it'll be for all of us."

"But Greg is in your room—" I tried again.

"I'm done. She's safe to head in now." His quiet voice sounded from behind me. I had no idea how long he'd been standing there or how much he'd overheard, but from the perfectly bland expression he was careful to wear, it had been long enough. He'd thrown a shirt on, but the fact that he was young, barefoot, and grumpily sleep-rumpled wasn't lost on Bella.

"Ew," she muttered as she pushed past us both, the larger of her two suitcases thumping behind her.

I watched her go with a sinking heart, repressed pleas so thick on my tongue I could taste them. Not surprisingly, they were bitter.

Greg moved wordlessly into the kitchen. I followed him, more out of a desire to get out of the hallway than because I wanted the company. There was something calming about the way he set about preparing the pot of coffee. He didn't say a word, his feet moving so soundlessly over the floor that he was like the ghost of a man rather than the real thing. It was the exact opposite of what I'd do in that situation, offering a ceaseless prattle of conversation to cover the pain, but it worked. By the time he held out a steaming cup of coffee, split fifty percent with my favorite caramel creamer, I was feeling much calmer.

"Okay, I think that's everything." Bella popped her head around the corner, her lips pursed tightly. "There wasn't much here to begin with. Just some winter clothes and my necklace organizer."

"You don't want to take your photo album?" I asked, unable to help myself. "Or any of your posters?"

"Ugh. Those are like five years old. I'm not into *Haikyuu* anymore."

"Oh. Right." The dignified thing to do now would be to give her a hug and send her on her way, offering nothing but my unquestioning support for the months ahead, but I couldn't. I just *knew* the second I opened my mouth, nothing but my emotions would spill out. So I channeled my inner Greg and sipped my coffee, waiting for her to make the first move.

But she wasn't the one to break the tense silence.

"We found your great-aunt Portia's treasure," Greg said, and in a conversational tone designed to entice. "In case you were wondering. It was in the attic."

I hid my smile behind my cup of coffee and waited to see if Bella took the bait. Even now, even after Greg had seen and heard how little she wanted to do with me, he was still willing to try. To keep her on the hook, to give her an opening so she could always come back home again.

"Great-Aunt Portia?" Bella echoed. For the longest moment, I thought it was going to work—that she'd take a step closer, let down her guard, say goodbye in a way that wouldn't break my heart—but all she did was frown without understanding. "Why would I care anything about her?"

15

—

A T ITS CORE, THE BOOK IS a love story." Sloane sat in her usual
spot at Arthur's feet, her legs folded under her and a cup of tea
at her elbow.

"Ha. You would think that." Arthur's lip curled. "Let me guess…
You wanted Stevens and his old housekeeper friend to live happily ever
after and drive off into the sunset together. She was the one who got
away, the soul mate who was destined to save him."

"I didn't say it was a love story between *them*. I meant between
Stevens and his work. In a lot of ways, he treated that butler job like
the great passion of his life. Loving blindly and without question,
dedicating himself body and soul to something he believed to be bigger
than himself. What is that, if not the love we try to sell to couples on
Valentine's Day?"

Arthur seemed physically pained at mention of the word *Valentine*.

"If you think great passion means refusing to see someone's flaws,
then you have no idea what real love looks like. It's not some game of
make-believe. It's messy and complicated and—" Arthur cut himself
off without bothering to finish. He stabbed a finger at me instead.
"What's wrong with the housewife? She hasn't strung more than two
words together all evening."

"For the last time, her name is Maisey. If you can't make an effort
to use it, we aren't going to invite you to our next book club."

"Fine. What's wrong with *Maisey*?" He turned a quelling eye on me. "You didn't finish the book, did you? Figures."

It was on the tip of my tongue to argue—I *did* finish, and with enough time left over to pull together a quiche so delicate it was practically melting in our mouths—but I didn't have the energy. For the past few days, it had been all I could do to eat and sleep, to go through the motions of giving people the benefit of my advice.

Weirdly enough, the book helped. I'd have normally drowned myself in *Flames of the World* reruns and that bottle of ice-cold Grey Goose, but it had been nice to spend some time with that dreary old butler instead.

"Well?" Arthur demanded. "Are you going to enlighten us with your profound psychic wisdom?"

"Don't." Greg glanced up from the foot of the stairs, where he'd been quietly repairing the broken boards for the past half hour. He'd been doing the same thing around my house, spackling holes in the wall and oiling hinges with a determination that bordered on the obsessive. "Leave her alone."

"Oho! So you're talking to us now, are you? Participating in the book club? What happened to change your mind?"

Greg rolled an indifferent shoulder. "She's had a rough couple of days, that's all. Be nice."

Sloane immediately turned contrite, but Arthur only narrowed his eyes in sharp appraisal.

"What could have possibly happened to her?" he asked. Turning toward me, he flashed a toothy and not-very-pleasant smile. "Uh-oh. Did your Amazon delivery get stolen off your porch? The bake sale committee make too many cookie demands?"

"Stop it," Greg commanded, and in a much harder voice this time. "You have no idea what you're talking about."

"She does look awfully pale." Sloane put a steady hand on my forearm. Her skin felt so warm against mine that it was almost unnatural. "Maybe you should head home and lie down for a bit, Maisey. We can always reschedule this for another time."

The thought of going home to my empty house and empty bed, to spend hours staring at the ceiling until the crushing weight of sleep finally overtook me, wasn't one I cared for. Now that Greg had oiled all the doors, I didn't even have their incessant squeaking to comfort me.

"Sloane's right," I said, forcing my attention back to the book we were supposed to be discussing. "It *is* a love story. A tragedy. Like *Romeo and Juliet*, only without all the death at the end."

Sloane flexed her fingers against mine in surprise.

"Bullshit," Arthur barked.

Sloane's eyes widened. "Arthur!"

"What? I taught *The Remains of the Day* for twenty years. It'll take more than the pair of you waxing poetic about star-crossed lovers to change my mind."

I shook my head, unafraid of either the fire in his voice or the challenge in his stare. That was one of the nice things I had to look forward to now—nothing had the power to hurt me anymore. My daughter was officially gone, her five-years-too-old posters the only things I had left to hold on to. Even though Cap said the movers weren't coming for another few days, Bella had made it clear that our goodbyes were already said. She made her choice, and that choice wasn't me.

It had never been me, only I was too stupid—too *unreliable* a narrator in my own life—to see it.

My copy of the book had been sitting listlessly in my lap ever since I got here, but I picked it up and rifled through the pages until I reached the ending. I hadn't started one of those quote journals that Sloane was talking about, but I knew exactly which passage I was looking for.

"'The fact is, of course,'" I read aloud, my voice surprisingly strong, "'I gave my best to Lord Darlington. I gave him the very best

I had to give, and now—well—I find I do not have a great deal more left to give.'"

Sloane nodded her understanding, her fingers still warm against my skin. "He loved his employer. Not *romantic* love—so don't start up again, Arthur—but the way a son loves a father. Fraternal love."

"No," I said flatly. "That's not it, either."

"Maisey, maybe we should save this for another time," Greg suggested. I didn't know when or how he'd managed to crouch in front of me, but he was there and clasping my hands between his. His palms were so enormous that I couldn't even see the tips of my fingers. "I'll walk you home."

"No." I didn't yank my hands out of his, but I didn't get up to leave, either. I liked it here—in this chair and in this house, even in the path of Arthur's annoyed stare. It was far better than what waited for me back home.

Nothing. What waited for me at home was nothing.

That was the thing I'd been avoiding for years, the thing that Bella recognized as soon as she'd grown old enough to see me for who I really was. I was a woman without hobbies or friends, who talked to strangers on the phone all day—not to help them with *their* problems, but so I could hear the sound of another human being's voice. For a while there, I got to be Bella's mom, and that was enough to hold up the pretense of more. As long as I was busy and active in *her* life, I could ignore the fact that I wasn't busy or active in my own.

"You don't understand the book," I said with a misty smile. "Not really. Not the way it's supposed to be understood."

"Now, see here," Arthur sputtered.

"Let her finish," Sloane said.

"Maisey, you don't have to do this." Greg's voice was the quietest and therefore the most powerful. I fixed my gaze on his and smiled to show I meant no harm.

"Except I do," I said. I peeked over his shoulder to where Sloane and Arthur were starting to show serious signs of alarm. "I know I'm not as literary as you two, but I still know things. I *see* things."

I laughed then, a crack in the facade that escaped before I could stop it.

"Actually, that's not true. I don't see things—not the things that matter. That's what I mean when I say it's a tragic love story. Because Stevens *did* love his boss. More than anyone else in the whole world. More than any person should love another living being."

My grip on the book loosened. It fell to the floor with a thump, but I didn't make a move to grab it. I didn't need it anymore—or ever again. I had no idea how Arthur had studied those pages for several decades and never gotten to the real heart of the story. It just went to show how useless some of these deep book discussions could be. All the literary devices in the world weren't of any use if you'd never known what it meant to love someone the way that butler had.

Purely. Deeply. *Selfishly.*

Because that was what his love was at its core—selfish. Stevens didn't love his employer for who he really was. He *pretended* he did, pretended so hard that he closed himself off to everything and everyone else in his life.

I saw the same thing in my clients all the time. Mr. Davidson was a prime example. He *knew* he'd never find true love until he shook off the years of self-doubt and self-satisfaction, made a real effort to turn himself into someone worth loving. But he was too far in it now. To admit he needed to change, to dig in and actually upend his life would mean admitting that the last fifty-three years had been wasted. He couldn't do that any more than Stevens the butler could.

Or me. I couldn't do it, either.

I reached my hand up to my cheek, surprised when my fingers came away wet.

"Maisey?"

Sloane was starting to sound really worried, so I tried for a smile and an explanation.

"She's been leaving me for years," I confessed. Her name stuck in my throat but I managed to get it out anyway. "My Bella. My daughter. I knew it was coming—of course I knew it—but I needed her too much to admit it."

"I'm sure she needs you, too," Sloane said. She was on the floor next to Greg, a white square of cloth in her hand. "Teenagers are tough, but you'll get through this. You both will."

"That's sweet of you to say, but it's a lie." I smiled mistily at her and accepted the handkerchief. Her initials were hand-embroidered in one corner next to a delicate pink rose. Bella's favorite flower—or so I always thought. For all I knew, she only liked dandelions now. "The poor thing. I never understood her the way she wants to be understood. Only the way *I* wanted to. Does that make sense?"

"No," Sloane said, but I could see Arthur watching me closely, his head bobbing slowly up and down. I latched onto that like it was my lifeline—like *he* was my lifeline.

"I poured so much of myself into her that there's nothing left now. Just a frumpy housewife who talks too much and thinks too little, an empty shell of a woman no one wants and even fewer people need."

"Greg, can't we *do* something? She's starting to shake."

"We can let her finish."

"Don't worry," I said as I began picking at the edges of the needle-point rose with my fingernail. A stray end came loose. I gave it a heartless tug, watching as it disappeared into a long pink thread. "I'll be fine, just like the butler from the book will be fine. Not happy, obviously, but that's the whole point."

"Of the book?" Sloane asked.

I nodded to show she was exactly right.

"I gave her the very best I had to give, and now…" I let my voice trail off, unable to say the rest, but that was okay. The nice thing about having literary friends was that they already knew.

I find I do not have a great deal more left to give.

MATEO

16

"MATEO, WE'RE GOING TO BE LATE if you don't hurry."

Lincoln popped his head into the bedroom where I stood in nothing but my underwear, three nearly identical outfits laid out on the bed in front of me. Black slacks, black button-down shirts, black socks—it looked like I was getting ready to attend the funerals for all three of Goldilocks' bears.

That one had a collar that was too big.

That one had a waistline that was too tight.

And that one... Well. It'd have to do. Like Lincoln said, we were running late.

"I don't know why you're so worried." Lincoln came up behind me, his arms around my waist and his head propped on my shoulder as I made my selection. "It's not like anyone's going to be looking at you. You know what happens the moment your mom takes the stage."

I changed my mind at the last second and grabbed the outfit that was too small around the waist. I'd be uncomfortable all night long, and there was a fifty percent chance I'd rip through the seams like a Jazz Age Hulk, but one had to suffer to be beautiful.

That was one of my mom's favorite sayings, so she'd have been the first to agree. She had four different embroidered pillows in her house warning of just such a fate.

"A bold choice," Lincoln said, his voice low with approval as I shimmied and squeezed my way into the pants. "Who are we trying to impress?"

"You," I lied as I sucked in a deep breath and snapped the button closed. I struck a playful pose and did my best not to feel like a sausage about to break free of its casing. "Is it working?"

He grinned in the way that won him friends and admiration everywhere he went. "You look perfect."

I didn't, but it was sweet of someone who *did* look perfect to say so. Hyperbolic as it seemed, Lincoln Jonas was walking, talking perfection. He stood six foot two—and not in the way that five-foot-eleven men sometimes refused to stand next to anyone but short people so they had the benefit of perspective. He was that tall in his socks in the middle of the living room. He also had the build—and the heart—to fill that frame. Add in a full stern-brunch-daddy beard and a tendency to wear flannel literally everywhere, and that was my boyfriend.

My love. My partner. The gravitational center of my universe.

"Ready?" Lincoln asked. "I promised your mom we'd be early enough to snag a table at the front. You know how much she likes being able to see us when she performs."

"The great Althea Sharpe?" I said, unable to resist the impulse. "How strange. I had no idea she cared so much."

Lincoln laughed, his barrel of a chest rumbling as he whisked me out the door and into the UberLux waiting outside for us. On her opening nights, my mom preferred as much fanfare as possible, which meant my poor little Fiat wouldn't cut it—and Lincoln's half-refurbished motorcycle was a *definite* no-go.

"The whole Sharpe family is known for their dramatic flair," Lincoln said as he scooted in behind me. The sleek black Jaguar oozed leather, class, and the indefinable scent of overcompensation. "It's kind of what I love about them. I don't know if you know this, but they're drawn to it like moths to a flaming inferno."

As always, that word—*love*—rolled off Lincoln's tongue like butter melting in a pan. The only thing he loved more than love itself was saying it out loud. And putting it in greeting cards. And blasting it from the rooftops.

If ever romance had a poster boy, it was Lincoln Jonas.

I should have been delighted about it—I *was* delighted about it—but that was the problem with dating a gravitational center. No matter what I did, his pull never wavered.

"That's not a real saying," I told him, but I could feel myself starting to relax. Especially once Lincoln started rooting through the UberLux candy selection until he found a roll of my favorite strawberry Mentos. "And we Sharpes don't love drama. Drama loves us. It's different."

The jazz club where my mother headlined was small, private, and known to just about every person living within a hundred-mile radius of Coeur d'Alene. What had started as a secret underground club had rapidly become the hottest spot to enjoy twenty-dollar cocktails and live performances, thanks in large part to the recent fame of our lakeside town.

Not too long ago, Coeur d'Alene had been little more than a sleepy resort wrapped up in a gorgeous Idaho forest and with a population that bleeds conservative red. In recent years, however, the town had been discovered by the Hollywood elite. A few Kardashian vacation snapshots on Instagram and all of a sudden no one could get enough of us. It was as though Hotel California had finally unlocked its doors, and everyone was streaming out to get a piece of the action.

Not that I meant to complain. All it took was one glance at my mother, the fringe on her flapper-style dress swinging as she belted out her favorite Édith Piaf hit list, and it was difficult to regret our city's recent descent into fame.

I'd never seen her so beautiful…or so compelling. Lincoln wasn't the only one who burned a little too bright in the limelight of my life.

"Can you believe we're seeing *the* Althea Sharpe live?" The couple at the table next to us had to shout to be heard over the big band, but they seemed to have no qualms about doing it. "With a voice like that, I thought she'd be a lot bigger."

"Did I tell you that I found one of her old records at a shop in town? An original. It's signed and everything. The owner said he had no idea where it came from or he'd have sold it on eBay years ago."

At this, I was careful not to meet Lincoln's eye, though he nudged me with his foot so hard that my restraint was rendered unnecessary. We both knew for a fact that my mom and Eduardo, the guy who ran the record shop, were in cahoots together. They'd sold more "original" records with that ruse than any decent person would be willing to admit. On a good day, half a dozen shoppers made the discovery and shelled out a hundred bucks for the privilege.

"I forgot to ask," Lincoln said as our server brought our martinis and placed them in front of us. I immediately pulled out Lincoln's olives and started munching on them. The salty brine tasted great after my strawberry Mento amuse-bouche. "How did it go with Sloane today? Did she officially ask you to be in her wedding party?"

"Nope."

"No?" he echoed, swiveling his head to stare at me. "I thought you said she called out of the blue because she had a favor to ask of you."

"She did."

"And that the only favor you could imagine doing for her was being in her bridal party."

I held up a finger. "I also said there was a chance she'd want the name of my brow tech. She didn't ask for that, either, which is a shame. Genevieve would love to get her hands on Sloane."

Lincoln laughed in the special, soundless way he had, his whole body shaking like Santa's proverbial bowl full of jelly. He'd have left the conversation there—Lincoln was good at knowing when to stop prying—but I could see that he was curious.

"Actually…she asked me to join in her book club," I said.

"Oh." He blinked, as confused by the request as I had been. "That was nice of her."

"No, it's not. Apparently, they were going to let me pick the next read as a reward for participating, but some lady in the group is having a hard time with her teenage daughter, so they've decided to read *The Joy Luck Club*. You know how I feel about that book." I rolled my eyes up toward the stage, where my mother was starting to shake her bosom for the appreciative crowd. Not for me the honored family traditions of our Filipino ancestors or the heartwarming story of a second-generation citizen coming into his own. I got a borderline burlesque show and three olives on a toothpick. "And it gets worse."

"Worse than the beloved tale of one of America's most celebrated authors?"

That time, I rolled my eyes at *him*. "The book club is at Arthur McLachlan's house. Remember that old guy I was telling you about? The one she lost her job over?"

"I thought you were scared of him," Lincoln said.

"I *am*. But Sloane said it's important for me to be there. Apparently, they need my professional insights to keep going."

I'd have been lying if I didn't admit to puffing up a little over this last bit. Even though I'd been a librarian for over a year now, I hadn't been born to the literary trade the way Sloane was. In fact, I hadn't been born to any trade whatsoever. My résumé read more like a hodgepodge of failed personalities than a formal document.

Nursing school had been my first destination, but I'd soon found that I didn't care for the smell of hospitals. In an attempt to throw off the shackles of my medical training, I next tried my hand at being a flight attendant. When it turned out I'm easily susceptible to altitude sickness, I flirted with personal training. *And* a personal trainer. That ended about as well as expected, which is why I'd become a cherished member of the Coeur d'Alene library team. In fact, I'd fallen so far into the literary world lately that I was trying my hand at writing a fantasy novel.

It was a pretty good novel, too. Or rather, it *would* be, if I could just find the focus to sit down and write.

"Are you going to join the book club?" Lincoln asked.

Obviously I was going to. "Are you kidding? I'm not passing up a chance to see the inside of Arthur McLachlan's house. Fifty bucks says he sleeps in a coffin under the floorboards."

Lincoln laughed out loud that time. The people who overpaid for my mom's record heard and shushed us. This, unfortunately, caused my mother to look down and notice me sitting there. She'd just warbled off the final note of "La Vie en Rose," so there was nothing stopping her from indulging in her every theatrical impulse.

As soon as her eyes met mine, I read the meaning in them as clearly as if Amy Tan had just plopped her best-selling novel in front of me. My mother lifted her hand and held it out to me, the glittering rings on each of her fingers beckoning like Blackbeard's treasure.

"Ah, my kittens—what a treat we have in store for us this evening," she crooned. She always referred to her fans as kittens even though she abhorred cats of all kinds. Dogs too. And gerbils and hamsters and any of the other living, loving creatures I'd been desperate to own as a kid.

I did have a goldfish once, but he only lasted three days before he died of a Hostess cupcake overdose. I'd tasted the fish flakes and thought it would be kinder to supplement his diet from my own lunch box.

"My darling, dearest, most precious son is here to watch his mama shine. Aren't you, baby?"

This scene had been enacted between us so many times before that I didn't need the cue. Twisting in my seat, I plastered on a smile and waved like a princess chained to a float.

"That's right," she said, still in that falsetto voice—the sound of a woman torn through the portals of time. "My own little Mateo."

Lincoln kicked my foot under the table again, this time in warning for me not to react. I did react, though—*viscerally*. It had been months since my mom had done this, mostly because I warned her that I wouldn't come to her shows anymore if she planned to drag me onstage and vaunt me around like a puffed collar. I was a thirty-three-year-old man, for crying out loud. I'd hung up my tap shoes years ago, long before flight attendant training or nursing school or any of the other fifteen careers I'd shed over the past two decades.

"As many of you can imagine, it's no small thing for him to be here with us today."

"Oh God," I groaned. "It's happening again."

"It was only twenty-five years ago that I thought I'd lost him forever."

"Just keep smiling," Lincoln whispered.

"Lots of you were there, I know. Watching with me. Waiting. Praying." She choked on a sob. This was the point where I could never *quite* tell if she was actually crying or not. Her performance was so convincing—in large part because she believed it herself—that it was impossible to say for sure. "Which is why I think we should urge him up on the stage, don't you? So he can repay you for all your kindness in his safe delivery."

A quick survey of the club revealed two possible escape routes: an emergency exit behind the bar that was likely to set off a full-scale fire alarm, and the men's restroom on the opposite side of the stage. I was calculating my odds of reaching the latter when Lincoln got to his feet and held out a hand to help me.

"No," I hissed, glaring at him in a warning to sit back down. He smiled and gave a small shake of his head, his expression rueful. *What can we do but play along?* that smile said.

I could think of several things. I could run. I could hide. I could jump down the nearest well and stay there for seventy-two hours while the whole world held its collective breath and prayed for my safe recovery.

"Mateo the Miracle, everyone!" my mother called.

As expected, a burst of applause rose up through the crowd. Half the people had probably never heard of me before, but such was my mother's aura of command. When she said to clap, people clapped. When she told them to cheer, they cheered. And when she ordered them to idolize her son as strongly as she did, they had no choice but to follow along.

"Don't be shy, baby. Show the people how you're thriving."

Lincoln's hand was around mine before I knew it. Since he, too, knew his role, he led me up the steps to the stage just as the big band struck up my theme song: "Forever Young."

A groan lodged in my throat and stayed there, choking me. If there was one thing I hated more than *The Joy Luck Club*, it was that stupid song.

The irony of the lyrics was lost on every person in that audience. The song had made a certain kind of sense back when I'd been *actually* young, my fresh-faced enthusiasm matching my mother's beat for beat, the pair of us tap-dancing our way into the hearts and minds of those who might otherwise forget our seventy-two hours of fame. These days, I mostly felt as old as Arthur McLachlan himself.

"Sing with me," she commanded, so I did. I *always* did, just like everyone seated around their tables, their whistles wet with vermouth. Even Lincoln joined in, his deep voice adding a depth to the song that couldn't be denied.

By the time we'd all finished promising that diamonds would last forever, I started to feel the button straining on the waistband of my slacks. Sweat beaded on my upper lip and under my armpits, leaving telltale marks of my discomfort behind.

"Mateo the Miracle!" my mother called again as the song petered out—along with my cracking, creaking voice, which had never been able to match hers for range. "My precious son! Saved by the hands of God and the kind wishes of people just like you!"

Lincoln was waiting for me as I stumbled off the stage, his eyes laughing and a devastating smile on his lips. "There now," he murmured as my mother segued into her next set, her energy unabated. "That wasn't so bad, was it?"

I glared at him as I brushed past, unable to stomach the too-close, too-hot nightclub a second longer. "You know how much I hate it when she does that to me."

The laugh left his eyes, his smile dimming from devastat*ing* to devastat*ed*. "She only does it because she loves you, Mateo. You guys sound so good together."

"There are much easier ways to show your affection for someone than public humiliation," I said, turning flippant. In situations like these, I always turned flippant. It was the only sure-fire way to stay safe. "A nice brunch, for example. Or a new Montblanc pen."

His eyes narrowed as if he wanted to speak, but he wisely kept his own counsel. Not that I needed to hear what he was thinking. I'd already heard it dozens of times before—the same argument we had time and time again, the one thing that kept us from a state of pure romantic bliss.

The second you get anywhere near a real emotion, Mateo, you hide as fast as you can. It's like you can't stand being loved for even a second.

"I'm going to get some air," I told him, but with a smile to show that I understood what he was thinking and how he felt, his frustration at my lack of emotional progress. One of these days, he was going to get fed up and leave me. I knew it, he knew it—even my mom had probably figured it out by now—but we very carefully refrained from discussing it. No need to name the specter until he was standing at our door.

As I headed toward the exit, a few people called out to ask me about my time at the bottom of a well, but I put my head down and ignored them.

I couldn't recall very many details about my fall, now a quarter of a century behind me. I also couldn't recall much about the desperation of the rescue team scrambling their resources to pull me out, though I'd heard the stories so many times I could recite them in my sleep. The only thing that stuck with me was the memory of staring up at the distant blue circle above my head. There'd been something beautiful about it—not the shape or the color, or even the occasional puff of cloud going by like chimney smoke—but in knowing how far away it was.

God, I missed that feeling. How relaxing it was. How *free*.

It was the first time I could remember stepping out of my mother's shadow and falling into one of my own.

———

"Filthy habit, isn't it?"

I was hiding out in the alleyway behind the nightclub, the air reeking of half-digested alcohol and freshly baked waffle cones from the ice cream shop next door, when my first fan arrived. He held a thin cigar between his fore- and middle fingers, but I wasn't fooled. On nights like this, when my mother was at the top of her game, someone almost always came out to ask me about my experience.

"I don't smoke." I held up my hands to show they were empty

of everything save for my phone. TikTok videos about puppies were the only things that saved me in moments like these. I needed their bland mass appeal to put everything back where it was supposed to be. "Sorry."

"Mind if I do?"

I shook my head and thought about shuffling off to the other end of the alleyway, but the smell was more regurgitation and less waffle cone in that direction, so I stayed in place.

"My doctor says these things will kill me." The man laughed softly as he lit up. The edge of a British accent added a pleasant crispness to his voice. "But we all have to go sometime—some of us sooner than others. I might as well enjoy myself in the meantime."

This was such an unanswerable thing that I didn't respond. Not that it prevented him from continuing.

"That was some performance in there. You were phenomenal, but you didn't seem to be enjoying yourself."

Since I could hardly stand in silence forever, I answered. "That's because I wasn't."

"Did you really fall down a well?"

I sighed. "Look, if you want an autograph or a selfie, we're going to need to go around to the front of the club where it's better lit."

"A selfie?" He chuckled. "Do I look like the sort of man who wants a selfie?"

I noticed then that he was much older than I at first assumed. The alleyway was so dim that I could only make out an impression, but my impression told me that he was in his seventies or eighties, his dark skin weathered into deeply carved lines on either side of his mouth. He was a little too gaunt to please my medical eye, and there was a yellowing about his eyes that wasn't being helped by his nicotine habit, but he was well-dressed.

Unable to resist the impulse, I chuckled. "Okay, maybe you don't want a selfie. But you'd be surprised how many people ask. I have a hashtag and everything. It's #MateotheMiracle. I trended once."

"I don't know what any of those words mean," the man confessed, and I found myself warming to him. "But I find your story to be vastly interesting. How old were you when it happened?"

"Seven," I said as I prepared to launch into my canned speech. It was the first thing I'd ever memorized, long before the words to "Forever Young" and the balcony scene where I once played Juliet. We'd been sticklers for original Shakespeare at the all-boys Catholic school I went to as a kid—mostly because we'd had no other choice. Although I'd killed it as Juliet, I was best as Ophelia. My drowning scene used to bring the parents to tears.

"We were visiting some family friends," I said, allowing my voice to wax poetic. "The farm they owned was huge, and I wandered off on my own in hopes of finding the goats. The well I fell into was old, empty, and unused for decades. Even after all these years, no one knows why the cover was off on that fateful day, but—"

"I remember that," he interrupted, even though I hadn't even gotten to the good part yet. Then, with a look of genuine concern, he added, "Were you aware that your nose is bleeding?"

"Oh geez. Is it?" I scrambled for the packet of tissues I always kept in my pocket for just such a situation, before I remembered that I was wearing the tight pants. "I'm sorry, it's this thing that happens—"

"Here. Take mine." A handkerchief was pressed into my hand before I could stop him. And stop him I would have, if given a chance. Did this man have any idea how many germs per square inch were carried in these things? I was always trying to get Sloane to give up on hers. Even if it was daintily embroidered, it was still gross. "Do you need to sit down?"

"No, I'm fine." I tipped my head back in an attempt to quell the sudden outpouring of blood. "It's from stress."

"I'm sorry. Does reliving your trauma bring it on? I won't ask any more questions." He promptly proceeded to do just that—to not ask questions or even mention the subject of the well again. It was such a rare thing in my life that I was completely floored...until he spoke up again. "Did I hear you mention a book club that you're a part of?"

"Um. Yes?"

"You'll have to pardon my inquisitiveness. I'm a book critic, so anything that smacks of literature piques my interest, even in a night-club." He smiled in a way that made me feel weirdly better about bleeding all over his handkerchief. "I'm Nigel Carthage. Perhaps you've heard of me?"

"Sorry," I said, shrugging. Sloane could probably name every single book critic and the news publication they worked for—in alphabetical order—but I'd always been more of an amateur. "It doesn't ring any bells."

"No matter. I only wanted to inquire if you were taking new members. I recently moved back to the area only to find that most of my old acquaintances are no longer here." He clucked his tongue. "Or alive. Take my advice and don't grow old. I find I can't recommend it."

"Oh. Um, I'm not in charge of the book club." I winced behind the handkerchief. Telling a man with dead friends that you didn't want his company was no walk in the park. "In fact, I haven't gone to any meetings yet, so I doubt I'm allowed to start writing out invitations."

The music from inside the club switched to a more upscale swing beat, which meant the dancing was starting—and that, if no one else was brave enough to kick things off, my Charleston was required.

"Look, I should head back in," I said with an apologetic shrug. I thought about handing the handkerchief back to him but decided this one would be better off at the bottom of my fireplace. Or the lake. "I'm sorry I can't be of help to you, but—"

"Take my card," he said. Like a magician, he reached into the same pocket that had held his handkerchief and extracted a single business card. The name Nigel Carthage sat boldly in the center, along with a line proclaiming him a contributing book reviewer at no less a publication than *The New Yorker*. I didn't have to be Sloane to be impressed by that. "If you find you have an opening, I'd love to be able to pop in and chat. You said you're reading *The Joy Luck Club*?"

"Yes, but—" I began feebly.

"Perfect." He beamed on me as if I'd handed him the golden ticket to a Wonka Wonderland. "I bet you have lots of interesting things to say on the subject. With a mother like yours, how could you not?"

17

PULLED UP TO ARTHUR MCLACHLAN'S HOUSE two days later, a copy of *The Joy Luck Club* in my pocket and two bottles of wine seat-belted securely next to me. Lincoln had assured me that one bottle would be plenty for an afternoon book club, but he'd never met Arthur, so I'd sneaked into the pantry and grabbed the red blend he'd been saving for our one-year anniversary. The temptation to crack it open and drink my way to the bottom before I got out of the car was strong.

As soon as I spotted the woman sitting in the middle of the sidewalk, with what looked like an entire platter of enchiladas splattered around her like the spray from an open artery, I knew the second bottle was a good idea. Also that the artery metaphor was *for sure* making it into my novel.

"Oh wow. That smells like it must have been really good." I walked up as nonchalantly as I could, trying not to startle her from her position on top of the thick, cheesy sauce. From the description Sloane had given me, I guessed this was the woman with the daughter problems. "Enchiladas?"

As soon as Maisey spotted me, she burst into tears. And not the soft, gently weeping kind. These were full-on, snot-bubbling, heart-tearing wails.

"Actually, it's a good thing you spilled them," I said, backpedaling faster than I'd ever backpedaled before. It was like I said before—no

matter what I did, drama always found a way into my life. "I'm deathly
allergic to chiles. If you'd made it inside with those, there's no telling
what would've happened."

"Really?" She glanced up at me through eyelashes caked with mas-
cara. Inky-black streaks ran in rivulets down her cheeks. They paired
well with her velour tracksuit, which would have been in questionable
taste twenty years ago when they'd actually been in fashion. She cast a
quick, anxious glance across the street, where an array of pink flamin-
gos in front of a small bungalow indicated that her questionable taste
carried over to her decor. "I didn't know. Maybe I should go home and
make a nice pasta salad instead."

She sounded so serious about this—as if she'd literally run across
the street and whip me up some rotini—that I didn't have the heart
to continue.

"No, not really. I just thought you might feel better if I lied."

She immediately burst into tears again and began wiping at her
face with her enchilada-y hands, adding glossy red sauce to the mess
of her makeup.

"Oh geez." I glanced around in search of help, but there was no
sign of Sloane anywhere. *Typical.* She lured me to this book club only
to abandon me before I even made it in the door. "If it makes you feel
any better, I have no self-control when it comes to homemade food.
I would've eaten half the tray and then felt bad about myself for days
afterward. It's better this way, I promise."

"You're j-just s-saying that. You're b-being n-nice."

"Well, yes," I admitted. "Look, if I open this bottle of wine, will
you promise to stop crying?"

"I c-can't!"

"What about money? I could give you some money." I made a big
show of searching my pockets, but the book took up most of the space.
The only other things I had were the freshly laundered handkerchief

from Nigel Carthage and a movie ticket stub that had been washed so many times it had formed a tight, tiny ball. "I'd offer you a stick of gum, but you look like a woman who learned a long time ago not to take candy from strangers."

"B-Bella used to l-love c-c-candy," she sobbed. "And n-now she's g-g-gone!"

I took an inadvertent step back, alarm tingling down to my toes. When Sloane mentioned this woman having problems with her daughter, I'd assumed it was the usual balance of teenage angst and white-lady drama. Not that the daughter was *dead*.

"Oh geez. Oh God. Oh fuck."

I didn't normally swear in front of PTA-mom types, but the situation seemed to call for it. There was a reason I always ran for hiding whenever Arthur McLachlan entered the library, and it wasn't just because I didn't get paid enough to deal with people like him.

The man practically pulsated with unchecked emotion. This lady did, too.

Since I could hardly leave her sitting in a pool of rapidly congealing enchilada sauce all by herself, I squatted to her level and held out Nigel's handkerchief. If she noticed the rust-colored spots where not even a mass infusion of bleach could get the linen clean, she didn't let it show. She blew her nose with so much force that she almost sent me toppling.

"Thanks," she said, her voice thick. "You're nice. I bet you always remember to call your mom on Mother's Day."

"I don't really have a choice," I admitted. "She's a difficult woman to forget."

"And you treat her well? Take her out to dinner? Surprise her with a nice spa day every now and then?"

"Sometimes, I guess. But it's not really necessary. She has a standing weekly appointment with her masseuse, and I'm pretty sure she has her hairdresser on retainer at this point. She's godmother to all six of her kids."

Something about this confession set the poor woman off again. With yet another sob, she said, "That's s-so s-sweet! I'm not g-god-mother to anyone."

"I'm sure you'll get asked someday." I remained awkwardly crouched in front of her, unsure what other comfort I had to offer. At this point, I mostly wanted to get her up out of the enchilada sauce, so I tried to find the driest spot on her velour jumpsuit and help her to her feet. We made it about halfway before a loud, angry male voice assailed us from behind.

"What the devil is going on here?"

I shot the rest of the way up to find myself facing a tall, broad-shouldered man who looked none too pleased to see me. Since I'd always been partial to tall, broad-shouldered men—pleased or not—I didn't let it alarm me.

"What happened? Maisey, are you okay?" The man turned to me with accusation in his dark eyes. I wasn't sure why, but something about them felt familiar. "What did you do to her?"

"Nothing, I swear. I came for the book club and found her like this."

"The book club?" the man echoed before something clicked and he relaxed. "You're Mateo, aren't you?"

I attempted a mock salute. "The one and only. And you are...?"

"That's Greg," Maisey said, sniffling. "He's Arthur's grandson. He's part of our book club, too."

I couldn't have been more surprised if the man had told me he was my long-lost brother. "Arthur has a *grandson*?" I asked. Then, before my remark even had time to settle, I laughed out loud. "Never mind. I see it now. The resemblance is uncanny."

"I wish everyone would stop saying that," the man muttered before offering me his hand. "And I'm sorry if I came on strong just now.

Tensions around here have been a little heightened, but I'm working on it. I'm Greg, by the way."

I took his hand and shook it. Already I was starting to see why Sloane hadn't mentioned this guy. *The sneaky little minx.* This man couldn't be less like the genteel, uptight Brett Marcowitz if he'd been written by a Brontë.

"If Arthur McLachlan's involved, heightened tensions are a guarantee," I reassured him.

"I'm s-sorry," Maisey said. She seemed to be regaining some of her color, her sobs slowing to a trickle. "I didn't mean to overreact. It's just that ever since Bella…"

I held my breath, certain her next words would confirm my worst fears. Fortunately, they only ended up being my fourth- or fifth-worst ones.

"Ever since my Bella moved away, I've been a bit…weepy. She hasn't called or even texted to tell me she's safe. I only know where she is because she forgot to turn the location tracking off on her phone." She tried handing me the handkerchief back, but I decided to be officially done with that abomination.

"How old is she?" I asked instead. "Your daughter, I mean."

"Sixteen."

"Well, that explains it."

"Explains what?" Maisey sniffled.

I pulled out my copy of *The Joy Luck Club* and brandished it like a Bible before my congregation. The enchiladas might be past salvaging, but I had hope for this poor woman yet. "I take it you haven't made it all the way through the book?"

"N-no. I'm not a very fast reader."

"Well, let me save you the trouble. The moms are overbearing. The dads are mostly hands-off. And the teenage girls, well, they're hard-core bitches."

At my truth bomb falling like a, well, normal bomb, Maisey gasped out loud. Greg looked like he wanted to laugh, but he managed to hold it back at the last minute. I took that to mean there wasn't as much of old Arthur McLachlan in him as appearances suggested.

"I'm serious. Have you ever met a teenage girl? They're awful." I flipped through the pages as if to prove my point. "One of the girls in the book refuses to play chess because her mom is too proud of her. Another one does the same thing with piano. And one of them literally watches her youngest brother die because she's annoyed at being put in charge of him."

"Are you sure we're reading the same book? Because I don't think that's what—" Greg began, but I cut him off with a flap of my hand. This Maisey woman was obviously starting to warm to me. Pesky logic and sound literary analysis weren't going to help her regain her composure.

"Now, I'm not saying you're an overbearing mom," I continued, even though it was written all over her. "But I'm guessing your daughter sees you that way. They all do. Every last one of them. They have to fabricate some kind of trauma as a part of growing up, and that one's the easiest to latch onto. There's a line about it in the book and everything."

Since both of them stood still, waiting for me to materialize this tidbit, I flipped through until I found the passage I meant.

"'I had stopped eating, not because of Arnold, whom I had long forgotten, but to be fashionably anorexic like all the other thirteen-year-old girls who were dieting and finding other ways to suffer as teenagers.'" I hesitated, since I sounded callous even to my own ears. "I'm not trying to gloss over eating disorders, obviously, but you see what she means. Those little vipers love drama. They feast on it. If they don't have any built into their lives, they'll keep looking until they find it. Usually in the shape of their mothers."

"Are you speaking from experience?" Greg asked, sarcasm and politeness wrapped up in one barbed drawl. "As a teenage girl and a mother?"

At that, I laughed out loud. This man had no idea how close he was. I'd never been a teenage girl, it was true, and parenthood was definitely not to my taste, but I knew a thing or two about surviving an encounter with a maternal behemoth.

"Not quite," I admitted. "Let's just say I'm still trying to outgrow my mom and leave it at that."

That seemed to clinch the matter. With a deep breath, Maisey scooped up the last of the enchiladas and steeled herself to face the trials ahead. "We might as well get this over with," she said. "If we get hungry, I guess we can always order a pizza."

"Oh, we're definitely ordering a pizza." Greg grinned. "Grandpa will *hate* that. He might even be so distracted that he won't notice Mateo trying to take his blood pressure on the sly."

"His blood pressure?" I asked, laughing. The only way I was going near that old grouch with a blood pressure cuff was if someone asked me to strangle him with it.

"Yeah." Anxiety touched the lines around Maisey's eyes. "I know that one'll be a stretch, but you should be able to get an idea about the rest, right? His pulse and breathing and stuff?"

"Uh, why would I want to do that? I'd like to leave here with all my limbs intact, thanks. I still need them."

Maisey and Greg exchanged a meaningful look. "Oh dear," Maisey said. "Didn't Sloane brief you on your duties?"

"My…duties?" I echoed, mistrusting the direction this conversation was taking. "I read the book. Isn't that enough? Or was I supposed to prepare a monologue? No offense, but I try to *avoid* the stage these days."

"No, it's not that." She dropped her voice to a conspiratorial whisper. "I meant the nursing stuff."

My Spidey senses started to tingle then—and by Spidey senses, I meant a prickling of tiny sword points up and down my spine. "What nursing stuff?"

Maisey took her lower lip between her teeth. "Sloane didn't tell you?"

"No, she didn't," I said. I was starting to get the feeling there was a lot Sloane hadn't told me. Blood pressure cuffs. Enchiladas. Tall, strange men who weren't her fiancé. This was turning into a *very* intriguing book club.

"Please tell me I was invited to this book club because of my wit and intelligence," I said.

"You were!" Maisey was quick to say. "You definitely were. It's just…Adult Protective Services is involved. We don't know what else to do."

I tipped my head back with a groan. I was going to *kill* Sloane for this.

Greg coughed gently. "You don't have to do anything you're not comfortable with, I promise. They're just asking us to get a licensed medical professional to sign off on his care. To make sure he's being properly looked after. Sloane thought you might be able to discreetly look over him while you're here."

Maisey clasped her hands in front of her. "We'd ask that chiropractor of Sloane's to do it, only he's…well…you know."

I flung up my hand. "Say no more. I'm in."

Both of them stared at me, understandably surprised at my sudden about-face. "Wait," Greg said. "Really? Just like that?"

"Brett Marcowitz is a lump of wet beige clay," I said by way of explanation. "If this plan is something he wouldn't approve of, then it has my full support."

Instead of finding anything strange about this, Maisey giggled. "You don't like him, either?"

I really didn't. I'd only met Sloane's fiancé a handful of times, but every encounter left me with a stronger feeling of distaste in my mouth. I was no authority on happy, thriving relationships, obviously, but even I knew better than to affix myself to a guy like that. He was bland and condescending, the sort of man who'd un-ironically wear a popped collar and read trade magazines about architecture.

I hated that Sloane was settling for that. I hated even more that I was oh-so-slightly jealous that she could.

"Let's just say he and I don't share a lot in common," I said. "I'm fun. He's not. I introduce joy and light into people's lives. He sucks everything good back out again."

Maisey clamped a hand over her mouth to keep from laughing out loud. Grinning along with her, I began to metaphorically gird my loins. I might have been lured here under false pretenses, and Sloane was going to owe me big time for this, but if there was one thing I was good at, it was pretending I knew what I was doing.

When you were a Sharpe, there was only one rule: The show must always go on.

18

A BRUSH WITH DEATH HADN'T IMPROVED ARTHUR McLachlan in the slightest.

"I *do* know who you are," he grumbled the second I set foot inside his cluttered, disorganized mess of a living room. It looked exactly like I'd expected—crowded with furniture and books, everything tilted as if shaken by a recent earthquake. Most of the furniture was well past its shelf life, but there was an umbrella stand by the door that I coveted with every part of my being. It was *gorgeous*—one of those old Victorian ones made from a real elephant's foot, all hollowed out and macabre. "You're the librarian who's always trying to get me to sign up to take needlepoint classes when I check out my books. I've never understood why you're so persistent. Do I *look* like I want to take needlepoint classes?"

Every instinct I had warned me to run for cover before he started to get really nasty. Every instinct except the one that had me locking eyes with Sloane, that is. One glance at her guilty, pleading flush, and I had no other choice.

Save me, that look said. *Protect me.*

And underneath it, a very determined *or else.*

"I have to ask everyone who checks out a book if they want to join that class," I said with an apologetic shrug. "The woman who runs it is one of the biggest donors at the library. We have to make her feel appreciated or she threatens to invest her money in the arts instead."

"Harrumph," Arthur said by way of reply. Like, literally. He enunciated both syllables. *Har-rumph.* Noun: A way for irritable old men who knew themselves to be in the wrong to avoid admitting it.

"Why don't you sit here next to Arthur?" Maisey said as she nudged me further into the house. I recognized this as a ruse to get me closer to the old man. Taking his temperature and oxygen levels without his knowledge would be impossible, but all I needed was proximity to listen to his breathing. It had been years since I'd done any actual nursing, and I'd never been all that enthusiastic about it to begin with, but he certainly looked like he was in full fighting form. "I'm sure you two have a lot to catch up on."

"I have nothing to say to that man." Arthur shifted to take up twice as much space on the cushion. "He can sit on the floor next to Sloane."

"Don't be such a grouch, Arthur." Sloane actually picked up a pillow and tossed it at him. "Mateo's here as my guest, which means we'll treat him with the respect he deserves."

She smiled at me in a way that made it impossible for me to flee. Like it or not—and I wasn't sure that I did—I was an official coconspirator now. Especially since Greg was blocking my only exit.

"Next to Octavia, Mateo knows more about literature than anyone," Sloane added. "Plus you need to kiss up to him if you want access to the good library books from now on. He recently got a seat on the acquisition board."

As I lowered myself to the couch, my whole body tensed against attack. Arthur rolled a knowing eye at Sloane. "Is that a fact? Are we talking about the same seat you quit your job over because they didn't give it to you?"

"Arthur!" Maisey's voice took a decidedly sharp turn. "She was fired because of *you*, remember?"

He sniffed. "I remember what she told us. But if a miserable old wretch like me is worth losing a job over, this is the first I'm hearing of it. I was her excuse, nothing more."

I wasn't sure how or why I found the courage, but I darted out my hand and grabbed the old man by the wrist. With a quick glance at the clock on the mantelpiece, I counted the beat of his pulse in time to the ticking seconds. His heartbeat was steady and strong, his body tense as he waited for Sloane to respond.

"The situation was more…complicated than that," she eventually said.

"Calculus is complicated. Quitting your job to take care of a useless old wreck like me is nothing short of foolish."

This exchange felt a little more earnest than the ones I usually witnessed between Sloane and Arthur. Less playful and barbed, more like the personal attack I'd overheard on that last day. But not, I thought, completely wrong.

Apparently, everyone else in the room disagreed with me.

"Well, if that isn't the biggest load of garbage I've ever heard," Maisey said. "After everything she's sacrificed, it'd serve you right if she walked out that door and took us with her, leaving you alone with your books and your attitude and your…your…"

"Your equally miserable grandson," Greg said, taking a firm stance. "Believe me, Pops, when I say that's the last thing either of us wants happening."

A stalemate might have descended then, but Arthur growled and yanked his wrist away.

"Let go of me," he muttered, rubbing his wrist as though I'd bruised it.

I wasn't displeased with my medical findings. As that yank proved, there was good muscle tone in him, and I could see his pupils flaring under the living room lights exactly the way they should. I might not have been as medically trained as, say, Brett Marcowitz, but I knew a healthy old man when one was flailing around next to me.

"I don't know why you're all ganging up on me," Arthur added mulishly. "This is *my* house and *my* book club. You're only here because I allow it."

He turned to me then, his finger outstretched in warning. I was so pleased with my ability to detect no wavering in that steady, unerring hand that I didn't realize he'd turned all his wrath on me until it was too late.

"You. Needlepoint Boy."

I ducked. "Um, can I pick a different nickname?"

"How much does that lady give you at the library? The one you kiss and scrape to every day of your life?"

Needlepoint Boy was bad enough, but that was taking things too far.

"As in, how much does she donate to the library?" I cast an inquiring look at Sloane. That sort of thing had always been more her purview than mine. Very little went on around the library without her knowing about, planning for, and wholeheartedly engaging in ahead of time.

Her next words proved it. "I couldn't give you an *exact* figure, but I know there are five of them," she said.

"Is that all?" Arthur gave another of those harrumphs, but this one felt more triumphant than antagonistic. "Fine. Go to your boss tomorrow and tell her I'll double that woman's donation, provided no one asks me to join one of their stupid classes again."

At the inevitable gasps of outrage that resulted, Arthur actually cackled.

"If I'd have known how easily you'd all pander to rich eccentrics, I'd have done this years ago," he said. "Can I make other stipulations, too? I think everyone should have to wear turtlenecks on Tuesdays."

"Arthur, it doesn't work like that—" Sloane began.

"Turtlenecks always make my neck look so short—" Maisey put in.

"Grandpa, you can't possibly be serious—" came the final protest. Since I assumed Greg was the heir apparent to this particular kingdom—up to and including that elephant-foot umbrella stand—his objection seemed the most valid.

"We're not taking donations at this time," I lied in an attempt to cut this argument short. "So it doesn't matter what kind of stipulations you want to make."

Since I doubted Arthur McLachlan had cut an argument short a day in his life, I added a clincher.

"But if turtlenecks are all you want, I promise to wear one to book club every week. Unlike Maisey, I look fantastic in them."

———

"Are you sure you should be drinking your wine that fast?"

I stood in Arthur's kitchen, hunched over the sink as I drained the glass of red blend I'd poured myself to steady my nerves. We were only an hour into this thing, and I'd already been called every bad word in existence since the Middle Ages. Say what you might about Arthur McLachlan, the man was erudite. I've never been called God's pestilent uvula before, but it was a phrase I intended to throw in at every dinner party I attended for the rest of my natural-born life.

"No offense, but I think I've earned it," I added as I poured myself a second and very generous glass. "You wanted me to join your book club, huh?"

Sloane had the decency to blush. "It's not as bad as it looks. I was going to ease you into the medical stuff, that's all. Let you get to know everyone first."

"You mean you were going to let me get attached to everyone first," I said, pointing the glass at her in warning. "You're such a liar. You told me you wanted my professional insight."

"I do want it! Just not the profession you're thinking of."

"You used me. Puffed me up with importance and then deflated me like a catheter balloon."

"Only because we were desperate," Sloane said. She disarmed me with a quick, mischievous smile. "Besides, I think you were enjoying yourself. I watched you in there. You liked getting the better of Arthur for once."

"I like a lot of questionable things," I retorted. "Including you. Who knew you were such a dastardly plotter under that quiet-librarian exterior?"

"Mateo, I'm not! I've never plotted anything a day in my life. It just seemed like the easiest solution, that's all."

I eyed her suspiciously, not believing a word out of her mouth. The Sloane Parker I used to work with might not have been much of a plotter, but this woman was. Sometime in the past month, she'd been doing her best to grow a backbone. It wasn't very big yet—more of a vestigial tail than anything else—but I could see her giving it a flex.

"Does this mean you aren't going to sign one eensy-weensy form for me?" she asked, turning a pair of soulful eyes my way. "And maybe check up on him a few times during book club meetings, just so we know he's getting better?"

We both already knew the answer to that. "Fine, but you're going to need to bring more wine to the next meeting. *A lot* more. That man is the worst."

She looked torn between throwing her arms around me and breaking out in a song and dance right there on the linoleum floor. Since she was still very much Sloane Parker, she settled for a smile.

"Thank you, Mateo. This means a lot more to me than you realize."

I could see her starting to get choked up—a thing that was only going to make *me* get choked up—so I bumped her with my hip. "Next time you want a favor, Parker, just ask. I'm always happy to help a friend."

Since that only seemed to make her want to cry even more, I grabbed my copy of *The Joy Luck Club* and started to head into the living room. We'd left the discussion somewhere on the streets of San Francisco and needed to get back to it.

"Wait. That's not your copy." She stuck a thumb out at the book, which looked for all intents and purposes exactly like the one I'd grabbed in town last week. Taking it from me, she rifled through the pages until a bright-yellow line popped out at me. "See? You didn't highlight this."

I glanced at the line in question before reading it aloud. "'All of us are like stairs, one step after another, going up and down, but all going the same way.'" I wrinkled my nose and glanced at the back of the book. It still bore the price tag from the Well-Read Moose, an indie bookstore in town, so I didn't see who else it could have belonged to. "Maybe someone took it back after they'd already read it. You know how many people think they can treat bookstores and libraries like they're the same."

She shook her head. "No, this is Arthur's. All his books are high-lighted like that—and I mean *all* of them. I've been cataloging his collection for weeks."

"Hey, Mateo. Have you seen my—" Greg poked his head into the kitchen and cut himself off the second he noticed Sloane. Without changing his expression, he nodded at the book in Sloane's hand. "That's mine."

"Oh. I thought it belonged to your grandfather."

"It doesn't."

He snatched the book back so quickly that both Sloane and I felt the stinging rejection of it.

"I'm sorry," she murmured. "I saw the highlighted sections and assumed—"

"You *read* them?"

"Yeah, but only a few. Did you know your grandfather does the exact same thing?"

"Don't touch my things," Greg said. After a brief struggle with himself, he added, "Please."

"Geez. What'd you do to that poor guy?" I asked as soon as the door swung to a close behind him. "He was perfectly nice to me before. Friendly, even."

The tight compression of Sloane's lips seemed to indicate that it wasn't a subject she cared to tackle right now, but she managed to pry them open long enough to speak.

"He doesn't like me very much. We didn't exactly meet under the best of circumstances. He thinks I…" Her voice trailed off and she shook her head. "I don't know what he thinks, to be honest. But it doesn't matter. Arthur needs him a lot more than he's willing to admit. The last thing I want to do is get in the way of whatever they're working out between them."

This was such a Sloane thing to say and do—to lay herself out on the railroad tracks to repair someone else's relationship—that I sighed. *My* problem might have been avoiding emotional entanglements of all kinds, but Sloane had never met an emotion she could resist. Most days, she bathed in them like Elizabeth Báthory undergoing a new skin-care regimen.

"Most people would have given up on Arthur McLachlan a long time ago," I said. "I'm not sure he deserves this much care."

Her voice grew quiet. "Why else do you think I'm so determined to make sure he gets it?"

19

—

"MATEO, YOU BEAUTIFUL LITTLE SNEAK. WHY didn't you warn me?"

I stood hunched over a box of art supplies in Area 51, the catch-all storeroom in the basement level of the library, when Octavia came rustling in. I should have known she was heading this way from the swish of silk over linen, but I'd been searching for the papier-mâché supplies for so long that I was starting to lose track of my senses.

"Warn you about what?" I asked as I straightened. This marked the last time I was volunteering to cover Sloane's Let's Make a Book Cover! class. It was back to straight story time after this, and I wasn't accepting arguments. Twenty wriggling kids asking questions about Little Red Riding Hood's life choices was bad enough; I didn't need mass quantities of newspaper and glue to make things worse.

"About the donation," Octavia said, beaming at me from the doorway. She didn't elaborate further, but I caught her meaning anyway. I caught it *hard*. "We haven't seen that kind of money from a single donor in years."

"No way," I breathed. "He did it? That old miser actually signed a check?"

"I don't know that I'd call him a miser, but yes. He dropped it off this morning—and sang *your* praises while he did it. If I hadn't already given you that promotion, you'd be next in line for it, no questions asked."

This seemed odd, since Sloane was the one who deserved most of the credit for any and all things related to Arthur, but I wasn't about to balk at the sudden influx of appreciation.

"Does this mean I can hand off Little Readers Corner duty to Janell?" I abandoned my attempts at finding the art supplies and shoved the box back on the shelf. "Because that seems like a fair trade for a five-figure Arthur McLachlan check. I hope he didn't say anything about turtlenecks, because I was kidding about that. Mostly."

This gave her a sudden pause. "Arthur McLachlan? Turtlenecks? What are you talking about?"

My pause was only slightly less sudden. "That depends. What are *you* talking about?"

"If you're implying that Arthur was the one who gave us the donation, you couldn't be farther off. This has nothing to do with him."

"Wait." I blinked. "Really? If we're not talking about Arthur, who gave us a donation? And what does it have to do with me?"

"Nigel Carthage." Octavia handed me a fluttering piece of paper. It took me all of two seconds to identify it as a receipt for twenty thousand dollars. "I had no idea you knew one of the reviewers for *The New Yorker*, but I can't say I'm surprised. I've always thought you had hidden depths."

I wanted to protest that my depths weren't the least bit hidden but my heart was thumping too heavily.

"Nigel Carthage?" I said, more to myself than to Octavia. "An older Black gentleman with a British accent? A little gaunt? Great clothes?"

"The one and only." Octavia stood back and crossed her arms with satisfaction. They crackled like they held entire bags of Doritos. "Where on earth did you meet a man like that?"

"My mother's nightclub," I said. My heart still thumped, but it was more like an anxious pitter-pattering now. This was starting to feel *very* sketchy. Nothing I'd said to that man should have resulted in an outcome like this. A phone call, maybe. A chance meeting outside another nightclub, sure. But that kind of money dropped without warning at my place of business? That was the start of a murder docuseries if I'd ever heard one.

I paused and added, "He stalked me outside and asked me to let him into my book club."

"Then by all means, let him in," Octavia said. "You know what this kind of donation can do for the library. For the *community*."

"Yeah, yeah, I know," I said, but without much conviction. Octavia's tone might have been light and her mood buoyant, but I felt pretty sure she meant every word. In her world, murder was a small price to pay for library funding. "When he dropped off the money, did he say anything specific about me?"

"To be honest, I wasn't paying close attention. There were too many dollar signs in my eyes." She paused. "Why? What's wrong?"

"I'm mostly just thinking aloud. But if I let him into my book club and end up at the bottom of a lake, make sure you pass this conversation along to the police, okay?"

She laughed to show her appreciation for my joke, but I was only half-kidding. The truth was a man in my position had very little to offer someone like Nigel Carthage.

Or, since honesty was the order of the day, very little to offer the world as a whole.

———

The attempted murder happened sooner than I expected.

I was halfway across the park leading out of the library when a dark figure barreled out of the tree line and hightailed it straight for me. Granted, it was only five o'clock, so the sun still hung well above the lake. Also this late in the summer, every family within a fifty-mile radius was out for an evening stroll, so there were plenty of witnesses around.

But the figure was big. And fast. I panicked, okay?

"My skin bruises easily!" I cried, throwing up my hand to shield the delicate bones of my face.

"Does it?" the figure asked as it came to a halt in front of me. He paused. "Taking vitamin C is supposed to help. Shouldn't a nurse know that?"

I brought my hand down, that gruff, friendly voice suddenly registering. "Greg? What are you doing here?"

"Jogging," he said as though it were the most natural thing in the world—which, considering how many other people were frolicking about in athleisure, it *was*. The only thing odd about this scenario was me. "Maisey told me where you work, so I thought I'd cruise by. Is that okay?"

"That depends... Is this about your grandfather?" Now that my life was secured for another day, I was more than happy to chat, but not if it meant dragging Arthur McLachlan kicking and screaming into the conversation. I tilted my head in a gesture for Greg to follow me to my car. He shoved his hands as deep into his pockets as they could go and followed, slowing to match his steps to mine.

"Um..."

Great. It *was* about Arthur.

I bit back a sigh. "Before you ask, no, I don't think he's going to keel over and die anytime in the next week. But if you're worried about him, I suggest you strong-arm him to an *actual* doctor. There's only so much I can do in a book club meeting before he picks up on it."

Greg shook his head. "No, it's not that." He colored slightly and added, "I mean, I *do* care that he's not going to die—and I appreciate you saying so—but I wanted to ask you about her. The girl. The woman."

He said this last bit as though rushing through a tunnel. *Her. The girl. The woman.*

"You mean Sloane?"

He hunched his shoulders as though trying to match his stature to mine. "Yeah. You know her well, right?"

I wasn't sure how detailed he wanted me to get—or how detailed Sloane would appreciate me being—so I deflected.

"She'll take good care of him," I said, "if that's what you're worried about. I know she doesn't look like much of a match for your grandfather, but they've been doing that whole cat-and-dog thing for a while now. I think they like it."

His grunt indicated that he'd come to a similar conclusion on his own, so I kept going.

"Until Arthur's collapse, it was all in good fun. We even had a secret scoreboard up in the break room to keep track of which one of them was winning. But that last day…" I let my voice trail off and shook my head. I'd never seen Sloane as shaken up as she'd been after Arthur's attack. "Let's just say he popped off some pretty awful things. Like, *cruel* things."

Greg nodded as though that made perfect sense. "Yeah, he would."

"Would he?"

"Knowing Grandpa? Absolutely." Greg's shoulders suddenly seemed less broad than they had before, as if they were getting tired of holding everything up. "The day he was rushed to the hospital was the anniversary of my grandmother's death."

I released a long whistle. That explained an awful lot about what I'd witnessed in the library—not an angry old man lashing out, but a *sad* angry old man lashing out. No wonder why we'd all been cowering in fear.

"If it helps, I'm pretty sure Sloane's forgiven him," I offered.

Greg didn't appear reassured by this. "I feel like she should be paid a lot more. For all the hours she's putting in, she should be getting like fifty hours of overtime every week. Won't she need to get a real job?"

That made me laugh. The one—and only one—thing that made Brett Marcowitz acceptable as a life partner was his bank account. "Eventually, maybe, but I don't think you need to worry about her. Her fiancé is a chiropractor."

"That Brett guy everyone keeps talking about?" he asked before shaking his head and moving on. "Never mind. Thanks again for all your help. I feel a lot better knowing Grandpa's being looked after. It'd be easier if he'd let me stay with him in the house, but…"

"You're not from around here?"

We'd reached my car by this time, but Greg didn't seem to be in a hurry to leave. I got the feeling it was because he didn't have anywhere else to go.

"No. I'm from Seattle. I'm only here because…" He shrugged. "It's a long story. I stayed in a haunted Airbnb for a bit, but now I'm living with Maisey."

"A haunted Airbnb?"

"Don't ask."

"Well, now I kind of *have* to." I grinned to show I meant no harm, though I had serious plans to pry that tale out of him later. "Look, if you don't know many people in town, did you want to grab a bite or something? Not"—I was quick to add—"that I'm hitting on you. But my boyfriend's probably cooking something with a lot of vegetables for dinner tonight. If I bring you home to eat half of it, he won't notice that I refuse to touch mine."

He eyed me speculatively. "What kind of vegetables?"

"Green ones." I shuddered. "Trust me—you'd be doing me a big favor if you came along and distracted him long enough for me to hide them in the fish tank."

———

I regretted my friendly overture before I even stopped the car.

"Oh geez." I pulled into my driveway with a feeling of deep foreboding and even deeper panic. Shifting quickly into reverse, I tried to zip out before anyone noticed me, but it was too late. Lincoln appeared in the doorway next to a woman wearing a fully lined mink coat despite the fact that it was eighty-five degrees outside.

"You didn't tell me this would be a *fancy* dinner," Greg said. There was enough laughter underscoring his voice for me to recognize defeat on all fronts. "Who's that?"

"Althea Sharpe." I cranked the parking brake and resigned myself to my fate. "My mother. She's a big-time lounge singer in these parts, so if you want to get on her good side, pretend you've heard of her. Otherwise, there's a good chance she'll put on a show in the living room to prove it."

"I haven't seen a good show in a long time..." The laughter was still in his voice as he appraised me out of the corner of his eye. "I didn't realize you were famous."

"I'm not famous." I bit back the urge to tell him not to google me, to warn him that the decades-old images of me granulating newspapers across the country weren't exactly flattering. In my experience, that only encouraged people to dive deeper. "But I'm not kidding about the likelihood of a sing-along. Lincoln's been learning some of her favorites on the piano so he can accompany her. Once the two of them get started, there's no turning back. I apologize in advance if you get roped into playing the triangle. Or the bongos."

Sighing, I stepped out of the Fiat. My only remaining hope was that the two of them hadn't been hitting the cocktails *too* hard. My mom pretty much ran on a steady drip of dry martinis, but Lincoln could usually keep her in check.

My boyfriend's surprise at finding a rugged, well-built man climbing out of my passenger seat was evident in the way his brows flew up to his hairline but not another muscle on his body quivered. My mother's surprise was, well, nonexistent. She'd have only been surprised if I *hadn't* rolled up to my own home on an evening she wasn't expected without a built-in audience to appreciate her. One of her favorite maxims—other than the one about suffering to be beautiful—was to always travel with an entourage.

"Mateo, my baby." She opened her arms to enfold me in her too-hot, too-musty embrace. Not even the gallon of Chanel No. 5 she seemed to have doused herself with was enough to cover the scent of sixty-year-old mink falling apart at the seams. "Thank goodness you're home. Lincoln and I were just about to get started without you."

She turned next to Greg, her hand outstretched in a way I recognized as a request for a papal kiss. I was in the middle of deciding how best to inform Greg about what was expected of him when he gripped her hand and pressed it warmly between his own.

"I can't tell you what an honor this is, Ms. Sharpe. My mom had all your albums. I grew up to the sound of you singing the blues."

I blinked, surprised by his fervor, but my mother accepted it as her due. "I hope you didn't listen to 'Bonjour, Baby' as much as the rest. I never did care for the way the producers overemphasized my vibrato."

"It was exactly the right amount of vibrato," he assured her before moving on to Lincoln. There, more restrained but still warm, he said, "I'm Greg McLachlan. Sorry to burst in on you like this, but Mateo's helping out with my grandfather. He said you wouldn't mind the extra company for dinner."

"McLachlan... McLachlan... That makes you Arthur's grandson, right?" Lincoln's brows bounced back a fraction. I was glad to see it. He wasn't a jealous man—not in the way most people got jealous—but it wouldn't do me any good to push him too far right now. Our anniversary was just around the corner, and we were both feeling the pressure.

Lincoln, because he loved anniversaries. Me, because I'd never had a relationship last this long before. We were breaking new ground together, and as recent events had proved, the going was rough.

"Does that mean you're part of the book club?" Lincoln asked.

"Something like that," Greg agreed.

My mother couldn't stand being upstaged for long, so she wound her arm through Greg's and began tugging him through the door. "I have no use for books, but my little Mateo has always been a reader. I gave him a thesaurus for his fifth birthday... Do you remember that, darling? He carried that thing around like it was a doll for *years*. He was so good with words that they wanted to move him up two grades but I wouldn't let them. 'Not my baby,' I said. 'He needs as normal a childhood as possible after the life he's had.'"

The only part of this statement that was even remotely true was the thesaurus for my birthday. I got it along with a Book of Mormon bound in blue leather. Both books had been given to us by a pair of polite, short-sleeved missionaries who'd spent more than three hours in our tiny apartment kitchen, listening as my mother recited her life story. She'd gotten all the way up to her first stage audition before they'd managed to extricate themselves—and a good thing, too, because once my mother got on the subject of her decision to chase her Hollywood dream against the odds and her parents' wishes, it was impossible to stop her.

To this day, I don't think they meant to leave the thesaurus behind, but they were so grateful to get out of the apartment that they didn't dare look back.

"I thought she told me you were a *mathematical* prodigy," Lincoln mused as we watched Greg and my mother enter the house. "And that your doll was a protractor, not a thesaurus."

"Don't start," I said, sighing. Once my mom started in on the lies, it was hard to keep track. "How many drinks has she had?"

"All of them. Every drop of liquor we have in the house." Lincoln paused to pull me into his arms and hold me there much longer than necessary for a simple greeting. For once—just a little once—I relaxed and let myself enjoy it. "How was work today?"

"Interesting." Since I could hardly relate the entire day's events while we had guests, I launched into an apology instead. "Sorry I didn't warn you I was bringing a guest home for dinner, but he stopped by after work to chat about his grandfather. I feel bad for the guy. Life can't be easy with a man like Arthur McLachlan for a relative."

Lincoln didn't say anything, but he didn't have to. The unspoken truth—that what I *really* meant was life with a relative like Althea Sharpe wasn't easy—rang loud and clear between us.

"It's fine. I'm sure he's great. I'll just throw another swordfish steak on the grill."

I entered the kitchen to find my mother bestowing her most dazzling smile on Greg. "I interrupted you just when you were getting to the good part. How old were you when you first heard my album?"

I cleared my throat, prepared to jump in and save him, but he answered easily enough.

"About ten, probably. I grew up here, so my mom and I had seen some of your posters around town."

I blinked, surprised by the authenticity of this reply.

"We didn't come across any of your albums until a few years later, after we'd moved to Seattle, but my mom immediately recognized you. She grabbed a copy of your first CD, fell in love, and bought everything you ever put out after that."

"Wait." I couldn't help myself. "You're serious? You actually *have* heard of her?"

My mom sighed. "My poor Mateo. You've never appreciated me the way I was meant to be appreciated."

She trailed over to the dining room table. It was located in a solarium off the kitchen, a back porch that Lincoln had converted and transformed with plants and twinkle lights. The room was almost always ten degrees warmer than the rest of the house, which was the only explanation for why my mom finally slid out of her coat and handed it to Greg.

He stood holding it awkwardly until Lincoln lifted it from his hands. If my boyfriend was smart, he'd toss it onto the barbecue the second he was done cooking dinner.

"That's what your little book club book is for, isn't it?" my mom continued brightly. "So all of you can better appreciate your mothers?"

"Mom, that's not what *The Joy Luck Club* is about. It's about children and their mothers better appreciating *each other*."

She waved this off with the unconcern of a woman who'd never once tried to understand anything about me. "It's the same thing. When do you get to the part where you take me on vacation? I remember that being in the book."

I threw up my hands in defeat. "The woman in the story flies to China to find her long-lost siblings, not to cruise the seven seas with her mother."

My mom barely blinked. Her ability to revise history to suit the particulars of her own memory was nothing short of miraculous. "Have you ever taken *your* mom on a cruise?" she asked Greg.

"No," he said quietly. "I always wanted to, but she passed away."

A feeling of discomfort immediately filled the air. My mom was the first to react.

"I'm sorry to hear that." She reached over and took his hand, but not before dropping the slightly lilting drawl of a songstress from her tone. "Every boy needs his mother."

"Thank you. That means a lot."

Lincoln waltzed in with our dinner before I could add my sympathies to my mom's, which was probably for the best. *If you can't say anything nice, don't say anything at all.*

It wasn't embroidered on a pillow, but that didn't make it any less true.

———

"What's another word for 'bubble'?"

A few days later, I sat in front of my computer, a whopping five more pages on the screen than there'd been a few hours ago. I hadn't been on a roll like this in a long time, the words pouring out of my fingers like a coffeepot percolating its heady brew.

"Never mind. 'Percolate.' That's perfect." I finished typing the sentence I was on and sat back, satisfied with my day's work. I'd just left my hero in the middle of a forest to battle a craggy dragon with an even craggier dragon grandfather, so things were starting to get good. "I guess my childhood thesaurus came in handy after all these years. Don't tell my mom. She'll never let me forget it."

When I didn't get an answer, I twisted away from my desk. In theory, my writing desk was just a plank of wood nailed into one corner of the living room; but when Lincoln nailed a plank of wood, it wasn't some random affair made with a hammer and a two-by-four. My particular slab was live-edge hickory braced with ornate hand-carved brackets and a built-in cup holder so I wouldn't spill my coffee.

Instead of looking proud of my success, Lincoln stood in the doorway with his arms crossed.

"Uh-oh," I joked. "Don't tell me. You lost our fortune on the Exchange. My mom decided to sell her apartment and move in with us. There's a lumberjack emergency, and only you can answer the call."

None of my guesses caused the muscles on Lincoln's face to move—not even to smile.

"You've been writing all day," he said in a tone as flat as his expression.

"Yes, and you wouldn't believe the progress I've made," I said. "Do you want to read my pages? I haven't proofed them or anything, but—"

"It's going well? Your book?"

"Yes. Isn't that weird?" My side was growing tight from twisting at an unnatural angle, so I pointed the chair outward and settled with one ankle propped on the opposite knee. It wasn't the most comfortable position, but Sloane once told me it makes me look like James Dean, so I adopted it whenever possible. And sometimes when it wasn't. "Poor Thaddeus was stuck in that stupid forest forever, but then he met a ferocious dragon who's part of a forest book club, and I haven't looked back."

"I'll bet he did."

There was no ignoring the bitterness in his tone, but I did it anyway. I had to if I was going to make it out of this conversation alive. It was the coward's way out, obviously, but cowardice was one of the few constants in my life. No matter how hard things got or emotionally overwrought they promised to become, I could always find a way to hide.

"By the way, I picked up a shift at the library tomorrow, so I'll have to meet you at the restaurant for our anniversary dinner," I said. My voice sounded falsely casual even to my own ears, but at least I was fitting all the words together properly. "I wish I could stay home and ride this literary wave for a while, but between the book club and work, I barely have time for anything. Octavia hasn't been able to replace Sloane yet, so the whole place is starting to fall apart. I don't think any of us realized just how much of the grunt work she used to do. Or how many bodily fluids she cleaned up."

"Mateo—" Lincoln began, but he cut himself off with a sigh. "I thought you hated the book you're reading for that fake book club."

It was on the tip of my tongue to say that the book club itself wasn't fake so much as my reason for being there, but I got the feeling that wasn't Lincoln's point.

"I do. It's all about a group of Chinese mothers who imprint themselves so deeply on their children's lives that there's no way to tell where one of them ends and the other begins. You understand my concerns."

"But you love your mom."

I hesitated. "Ye-es."

That hesitation was my undoing. Even though it was true—I *did* love my mom, and she *had* imprinted herself on my life in ways I'd never be able to undo—the battle that was waging itself inside Lincoln's heart had nothing to do with her and everything to do with me. He opened his mouth, shut it again, muttered something incoherent, and eventually turned on his heel.

"I take this to mean you don't want to read my pages?" I called to his retreating back.

His only answer was to turn around and level me with a long, thoughtful stare. There were a thousand different ways to interpret that stare, but I only needed one. He was trying with every fiber of his being not to push me any further than I could go.

And he was failing. We were both failing.

"Suit yourself," I said. "You'll have to hack into my computer if you change your mind. My password is Lincoln&Matco4Ever, in case you need a helping hand."

20

—

THE NEXT EVENING, I ARRIVED AT Bardenay, a rustic-chic restaurant overlooking the water, to find that my anniversary dinner with Lincoln had expanded by two.

And not just *any* two. Whether by design or the machinations of fate, Sloane and Brett sat opposite my better half at our favorite corner booth. Under normal circumstances, the idea of spending a whole meal listening to Brett Marcowitz wax poetic about the benefits of the Gonstead technique was one that would put me off eating forever, but these circumstances weren't normal.

For one thing, Lincoln and I hadn't yet admitted that the unnamed specter had officially reached our door. For another, I was dying to talk to Sloane about the donation to the library. Apparently, the check had cleared that morning. We were practically Rockefellers.

"Sloane, what do you know about a man named Nigel Carthage?" I asked by way of greeting. I paused long enough to drop a kiss on Lincoln's cheek. The woodsy scent of him sent a pang through me—of regret, maybe, or longing. Or possibly just pain. "Offhand, do you recognize the name?"

Sloane found nothing odd in my question. Brett was obviously affronted at being so casually dismissed, but I didn't care. Some things were more important than Brett's feelings.

Okay, literally everything was more important than Brett's feelings. But I could hardly say that to the man's face.

"Nigel Carthage?" she echoed with a wrinkle of her nose. "Why does that sound familiar?"

"That's what I want to know." I propped my chin on my hands and blinked expectantly at her. "Take all the time you need. This is important."

"Wait. He's a literary critic, right?" She got to the answer much quicker than I expected—and without once having to resort to her phone for clues. "Does lots of reviews for big-name books and big-name publications?"

"Geez, Sloane. You really need to get a life."

She blushed and began toying with the tacky purple brooch on her collar. I'd noticed her wearing that thing at book club, but time wasn't doing anything to improve it. Seasonal Halloween stores sold better quality stuff than that.

"It's not as pathetic as it sounds. His name pops up in the library review journals all the time—a thing you'd know if you ever picked one up. Did you know he used to live here?"

"He still does." I let the news settle before spilling the *real* cream. "I met him at my mom's club the other night."

Lincoln cleared his throat. "You didn't tell me you'd met a book reviewer."

"Not just a book reviewer," Sloane corrected him. "*The* book reviewer. A good quote from him can launch an entire career. But I don't understand. What does Nigel have to do with anything?"

"He donated twenty thousand dollars to the library—and get this, he mentioned me by name when he did it."

It said a lot about Sloane as a human being and my friend that her expression showed nothing but delight at this piece of library gossip. There was no envy in that wide-eyed stare of hers; no regret that hers hadn't been the name on the golden ticket. She was the only person I knew who was capable of genuine, un-ironic joy in other people's triumphs.

"Mateo, that's fantastic." She stopped playing with the brooch and clasped both my hands instead. "Are they letting you have a say on how it's spent? Because there's that used car lot on Sherman that promised me two vans at a discount if we bought them before the year's out. They'd be perfect for expanding the bookmobile program. I'd be happy to pop in and—"

Now it was Brett's turn to clear his throat—though he did it with much less finesse. "Sloane, love, you don't work there anymore, remember? It's Mateo's job to handle that kind of thing now."

She sat back with a flush, her eyes downcast. "I didn't mean it like that. I only wanted to introduce Mateo to my contact at the lot. I'd hate for the library to lose out on the deal just because I chose to walk away."

A waiter approached the table before any of us could make an attempt to dispel the sudden heavy tension. I was inordinately proud of Lincoln for glossing things over by ordering a pitcher of sangria and a smoked trout spread for the whole table. The world could be falling apart around him, but he'd still remember his manners.

"I doubt Octavia will let me anywhere near the money, so it's not like it matters," I said as soon as the waiter disappeared from view. "Besides, that's not the strangest part."

"Maybe we should save the work talk for another time," Sloane said with a quick, anxious glance at her fiancé. I cast a quick, anxious glance at my own beau to find that he was watching me with an intensity that seemed a little too heavy for the circumstances.

"Actually, I'd like to hear this," Lincoln said, his voice carefully neutral. "How does this tale get stranger?"

I ignored the warning thrum in my veins and answered, "I'm pretty sure the twenty thousand bucks was meant to be a bribe."

Sloane frowned. "For what? Nothing in the library is worth that much."

"He wants in our book club."

My news wasn't received with the excitement I'd been angling for. Instead of an outburst of intrigue and drama, I got laughter—and lots of it.

"I'm serious, you guys. I know how it sounds, but I have proof. Look." I pulled out the business card he'd left me and flashed it at my incredulous audience. "He gave me this and told me to call him if we ever got an opening. I think he must really love *The Joy Luck Club*."

Lincoln was the first to recover. "No one loves a book so much they'd pay that kind of money just to talk about it with a group of strangers."

"A billionaire might. That's like twenty bucks to them."

"But Nigel Carthage isn't a billionaire," Sloane pointed out. "I doubt he's even a millionaire."

The waiter arrived with our drinks and the appetizer. Grateful for the distraction, I took the biggest slice of bread I could find and liberally dished a scoop of trout spread on top.

"You don't know his financial situation," I said around a mouthful of the smoky dip. "He could be sitting on piles of money. Besides, what other explanation is there? He cornered me in a dark alley. He all but begged me to let him into our club. Then, when I refused, he showed up at my place of business with a huge check. I think we should let him in. To see what happens."

Sloane shook her head. "I had a hard enough time selling Arthur on you being there. It'd never work."

"I'm with Sloane on this one," Brett agreed. I watched as he arranged a plate for Sloane and put it in front of her before helping himself. It was a sweet gesture, if uncomfortably paternal. "You guys have already taken over that poor man's house and life. I think you should just cancel the whole thing."

"Haven't you overlooked the most obvious explanation?" Lincoln asked.

"You mean that he might be after my mom?" I shook my head. "I considered it, but if that's the case, he'd be much better off signing the check over to her. I don't think she's ever set foot inside that library."

"No, not Althea," Lincoln said, his expression mirroring Brett's for severity. "Maybe what he wants isn't your mom or the book club, but...you."

This time, it was *my* turn to laugh—a thing I did so loudly and so thoroughly that the entire restaurant seemed to be listening in. "Lincoln, he's like eighty years old."

"So? When did that ever stop someone? Hugh Hefner kept his mansion going all the way into his nineties."

This only added to my hilarity. In another few minutes, Lincoln would be accusing me of having romantic interludes with old Arthur himself.

"Listen to what you're saying. I met him once. In my sweaty, too-tight pants. After my terrible performance onstage with my mother. No one is transported to euphoric heights by the sight of a poorly dressed librarian in his thirties tap-dancing to 'Forever Young,' I promise."

"*I* am."

At that, my laughter stopped short, my whole chest heaving with a sharp, unyielding pang. It was what I'd always imagined being inside a vacuum would be like—a sudden, terrible nothing.

"Lincoln," I said, but it was obvious from the expectant way he was watching me that more was necessary. An apology, maybe? An avowal of love and affection? A reassurance that in the contest between his emotionally supportive, generous affection and literally every other human being on the planet, he'd always be the winner?

"Mateo," he replied, waiting.

Suddenly, it didn't seem to matter that Sloane and Brett were at this anniversary dinner with us. All the double dates in all the world wouldn't save us now. The knocking at the door was going to have to be answered one way or another.

"You know how I feel about performing," I said, my gaze fixed on my plate. I think I was mumbling, but I couldn't be a hundred percent sure.

"No, I don't," he said. "I know how you *say* you feel. That you hate it and would rather do anything else in the world. That you'd prefer to be a flight attendant or personal trainer or librarian or anything other than a singer."

I blinked at him, unsure where all this heat about my job was coming from. Our problems were emotional, not professional.

"So what? They're just jobs. They're temporary. They don't mean anything."

Lincoln got to his feet so quickly that it left *me* feeling dizzy.

"I'm sorry, you guys," he said. He threw his napkin to the table and jerkily extracted a hundred dollar bill from his wallet. It fluttered to the table. "Enjoy your dinner on me tonight. I'm not hungry anymore."

"Please don't do this," I begged, but it was no use. Lincoln was already moving toward the door with his long, massive strides. When I turned back to the table, it was to find that Brett looked as uncomfortable as I felt.

Which, ugh. He *would*.

"Oh, don't look so worried," I said as I threw my own napkin on the table. I was suddenly very tired of pandering to a man I didn't like and barely even knew. "Relationship drama isn't contagious. You and Sloane aren't going to suddenly start shouting at each other over the trout spread. I doubt you even know how."

21

INSTEAD OF WALKING OUT OF THE restaurant to find my scornful lover staring moodily out over the water or angrily punching holes into walls, I discovered him bent on one knee as he changed the tire of a stranger in the parking lot.

"Spares aren't meant to carry you for long, so make sure you head straight to a mechanic," he said to the group of college-aged teens standing uselessly by as they watched him. He finished tightening the lug nuts and stood back to survey his handiwork. "That should hold you for now."

The teens thanked him for his help, one of the girls even going so far as to offer him either a twenty-dollar bill or her phone number—from my distance, I couldn't tell which—for his trouble. He declined and stood watching to make sure the tire held as they piled into the vehicle and drove away.

"The last true white knight," I said, the whole of the Sahara in my tone. "Always coming to the aid of the down and downtrodden."

He didn't turn to greet me. "They were stranded. What else was I supposed to do?"

"Call them an Uber? Tell them to ask their mommies and daddies for help? Make them figure it out on their own?" I gave up with a sigh. Lincoln would no more pass by a stranded motorist than he would fail to help children cross the street or call out people speaking rudely to customer service workers. "Do you want to tell me what that was about in there? Brett looked ready to pull the fire alarm to keep people from staring at us. I don't think he's used to drawing a crowd."

Lincoln chuffed on a laugh, but he didn't unbend enough to actually smile at me. "I know you think he's a little on the dry side, but compared to you, *everyone* is on the dry side. I didn't think you'd mind if I invited them to join us."

"I don't mind," I said, my heart starting to pick itself up from the pit of my stomach. Being called wet wasn't much of a compliment, but it was better than nothing. "Seriously, Lincoln. You just accused me of leading on an eighty-year-old book reviewer I talked to for all of ten minutes. What's going on?"

He sighed and glanced off in the distance, looking so much like an Instagram model that I could kick him. Or kiss him. Possibly both.

"I wish you'd tell me why you hate *The Joy Luck Club* so much," he said.

This was such a strange request that I couldn't help pushing a little harder. "Is this your way of saying you want to join the book club, too? Because the going rate is twenty grand. I don't think you can afford it."

No smile that time, either. I gave up.

"Look—what do you want me to say?" A fully public parking lot was a strange place to have this conversation, but if Lincoln wanted to do it here, I had no other choice. "It's just a book."

"That's a pretty strange thing coming from the mouth of a budding author."

He said those last two words—*budding author*—like he had to physically slice them from his tongue in order to get them out.

"Are you...mad that I'm writing?"

He was careful not to look at me, his gaze fixed instead on a crushed paper cup teeming with ants. "I'm not mad. I'm just trying to get ahead of this thing, that's all."

I had no idea what *thing* he was talking about—or why it was getting him all hot and bothered—but something about the tight coil of his posture warned me to tread lightly.

"It's pretty obvious why that book annoys me," I said. I watched as the ants discovered a patch of sticky residue and started crawling over each other to get to it. "It's the most cliché thing in the world for a gay little mama's boy from the Philippines to see himself written so clearly in those pages, but there you have it."

Lincoln looked over at me, startled. He'd never heard me talk so bitterly about myself before, but that was because I'd never opened this particular wound. Not where he could see it, anyway.

"'Oh, her strength! her weakness!—both pulling me apart,'" I said, grimacing wryly. Like the way I'd pulled the quote for Maisey the other day, this one came easily. Obviously, I'd spent more time in Tan's complicated world than I liked to admit.

"Is that from the book?"

"I asked my mom once what would have happened to us if I hadn't fallen into that well when I was seven," I said by way of answer. "Did you know that? Came out with it, point-blank. If my literal descent into fame had never occurred, what would we have done? What would have become of us?"

"And what was her response?"

I laughed. There was no humor in the sound, and I could feel the nausea rising up from somewhere deep inside me, but I couldn't stop now. Lincoln had asked, so Lincoln would be answered.

"She told me to try again."

"To try what again? Falling into a well?"

I scoffed. "Of course not. She wanted me to try my *story* again. To reach back through time and really remember what happened that day." I'd never said the words out loud before, even though I'd been sitting on them for a long time.

"Mateo…"

"For years, I thought maybe she'd done it on purpose, you know?" My question was purely rhetorical. Of course Lincoln knew. He knew everything—or, rather, he *would* in about two minutes. "I thought she might have manufactured the accident as some kind of PR blitz to catapult her into the fame she so desperately wanted."

"Mateo," he said again, more determined this time. "Althea wouldn't have done that. She worships the ground you walk on."

I flung up a hand to stave him off. I had to get this out now or I wasn't sure I ever would.

"Please. You know as well as I do that the only hallowed ground in our family is wherever *she's* standing." I paused, wanting to take a moment to corral my thoughts but afraid of what else Lincoln might say if I left him the space. "I know that's a stupid reason to hate a book, but I can't help it. Every time I crack those pages, I can't help thinking how much easier my life would be if my mom was a little bit less…"

Lincoln supplied a few possible answers. "Glamorous? Fun?" The last one came out hard: "*Loving?*"

"It was me," I said, forcing my gaze to lock on his. What I saw there scared me more than anything else in the world—even spending three days at the bottom of a well.

Especially that.

"I was me," I said again, more determined this time. "I'm the one who manufactured it, not her. I needed to get away from her, and at that age, the only place I could think to do it was twenty feet underground."

When Lincoln didn't respond, I dropped my voice and let the rest of my restraint go.

"What kind of kid does that?" I asked. "What kind of person? I spent *three days* down there, Lincoln. I could have died. And all I cared about was how nice it was to look up and see the sky."

For the longest time, Lincoln didn't say anything. We both stood there, watching but not watching the march of those hungry ants.

"It's me, isn't it?" he asked so suddenly that I twitched. "That's why you're so fixated on writing your book all of a sudden?" Misreading my twitch as one of guilt rather than surprise, he was quick to add, "I'd rather hear about it now than a few months down the line. You don't owe me anything, but I need to know. So I can protect myself."

"I don't know what you're talking about," I said, but it was a lie. I knew. I knew down to my very bones.

"You're moving on," Lincoln said. "You're pursuing a new career and new friends, closing the door on your old life before it gets to be too much. And the only thing I can do is stand back and watch it happen."

The things Lincoln was saying were hurtful for the sole reason that they were so much truer than he knew. Every career I'd had in my life had been in pursuit of something—anything—other than the thing I really wanted. My nursing career? A great way to stay fit and meet cute doctors. Flight attendant? What could be wrong with hitting the skies with promises of a nonstop party lifestyle? The stint with personal training, an MLM menswear scheme that had been a borderline cult, even a few bizarre weeks as a mascot at a theme park in my teens— they'd all been a way to avoid the thing that was staring me in the face.

I'd climbed into a well to hide from the overwhelming influence of the woman who'd given birth to me. Who'd raised me. Who loved me so much that I was terrified of what would happen if I let myself love her back.

And I'd been hiding every single day of my life since.

"You could be an amazing author, Mateo. There's no doubt in my mind about that." Lincoln smiled then, but there was no warmth in his expression. "You could be amazing at anything you put your whole heart into. I just wish the thing you were willing to put your heart into was me."

In that moment, standing in a parking lot with a man I adored, my world expanding and contracting like a breath that wouldn't end, I was having the hardest time deciding what was happening. Was I being dumped? Chastised? *Begged?*

I wanted to believe that Lincoln was about to pull me into his arms and declare his everlasting devotion, to promise to climb down the well with me the next time I needed a break from the too-bright colors of the world, but he mostly looked exhausted. That expression only got worse when Sloane came rushing out of the restaurant, Brett a few paces behind her.

One look at her stricken expression, and I knew something terrible had happened.

"Arthur?" I asked, what was left of my heart thumping wildly.

"We have to get over there. Maisey said she found him collapsed in the living room. I'm afraid we might be too late."

GREG

22

ONCE UPON A TIME, THERE WAS a boy who loved his mother very, very much. His love for her was so great that when she lay on her deathbed, clutching her son's hand with all the strength that remained in her racked, wrecked body, she extracted a promise from him.

"Fix it," she'd said, her voice surprisingly strong. The hospice nurses had said to expect that, a final burst of energy before she slipped into the coma that would eventually claim her, but I'd assumed she'd request a cheeseburger or remind me to turn off the stove, not send me across the state to repair a relationship she'd broken a long time ago. "He's all you have left. You owe it to him—and yourself—to try."

Such was the boy's love for her that he did what she said. Not right away, and not with anything approaching enthusiasm, but when fate left him with no other choice.

Fuck. What a mess that was turning out to be.

"Ha! I knew it. This is a trap. This has been a trap from the beginning."

I sat at the far end of my grandfather's living room, my feet swinging from the end of the hospital bed that he refused to sleep in. It was similar to the model we'd had installed in my mom's house once she'd entered hospice. If you could ignore the way the plastic mattress crinkled and crackled every time you moved, it was pretty comfortable.

"What kind of librarian has a stethoscope in the trunk of his car?" my grandfather asked as Mateo sat on his haunches, listening to the thump of a heart that had stopped doing anything beyond the basics years ago. Pump and squeeze, keep the body alive.

But never, under any circumstances, relent.

"This doesn't work if you're shouting at me the whole time," Mateo said as he ran through what remained of his medical checklist. He'd already taken my grandfather's temperature and blood pressure—both normal—and was now moving on to his breathing. "I need to listen to your lungs, but I can't do that unless you calm down first."

I swung myself from my perch. In my experience, telling anyone— especially a man with as little patience as this one—to calm down rarely resulted in anything but an increase of hostilities. Placing myself carefully at Mateo's back, I crossed my arms and glared. It was a look I'd inherited from my grandfather, so I knew how effective it could be. He opened his mouth, saw me standing there, and closed it again.

He might have been a bastard of the highest degree, but he was no fool.

"Fine," he grumbled. "Listen to my breathing, if that's what gets you through the day. But I'll be damned if I'm letting you stay in my book club after this."

"*Your* book club?" Sloane asked. She'd come in with Mateo, but so far she hadn't done anything more than hold Maisey's hand and pat it in a soothing way. "You didn't want anything to do with it, remember?"

Since Mateo was listening intently to my grandfather's breathing, no one bothered to reply to this. With an efficiency that spoke well of his experience, Mateo sat back and draped the stethoscope around his neck.

"Well, I can't hear anything wrong with him. There's a bit of a rattle to his breathing, but that's typical for someone recovering from edema." He swept a glance around the living room. "Where was he when he fell?"

"I didn't fall. I tripped over that goddamned umbrella stand. Someone must have moved it."

"Is *that* what it is?" Maisey asked with a glance at the monstrosity in question. Like most of the furniture in my grandfather's house, the elephant's foot was old, grotesque, and probably purchased just to rile people up. "I thought it was a planter. I was going to put it out front to hold the dahlias I brought from my garden."

It was difficult to tell whether the idea of fresh flowers or someone touching his old, decrepit crap without his permission upset my grandfather more, but it didn't matter. No way in hell was I letting him take his wrath out on poor Maisey. The woman was having a hard enough time as it was.

"It's hideous, and we're getting rid of it," I said in a tone that brooked no argument. "There's too much clutter inside this house as it is. I'm sure someone on the internet will haul it away for a couple bucks."

"Don't you dare," my grandfather and Mateo both said at once. My grandfather's outburst was predictable, but Mateo's took me by surprise. From the look on his face, it took him by surprise, too.

"I'm taking it as payment for services rendered," he said. "If I have to drop everything and come running every time Arthur feels a palpitation coming on, I expect to be compensated accordingly."

"*Palpitation?*"

Mateo nodded. "That's all it was. Maybe if you spent less time stomping around your house like a giant at the top of his beanstalk, you'd recover faster. As it is, I suggest more fluids and a daily blood pressure check."

The amount of collective relief brought by this all-clear would have astounded me a month ago. When I'd first arrived in Coeur d'Alene, it had been to find my grandfather running off caretaker after caretaker, refusing all efforts of assistance or—God forbid—kindness. I'd been a coward, I knew, hiding out in my car while everyone else was forced to carry the burden of his temper, but what other choice did I have? Almost a month had passed since then, and I *still* couldn't set foot inside the house unless Sloane was here to act as buffer. I was allowed to be present for the sole reason that my grandfather didn't want to look bad in front of his new friend.

Why he was so concerned with Sloane's good opinion, however, remained to be seen. And it wasn't like I could just come out and ask the guy. I had a closer relationship with the dental assistant who cleaned my teeth twice a year.

"So he's going to be fine?" Sloane asked, her mouth touched with lines of anxiety. "It was just an…accident?"

My grandfather snorted. "That was no accident, young lady. That was me ferreting out the truth. I knew something about this whole Mateo situation smelled off. Fish and company always start to stink after three days."

I couldn't help laughing. It wasn't something I'd been doing a lot of lately, so it was no surprise that everyone turned to stare.

"I'm sorry," I said, not sorry at all. "You want us to believe that you tripped over an elephant's foot as part of a plot to uncover Mateo's secret identity as a nurse brought in to check up on you against your will?"

My grandfather set his jaw. "No one asked you."

"No, you didn't," I agreed in the bland, mild voice I'd learned to adopt a long time ago. My natural state was as blustery and unpleasant as my grandfather's—as tensions around here were doing their best to prove—but my mom had been careful to instill in me a sense of control over it.

"You're a pit bull, my little one," she'd said the first time I'd realized that being oversized and rough around the edges meant that I couldn't just swagger my way through life. I'd probably been all of thirteen at the time, still growing into my limbs and careless about where they'd landed.

Fine. They'd landed into this other kid's face, but in my defense, he'd deserved it. He'd been terrorizing the younger students at the bus stop on the corner all year. I'd been unaware of my own strength—or at least of what that strength could do when riled up with the fury of seeing yet another seven-year-old with a face full of gravel and nothing left to eat at lunch that day.

"It's not fair, but pit bulls have to be extra careful about everything in this life. Smaller, cuter dogs can growl and snap. Elegant, well-groomed dogs can tear apart the furnishings and suffer no consequences. But you have to watch everything you say and do, or the world will put you down without a second thought."

Later, I'd come to realize that what I suffered was only a fraction of what similarly sized men with more melanin in their skin suffered, but the warning had been an effective one. So had the boxing classes my mom had immediately signed me up for. According to her logic, it was better to be trained in the use of weapons than to walk around with them balled up at your sides, uncontrolled and angry at everything.

My grandfather, I hardly needed to say, was uncontrolled and angry at everything.

"Does this mean I get to keep the umbrella stand?" Mateo asked.

My grandfather set his jaw. "Absolutely not."

"Okay. Then my rate is five hundred dollars an hour, backdated to my first visit. I'll have my accountant send you a bill once I'm satisfied with your overall condition."

This was as much of a lie as the idea that my grandfather had tripped on purpose, but no one pointed it out. Two things were becoming rapidly clear around this place: one, that against all odds, my grandfather had fallen into the hands of a kind, caring, supportive group of people he'd done nothing to deserve; and two, that it was starting to look more and more like I'd have to become one of them.

"I don't know why everyone is conspiring against me like this," my grandfather said, his face screwed up like a toddler on the brink of a tantrum. When no one bothered to enlighten him, he gave in. "Fine. Take it. I hope you and the elephant's foot will be very happy together."

A smile of smug satisfaction crossed Mateo's face. "Thank you. We will. I know exactly where I'm going to put it." The smile faltered. "At least, I *think* I do."

If my grandfather noticed that flicker of emotion on his fellow human being's face, he was determined not to let it bother him. It bothered me, though. A lot of things about this situation did, including the fact that Mateo really should be getting some kind of compensation for his time. Not to mention Maisey and, even though she assured me she was faithfully logging her hours, Sloane.

Despite appearances and habits so miserly they were steeped into his marrow, my grandfather wasn't hurting for money. Neither was I, but anytime I tried to offer anyone in this room so much as a free lunch, they acted as if I'd personally offended them.

"So, it's decided?" Sloane asked with a glance around the room. "Mateo can continue to check in on Arthur as his official nurse—for the bargain rate of a piece of furniture I'm pretty sure is cursed—and the book club will go on as usual?"

I was careful not to meet that authoritative look of hers head on—which, yes, was even more like a cowardly lion than sitting in my car outside this house for days on end, but what could I say? I was way too much of a chickenshit to let that woman know how much she threw me off.

The irony was unmistakable. That first day we'd met, when I'd been wound tight with worries about my grandfather and how best to approach him, I'd been the one to scare *her*. In my defense, there was something seriously wrong with her parents, and I'd had no way of knowing about that trick with the elevator, but that was no excuse.

I was a pit bull. A lion—cowardly or otherwise. A man who gave off the impression of fierce, stoic independence even though most days all I really wanted was a hug.

"I'm amenable," Mateo said, though his attention was only half on us.

"Yes, *please*," Maisey said. "I don't know what I'd do if the book club wasn't here to keep me going. You guys are all I have."

"Fine," my grandfather grumbled. Like me, he was careful not to look Sloane in the eye. "It's not as if any of you listen to me anyway."

Everyone turned in my direction. I had no idea when I'd become an official member of this book club/support group for the down and downtrodden, but it seemed my vote was needed to clinch the deal.

Emboldened by this feeling of being needed—of being *wanted*—I added a concession.

"I'll only agree if I can stay here with you." My words fell onto a silent room rendered even more silent by the narrowing of my grandfather's eyes. We'd all spent enough time with him to recognize the signs of an incoming storm.

"And where the devil do you think you'll sleep?"

"Calm," Mateo murmured. "Remember to breathe."

My grandfather followed the second command, but through nostrils so dilated I doubted the first one was taking hold.

"There's a perfectly good hospital bed right here," I said, pointing.

His expression became downright dangerous. "If you think I'm going to climb into that Orwellian torture device of my own volition, so help me—"

I couldn't help laughing at how eloquent my grandfather was even in the throes of his worst temper. Mom always used to say that he wielded his intellect like a shield, a way to keep himself above—and therefore distant from—people. I was starting to think she had a point.

"I meant that *I'll* sleep in the bed," I said. "I'll have to abandon Maisey in order to do it, but..."

Maisey nodded at me, a wistful smile touching her lips. "You're right. It's better this way. I'm going to have to learn to live on my own eventually. Might as well do it while there are friends across the street."

"That's right." Sloane squeezed Maisey's hand. "And if Greg is staying here, then maybe I can have a few sleepovers at your house. Just to keep you company on the nights you need it. Or the nights *I* do."

Maisey looked in danger of bursting into tears, so it was probably for the best that my grandfather took one look at the heartfelt, touching scene in front of him and let out a grunt of disgust.

"If I'd known my house was going to turn into the setting of a Jojo Moyes novel, I'd have let them put me in a nursing home in the first place," he muttered.

Sloane didn't bat a single eyelash. "Why, Arthur, I didn't know you'd read Ms. Moyes. Which is your favorite? I know *Me Before You* is popular with readers, but I find that her early work in *Ship of Brides*—"

My grandfather got up with a sudden, jerky start that left no room for misinterpretation. Neither did his parting shot.

"Bah!"

23

—

I T TOOK ALL OF THREE MINUTES to pack up my worldly possessions
and throw them into a knapsack to carry across the street to my
grandfather's.

To be fair, I had plenty more worldly possessions in storage in
Seattle, but I was finding it increasingly difficult to remember why I'd
bothered to save any of them. One mattress, oversized and overpriced,
bought because of an enticing Instagram ad. Way more shoes than
any man needed to own, also oversized and overpriced, mostly bought
because of enticing Instagram ads. The list went on, but it only contained more of the same.

My life now was reduced to a single bag containing a few clean
shirts and changes of underwear, a newly purchased copy of *The Joy
Luck Club*, and a slip of paper with my grandfather's address scrawled
on it. I didn't need the address, since he'd been living in the same house
forever, but I liked that my mom had been careful to write it out for
me. She'd known that I wouldn't be able to throw it away, that it would
flutter on the empty fridge like a nagging string hanging from my
collar.

"I'm going to miss you," Maisey said as she stood in the doorway
to her daughter's room, still weirdly loath to cross the masking tape line
that lay across the floor. "Is that sad?"

"If it is, then we're both sad, because I'm going to miss you, too."

I patted for her to join me on the foot of the bed, but she stayed put. She was itching to get in here and rifle through the few meager remains of her daughter's belongings, but she probably never would. Not while the pain was so sharp, anyway. "Still nothing from Bella?"

"No. But I heard from Cap and he gave me a full update." She sighed and scuffed the tape line with the toe of her sneaker. "Do you think what Mateo said the other day was true? About teenage girls being—what did he call them?—heinous bitches?"

She said that last bit as though there was a chance that Bella might overhear, like the girl was so ingrained in this room that a part of her lingered. I answered with equal care. As much as I appreciated Mateo's attempt at comfort, I don't think he quite understood the depths of Maisey's despair.

"Do I think all teenage girls are like that? No. Do I think Bella might have a little bit of heinous bitch in her?" I hesitated. I'd overheard enough of the conversation between the two of them to make lying impossible. "Maybe. You deserved a better goodbye than that."

Maisey adopted the voice all of us were starting to use whenever we quoted a passage from the book we were reading. "'I am ashamed she is ashamed. Because she is my daughter and I am proud of her, and I am her mother but she is not proud of me.'" She sighed and sagged against the doorframe. "I finished reading between my calls this morning, in case you couldn't tell. Maybe Bella will be like Jing-Mei and finally come around to loving me once I'm dead."

Suddenly remembering who she was talking to, Maisey slapped a hand over her mouth. "Oh God. I'm so sorry, Greg. I didn't mean—"

"It's fine," I was quick to say. It *wasn't* fine, obviously, but I mostly wished another member of the book club was here to help. Mateo would say something irreverent and caustic. Sloane could pull out some sentimental, deeper meaning from the text. Even my grandfather might have been able to put things in an academic context. But the only thing I'd been able to glean from the book was mothers were one hell of a gift in this world, and we all just fucking wasted them.

"My mom and I got along really well," I said, since it seemed like I needed to say something to divert her attention. "*Too* well, according to all the Freudian scholars out there, but she always said she had a great role model to mold herself after. Her mother. My grandmother."

"Really?" Maisey took a step into the room, her toes nudging across the line. "Arthur never talks about any of this."

I grimaced. "He wouldn't."

Maisey made a gesture for me to continue. It was so nice to talk about my mom with *anyone* that I doubted I'd have been able to stop even if a train had burst through the room.

"My grandmother died young. Too young, a few weeks after my mom turned twelve." From breast cancer, but I didn't want to say that part out loud. Too many women in my family had fallen on that particular sword. "It would've been tragic for *any* little girl, but my mom was left alone in that house with Arthur. For six whole years, it was just the two of them facing their grief alone."

I let the words settle for a moment, feeling the real weight of them for the first time. I'd always known that my grandfather was a difficult man, even as a kid when the only difficult thing I had to do was remember to make my bed every morning. On the few instances when I'd met him, he'd always seemed more of an ogre than a person, the wicked wizard in the fairy tales my mom used to read to me at bedtime. In fact, she used to spin him exactly like that, building him up to be a creature to be vanquished by anyone brave enough to try.

Now that I knew him less as a mythical being and more like a hard, tyrannical man who could only be reached on an intellectual level, I understood what my mom must have really endured. Not evil in the way the books made it out—a twirling mustachioed bad guy plotting the hero's downfall—but the pain of a thousand imperceptible cuts. Of closed doors and angry meals, of a pain she'd been forced to endure alone.

I knew, because I was enduring that same pain. I'd been enduring it for five long months.

"Your poor mother," Maisey said now, the words coming out in a whoosh of air. She stepped even further into the room. "And poor Arthur. Some men get like that, you know, when they lose the person they love most. I get their calls a lot. They have all these jumbled-up emotions— anger and grief and deep, overwhelming despair—but the one person they trusted with those emotions is gone. It's the saddest thing. What are you supposed to do with your heart when it's already been buried six feet deep?"

"You pretend," Sloane said, suddenly appearing behind her. I had no way of knowing how long she'd been standing in the hallway listening, but from the quiet way she spoke, it was long enough. "You go through the motions as best you can, knowing deep down that you'll only experience half the life you were promised."

"Oh good." Mateo popped up before any of us could respond. He clearly hadn't heard a word of what we'd said, because he rubbed his hands together and cast a glance like a lasso roping us all in. "Everyone's here. We need to talk."

I didn't know whether or not I was relieved that our conversation was interrupted, but there was no chance for me to decide. Throwing himself across the masking tape line and onto Bella's bed, Mateo broke every barrier we had.

"Our book club is being infiltrated from the outside, and I need your help figuring out why."

—

"According to Google, Nigel Carthage is an award-winning Shakespeare scholar. Never married, lots of review publications under his belt, no controversies to speak of. Though he did have one very sassy exchange with Stephen King over Twitter."

Sloane turned her laptop to face us. Sure enough, the saturnine face of America's favorite horror writer stared out at us from across Maisey's living room. Maisey had somehow managed to materialize a full plate of tea sandwiches, but no one was doing much in the way of eating.

"Apparently, they disagreed about the recent influx of television adaptations of Shirley Jackson books," Sloane said. "The whole thing is kind of funny, actually."

"Ugh, Sloane. You're terrible at this." Mateo yanked the laptop from her and started furiously typing. At least, he typed as furiously as anyone using the one-finger hunt-and-peck technique could. Each press of the key clacked loud and determined. "If we want to find out what this guy is really up to, we can't look on the nice parts of the internet. We need to go to the dark side."

"Twitter *is* the dark side," she protested. "People get really mean on there sometimes."

Mateo ignored her and peered closer at the screen. "Hmm. He speaks fluent French. His middle name is Bernard. Oh, ew. He really needs to visit a podiatrist. And for the bargain price of $19.99, we could run a full background check. Just in case anyone wants to volunteer their credit card information."

No one did. Heaving a long sigh, Maisey held out her hand. "Give me the laptop."

Mateo held the laptop closer. "Uh, no offense, Maisey, but I doubt you'll find anything except more fungus on his toenails."

Instead of saying anything, Maisey waggled her fingers.

"Fine, but don't say I didn't warn you," he said, handing it over. "It's ninety percent book reviews."

We all sat and watched as Maisey started scanning the computer screen, her lips pursed and an intent expression narrowing her eyes.

Whatever she was looking for seemed to be taking a while, so I took a moment to set my knapsack by the door, careful to fold the address and tuck it in the front pocket.

Instead of asking about it—which I could feel both Mateo and Sloane straining to do—they steered the conversation back to the topic of Nigel Carthage.

"Mateo, I still think you're overreacting about this whole thing," Sloane said. "People donate money to libraries all the time without ulterior motives. And the man is obviously a big reader, so what could be more natural than for him to join a local book club?"

"Are you kidding?" Mateo countered. "He once ripped Jonathan Franzen to shreds during an awards ceremony *to his face*. Why on earth would a man like that beg for a chance to discuss *The Joy Luck Club* with a bunch of nobodies from North Idaho?"

This appeared to be so unanswerable that Sloane grew silent once again. I wanted to add something useful to the conversation but I didn't know what to say, so I picked up a cucumber sandwich and ate it. At least chewing gave me something to do with my mouth.

"Oh, wow." Maisey sank back against the couch cushion. "I didn't see that twist coming."

"What is it?" I asked.

Sloane wasn't far behind. "What did you find?"

Mateo was the only one not buying it. "Really? That fast? How'd you get so good at internet searching?"

Maisey chose to address Mateo's question first. "I do it for it work all the time." A sheepish smile touched her lips. "I'm not supposed to look up my clients, obviously, but it can help when I'm trying to give more personalized advice. I don't search for things like pet names or dead relatives or anything—I'd never do something like that—but little things. What their interests are and how they interact with the world. Ways to help them better understand themselves."

"Shady." Mateo nodded. "I like it."

"It's not shady." I was quick to rise to her defense. I'd spent enough time with the woman to know that there wasn't a shady bone in her body. No one loved the way Maisey Phillips did—unabashedly and with zero trace of irony. "It's *kind*. She only wants to help people."

"By Google-stalking them?"

"No." I set my jaw. "By taking the time to care."

Sloane cleared her throat. "Uh, I hate to interrupt, but am I the only one who's dying to know what she found?"

Maisey turned the screen around so we could see what she'd pulled up. It didn't look like much—just a résumé so old that it had been scanned and uploaded by hand—but Sloane gasped out loud at the sight of it.

"Does that say what I think it does?" Her eyes widened, their soft hazel depths growing green from the reflected light of the screen. "No way. He was a professor at North Idaho College back in the seventies?"

"Does that mean something?" Mateo demanded. "What am I missing?"

For the first time, I found myself taking an interest in this Nigel Carthage character—and not just because he gave me a concrete excuse to engage Sloane in conversation. "My grandfather taught English literature there for almost his whole life." I answered the question I knew was coming next. "Starting in the 1970s."

Excited voices broke out all around me. Mateo's was the most triumphant and therefore the loudest. "I *knew* there was something more to this. That night Nigel overheard me in the club...I mentioned Arthur by name, I'm sure of it. In fact, Nigel even admitted that he was feeling lonely because everyone he used to know was either dead or gone. He must have heard me say Arthur's name in conjunction with the book club and hoped to reconnect."

"Then why didn't he come out and say that?" Maisey asked. "I'm sure Arthur would love to meet up with an old friend."

I snorted out loud at that.

"Well, he *might*." A self-conscious look crinkled the edges of Maisey's eyes. "Everybody likes to chat about their youth. Nostalgia is big in my line of work."

Sloane tugged gently on my sleeve. "Have you ever heard your grandfather mention him before?"

I hadn't realized she was so close to me. Surprise locked my muscles tight and made my voice gruffer than usual. "My grandfather and I have shared all of twenty minutes' worth of conversation in the entire course of my life. I'm afraid an ex-coworker from the seventies didn't make the list."

Her hand fell, and I cursed my clumsiness. I hadn't meant to sound so defensive but, well, I was defensive. Every single person in this room knew more about my grandfather than I did, even though he was my sole living relative. I was an only child, my dad a nonentity who wasn't even listed on my birth certificate, and no other family had reached out to claim me once my mother passed. Forgive me for coming across a little harshly.

"I'm sorry," I said, since my solitary state was hardly Sloane's fault. "I wish I could help, but he's as much a stranger to me as he is to you. *More*, probably. You've had more than three months to get to know him. So far, I've had three weeks."

"And not a very good three weeks, huh?" she asked. The question must have been rhetorical because she clucked her tongue in sympathy before turning to address the group. "Well, I hate to break up the party, but we should call it a night. It's getting late, and if Greg is going to stay with Arthur tonight—"

She broke off to look at me. I ducked my head in assent. As little as I cherished the thought of sharing a roof with that man, it was better for a family member to do it than any one of these three. He could hardly murder me in my sleep.

At the very least, he could only try.

She nodded. "Then you should get settled in before it's time to put Arthur to bed. He won't like it, by the way. He never does, so be sure not to offer him anything other than his meds. Not a hot-water bottle. Not tea. *Definitely* not a bedtime story."

I couldn't helping laughing at that last one. "You didn't."

A light brush of color touched her cheeks. "It's not how it sounds. I thought he might want to do the book club reading together. I was...incorrect."

Mateo closed the laptop and handed it to Sloane before starting to roll up his sleeves. "Since I'm already outed as his nurse, I might as well get him settled for the night."

"You don't have to," I was quick to say. I looked to Sloane for confirmation. "He doesn't actually need anything, right? Just someone there in case of an emergency?"

"It's best if he sleeps sitting up, or at least with a few pillows prop-ping him up to keep his lungs clear. If he wakes up and it's still dark out, he might be a little disoriented, but it passes quickly. You just have to make sure he doesn't try to navigate the stairs on his own." She pursed her lips, unaware of the feelings of terror she was raising in my breast. Things were *that* bad? And she'd been carrying the bulk of that burden this whole time?

Mateo nodded as if this made perfect sense. "Until his strength is back up to normal—which could take weeks, by the way—he may continue to struggle with simple day-to-day tasks. But the good news is it won't last. He'll be back to living alone and antagonizing perfect strangers in no time."

The thought of this was so depressing that the entire room fell silent. The antagonizing-perfect-strangers part was fine—expected, even—but the living-alone part stung. It was a stark reminder that this thing we were doing together had an expiration date—that soon we'd all have to return to our regularly scheduled lives.

Our regularly scheduled separate lives.

Our regularly scheduled separate *isolated* lives.

Mateo was the first to break the silence. "Come on," he said, heaving a sigh and the full weight of his body up off the couch. "I'll show you a trick for how to physically subdue a patient in danger of self-harm. It's easy once you get the hang of it."

I couldn't help being amused by this. "What makes you think I can't physically subdue someone?"

Mateo stopped and swept a glance up and down my body, his lips curving as he took in my full height and frame. "Fine. I'll show you how to physically subdue someone without crushing his bones. How's that?"

"You never offered to teach me that," Sloane said.

"Or me," Maisey added. "I've always wanted to learn self-defense."

"If either of you find yourself facing a man like Arthur McLachlan in a full-body rage, my advice is to run," Mateo said.

Maisey considered this for a moment. "And what's your advice if we're facing a man like Greg?"

"That's easy." Mateo winked. "Run faster."

———

"I wish you'd let me pay you for this."

I stood on my grandfather's front porch, talking to Mateo in a voice too low to be distinguished by the man currently propped upstairs in his bedroom with twelve pillows and a hefty stack of books. Despite repeated entreaties to go to sleep, my grandfather was determined to work his way through the complete works of Oscar Wilde before morning.

"Are you kidding?" Mateo countered. "I can't remember the last time I enjoyed myself this much. Did you see how quickly I dodged that copy of *The Picture of Dorian Gray*?"

Yes, I had. I'd also been fairly sure that my grandfather intended to miss. Even though he'd never admit it, I was pretty sure he felt better knowing there was a nurse on hand—one he knew and trusted, one he *liked*, even. It was a feeling I shared. Mateo was an absolute whirlwind of a man, vibrating with more energy than anyone I'd ever met, but I appreciated that about him. As someone who was the exact opposite—slow to think, slow to act, even slower to charm—I could see why people liked him so much.

"It's not right for you to be giving up your free time like this," I insisted. "You and Sloane didn't even get to finish your double date."

He brushed this off as easily as he had all the rest. With a playful waggle of his eyebrows, he said, "Please. I was born for intrigue. I'm thinking about calling Nigel up and asking him to meet me for coffee."

"Why?"

"To see what I can uncover, obviously. There's some kind of mystery between him and your grandfather, and I intend to find out what. Maybe I could become a private investigator. You don't need a degree for that, do you?"

"In Idaho?" I huffed on a laugh. "I doubt it. They pretty much let you do anything you want. I've seen a bunch of people riding motorcycles without helmets on."

"Mateo Sharpe, PI." He tipped an imaginary fedora. "I like the sound of that."

Before I could ask how many careers he intended to have in his lifetime, his ringtone cut through the night air. I tried to step into the house to leave him to his call, but he put out a hand to stop me.

"It's Lincoln. I'll only take a sec."

The last thing I wanted to do was intrude on a private conversation between this man and his boyfriend, but all that waited for me inside that house was a crinkly hospital bed and my grandfather's indifference, so I stayed put.

"I was just finishing up with Arthur before heading home. Yeah, he's fine. False alarm." There was a pause and a sudden tension around Mateo's mouth. "Greg is here with me right now, actually. We're making plans to stalk Nigel Carthage together."

I didn't recall offering to stalk anyone, but Mateo sighed heavily before saying, "If you must." He held the phone out to me. "Here. Lincoln wants to talk to you."

"Me?"

He shook the phone. "We're in a weird place, so it's probably best if you play along. I can load up my new umbrella stand while you chat."

"Hello?" I said as I watched Mateo struggle to lift the elephant's foot and drag it to his car.

"Greg. Hey. Thanks." Each of his words was uttered as a complete sentence, although I couldn't make out the meaning of any of them. "What are your plans for tomorrow evening? Are you free?"

"Um, I think so. Why? What's up?"

"Althea's performing at the Lofthouse, so I thought I'd see if you want to join us. Mateo said you don't know a lot of people in town, and you seem to be a fan of her music, so…"

I'd received invitations to funerals with more enthusiasm. "Thanks, but I should probably be here in case my grandfather needs me."

There was a long pause. "Look, I wouldn't ask if it wasn't important. Mateo is…" He sighed. By the time he started speaking again, there was a lot more animation in his voice. "He seems to be really invested in whatever is happening with you and your grandfather. I know he'll have a better time if you're there to take the edge off. It would mean a lot to me—to us both—if you came."

I was pretty sure all the social rules dictated a firm and resolute "no" in situations like this, but Mateo had returned and overhead enough to put the pieces together. He flashed a thumbs-up to show his approval.

"Yeah, sure. That sounds like fun. I'll see you tomorrow."

Lincoln rattled off the details before hanging up. I handed the phone back to Mateo with a questioning lift to my brow.

"It's too complicated to explain," he said. In defiance of this, he went ahead and explained it anyway. "Lincoln's afraid I'm going to leave him to become a famous author."

"I thought you were going to be a private investigator."

Even though Mateo shrugged, it was obvious—to me, at least—that his indifference was feigned. That was one of the things no one told you about losing someone you loved. I'd always thought that grief turned people inward, forced them to clutch their memories around them like a cloak against a gathering storm, but the opposite was true. The moment my mom had closed her eyes for the last time, it was as if I'd been plugged into some vast network of other people's pain.

"I don't want to be a private investigator," he said. "Or an author. Or a librarian. That's the problem."

"Have you tried career counseling?"

His laughter came out as a short, sharp burst. "No, but I'll put it at the top of my to-do list. You're sure you don't mind? I can make your excuses if you'd rather avoid the drama of my personal life."

I shook my head with a desperation I barely recognized in myself. Truth be told, being plugged into this network was the only thing keeping me going right now. It was good to take an active part in things, even if all I was doing was eating everything Maisey cooked and listening to torch ballads from the forties with Mateo and his boyfriend.

"I don't mind," I said. "I'd like to see the great Althea Sharpe perform live. It was one of the things my mom never got to cross off her bucket list."

"Okay, but don't say I didn't warn you. And if she invites you up onstage to join her, I suggest you put your foot down or you'll never be able to face a spotlight again."

24

—

"WHERE THE DEVIL DO YOU THINK you're going?"

I paused in the act of buttoning my shirt—one of the five I was wearing on rotation, courtesy of the small wardrobe I'd brought with me. On Tuesdays, I wore my Henley. On Wednesdays, it was my favorite T-shirt showcasing two T. Rexes in a boxing match. Today was Thursday, which meant I was wearing a faded fisherman's sweater that was way too hot for any weather but Seattle's.

"Um. Out?" It had been a long time since I'd been asked to account for my nocturnal activities, so I wasn't sure about the standard protocol. I sprinkled in a few details. "Mateo's mom is performing at some club tonight, and his boyfriend invited me to come along."

My grandfather watched as I poked my head through the neckline of the sweater and tugged it into place.

"What?" I said, feeling more self-conscious than I cared to admit. My grandfather's stare was like a pair of lasers aimed at my chest, which was already starting to swelter under the heavy knit. "You think I should wear something else?"

"I don't give a tinker's curse what you wear." He paused. "Wait here."

I *did* wait, but that was mostly because there were still a few minutes before I needed to leave. The evening was going to be awkward enough as it was; I didn't need to roll up early and invite trouble.

Unfortunately, it looked like trouble planned on inviting himself.

"If I have to spend another minute inside this house, I'm going to start tearing the wallpaper from the walls." My grandfather turned a malevolent eye on me. "That's a literary reference, in case you were wondering."

I didn't point out that I had a four-year degree from a university that boasted several great undergraduate liberal arts courses, or that I'd grown up under the care of a woman who'd learned early on that books were the only way to communicate with her father. My grandfather had decided that I was exactly like the lumbering jackass who'd impregnated his only daughter and then run off, and I doubted anything I said or did would change that.

"There's no need to tear the wallpaper on my account," I drawled, one small step removed from chewing a cud. "If you want it removed, a spray bottle and a scraper'll do the trick."

He shuddered his revulsion as he struggled to get into a sweater with huge leather patches on the elbows.

"Oh, no you don't," I said, holding up my hands as if to ward him off. "You're not coming with me."

"Why not? It's a public club, isn't it? I have as much right to be there as anyone."

The way he spoke gave me pause. That wasn't the sound of a man who was hell-bent on pushing his way where he wasn't wanted; it was the sound of a man who was almost—*almost*—begging for the door to be opened to let him in.

"It's going to be dark inside," I pointed out. "And loud. And full of half-drunk people who haven't picked up a book in years."

"Good," he said with predictable contrariness. "That sounds perfect."

I strove to come up with an excuse for keeping him at home, but this was a man who was used to getting the last word—and keeping it.

With a harrumph of triumph, he reached for his cane and headed for the door.

———

I hadn't been prepared for the royal treatment we got at the door of the Lofthouse.

"You can follow me right this way," the hostess said, beckoning us past a long line of people waiting to get in. "You're expected."

As I'd threatened, the club was dimly lit and full of people tipping back martinis like they were Gatorade, but neither of these things seemed to stop my grandfather as he pushed and poked his way around the tables crowding the floor. He looked as out of place as I felt in my thick cable-knit sweater, but when we approached a table near the front, Mateo jumped to his feet to greet us.

"You came! I wasn't sure if you actually would." Mateo blinked at the sight of my grandfather. "And you brought…company."

"You're the one who's always acting like I'm knocking on death's door," my grandfather grumbled, his jaw set for battle. "You should be happy to see me out and about."

"I mean, it might have been better to start with a trip to the pharmacy for a blood pressure check, but sure." Mateo offered him his chair. He nodded at Lincoln, who I could see carefully appraising us both. "This is my boyfriend, Lincoln. Lincoln, this is the patient I was telling you about, Greg's grandfather. He's the one who gave us the umbrella stand."

I half expected us to be berated and driven out for this crime, but Lincoln relaxed enough to smile. "Thank you. It's quite a piece."

My grandfather narrowed one suspicious eye. "If you don't like it, that's too bad. We already agreed on payment."

"If it makes Mateo happy, then it makes me happy," Lincoln said.

He was careful not to look at the man in question while he spoke. "Should we order drinks?"

I was surprised to find my grandfather greedily appraising the cocktail menu, and even more surprised when he chose something nonalcoholic and bearing a floral garnish.

"What?" he demanded as he hooked his cane on the edge of his chair and settled himself comfortably in place. He was so close to one of the speakers I felt sure he'd end up blowing out an eardrum. "Mateo said I can't have anything stronger than tea until I'm off these worthless medications."

"I didn't say anything."

"You looked at me. It's enough." My grandfather turned to Mateo for confirmation. "Unless you're ready to change your medical opinion?"

"Not a chance, old man," Mateo said. "It's nothing but fruit juice and sparkling water for you. Nurse's orders."

"See?" My grandfather sat back with triumph. "You're not killing me off that easily. If you want me dead, you're going to have to hire a hit man like everybody else."

Lincoln blinked at the sudden turn this conversation took—and at the playful spirit with which we took it. "Do, ah, a lot of people hire hit men to take you out?"

I had to bite back a snort. I imagined the idea had occurred to just about everyone my grandfather met.

"We actually discussed it during a lull at the library once," Mateo said. "You'd just told one of the new hires that her views on Kierkegaard rivaled that of a toddler finding his toes for the first time. It took all Octavia's powers of persuasion to keep her from quitting on the spot."

This time, my snort managed to escape.

"After that, we considered murder, a professional hit, giving you a stern talking-to, and banning you outright." Mateo smiled at the memory.

"Well?" my grandfather demanded. The only offense he seemed to take was the length of time Mateo needed to relay the tale.

"Well, what?" Mateo shrugged. "You're still here, aren't you? Sloane talked us out of it. She's always had a soft spot where you're concerned, though I'll be damned if I can figure out why."

It was a sentiment I'd shared so many times that I felt myself straining to hear my grandfather's response. I'd long since discarded my theory that Sloane was using him for money, but what other reason could she have for sticking around? She was well-educated. She had a fiancé. She made no demands of anyone, asked for nothing for herself. Thanks to her methodical and painstaking book-cataloging system, my grandfather's house was actually starting to look—and feel—like a home. And as far as I knew, he'd never once said thank you for any of it.

I didn't get my answer. The lights flickered before going all the way dim as the big band filed out to take the stage. Despite myself, I found my breath catching in my throat as Althea walked out.

"You're in for a treat." Lincoln leaned across the table toward me, but his voice was loud enough for the whole table to hear. "Have you seen her perform live before?"

"No, but my mom was a big fan of her music. When I was growing up, there was almost always something sad and French playing in the background."

Since the band was striking up, I assumed this would be the end of the conversation, but my grandfather spoke up. "She got that from your grandmother," he said.

It was hard to distinguish his words in the cacophony of half a dozen brass instruments blaring to life, but then, it might have been the roaring of my own blood that covered the sound of his voice. To hear my mom tell the tale, my grandmother had been a living saint, a woman too good for this planet and for the people she chose to share it with—the exact opposite of the man she'd married. And not once had I heard my grandfather refer to her, even in passing.

"She loved this kind of music," he added. "Not a day went by without the melancholia of ennui setting the tone."

Instead of showing his own melancholy or ennui at this, my grandfather smiled. Actually *smiled*—a small, content compression of the lips that seemed to carry some secret meaning.

"Sentimental nonsense, all of it," he added with a stern look around the table, lest any of us get the wrong impression.

But it was too late. My impression was intact, and all I could feel in that moment was that it was very, very right.

———

Mateo had warned me ahead of time that there was a good chance he'd be pulled up onto the stage and forced to perform like a dancing monkey, but I'd thought he was kidding.

"Holy shit."

Several people turned to glare at me at the sound of my outburst, so I did my best to hunch my shoulders and disappear. I also lowered my voice, but there wasn't any need. As Mateo and Althea launched into a duet of "Forever Young," I could have shouted at the top of my lungs and not taken away a fraction of their allure.

"I know." Lincoln sighed. For a man who was apparently dating the living reincarnation of Frank Sinatra, he seemed awfully sad. "He's amazing."

I had no idea how such a small, slight man could carry that powerful of a baritone in his throat, but there was no denying he had talent. Talent *and* presence, if the way he held the whole audience captive was any indication.

"Just make sure you don't congratulate him afterward," Lincoln said. "He hates hearing how good he is. He hates everything associated with the stage, actually."

My grandfather let out an annoyed huff. "False modesty is something I have no patience for."

"I wasn't aware you had patience for *anything*."

He ignored me. "What the devil is he doing working as a librarian?" he demanded of Lincoln. "Or a nurse, for that matter? If I had a set of pipes like that, I'd be out using them every chance I got."

A look of pain crossed Lincoln's face. "It's complicated."

"Balderdash," my grandfather said. This was so woefully inadequate—and also somehow so exactly right—that I found myself echoing the sentiment.

We turned our collective attention back to the stage, watching and listening as the pair of them finished up their song. An inexpressible sadness filled me at the sight of it—the rich sound of Mateo's voice, his mother's obvious pride in him, the way the audience roared its appreciation—followed almost immediately by anger. I wasn't a man given to jealousy very often, but I felt it now, and I felt it hard.

My mom and I had never been a singing sensation, obviously, and that weird speech Althea gave about Mateo falling into a well puzzled me, but I'd have given everything I owned for a chance to trade places with him. I'd heard from plenty of people who promised that my mom was still with me—forever in my heart, watching from afar, that sort of thing—but no amount of faith could replace actual human warmth.

"I'm sorry about before," Lincoln said before I could fall too far into the quagmire of self-pity. I was more grateful for the interruption than I could say. Self-pity always felt like a wool blanket tossed over my head—not suffocating me, but making me uncomfortably aware of each breath.

"Before?" I echoed.

He waved a hand as if to encompass the entirety of everything we'd ever said or done. "At my house the other day, at dinner."

"I didn't notice anything," I said. "In fact, I'm the one who should be apologizing to you, showing up unannounced like that."

He shook his head, his frown deepening. "I'm usually better than that. You're new to town, you don't know many people, and I should have made more of an effort. Especially if you're going to be sticking around for a while." He glanced at me. "Are you? Sticking around, I mean?"

My grandfather was so still and quiet next to me that I knew he was waiting to hear my response. I felt unaccountably annoyed by it. He hadn't extended anything even remotely approaching an invitation— had done even less to indicate that he wanted me to stick around. Not once had he asked about my mother's death, what I was doing for money, if I had somewhere to go home to.

Not once had he asked if I was doing okay.

I was struggling to come up with an answer when Mateo trotted back toward our table, refusing all pleas for an encore. He was also, I quickly noted, bleeding from his nose.

"Oh geez. Not again." Mateo tipped his head back with a groan, but it was too late. The bright red trickle had already taken hold. "Quick. Does anyone have—"

I pulled a handkerchief out of my pocket and handed it to him. A grimace of distaste crossed Mateo's face at the sight of it, but his wasn't the expression I paid the most attention to.

"Where did you get that?" My grandfather snatched the handkerchief out of his hand before it could be used to stanch the blood. Lincoln was forced to wad up a handful of booze-splashed cocktail napkins and hand them to Mateo instead.

"It's Mateo's," I said, bewildered. "Maisey asked me to give it back to him after she dropped a pan of enchiladas. She did something with hydrogen peroxide and what I'm pretty sure was holy water to get the stains out."

"Why would Mateo have a handkerchief embroidered with the initials NC?"

"Mateo doesn't have any handkerchiefs. Mateo thinks they're disgusting and should never be used in polite society. I got that one from—" He cut himself off before casting a glance at me so full of meaning that I knew we'd stumbled onto something big. "From a stranger I met at this very club."

He didn't have to say the rest. Neither one of us was a private investigator, but that didn't mean we were willing to overlook a clue as big as this one: *a stranger by the name of Nigel Carthage.*

25

—

I STOOD HOLDING A TRAY OF FOUR coffees in front of the North Idaho College library, trying to look as though I belonged.

Technically, I *did* belong just as much as every other person streaming past the old fort building or tossing Frisbees on the green lawn across the street. This wasn't one of those highly academic colleges where hushed tones and marble reverence were required every time you walked in the door. The students' average age was midtwenties, and most graduates went on to work in administrative offices. No one would ever call these halls hallowed.

Then again, most of the people here weren't about to launch an investigation into their estranged grandfather's past alongside a group of people he'd known all of a month. At least the coffee gave me something to do with my hands.

"Oh. You brought coffee, too."

I turned at the sound of Sloane's voice. A paper cup was clutched in each of her hands. The sight of those two cups—only two—filled me with a sense of dread that brought out the pit bull in me.

"Where's Maisey?" I demanded in a voice that even made *me* wince. "And Mateo? Weren't they supposed to come with you?"

To my relief, the gruffness of my tone only seemed to make Sloane relax. She even smiled, though it was the same smile she wore when my grandfather was on his worst behavior—a kind of sympathetic curve of the lips that made both of us McLachlans look like the asses we were.

"Sorry. It's just me today. They both had to work this morning. Maisey couldn't get anyone to cover her shift, and Mateo..." Her voice trailed off. Her smile became less sympathetic and more like the Cheshire cat from *Alice in Wonderland*, which was fitting considering she was wearing a blue dress with what looked like lace napkins attached at the collar.

Not in a bad way, though. She looked...sweet. Like you could trust her to hold your place in line or the secrets that were buried deep in your heart, depending on the demands of the situation.

"Mateo said they're really floundering to replace me." She took a satisfied sip from the smaller of the two coffees. "Is it bad that I'm happy about it? I literally cackled when he texted to tell me he'd been called in at the last minute. I think your grandfather is starting to rub off on me."

"I don't think that's possible," I said with perfect honesty. My grandfather didn't have a kind word for anyone; Sloane had never uttered anything but. It was like comparing apples and...rotten apples. "Would you go back to work if they offered?"

"In a heartbeat. It's the only place I've ever really belonged."

Words of ready sympathy sprang to my tongue, printed and placed there by every greeting card company known to mankind. "I'm sure that's not true."

Her expression told me what she thought of my attempt.

"Look, I know you keep saying you don't want to be paid for taking care of my grandfather, but—" I began.

She cut me off with a *tsk* of annoyance. "I know you mean well, Greg, but you have to stop offering us cash." She moved toward a nearby garbage can and tossed the extra coffee in. It was on the tip of my tongue to cry out—I wanted to know what she'd picked for me, if it was dark and bitter or light and sweet—but I fortified myself with a sip of my own drink instead. I'd gotten myself a pumpkin spice latte, out of season and cloyingly spiced, but comforting all the same.

"I can't help it," I said as the cinnamon and cloves rolled over my taste buds. "I don't know how else I'm supposed to show my thanks."

We headed into the library shoulder to shoulder, our bodies careful not to touch as we squeezed through the door. I offered the tray of extra coffees to the woman standing at the checkout counter, an action that caused Sloane to look sideways at me.

"What?" I said uncomfortably. "I didn't want to just throw them away."

"You're nothing like your grandfather," she said, and in such a way that there was no option to refute her.

My feeling of discomfort only grew. "Of course I'm not. I barely know the guy. I don't understand why everyone keeps expecting me to have all this insight into how he thinks or what's going on with this Nigel Carthage business. As far as my grandfather is concerned, I'm just some random man his daughter gave birth to and who's suddenly pushed his way into his life."

Even though we were in a library and all my childhood training called on me to whisper and tiptoe, Sloane seemed perfectly at ease in her surroundings. Which made sense, considering how much time she'd spent in one.

"Do you know how I left him this morning?"

I was guessing she left him much the same way I had—by slipping out the door as soon as the coast and her conscience were clear—but she only kept watching me in that quiet, intensely scary way. If she'd been my librarian when I was a kid, I'd have probably given up on reading and taken to a life of crime instead. It would have been safer.

"I walked him over to Maisey's house so he could spend the day with her," she said.

"Wait." I blinked. "Really? I thought you said she had to work."

"She does. He wanted to, and I quote, 'see a real charlatan in action.'"

I didn't want to laugh in this place of reverence and stern librarian stares, but I did anyway. "That wasn't very nice to poor Maisey."

She answered me with a smile of her own, but there was something about it I didn't quite trust. There was irony in that smile—irony at me. *For* me.

"Are you kidding?" she said. "It was poor Maisey's idea. She thought your grandfather might benefit from seeing human kindness being put into action. A few hours of listening to her patiently and gently helping people with their problems will do him a world of good."

"Um…"

"He'll argue with her, of course, and call her mean names, but I can't think of anything better for Maisey right now. She'll stand up for herself, and feed him, and with any luck not think about her daughter once all day."

This was such a naively terrible idea that I couldn't help but pause. "You think?"

"I *know*." She reached for my hand—the one not holding the coffee—and squeezed it. This marked the first time she'd touched me, the first time she'd crossed over the barrier that surrounded me like a junkyard dog, and I felt it. So did she, if the quick way she dropped her fingers was any indication. Her color heightened, she added, "Objectively, it doesn't make any sense—throwing the two of them together and hoping for the best. But Maisey *likes* spending time with your grandfather, and strange though it seems, he likes spending time with her, too."

I suspected that what they both really liked was pleasing Sloane, but I didn't say so. For one thing, we needed to start our research if we wanted to uncover any answers about my grandfather and Nigel

Carthage. For another, I wasn't about to sit this woman down and explain how someone with soft eyes and a softer heart could make everyone around her better—not because they wanted to impress her or because they secretly feared she was taking advantage of an ornery old man, but because she was the only thing holding the entire world together.

"Well," I said, drawing a deep breath and surveying the rows upon rows of books ahead of us. "You're the expert. Where do we start?"

At the prospect of all this literary and encyclopedic splendor, Sloane grinned. "We start with the librarians, obviously. No one knows more about anything than they do."

———

I could've spent three days inside the North Idaho College library poring through old alumni records and class schedules from the past five decades and not come up with a fraction of the information Sloane was able to get out of the college librarians in half an hour.

"I can't believe you're Professor McLachlan's grandson," said one of the librarians. We'd accosted him on his break, but he didn't seem upset about it. If anything, he was almost starstruck to have met me. "I failed his Literary Theory class three times. *Three.* He was the best teacher I ever had."

"That doesn't sound like a very good teacher to me. I feel like I should offer you a refund."

Sloane pushed her reading glasses to the top of her head. We sat around a conference table, stacks of papers from the seventies in front of us, and she couldn't have been more delighted about any of it. Library people were weird. "Don't listen to him. He's always trying to give people money to make up for his grandfather's terrible personality."

"That must be an expensive habit," said another librarian, this one carrying an armful of college yearbooks, their leather covers yellowed and cracking with age. She placed them reverently in front of me. "What would you pay if I told you he once called me a feckless waste of space?"

I sighed. That sounded exactly like something my grandfather would say, if only because I had no idea what that word meant. "I don't know. Does fifty bucks sound fair?"

All three of them—Sloane and her two new library friends—laughed.

"At that rate, you'd better be Jeff Bezos," the male librarian said with a grin. "Your grandfather was a teacher here for over forty years. You might want to start with a lower bid and work your way up."

"Hey." Sloane's hand covered mine with a quick, friendly squeeze. "It's okay. You don't have to keep apologizing for him. My parents are just as unpleasant, and I haven't tried reimbursing you for your Airbnb yet, have I?"

My fingers twitched underneath hers. As if by unspoken agreement, we'd never mentioned the day of our meeting—of the tight-lipped way she'd ridden that elevator, of how small and scared and *sad* she'd seemed during that visit to the basement.

"No," I said slowly, as if once again hiding in a corner to avoid startling her. "And now that you mention it, I *did* pay through the whole month."

She slid her hand away, but with a smile that I had no choice but to return. For weeks, I'd been terrified of what would happen if I found myself alone with Sloane again, but this was good. This was better than good, actually.

We were being friendly. We were being *friends*.

The female librarian tapped the stack of paperwork with the tip of her pen. "Okay, so everything here is admin—class registers and syllabus information, things like that. And over here"—she touched the yearbooks—"you'll find stuff about extracurriculars, clubs, et cetera.

We're working on pulling up his academic research and publications, but that could take a little longer."

"What are we hoping to find?" the male librarian asked with an eagerness that seemed misplaced, given how dull the subject matter was.

"We aren't sure yet," Sloane said as she dived into the paperwork. "But we'll let you know when we find it."

We found it five minutes later.

It was a little disappointing, to be honest—not that I was able to uncover the mystery so quickly, but that the answers were so easily available…and that my latte didn't even have time to grow cold first. I wasn't ready to say goodbye to this fun, playful version of Sloane. Or, to be more specific, to this fun, playful version of *me*.

I hadn't seen this Greg in a long time. I missed him.

"Look at this." With surprisingly steady hands, I turned the year-book from 1973 around to show Sloane. A black-and-white photo of a faculty dinner sat in the center. My grandfather, looking robust and happy in a checkered scarf and voluminous pants, stood next to a bespectacled Black man in pants of equally alarming breadth. The caption underneath identified them as clearly as if they were in the room with us—Arthur McLachlan and Nigel Carthage, PhD.

Which, okay, wasn't the most illuminating thing in the world. Obviously, they'd known each other, and obviously, this college was where it had happened. But the fact that they both had their arms around a slight, pretty woman in a pinafore—and that they were both smiling at her as if she were the only person in the photo, the room, the *world*—told its own tale.

Especially since I recognized her at a glance. I'd never met her and never would, but I knew that slightly upturned nose and wide forehead as if they belonged to me.

Mostly because they did.

"Oh, what a nice photo of your grandfather," Sloane said, unaware as of yet that the world was slipping and sliding beneath us. "He looks so happy—he and Nigel both. This proves they must have been friends once upon a time…but I don't understand. Who's this woman? Her name isn't captioned."

"Her name is—*was*—Eugenia Pittsfield."

Sloane must have picked up on the emotion in my voice because her expression became immediately subdued. I don't know what it was about her that could so easily echo the numbness in my veins, but she seemed to know instinctively that my blood had gone cold. "Was?" she echoed.

"My grandmother."

26

—

"T'S A LOVE TRIANGLE! I *KNEW* it was a love triangle." Maisey held her hand to her chest and swooned so hard she fell across my grandfather's couch. "I love love triangles."

"Slow down." Mateo lifted Maisey's feet and settled himself on the cushion next to her, neither one of them finding anything odd in the familiar, comfortable position. "It's one picture, not a written confession. For all we know, Arthur and Nigel are looking longingly at a cake. Or each other."

Maisey lifted her head long enough to glare at Mateo. "Don't ruin this for me. This is the closest I've gotten to real romance in years."

"The two of them looking longingly at each other *is* romantic. Maybe Nigel has come to claim Arthur after all these years."

Sloane intervened before the two could take their squabble any further. "Whatever it is, can we please keep our voices down? Arthur will be up from his nap any minute, and the last thing we want is for him to know about this."

"Is it?" I asked, unable to help myself. It wasn't my fault. This whole thing with my grandmother had thrown me for a serious loop. "What would happen if we just came out and asked him about Nigel? What's the worst he could do? Call us names? Throw us out? Disband our book club once and for all?"

Since these were all things he'd done and/or threatened to do on multiple occasions, I felt pretty confident about throwing caution—and my grandfather—to the wind. Until, of course, he spoke.

"What about Nigel?"

Everyone in the room turned to find my grandfather standing a few feet away, clutching the doorframe so hard that we could count each vein on the marbled topography of his hand.

"Arthur!" Sloane exclaimed. She started up as if to help him but changed her mind at the last second. "We thought you were asleep."

"I'm sorry. Do you need me to leave so you can sit around and talk about me like I'm a feeble old man? To hatch and scheme and conspire against me?"

This speech seemed a touch dramatic, even for a man who could create drama out of the daily delivery of the *Coeur d'Alene Press*.

"No one is conspiring against you," I said. "We were just discussing the possibility of expanding the book club. Who's Nigel Carthage?"

All of the heat of the room seemed to vanish at once, which was odd considering how inflamed my grandfather got. In an instant, he went from a slightly stooped, sleepy curmudgeon to the devil himself. His nostrils flared and his color heightened, his blood boiling over for everyone to see. Even before he started speaking, I could see everyone wincing at what was to come.

That was the man my mother had run from. *That* was the man she'd begged me to return to.

"Don't you dare speak that name out loud again," he said.

I dared. After all, he and I were cut from the same coarse cloth. "Nigel Carthage? Why? What did you do to him?"

"That man is never to be mentioned inside this house again, do you understand?" My grandfather lifted a finger and pointed it around the room like a witch cursing a blasphemous kingdom. "I've borne the four of you taking over my house and my bookshelves, listened to you share your wrong opinions on literature and sob endlessly about your personal problems, but this is where I draw the line. It's down, it's permanent, and I won't hear a single syllable otherwise. Got it?"

I didn't agree with almost everything my grandfather had just leveled at our heads, but I knew a dressing-down when I heard one. So, it seemed, did everyone else.

"I'm sorry, Arthur." Maisey swung her legs from Mateo's lap and sat contrite, her head hanging. "We didn't realize he was a sore subject."

Her quick apology did little to alleviate my grandfather's wrath. "He isn't a sore subject. He's a man who belongs buried in the past where I left him. How would you like it if I brought up how badly you'd mishandled your relationship with your daughter?"

"I don't know what you're talking about," Maisey said, her color bright.

Even though she obviously *did* know what he was talking about—and wanted to shut the conversation down as politely as she could—but my grandfather kept going. "For God's sake, woman. You call yourself a psychic, but you're the most obtuse person I've ever met. Dandelions have more introspection than you."

A pained expression twisted her features. "That's not true."

"Any idiot could see that what that child needed was *space*, not some overbearing helicopter mom without a life to call her own. It's no wonder she went to another state to get away from you. How else was she supposed to escape your endless prattle?"

"Now, see here—" I began, but my grandfather only turned to Sloane next.

"And you." He laughed with a callousness that felt foreign, even for him. "What if I mentioned the promotion that your boss gave to Mateo instead of to you, even though you're vastly more qualified for it?"

"Hey! I'm just as qualified as she is," Mateo protested, but my grandfather wasn't done yet. His cruelty was only starting.

"Both of you run around and yammer on about books like they

mean something, but it's obvious you've never learned a thing from them. If you had, you wouldn't waste your time following dreams that belong to someone else. Sloane, marrying a man who will bore her to tears within six months. Mateo, shuffling through careers that mean nothing to him." He opened his mouth in a soundless laugh. "And why? Because you're too chickenshit to do something that really matters? So afraid of failure that you're both willing to lie down before you even try to stand? I thought we were finally starting to get somewhere, but I see I was wrong."

"Grandpa, you've done enough—"

It was no use. He turned his ammunition toward me next. I knew, even before he spoke, what was coming. Already, I could feel myself flinching away from him, curving my body in an effort to prevent the blows from landing on my vital parts.

"And you. My grandson. My legacy." He practically spat the last word out at me. "It took you all of six months to come crawling back after your mother died."

Five. It was five.

His upper lip curled. "Hannah would have been ashamed to see you hunkering on that hospital bed in the corner, begging for whatever scraps of affection I decide to give you. Thank God she can't see you now. The day she left, she swore she'd never willingly cross my threshold again—not for all the money in the world, not if I got on my knees and begged. Dammit if she didn't stick to her word to her dying breath. You might be twice her size, but you'll never be worth half of her."

There were no defensive maneuvers for this kind of attack—at least, not any that I'd learned. I could parry and slip with the best of them, but there was nothing I could do to stop his words from driving hard and deep.

"What would she say if she could see you now?" he demanded. "What would she think if she knew how quickly you'd fall?"

I had no idea when everyone in the room had started moving, but when I finally managed to breathe, it was to find that Maisey, Sloane, and Mateo had formed a protective arc in front of me.

"Don't you dare say another word," Sloane said in a voice so hard and distant that it sounded as if it was coming from someone else. "I don't care if this *is* your house. You have no right to speak to another human being that way."

My grandfather opened his mouth to argue, but Maisey spoke up before he could make the attempt.

"Shame on you, Arthur," she said. "Do you have any idea what I'd give to have my daughter in the same state as me, let alone the same room? This young man picked up his whole life and traveled across the state to take care of you, and you're wasting it. You're throwing it away."

"I always knew you were a mean, miserable old man," Mateo said. His voice was sharp and pointed, like a needle stabbing into the same hole over and over again. "But I didn't know *how* mean and miserable until this exact moment."

And then they left. Not in a single-file line or one at a time, but as a pack and without once moving from their positions around me. Dazed, I had no choice but to fall into their protective cocoon, to be pushed and prodded out the door until I stood in the incongruously cheerful August sun. Blinking, I tried to gain control of my senses and my surroundings, but there was no need. For the first time in five long months—and, if I was being honest, for the six painfully drawn out months ahead of that—I wasn't being asked to carry anything.

"Well," Maisey said with a comprehensive whoosh of breath. "That Nigel Carthage man seems to have touched a nerve."

Sloane released a shaky laugh and pushed her hair from her face. She was starting to regain her color, but she looked about as rattled as I felt. "You can say that again. I wonder what went on between them to turn Arthur so feral." She turned to me then and gripped my arm with a surprising show of strength. "You know that was what happened in there, right? It had nothing to do with you or your mother. That was your grandfather lashing out like a wounded animal, protecting himself the only way he knows how. He didn't mean it."

"That's not true," I said, starting to regain my bearings. "He meant every word."

And he was right, too—that was the thing. I *wasn't* worth half of my mom and I never would be. The part he'd gotten wrong was the why of it. I wasn't weak because I'd come to this house; I was weak because now that I was here, I didn't think I'd be able to leave. This was the house that had forged the best woman I'd ever known, the only place where I could access the memories that existed outside my own heart. This building—and the man contained within it—was old and decrepit, held together by a mass of emotions that had gone unrecognized for too long, but that didn't matter.

It was still the only thing approaching a home I had.

Mateo's sudden laugh rang out, a staccato burst that drew all our attention.

"What's wrong?" Maisey asked.

"Nothing's wrong," he said. "I just think we all know what has to happen now. There's only one way to make Arthur pay for an outburst like that."

Mateo's meaning didn't become clear until Maisey gasped and Sloane slapped a surprised hand over her mouth.

"You know I'm right," he said. "It's the only way to show that old bastard that he doesn't get the final word."

"Wait." I swallowed. "You mean—?"

"It's high time the Racing in the Rain Book Club made the formal introduction of our newest and most illustrious member." Mateo rubbed his hands together with a greedy—and welcome—crackle. "Arthur McLachlan isn't the only one around here who knows where to hit so it *really* hurts."

27

—

I KNOW WE TOLD YOU TO TAKE as long as you need, but we lied. The situation is getting desperate. We're drowning without you."

I shifted my position on the bed, crunching and crackling the mattress under my weight. The noise sounded preternaturally loud in the determined silence that filled the living room. So did the voice continuing on the other end of the line.

"We're supposed to be launching the website in two months, but our new guy is starting to break down under pressure. Where are you with the whole grandfather situation?"

Under normal circumstances, I'd have politely taken this call outside, where my voice wouldn't disrupt my grandfather trying to read from the couch. Under *these* circumstances, I didn't give a damn. It had been more than twenty-four hours since his temper tantrum, and he had yet to say a single word to me. Not "hello," not "What should we eat for breakfast," and definitely not "I'm sorry for all the terrible things I said."

I crunched and crackled even louder.

"He's in pretty bad shape, actually," I said, allowing my voice to travel to the other side of the room. My grandfather didn't look up, but his whole body grew motionless in an intent, listening way. "We're starting to suspect he's in some kind of mental health decline."

"Oh. *Oh.* Shit, Greg. I'm sorry to hear that." Wayne, the man on the other end of the line, was my project manager and a friend of long standing. He clucked his tongue in sympathy. "After everything you went through with your mom, I was really hoping this one would be easy."

"That makes two of us," I said grimly. "I'm thinking about cutting my losses and putting him in a home. There are some nice ones around here with bingo game nights and group trips to the children's theater."

That got my grandfather's attention. "Bingo?" he demanded. Louder and more irascibly, he added, "Children's theater?"

"I don't want to have to do it, but the last thing I ever gave my mom was a promise to take care of him. Even after all the terrible things he did to her, she never stopped loving him." I sighed. "But if you guys want to get that website debugged in time…"

"Oh, we do," Wayne said. "But it sounds like you have your hands full. You know what? Forget I called. This is our problem, not yours."

A pang of guilt spiked through me at the deception. True, my grandfather *was* worse than I'd expected, but not in a his-health-is-deteriorating way. This was more of a how-can-one-man-be-so-awful situation. Unfortunately, we didn't have a workplace policy to cover that.

"Take it back," my grandfather said. He'd risen to his feet with the aid of his cane and was hobbling toward me. "Tell whoever you're talking to that I'm not going anywhere near a children's theater. I'd rather be chained up and bricked behind a basement wall."

"Is that him?" Wayne asked. "Chains? Bricks? He doesn't sound so good."

I couldn't help laughing. Wayne might not have caught the Poe reference, but I did.

"Don't worry. He's going to live." I locked eyes with my grandfather's. They were like a reflection of my mom's—the same gray color, the same steely flash of determination—but without a fraction of her warmth. "If I accomplish nothing else while I'm here, I can at least do that much."

Wayne had no way of knowing what I was talking about, but he knew enough about my situation to accept my words at face value. I felt like an ass for leaving him hanging, but he was used to it by now. Unsurprisingly, the past few years had been pretty touch and go in terms of employment. When my mom had first gotten sick, I'd gone down to part-time hours so I could move in with her and take on as much of her care as possible; toward the end, I'd been on full family leave. It was only recently that I'd started to get back in the swing of things.

And then...this. A late-night call from the hospital. The burden of a promise I'd made my mom weighing heavily on my shoulders. A group of unexpectedly friendly strangers offering to share that burden with me.

"Well?" my grandfather said as I hung up the phone and tucked it back in my pocket. "Are you going to tell me what that was all about?"

"That depends. Are you going to apologize for what you said yesterday?"

He set his jaw. "I don't have to explain myself to you. Hannah was my daughter long before she became your mother."

Since he'd already carved out a hollow in my chest, his words didn't have nearly the impact he'd hoped.

"Yes, and we both know how well you used the time you had together." I felt proud of the way my voice didn't waver. "But I wasn't talking about an apology for me. I meant for *them*."

He couldn't pretend to misunderstand me. "I didn't say anything that wasn't true."

I kept my mouth shut.

"Dammit, Greg. You've been here long enough by now. You've seen them. You know I'm right."

It was true. I did. But the difference between me and my grandfather was that I'd never use that knowledge to hurt anyone.

He drew an irritated breath and kept going. "I stand by all of it, you hear? Every single word. Maisey is suffering from the same growing pains every mother feels at that age, only she's so bored and lonely over there that she can't see a way out of it. Mateo is shuffling through careers he doesn't give two licks about, and all because he doesn't want to give his mother the satisfaction of seeing him follow in her footsteps. And Sloane..."

I didn't move, not even to breathe. From the way my grandfather's voice started to vibrate, I could tell we'd reached the real heart of the matter—and the real matter of the heart.

"She's only marrying that man because he's offering her the easy way out. He has money and a roof over his head and a built-in family she doesn't have to work to earn."

All of those sounded like perfectly reasonable—if dry—reasons to marry someone, but it was obvious my grandfather felt differently.

"She doesn't know what she's worth. She doesn't think she can do anything better with her life." He threw his copy of *The Joy Luck Club* across the room. It hit the opposite wall with a thud. "But she can, by God. She can and she *will*."

To my surprise, my grandfather suddenly started crumpling into a heap. Leaping up from the bed, I had my arms around him before either of us knew what was happening. The fact that he didn't fight me was bad enough—that he actually let out a sound almost like a sob as I held him was even worse. He felt much more fragile than his size seemed to indicate, as though his body was just a projection to distract from the real man inside.

I was debating between calling Mateo and 911 when he took the decision out of my hands.

"Did she really ask you to come here?" he asked, and in so quiet a voice I almost had to put my ear to his lips to hear him. "It was her idea?"

"Yes," I said, my own voice low and tight. I didn't have to ask him to explain. I knew very well that we weren't talking about Sloane anymore. "It's the only reason I came, and the only reason I'm still here now. If it had been left up to me, I'd have buried you alongside her."

I expected a series of follow-up questions, but he merely nodded and closed his eyes, his whole body sagging into the couch.

"Do you need anything?" I asked as I continued examining his face, looking for any of the signs Mateo had warned me about. I didn't see anything to alarm me. His lips were just as pink as they usually were, and although he looked pale, his skin wasn't clammy or cold. "Something to drink, maybe, or—"

"I'm fine."

That was all he said—just two words, two syllables—but it was enough to lay my fears to temporary rest. He was fine. I was fine. We weren't good and we weren't whole, but we were getting by.

For now.

———

A few days later, I paced the length of my grandfather's kitchen, my long steps eating up the linoleum and spitting it back out again.

One-two-three-four. I stood in front of the window overlooking the backyard, where a huge expanse of dead weeds threatened a fire hazard for the whole neighborhood. Lately, Maisey had been spending quite a bit of time out there, and her efforts were starting to show. A newly turned-over strip of dirt was ready for transplants from her own yard.

Four-three-two-one. I was back at the pantry, where we'd stored enough foodstuffs to carry my grandfather through the apocalypse and back again. And not just dried beans and boxes of powdered eggs, either. This was the good stuff. I'd never even heard of half the food being kept in here. What were you supposed to do with hearts of palm?

One-two-three-four. I was back at the window again, only this time—

"What's wrong with you today?" My grandfather poked his head into the kitchen, his reading glasses perched on the end of his nose. "It sounds like a herd of cattle is running through here."

"Sorry," I said, my response automatic.

"Are you hungry?" he demanded. "Because book club starts in an hour. You know that infernal woman never comes without a five-course meal in hand. You can eat then."

"I'm not hungry," I said meekly.

"Are you bored?" he tried again. "Because there's that patch of rotting drywall in the bathroom you could touch up if you can't find anything else to do."

Since I'd already replaced, spackled, and painted that particular patch, his offer didn't hold much weight.

"It's not boredom," I said.

"Well, get whatever's happening to you under control. I can't concentrate on my reading with you thumping around." With those parting words, he took himself off again. And a good thing, too—if he'd stuck around a few seconds longer, I might have told him what was really bothering me.

I was nervous.

There had only been a handful of times in my life when I'd let anxiety get the better of me. One of them had been my very first date—a high school dance with the girl who'd sat next to me in math class. She'd gotten an A on the midterm thanks to the depths of my devotion and the fact that I could program our graphing calculators to hold all the answers to the test questions. I doubt she'd have given me the time of day under any other circumstances, but I'd won her over with my technical skills and questionable morality.

I *hadn't* won her over with my gangly limbs and overindulgence in body spray the night of the dance, but that was a totally different story—one that ended with my mom picking me up early, taking me to three different McDonald's until we found one with a working ice cream machine, and eating my sorrows together until we were practically floating along on a cloud of McFlurries.

Anxiety had also been there the day I'd graduated from college with a flimsy computer science degree in hand. That slip of paper had been my ticket to a bigger, brighter future—but it had also been accompanied by my mom's first breast cancer diagnosis. She'd beaten that bout, and I'd landed a job that paid well enough to support both of us while she did it, but my life had been on an irreversible course since that date. All those other hallmarks of young adulthood—dating and cohabitation, trips abroad and whirlwind weekends in Vegas—had been put on the back burner.

It was hard to build a life of your own when you were trying, desperately, to help your mother hold on to what remained of hers.

"Psst. Is he here yet?"

My anxiety ratcheted up a notch at the sound of a soft female voice at the back door to the house, which led in through the aforementioned garden. If it had been Maisey or even Mateo who'd come popping in like this, I might have been fine, but that conversation with my grandfather was still at the forefront of my mind.

He didn't want Sloane to get married—didn't want it so much that it superseded every other emotion he had, made him accept her with a willingness he'd never shown to another living being. And I *still* didn't understand why.

"Not yet. You're the first to arrive." I ushered her inside. With a quick peek to make sure she'd come alone, I snicked the door closed behind her. This was it, then. The moment of truth.

"Everything's a go?" I asked. "Nigel will be here?"

"Oh, he'll be here." Sloane didn't have to lower her voice to a whisper to avoid being overheard; the whisper was ingrained within her. "Mateo texted and said he stopped by Nigel's house an hour ago. He is going to drive him around the city to kill some time until book club starts."

"Good. We don't want to scare him away too soon." I hesitated, assailed by sudden doubt. "Should we have Mateo tell him how my grandfather is likely to react? It seems cruel to throw the guy into the lion's den without some kind of advance warning."

Sloane paused to consider this. I'd noticed her doing it before—taking her time to respond to things, thoughtfully giving weight to each query made of her—and I liked it more and more each time. That quality might have made her seem out of place in a society that was constantly striving for more, but it fit her. I got the feeling she didn't say—or do—anything she didn't mean with her whole heart.

"I think he already knows," she eventually said. "The fact that he approached Mateo and resorted to bribery instead of just calling up Arthur says a lot."

"Like he's scared out of his mind?" I suggested.

She laughed. "I was going to say 'like he's circumspect,' but yours works, too. It's obvious that *something* happened between them, and it's equally obvious—to Nigel, at least—that he can't just walk in unannounced. Your grandfather would have him forcibly removed before he got a foot in the door." The laugh fell from her lips, and I felt something shift in the air between us. Her next words confirmed it. "I'm sorry about your mom, Greg. About her death and about the way your grandfather treated her."

I started to roll my shoulders down, to shrink into a snack-sized version of myself, but Sloane stopped me.

"I wish you wouldn't do that." A small, sad smile touched her lips. "I'm not scared of being trapped in a room with you anymore, and I promise there's no reason for you to be scared of me."

I didn't unfurl my stance all the way. I wasn't so sure I agreed with that last part.

"Will you tell me about her?" She hopped up onto the counter, her floral skirt fluttering around her ankles as she settled one prim knee over the other. I had no idea how a woman could make sitting on formica seem like a lesson in decorum, but she managed it. "If it's not too painful, I mean."

"My mom?"

She nodded, and with such earnest friendliness that I knew she wasn't just offering for form's sake. People did that all the time—murmured condolences and made vague promises of assistance—but Sloane was different. When she fixed those big, knowing eyes on me, I knew she was actually looking. Actually *seeing*.

"I wouldn't know where to start," I said, leaning back against the opposite counter and allowing myself to relax.

"How about the sound of her voice?" Sloane suggested.

This was such an unusual request that I answered. There was no time to put up a filter or any kind of emotional blockade first. One second I was standing alone in the kitchen with a woman who made me feel every inch of my skin. The next my mom was there with us, and all I felt was good.

"It was an ordinary voice, for the most part. Lower than most women's, raspy when she was tired and almost like a growl when she got annoyed." I smiled, remembering how often that growl had been directed at me in my teens. Being a single mom with a kid like me had been no treat. "Her laugh, though, that was anything *but* ordinary. It was like it always took her by surprise—a shout that popped so suddenly out of her that everyone else was just as surprised. God, I miss that sound."

"It was cancer that took her?"

I nodded. "She got it twice—right after I graduated from college, and then again last year. In a lot of ways, we were lucky to have that space in between. We'd lost enough time to value the little bit we had left."

"Any smells you associate with her?"

Huh. That was another unusual question. Unusual but nice.

"Coffee," I said, landing on the first thing that popped into my mind. "Maple syrup. And…cotton balls?"

"Favorite memory?"

"Um…would it be pathetic to say it was a trip to the zoo we took when I was a kid? I feel like everyone's favorite childhood memory is at the zoo."

"This isn't a test, Greg. There aren't any wrong answers."

The speed with which she asked her questions was starting to feel *exactly* like a test, but I didn't say so. I was afraid she might stop asking them if I did.

"What would you say to her if she was standing here right now? Just the two of you?"

I felt my eyes mist over. If my mom were here—in the kitchen where she'd grown up, the kitchen where my grandfather's anger had sucked up every last bit of happiness she'd been able to hold onto—I wouldn't be saying anything at all. I'd be getting her as far away from this place as possible.

"I'm sorry you had to live here," I said. It was as close as I could get. "I'm sorry you had to leave. I'm sorry I don't know how to help him."

Sloane didn't say anything then, only sat with me while I absorbed the enormity of the moment. It was strange. For a few minutes there, I'd felt as though my mother were alive again, her memory awakened by a few simple questions and my just-as-simple answers. In the five months since I'd lost her, no one else had done anything like that. It was as if Sloane knew that what I needed more than sympathy and support—more than all the condolences in the world—was a chance to talk about her.

I was about to thank her for it when I remembered something she'd said the other day, when Maisey and I had sat in her daughter's room discussing my mother's death. She'd mentioned burying her heart six feet deep. I'd felt then that she understood something of loss, of the gaping hole that was left when someone you loved was cut out from your life.

Now I *knew* it.

"Who did you lose?" I asked.

She blinked, startled by the sudden shift, but not in the same way I'd startled her upon our first meeting. "My sister, but it was a long time ago—a lifetime ago."

I nodded to show my understanding. In many ways, every death was separated by a lifetime. There was before and there was after, and the only thing that linked them was a wisp of a memory that seemed to be fading with every passing day.

"What did her voice sound like?" I asked, since it seemed like the only way I could repay her.

A quick smile of understanding crossed Sloane's face. "It's been twenty years, so I barely remember anymore. Let's see... It was like mine, probably, but more assured. More confident. She was my older sister, and she never once let me forget it."

"Associated smells?"

"Popcorn. Chewing gum." Her smile fell. "Antiseptic cleanser. We had to be really careful about germs toward the end. Her immune system couldn't handle them."

Every part of me wanted to wrap my arms around her and pull her in for a hug—not romantically, but because I'd never seen anyone who looked like she needed it more.

"She had a congenital heart defect," she added before I could ask. "She was born with an early expiration date."

Suddenly, those angry parents reenacting *The House on Haunted Hill* were starting to make a lot more sense.

"Favorite memory?" I asked.

She must have known this one was coming, because she fingered the old Victorian-looking pin she always wore. "She made this for me. It's from our favorite book. Once things got bad, we didn't get outside a lot, so reading together was our only way of experiencing the world. Even though our surroundings were confined, we went so many places together, shared so many adventures. And after she was gone, well…" Her voice trailed off and she looked out the window toward the backyard I'd been examining for myself less than an hour ago. When she glanced back at me, it was with a look of self-deprecation that brought out a small dimple I'd never noticed before. "I'm a disgraced former librarian so desperate to find that feeling again that I forced a book club on an unwilling old man. Clearly, I haven't changed much."

It was the answer I'd been seeking from the moment she'd walked into my grandfather's house. What she was doing here and why—how a woman with a fiancé and a life of her own could spend so many hours taking care of a man who didn't deserve it—but I didn't feel a fraction of the satisfaction I'd expected.

"What would you say to her?" I asked, my next line just as clear as all the rest. "If she was with us right now?"

I'd never know the answer. As she took a deep breath and prepared to unburden her heart, we heard the sound of a car pulling into the garage around the back. She slid off the counter and ran to the window, both of us watching as Mateo jumped out of his car and ran to open the door for a well-dressed older gentleman. I immediately recognized him from the snapshot in the yearbook.

"I can't believe we're actually doing this," Sloane said as her hand shot out and sought mine. I recognized her sweaty, tenacious grip for what it was—a friendly gesture meant to soothe and be soothed—but that didn't stop my stomach from doing an actual somersault. I liked how hot she felt, how *real*. "Are we sure this is a good idea?"

"Not even remotely," I said, not daring to move until she did. "But there's nothing we can do to stop this train now."

ARTHUR

28

———

MOST OF THE BOOKS I'D READ in my lifetime started with an origin story. People loved that kind of garbage when they were looking back on the wreckage of their lives, of years wasted and pain suffered, of opportunities that whizzed past because they were too scared to reach out and grab them.

So, fine. This was mine.

I was born in Coeur d'Alene, Idaho, back when the city first started to fall from its mining glory to become a tourist trap for people who didn't have the means or the mettle to leave. No one around here remembered those times anymore, but that was typical. Memories were short when it came to anything unpleasant, and those rough, tough, ramshackle days of turmoil hadn't been pleasant for anyone but the mine owners.

As for my lousy childhood, well, it was too late to start crying about that now. What was the use of blaming my mother for decisions she'd made seventy years ago? Life was different then. Harder. Leaner. Whittled down so sharply there was no way to reach out and grab it without getting hurt.

That was the thing I couldn't get these kids to understand about *The Joy Luck Club* no matter how hard I tried. Or about *The Remains of the Day*. Of course there was a chasm between generations—between past and present, the people we were long ago and the people we were now.

Life stories were written in ink, not pencil. Once they were down, the only thing you could do was turn the page.

"Ah, Sloane. There you are." I struggled to my feet as Sloane pushed her way out of the kitchen, my grandson following doggedly at her heels. He'd been doing that a lot lately, nipping along wherever she went, his eyes never straying far from her face. I'd have berated him for it if I wasn't guilty of the same.

It was pathetic, really. I'd lived alone in this house for almost thirty years, and I'd done fine with each and every one of them. I had a routine to keep me from getting bored, my books to keep my mind active. I'd gone for days at a time without having to speak a word to anybody, and I regretted none of them.

All that had changed the day I met Sloane Parker pushing her little library cart down an aisle in the Fiction section. She'd played book-title games and sweetly suggested the most basic reading list possible, and I'd fallen for it. Me, a professor of literature. Me, a man who'd been reading Dumas in the original French for longer than she'd been alive. It had all been a snowball barreling down the hill from there, her presence in my life building up until there was no escaping its path.

"I want to talk to you about the next book we're reading for the club," I said before she could tell me to sit back down or drink a cup of tea or otherwise act like the old man I had no intention of being. "There's this new treatise on mathematical principles I'd really like to—"

"A math treatise?" Sloane laughed and brushed me off without letting me finish my proposal—and it had been a good one, too. We needed something with logic and reason, something that demanded we sink our teeth in and refuse to let go. "Sorry, Arthur, but there's no way you're getting Maisey and Mateo to sign off on something like that."

"Dumas, then," I said, unwilling to give up without a fight. "Or even Vikram Seth. A rich cultural context could really—"

"Maybe you should sit back down." Greg was the one who interrupted this time, only he didn't soften it with a laugh. He folded his arms like he was about to escort me off the premises. Of my own house. *That* was how much respect I was garnering these days. "Mateo is on his way in."

"I don't give two figs what Mateo is doing. I want to talk about the next book. It's my turn to pick, and I say we dig deeper. No more of this light fare. I want something with meat on its bones."

I didn't mention that I also wanted a book that couldn't be finished in a night or two. *A Suitable Boy* was a good fifteen hundred pages long. *The Count of Monte Cristo* only missed that mark by about fifty pages. Once we started something like that, it would take months to finish reading and discussing, especially if we let Maisey set the pace.

They couldn't just walk away in the middle of a book. They wouldn't. No matter how strong the provocation.

Or how terrible the man.

A knock sounded at the front door. Even if Greg and Sloane hadn't glanced at each other in a quick, meaningful way, that sound would have put me on my guard. None of these people knocked. They waltzed in and out of my house like they owned it, sleeping and eating, rearranging things however they saw fit. Feral pigs had better manners.

"What is it?" I demanded. "Who's here?"

"We told you already," Sloane said. "We saw Mateo drive up. He's bringing a guest with him tonight."

"It's that mother of his, isn't it?" I asked, though I wasn't nearly as upset at the prospect as I sounded. Althea Sharpe had been gifted with a set of pipes—she and that son of hers both. Genie used to love those old French standards. Couldn't sing worth a damn, that woman, but that had never stopped her from belting her heart out anyway. I could still hear her standing over the sink as she did the dishes, butchering half the words to *La Bohème* and forgetting the rest.

As was always the case when I let Genie slip into my memories, I felt myself hardening into stone.

"She can come today, but I won't have it anymore." I thumped my cane on the floor for good effect. Once upon a time, I used to be able to command attention with my voice and my words, but those days were rapidly dwindling. I was starting to realize what Teddy Roosevelt saw in that big stick of his. "I'm getting tired of my house being turned into your personal playground. If you want to keep throwing parties, I'm charging you rent."

I drew a deep breath and waited for the inevitable backtalk. I looked forward to it, even. Back when I'd been a teacher, none of my students would have dared to speak to me that way, all of them so worried about getting the right answers that they never let themselves enjoy the deep, satisfying process of being wrong.

Sloane was wrong all the time. Maisey, too. Mateo and Greg didn't put forth their opinions very often, but I felt pretty sure they didn't have one good literary theory between the two of them.

But damn it all if I didn't like every last one of them for it, for doubling down on their errors and trying to talk circles around me, for taking enough interest to *try*. I hadn't felt this good about arguing with people in decades. Not since…

"Are you going to open the door and let them in, or do I have to do everything around here?" I stalked forward and yanked on the doorknob before I went too far down that road. Standing around and dwelling on the past wasn't doing me any favors—not the standing part, and *definitely* not the dwelling part. "You're welcome to join us this time, but there will be no singing until after we pick the next book club book. That's my final word on the subject."

I only got the door halfway open before it happened again—that sense of drowning, of sinking to the bottom of the ocean with an anchor tethered to my chest. This time, however, I wasn't lying alone on my mattress. Instead, there were people—so many people, all of them crowding around me at once.

"I knew this was a bad idea."

"Let's get you somewhere comfortable, Arthur."

"He doesn't look too good."

"Didn't you warn him I'd be coming? I thought you said he was expecting me."

"Just give the man some space to breathe. He'll be all right in a second."

This last one was uttered by Mateo, my favorite by far. All the other nurses that had been sent here were more like angels of death than medical practitioners, each one listing the ways and means of my inevitable departure from this world.

Do this or you'll die a cold, miserable death.

Eat this or you'll slip into a coma and die a cold, miserable death.

Measure your urine output or I'll do it for you, and then we'll both die a cold, miserable death.

Mateo didn't do any of that. He was begrudging but efficient, more concerned with his own affairs than anything that was happening in my life. At least, that was what I'd always assumed. When I blinked and risked another glance at the man next to him, all of my good feelings fled.

"Get him out of my house," I croaked, my voice sounding as if from twenty thousand leagues under the sea. "Whatever it is you think you're doing, you're wrong. It's all wrong."

"Now, now, Arthur," came the smooth, dulcet voice of Nigel Carthage. The years had done nothing to change the insufferably uptight look of him. Oh, he was older, of course, as we all were, but neither time nor trouble had touched him the way it touched me. His tie was too tight, his belt chosen to match the exact sheen of his shoes. "Is that any way to greet an old friend?"

"You're not my friend," I said as Mateo thrust me down to the couch and pulled out his blood pressure cuff. As the Velcro ripped open and he unceremoniously wrapped the cuff around my arm, I added, "None of you are my friends. I regret the day I agreed to any of this."

For some strange reason, this made my grandson laugh. "You haven't agreed to a single thing since I've been here. In case you haven't noticed, that hasn't stopped us yet."

I tried to turn a glare on him, but it didn't work. Ever since I'd broken down and asked him about his mother, begged him to tell me if she'd really sent him here, if she hadn't forgotten me in her final moments, I'd lost my power.

And distance. I'd lost my distance most of all.

———

Nigel Carthage had been born with a silver spoon in his mouth and a complete Shakespearean library at his feet. In addition to a trust fund and an estate in Surrey that he almost never visited, he had a family friend so high up the publishing chain that he was practically the anchor link.

"You look rough," Nigel said as he took the chair opposite mine. Even in my hazy, half-lidded state, I could see him carefully hitch his pants, his eyes never straying around the room. He noticed it, though—I knew he did. The tumbling, dusty books and the hospital bed, the faded curtains and patterned rug that I'd never had the heart to replace.

Oh, how the mighty had fallen.

"Who are you calling rough?" I grumbled. Of course I looked rough. I *felt* rough. Unlike Nigel, life hadn't seen fit to place me on a marble pedestal and leave me there. "And why the devil are all of you watching me like I'm about to keel over and die? If the shock of seeing my old nemesis come waltzing into my house uninvited didn't kill me, then nothing will. I'm immortal."

I crossed my arms and sat back, satisfied I'd had the final word. Unfortunately, no one else seemed to have gotten the memo.

"Of course you are, Arthur," Sloane soothed.

Maisey winked at me. "Like your Byronic vampires."

"I predict you'll outlive us all," Mateo agreed with a nod.

Only Greg stayed silent, watching me with an expression so much like Hannah's that it was all I could do to stay seated. That look of reproach was a knife to my tottering *un*-immortal heart.

I didn't mean it, I wanted to say. *All the things I said, all the things I didn't. Please don't leave me the way she did.*

"I apologize for stopping by unannounced, but I was hoping to join your book club," Nigel said as though there was nothing strange about any of this. "It's been ages since I had a good literary discussion with friends."

Yes, because he'd spent the past five decades sitting in a glass castle and sending forth his literary decrees from on high. They were terrible decrees, most of them. Nigel had always been scared of anything that smacked of progress, preferring to cling to classics and anything that reinforced the status quo. God forbid he relax his standards enough to actually enjoy *The Art of Racing in the Rain.*

There. I said it. That book was a goddamned delight to my soul.

"Well, you're just in time," Sloane said with that soft, sweet smile that had gotten me to pick up many a book against my will and better judgment. "We're about to select our next book."

"It's *The Count of Monte Cristo,*" I said.

Mateo groaned. "Can we please pick something from the twenty-first century this time? Not all of us are into the duels from our early childhood days."

Nigel released a sound that echoed the grumbling deep in my gut. "Watch yourself, young man. *Monte Cristo* is a classic."

"Is that the one that Sloane's been using as a doorstop to keep the upstairs bathroom door from slamming shut?" Maisey asked with a nervous wring of her hands. "Because that one looks...long."

"It's much too long," Sloane agreed cheerfully.

Her sunny mood had the same effect it always did on me, which was to turn me as contrary as humanly possible. True, I was contrary by nature, but Sloane had a way of bringing out the worst of it.

And the best of it. That was the thing she couldn't see—the thing I didn't know how to make her understand.

"Too bad. It's my turn, and I want a good revenge story. One where the wronged man wins in the end." I looked straight at Nigel while I said this.

"I agree," he said, his eyes locked on mine. "No one understands the dastardly twists and turns of fate better than Dumas."

I nodded. "Enemies rising from the grave."

"Decades of denial for the sake of one moment of triumph," he countered, nodding harder.

"A man who knows himself capable of the worst sins."

"A woman who loses everything because she refuses to see those sins for what they are."

I felt like we were getting somewhere, Nigel and I, but Sloane laughed softly. "Yeah...no. We're not doing any of that. I think we should read *Anne of Green Gables*."

And just like that, the air left my lungs. It wasn't like the edema that had brought all this on in the first place, that buildup of fluid that I ignored for too long, the same way I ignored every other ill—bodily or otherwise. This was more like a punch to the chest, so deep that it stopped my heart cold.

If Sloane saw the way her words hit me, she didn't let it show. She smiled at the gathered assembly instead. "I know it seems a bit childish, but it has something for everyone. It's a classic, which should fit right in with Nigel's literary background. Maisey, it's not a difficult book, and I think you'll really like the sense of community that's built up in it. Mateo, you know it's on the list of books all librarians should read. And Greg, well…" She glanced at my grandson—that gruff, tough, surly chip off the old block—and laughed. "Sorry, Greg. I can't think of anything you'll like about it. But maybe you could take one for the team?"

He returned her laugh with one of his own. "Of course. That was one of my mom's favorites. I'd love to read it with you." Flushing to the tips of his ears, he hastily added, "With everyone, I mean."

"Pick something else," I said. I would have shouted it, but my lungs still felt curiously tight. "Anything else. I'll read that book over my dead body."

When that didn't do more than bring out a series of knowing looks, I doubled down.

"You mentioned everyone but me." I crossed my arms and did my best impression of a man who refused to be beaten. By life. By kindness. By *anything*. "If you want me to agree to that saccharine, antiquated piece of girlish nonsense, then you need to include me on the pitch list. What do I get out of it?"

When Sloane turned toward me, her smile now permanently fixed, I realized my error. I'd given this girl carte blanche to ransack my piles of books, to nose through my home for as many hours as she pleased. And she *did* please. Many a morning, I'd come down to find her sleeping on the couch, one of my prized first editions lying open on her chest. For a woman who'd dedicated her life to the care and keeping of books, she was alarmingly lax in the way she treated mine.

There was only one other woman who'd dared to treat my books like that, sweeping them into her arms with a laugh on her lips and the light of battle in her eyes. Sloane didn't look a thing like my Genie, but their souls had been forged of the same liquid fire. It was the only thing to ever penetrate the hard protective exoskeleton that bound me.

"That's easy," Sloane said. "Of all the books you have in your personal library, that one has the most highlighted passages. It obviously means something to you. Something big."

That was when I knew I was done for. If Sloane had seen my highlights, if she'd flipped through those pages and pieced the words together, then she knew.

Unfortunately, she wasn't the only one. Nigel crowed out with triumph and a slap of his hand on his knee. "The secret's out now," he said, thus sealing my exoskeleton shut forever. "That saccharine, antiquated piece of girlish nonsense is his favorite book in the whole world."

———

"I'm sorry to have taken you by surprise, old chap." Nigel cornered me on the way to the bathroom—the one place I was allowed to go when I needed to be alone. Not even Mateo playing nurse was brave enough to follow me there. "But I knew you wouldn't agree to see me any other way."

"You didn't take me by surprise," I grumbled. "Do you have any idea how transparent that group of children back there is? They've been skulking around here for weeks, waving your dirty old handkerchiefs around and pretending like I'm hard of hearing. I knew it was only a matter of time before you pushed your way in here."

He smirked in a way that yanked me back through time and dumped me unceremoniously on the floor. That smirk had been a cause of extreme jealousy in my twenties; I could scowl and frown with the best of them, but Nigel was too smooth for that. He was all affectation and cool disdain, James Bond the way Ian Fleming intended him.

"Twenty thousand dollars to a small local library, Nigel?" I grunted to demonstrate what I thought of his tactics. "Don't you think that was a touch heavy-handed?"

"It got your attention, didn't it?"

"So would walking naked down Sherman Avenue, only it would have been a hell of a lot easier on your retirement plan."

He had the audacity to laugh at that. Or at me. I couldn't tell which.

"I'm not so hard-pressed that I can't spare a little of my savings for a good cause." He peered down the dark hallway, which had only grown darker as of late thanks to the stacks of books lining the walls. Sloane was making great progress on my collection, but her organizational approach was somewhat…haphazard. "I could write you out a check, too, if you want one."

"I don't need your charity," I said. Lest he get the wrong impression, I added, "Or your profound insights into *Anne of Green Gables*, so don't bother coming back. Our book club isn't currently taking members."

"Please, Arthur?" Nigel asked, this time without a trace of Bond in him. "I know we didn't part on the best of terms"—he paused at the sound of my loud harrumph before trying again—"but it would mean a lot to me."

I wasn't sure what to do with this. Sincerity wasn't a thing Nigel and I had ever shared before. Competition, yes. Antipathy, you bet. That was just the way of academia, even back in the seventies. There were only so many slots at the top, and Nigel and I had both been determined to secure one.

"I was sorry to hear about Eugenia's passing, by the way," he said. From his choice of words, I could tell he was posing this as an afterthought, but there was nothing *after* about it; Genie had been dead these thirty-three years and more. This was a calculated attack, even if I didn't understand where it was coming from.

I had nothing this man wanted. Not anymore.

"Hannah, too," he added. "She was so young. They both were."

That was as far as I was willing to go. Trapped in a hallway or not, I wasn't going to stand here and listen to him list all the people I'd lost.

"That's right," I said, my spine stacking until I almost stood upright. "You win. I'm all alone in the world now. T. S. Eliot was always one of your favorites, wasn't he? 'Hell is oneself, Hell is alone.' Truer words have never been written."

Laughing, cheerful voices from the living room carried down toward us, swept along on the scent of the homemade rosemary focaccia that Maisey had baked that morning.

"Maybe not *all* alone," Nigel said softly.

I could have cursed the book club for choosing that moment to revel in their hilarity. In fact, I *did* curse it, though Nigel had heard those words so many times they didn't hold much weight.

"Is that your way of saying I can stay?" Nigel said. For some reason, he suddenly looked about twenty years older. "I hate to beg, but it would mean a lot to me. I haven't read *Anne of Green Gables* in ages. Not since—"

I flung up my hand, unwilling to let him take one step closer to the edge—or to drag me with him. "Fine. If you insist. I'm not going to kick a dog when he's down."

"Not even when the dog in question is me?"

That wrung a reluctant smile from me. "I've always had a soft spot for a mangy old cur."

"And for a soft-spoken woman with big words and even bigger ideas?"

I hesitated, thinking of the girl sitting in my living room right now, a purple brooch at her neck and the whole world at her feet.

"I already said you could stay. Don't push your luck."

29

—

'D ALWAYS KNOWN I WASN'T A particularly likable man. Like Dostoyevsky's Underground Man, I was sick and spiteful, two qualities that were so much a part of me that there was no way of killing them without killing the man they belonged to. I was unpleasant to be around, incapable of change, and—unlike Maisey—there was nothing unreliable about my narration.

But, oh, how I wished there was. To turn a blind eye to my faults, to sail through life on a sea of ignorance—now that was bliss. People with no introspection had no idea how good they had it.

"I'd like to see the nurse I threw out of my house," I said as I hobbled through the door to the home health services company listed on the bottom of my hospital release form. Not surprisingly, the woman behind the counter blinked and asked me to repeat this request.

"Come again, sir?"

"You heard me just fine," I grumbled. Then, remembering my errand, I took a deep breath and tried again. "I don't remember her name, but she liked Doris Day. The early years. And she had no idea who Virginia Woolf was even though I explained it to her three times."

A heavy cough sounded from behind me.

"What I mean is," I said, doing my best to moderate my tone the way Maisey had instructed me, "I'd appreciate it if you could pull up my account and tell me the names of the nurses who came to my house to help me. One of them was a Doris Day fan."

The woman snapped her gum. "Sure thing, hon. Did you say you threw her out?"

This time, the sound behind me was a laugh.

"His name is Arthur McLachlan," Maisey said with all the efficiency of a woman who regularly interacted with strangers. "He opened his account sometime in June after he left the hospital against medical advice. You were nice enough to keep sending replacement nurses even though he did his best to run each one off."

"Ohhh. I remember you." The woman narrowed her eyes at me. "There's no way I'm giving you their personal information. Do you have any idea how hard it is to retain qualified nurses as it is?"

Since this was no more than I'd expected—and, yes, *deserved*—I sighed and gave in. "It's fine. I'm not here to yell at them. I'm here to apologize."

"Apologize?"

"Make amends."

"Make amends?"

I turned to Maisey, feeling my frustration start to mount. She immediately began lifting her hands before lowering them again like a mime mimicking the waves of the ocean. "Breathe in and out. Remember what we talked about. Use your words."

I breathed. I remembered. I used my words.

"I'm also here to recompense them for their loss of work. It wasn't fair of me to dismiss them early from their shifts. I'm sure they rely on that income to get by. I'd like to ensure they don't suffer for my bad manners."

"Oh. Um. Wow." The woman's eyes returned to their normal size. "No one has ever done that before. Are you sure?"

"Of course I'm sure. Would I have come all this way otherwise?"

At this, Maisey sighed. I was tempted to join her, but I knew I wouldn't get any sympathy. When those nurses had come to the house, I'd behaved like the angry, irritable, *scared* man I'd been, and now I had to pay for it. Literally.

I had Greg to thank for this. Greg and Maisey both, though only Maisey knew about it. For some godforsaken reason, my grandson seemed to think that the burden was on *him* to cover the cost of my mistakes. I'd overheard him trying to pay off Mateo, Maisey, and Sloane so many times that even I was starting to get sick of the offer. I was here purely as a preventive measure. The last thing I needed was for him to go into debt because I lacked the ability to say what I really meant.

"I'm sorry," I said. "I'm not very good at this."

"No kidding," the woman muttered under her breath.

"Since you won't give me their names, could you at least see that they get these checks along with my sincerest apologies?" I resolutely ignored her outburst as I handed over the four cashier's checks. "My medical emergency took me by surprise, and I didn't act as well as I should have."

The woman didn't make a move to grab them, but I wasn't surprised. Maisey had prepared me for these difficulties ahead of time. She'd prepared me for a lot of things, including the likely possibility that I'd be shown the door and/or escorted off the premises by a policeman.

"You're never going to be the kind of man they throw parades for," she'd said with what I could have sworn was a twinkle in her eye. "But it won't kill you to go to a few just to see what all the fuss is about."

It was the closest thing to a psychic reading I'd been able to get out of her. Not that I'd given her my palm or anything mystical like that. I'd just let her probe the recesses of my brain a little. For research. To make sure all those poor saps were getting their money's worth when they called her up and handed over their credit card numbers.

I'd warned her ahead of time that I had no problems lodging a complaint with the Better Business Bureau if I found anything sketchy in her reading of my character, but it hadn't been as bad as I'd feared. Other than that bit about parades, all she'd gotten out of me was the recipe for my favorite childhood dessert and a reluctant admission that I owed these nurses an apology. And even *that* wasn't terrible, since she'd promised to drive me over here herself. No one else would have to know about it.

"Are you sure, hon?" The woman eventually reached for the checks, but not nearly as greedily as I'd expected. "The money is appreciated but not at all necessary. It happens a lot more than you'd think."

"What does?" I didn't let go of the checks right away, but only because I needed them to keep me from keeling over. "People run your nurses off?"

"Well, they don't run them off *specifically*, but we get some pretty strong reactions. It's not easy, opening your home to a perfect stranger and inviting them in for the most intimate level of care. Especially when a scare is unexpected like yours was. You're only human, after all."

I gave up on the battle over the checks and tottered backward. I could feel Maisey behind me, but the woman was blessedly silent for once in her life.

"'Man is the only creature who refuses to be what he is,'" the woman added with a cluck of her tongue. "Don't worry. I'll see that these get where they need to go."

I blinked at the woman, unsure if I could possibly be hearing her right. "I'm sorry. Did you just quote Camus at me?"

"I don't know. That's what it says on the wall at my therapist's office. That and 'Be the change you want to see in the world.' I can never decide which one I like best." The woman beamed at me as though she hadn't just committed sacrilege of the highest order. "By the by, who did you end up finding to take care of you? I processed your at-home care forms for the hospital, but I didn't recognize the name. He's not one of ours."

"You mean Mateo Sharpe?" Maisey asked.

The woman snapped her fingers in recognition. "That was it. He worked out all right? You were happy with his level of care?"

"He kept me alive, didn't he?" I demanded in my usual manner, but my heart wasn't it. I sighed and added, "He's a good kid. A little driftless, but who isn't at that age? I like him."

The woman's interest perked. "Really? Do you think he'd be interested in applying for a job? We offer super-flexible hours. Qualified nurses are always hard to come by." She grinned at me in a way I neither trusted nor cared for. "Especially when our patients do everything they can to scare them away."

It behooved me to put this woman in her place, but my heart wasn't in that, either. I'd never realized before how much effort it took to keep up all that bluster—to fight everything and everyone, to treat every square on the pavement like a battleground. If I looked anything like Nigel Carthage these days, my energy could be expended on much better places.

And much better people.

"Go on, then." I waggled my fingers. "Give me an application. I'll see that he gets it, but I'm warning you right now—he's too good for this job. I went to hear him sing at a nightclub last week, and it was like being transported through time."

Maisey snatched the application out of the woman's hand before I could make the attempt. "Arthur, you old softie. You didn't tell me you saw Mateo perform."

"I had to get out of the house," I said.

I hoped that remark would shut her down, but I needn't have bothered. Shutting Maisey out of anywhere she wanted to go was an exercise in futility, and "there is no more dreadful punishment than futile and hopeless labor."

That was Camus, too.

"Tell me everything," she said as she wound her arm through mine and dragged me out the door. "What did he wear? How did his mother look? And—oh—did Lincoln swoon the moment Mateo took the stage?"

———

"What do you think you're doing?" I asked Maisey as she steered her minivan down a street I didn't recognize. We were supposed to be heading home, but she drove the same way she talked—wildly and without direction—so it was no wonder we'd ended up on the far side of town. "You silly woman. You've forgotten the way home. And everyone thinks *I'm* the one in a decline."

"Relax," she said as she flipped the radio down and pulled up in front of a cemetery that had seen better days. "We're taking a detour."

"To where? An early grave? Thanks, but I'd rather stay on this side of the grass, if you don't mind."

She pointed at a house on the other side of the street. "No. We're taking a detour to there."

I followed the line of her finger to an abomination against architecture, a white box of a building with high-tech panels and a fence that looked to be made of plastic. The only decoration on the exterior was a potted palm tree that might look fine *now*, but would almost certainly die the moment the bitter Idaho winter settled in. I was about to enlighten Maisey about my feelings on anyone who found it acceptable to live in such a place when I realized there was no need.

Because I saw who was living there, and because Maisey already knew how I felt about him.

"Have you lost your ever-loving mind? I don't want to pay Nigel a visit. I want to stay as far away from that man as possible."

"We're not visiting him. We're checking on him. Just taking a peek to make sure he's okay."

"Why wouldn't he be okay?" I asked. Without waiting for an answer, I spoke again. "And what kind of puerile fool parks a car directly in front of the house they're staking? Haven't you ever done this before?"

Maisey had the audacity to laugh as she started up the van and crept it a few houses ahead to avoid suspicion. It was all well and good for *her* to get caught sitting outside the house of my greatest adversary, but what was I supposed to do if he stepped outside and caught me? Admit to vulgar curiosity? About *him*?

"What happened between the two of you?" Maisey asked as we sat hunched in our seats, watching as Nigel shuffled across his living room to water a few plants that looked just as incongruous as the palm tree out front. "If you don't mind my asking."

"Of course I mind you asking. It's none of your business. What kind of question is that?"

Instead of taking offense or even cowering, as the Maisey of last month would have done, she shrugged. "I thought it was worth a try. Greg once told me that he'd rather I come out and ask him about his past instead of trying to poke around in his business and find out that way. I figured you might feel the same, seeing as how you're related and all."

"Greg said that?"

Rather than answer me, Maisey pulled open her glove box and pulled out a pair of binoculars. "He looks kind of lonely in there, don't you think?" She pressed the binoculars to her eyes. "All by himself in that big, ugly house. I bet it has one of those toilets that talk to you. I've always wanted to try one of those. It's like having a friend hold your hand while you pee."

"Maisey!" If my cane hadn't been stowed in the back, I'd have used it to rap on her knuckles. "I know what you're doing, and it won't work. I don't care how Nigel feels or who holds his hand while he uses the facilities. What do you mean about Greg? You asked him about what he's doing here? And he told you?"

"Yep. From something he said at the time, I get the feeling he'd tell you, too, if only you'd muster up the nerve to ask." She gave an excited leap in her seat. "Aha! Look! He's pulling out a book... Isn't that sweet? It's *Anne of Green Gables*. He must be getting ready for our book club."

"Give me those." I pulled the binoculars out of her hand. Sure enough, a blurred image of Nigel turning the pages of the book filled the lenses. "Ha! He looks even older and more tired when he's not trying to impress me. I guess he never got around to hiding that portrait of his in the attic."

"What portrait?" Maisey asked with predictable ignorance. With less predictability and more of the intuition I was starting to realize was no sham, she added, "Oh. You're making a literary reference again, aren't you? You know who would probably appreciate those more than me..."

I dropped the binoculars and pointed at her. "Don't start. I already gave those nurses the blood money you demanded of me."

"I'm just saying he looks like he wouldn't mind the company."

Unable to resist, I peeked through the binoculars again. Nigel sat in the same attitude as before, the book open on his lap, but he wasn't turning the pages. He wasn't doing much of anything except staring off into the distance as his shoulders gave light, heaving shakes.

I dropped the binoculars and shoved them back in the glove box before Maisey could ask for another peek. "I've had enough of this. Let's go."

"Wait. Don't you want to at least say hello first—"

"I mean it," I said as I stared straight ahead. "I want to go home now. I'm tired."

Using my so-called fragility as an excuse was a juvenile trick, but I didn't regret it as Maisey started up the van and pulled back onto the road without argument. There was no way in Hades I was *ever* knocking on Nigel's door, and the last thing I wanted was to drink instant coffee while we chatted about the past, but I wasn't a total monster.

I could at least give him the privacy he needed to sit in his living room and cry.

30

———

HAD NO IDEA HOW I GOT roped into the dinner.

Even in my glittering, ebullient youth, I'd never been much of a hand at dinner parties. There were always too many people invited, as if an empty seat at the table was a sign of personal failure. Or worse, weakness. Every host and hostess I'd ever known went above and beyond to avoid that calamity, which meant they threw together all the wrong people—a cacophony of bad opinions and worse personalities, all of them jumbled together to stave off that horror of all horrors: a conversational lull.

"Francine, I'd like you to meet my dear friend Arthur McLachlan." Sloane hooked her elbow through mine and practically dragged me across a hideous geometric rug that looked like my worst Cubist nightmare. "He used to be a professor at North Idaho College and is now a part of the book club I was telling you about. Arthur, this is my future mother-in-law."

The woman offered me her hand as though extending a dead fish. "You're awfully old."

"You're no spring chicken yourself." I took her dead fish and shook it. "But I wasn't going to mention it."

My lapse of good manners was worth the choke of Sloane's stifled laughter. Good God, was I really going to be subjected to two hours and a pot roast of this? They'd better have me sitting next to Sloane at the very least.

The Francine woman's nostrils tightened into two pinpricks. "I only meant that you seem a little advanced in years to be hanging around with a bunch of twentysomethings."

"Mateo is in his thirties," Sloane said. "And Maisey's forty-four, but she has an old soul, so it's really closer to seventy-four."

A snort escaped me. "Maisey's soul is no older than a flatworm."

Sloane shook her head, as unwilling to submit to me in this as she was in everything. "No way. You don't gain her kind of insight into people without some kind of mystical force at play."

We were interrupted by the arrival of Brett: the doctor, the fiancé, the man I loathed with every fiber of my being. He pecked a chaste kiss on Sloane's cheek and smiled down at her with a look that I'd have wiped right off his face if I were twenty years younger.

"How old is *my* soul?" the fiancé asked. "Or is it better if I don't ask?"

"Yours is brand new," she said, and so quickly that I knew she'd thought about this before. "Everyone in your family is. It's what I like best about you."

"About me?" Francine echoed. She teetered on the edge of offense, unsure whether or not she was being insulted and unwilling to commit until she knew.

"Yes, about you. About *all* of you." Sloane swept her eyes around the room. I had yet to be introduced to any of the rest of this family, but there was no need. My soul was plenty old, so I knew exactly what I was looking at. Pomp and self-consequence at every turn. Everyone was well-dressed and far too pleased with themselves considering the only books on the shelves were Reader's Digest collections. "You're never anything except what you advertise."

The woman's nostrils pinched even tighter. "And what's that?"

Sloane smiled blandly up at her fiancé. "You're accepting. Uncomplicated. Kind."

Each of those words cut through me like the swing of a scythe. Those were the worst three words I'd ever heard used to describe *anyone*, let alone the man Sloane was a few short months away from chaining herself to forever. I was no phone psychic, but even I could see what the future held for her.

A life that was accepting and uncomplicated and kind, sure. But also one that wasn't worth living.

"Bah!" I said, since I didn't have the words to say what I truly felt. Maisey would have been ashamed of me, but this wasn't like apologizing to a few nurses for my bad temper. *That* was just a matter of stringing the right syllables together and forcing them out. This was something else altogether, something I'd never been able to do.

That was the truth of the matter, and it had to be said. I, Arthur McLachlan, didn't have the right words. I'd read thousands of books, absorbed the wit and wisdom of thousands of authors, but I'd never be able to do what they did. To bleed onto Hemingway's oft-quoted page, to take a piece of myself and hold it up for everyone to see.

I *needed* that blood. I *needed* that part of myself. I'd already lost so much as it was.

At the sound of my outburst, one of the well-dressed, self-consequential family members laughed out loud. Out of all of them, she seemed the least obnoxious. She had the same twinkle in her eye that had first drawn me toward Sloane.

"I couldn't have put it better myself," she said as she came forward, her hand outstretched. "I'm Rachel, by the way. I don't think we've formally met."

I didn't take her hand. To encourage familiarity with this group would only lead to a repeat invitation. Unfortunately, this only caused her to laugh harder.

"Oh, wow. You're every bit as rude as Sloane said."

"Rachel, I didn't! I said he was…difficult, that's all."

"Don't apologize on my behalf, girl," I said. "I *am* rude. And difficult. I find it's the best way to avoid dinner parties like this one."

The new girl—Rachel—wound her arm through mine and gave my hand a friendly pat. I was so startled by this overture that I forgot to fight back until it was too late. She had a grip like an Amazonian.

"It's official," she said. "When Sloane's gone, I'm adopting you in her stead. My friends will get such a kick out of you."

I ignored the implication that I was a stray dog who needed to be swept up off the streets to focus on the more important half of that statement. "Gone? What do you mean, gone? Where's she going?"

"Oh!" The Amazonian grip relaxed enough for me to get my limb back. "Didn't she tell you? She and Brett are—"

"Rachel, *don't*." Sloane spoke with the same severity she'd used the other night at my house, when I'd felt the world slipping out from underneath me and had lashed out at all of them. The world was slipping again—and taking me with it—but there was nothing to lash myself to this time.

"Wait—you haven't told him yet?" The fiancé spoke with a severity that suited his surroundings, an assumption of power that had nothing to do with merit and everything to do with circumstance. "I thought we decided on this, my love. The sooner the better. In the best interests of everyone involved."

"If that isn't just like you, Sloane." Francine tsked. "You'd forget your head if it wasn't attached. It's always up in some cloud."

I took umbrage at every part of this speech, but I had no time or energy for a woman so comprehensibly wrong about Sloane. Her head wasn't in the clouds; it was bent low to the ground, refusing to see anything but what lay in her direct path.

"If you must know, Mr. McLachlan, Brett has been offered an incredible opportunity on the East Coast." Francine turned toward me, puffing up with enough maternal pride to inflate a hot air balloon.

"Some old college friends of his are starting up a health and wellness center, and they can't do it without a doctor of his stamp to lend them credibility. He's very sought after."

It was clear this barrage of nonsense required a response. "A doctor? I thought he was a chiropractor."

The hot-air balloon began to overheat. "He *is*."

"Please. He might as well answer phones at a psychic hotline and have done with it. At least Maisey doesn't pretend to be anything other than what she is. I can respect that."

Rachel laughed again, but I was growing tired of her irreverence. Any other day, I might have been able to appreciate a young woman who was so quick to see the absurd in the world around her—Jane Austen and I had that in common—but this was too important. Sloane was moving to the other side of the country? She was leaving?

The room started to spin, my lungs tightening so suddenly that it felt as though a metal band had been wound around my torso and clamped into place.

Before I could break free of the cage, a cushion appeared underneath me. When I glanced around, I was surprised to find myself on the couch with Sloane seated next to me, her hand rubbing warm, soothing circles on my back.

"In and out," she soothed. "One breath at a time. It's going to be okay."

No, it wasn't. Everything was wrong, and I didn't just mean that I was wishing for my bed and my oxygen tank.

"What. Are. They. Talking. About?" I wheezed. Sloane tried to shush me, but I drew on every ounce of strength left in me to keep talking. "Where. Are. You. Going?"

Instead of answering, Sloane cast an accusing glance around the room. Her hand was still on my back, still patting me like I was a child who'd woken up from a terrible nightmare. I didn't shake her off as instinct warned me to. It was too nice to feel that press of her hand, to know the comfort of a sympathetic touch. One of the things they never told you about growing old alone was how desperate you'd get for that simple human right—or how hard you'd cling to it once you found it again.

"I told you to let me talk to him on my own terms. I warned you he wasn't back in full health yet." Her face appeared in front of mine, lines of worry crisscrossing over her forehead. "Arthur, nothing has been decided yet. It's just something we're discussing, okay?"

"Still discussing?" came the echo of Francine's voice. "Brett, honey, is that true?"

"Leave the kids alone, Francine," said the man who'd been introduced to me as the fiancé's father. "They know their own business."

The fiancé coughed. "We're working out the kinks, that's all." He appeared next to Sloane, and I'd never hated the sight of a face more. Not content with shoving Sloane down the narrow confines of the altar, he was now purporting to carry her off against her will and inclination. "He looks fine to me. A little tired, but that's no surprise. Remember what I told you the other day, Sloane."

When Sloane didn't answer, I forced myself to speak again. I was pleased to find that my breath—and my voice—came a little easier this time around. "What did he tell you?"

"See?" the fiancé said. "He's coming around already."

"What did he tell you?" I demanded again, my eyes scanning Sloane's face for signs of distress. Most days, they were easy enough to find; her pinched, white face was as easy to read as a book. Sure enough, her eyelashes started fluttering like a kidnapping victim pleading her case from afar. "Sloane, tell me, or I'm going to keel over and have a heart attack right here and now."

The fiancé coughed again, this time with heavy emphasis.

"It's not a big deal, Arthur," Sloane said in a voice that felt—to me, at least—like a big deal. "Brett thinks you might be exaggerating some of your symptoms as a way to keep me around longer, that's all."

There were so many things wrong with this statement that I felt a thousand fiery spikes forcing me to an upright position. Admittedly, this gave credence to the fiancé's claims, but I didn't care.

"My health has nothing to do with this," I said, turning toward him. "Sloane is organizing my book collection, remember? She's *working*."

The fiancé snorted like a horse about to break out of its stall. "You haven't paid her a single penny since she showed up there."

"The check is in the mail," I lied.

"You're taking advantage of her generosity, and you know it. Sloane is a *good* person, Mr. McLachlan. Better than anyone I know. Some men might be willing to stand by and watch as the world tries to crush her underfoot, but I'm not one of them. She put herself in my hands, and I intend to make sure she's taken care of for as long as she stays there."

Sloane's lower lip quivered. "Brett?"

"What, Sloane? You know how I feel about you."

Two things happened in the sixty seconds that followed this declaration. One of them was a complete overhaul of Sloane's expression. There was such a softening about her mouth—and such a hardening around her eyes—that I thought I must have been imagining things, so incompatible with one another were they. The second was that the band around my chest started squeezing again, this time refusing to stop until it was encased around my heart.

"I think I need to lie down," I muttered, but my voice had grown so faint that the words may have only existed inside my head.

I had no way of knowing how much time passed between my fainting spell and my unceremonious departure from the too-big, too-ostentatious house full of the too-big, too-ostentatious family that

Sloane was purporting to marry into. It felt like hours, but I suspected I'd been carried out and deposited into Sloane's car within minutes. People were always happy to see the back of me, but never like this—like I was a burden they were unwilling to bear, as if my very existence was an affront to them.

Goodbyes were said and apologies made on my behalf, but my heart remained tightly bound. Especially when Sloane didn't start the car right away. Her hands tapped on the steering wheel, a random beat designed to irritate.

"What?" I asked as I closed my eyes and followed the instructions Mateo had given me a few days before. Breathe slowly and deeply. Focus on the way my lungs expanded and deflated. It felt an awful lot like mediation, but the kid must have known what he was talking about because it helped. "I thought we were leaving."

"We are. Do you want to go to the hospital?"

"Of course I don't want to go to the hospital."

"Should I take you there anyway?"

"You're more than welcome to try."

I could feel her gaze on me as she started the car and began slowly backing out. The drive was a long, circular path to nowhere, so she had ample time to examine me for signs of distress. Since there weren't any—I was *fine*—she eventually gave up and moved the car at a normal pace.

We continued on this way for much longer than felt comfortable, which was odd considering it couldn't have been more than ten minutes. Sloane and I often sat in silence for hours at a time—usually when I was reading or pretending to nap while she endlessly sorted my books—but there had never been anything odd about it. It was one of my favorite things about her, how she didn't always feel a need to fill the silence, how soothing a companion to a man who'd long grown accustomed to living without one.

"Aren't you going to say anything?" I asked when I could not take the interminable weight of that silence a second longer.

She showed me the neat line of her profile. "About what?"

The answer to that was as clear as if he were sitting in the back seat. "You don't love that man."

She jerked with surprise, the wheel turning quickly under her hands. I had to reach over to steady our path, and even then it was a close-run thing with an eager squirrel darting across the street.

I expected her to defend herself—or at the very least to ignore me and continue driving without saying a word—but she heaved a sigh and spoke three words that chilled me to the bone.

"Does it matter?"

My foot pressed hard against the floor of the car, as if I were hitting an imaginary brake to bring everything to a halt. But I had no brake and even less power.

"What the devil do you mean? Of course it matters! It's the only thing in this world that does."

She looked at me then, a turn of her head that seemed to take every ounce of strength she had. "The job offer he got is a really good one. It's right outside Boston. I've always wanted to visit the sights around there. The House of Seven Gables, Orchard House…you can't tell me that doesn't sound like something I'd love."

"So go visit them," I said. "Stay for a few weeks. Stay for a month."

"Stay for a lifetime?" she suggested, and so gently that the last of my fight ebbed away. I'd been fighting for too long—three decades too long, in fact—and I felt each of those years like they were a century.

"When?" I croaked, the single hoarse syllable all I could manage in the sudden clenching of my throat.

"Soon. Right after the wedding. Brett doesn't want to lose any time."

"But you said it wasn't decided. You said you were still discussing it."

She laughed at that, a sound that felt as brittle as my heart. "Brett doesn't discuss things. He decrees. At first, I wasn't sure it was what I wanted, but…" Her voice grew thick. I felt my own responding in kind, choking me from the inside. "What's the point of fighting him? I don't have my job at the library anymore. My parents have no interest in whether I stay or go. And you heard Brett back at the house, Arthur. He cares about me. He takes care *of* me. How many people get to spend their lives in the keeping of someone who wants to shield them from every strong wind? How can I refuse something that most women would kill to have?"

I didn't have an answer for her. Everything about this situation felt so familiar—so painfully, unalterably recognizable—that I was starting to lose track of time. My own Genie had posed this same question so many years ago that I sometimes wondered if I'd imagined the whole thing—our love and our life, the daughter she'd adored and the daughter I'd failed.

"I think I'd like to go home now," I said.

"Arthur…"

I leaned back in my seat and closed my eyes, squeezed so tightly that no crack of light shone through. "I'm tired," I said—and I was. Tired of going through the motions, tired of pretending that something terrible hadn't been happening to my heart ever since my stay at the hospital. Physically, that heart was the same as it had always been—consistent and strong, a sturdy organ that I could rely on for years to come.

Emotionally, however, I was broken. I'd been broken for a long time, and I'd done my best to make sure that everyone around me was broken, too.

"I've done so many terrible things," I said. "I've *said* so much even worse."

I don't think Sloane heard me, but that was okay. For once in my life, words weren't going to cut it.

31

—

THOUGHT YOU CALLED ME HERE FOR an emergency book club meeting."

I threw open my front door and ushered Nigel inside with unseemly haste. I'd told the narcissistic weasel that he needed to sneak in through the back in case Maisey had her spyglass out, but he obviously hadn't listened to me. He'd *never* listened to me, even though I'd been the one to win our collegiate knowledge bowl every year while we were in graduate school.

"Have you no common sense?" I asked. "If that infernal woman sees us, she'll come over with cupcakes and a determined plan to reconcile our differences."

"I like cupcakes," Nigel said, unperturbed. He swept a quick glance around the mess of my living room, his gaze eventually falling on the only tidy spot: Greg's corner. The hospital bed had been made up so neatly it looked as if it were awaiting its next surgical patient, and his small shelf was organized with the five earthly possessions he seemed to own.

Those five meager things reminded me a lot of when Hannah had moved out, storming out of the house after a particularly bad argument about her plans for the future. I'd wanted her to live at home with her as-yet-unborn baby, raising him in the only home any of us had ever known, but she'd laughed at that. Laughed and left, and with little more than the clothes on her back. I'd been sick for months after she'd gone, my whole body racked with guilt and worry about what would become of her.

Maisey knew something of that pain. It was why I left the front door unlocked, why I'd been leaving it unlocked all this time. Hugs weren't my style, and she hardly needed the benefit of my advice, but until that girl of hers reached out, Maisey was in for a rough ride.

She'd survive, though. We all did.

"We're alone?" Nigel asked as he returned his attention to me. "No one else is here?"

"Afraid to be trapped with me without the benefit of witnesses?" I snorted. "Don't worry. I don't have the energy to murder you."

"Do any of us?" Nigel laughed, and damn it all if that sound didn't take me back through the years. "I barely have the energy to tie my shoes anymore. Loafers are a gift from God."

I fought against the urge to agree to this—and to all other conversational gambits he might be willing to throw out in hopes of winning this round. I wasn't here for a friendly chat about the vagaries of age; I was here because I needed help. And Nigel, sanctimonious popinjay that he was, was the exact man to give it to me.

"Sit down and stop pretending you're here for any reason except to thwart me," I said as I fell into my favorite armchair. The spine of a thin, leather-bound volume—*Jonathan Livingston Seagull*, I presumed—jabbed into my back, but I didn't care. In fact, I welcomed it. The less comfortable and settled I got around this man, the better. "I'm having a personal crisis, and I need you to fix it."

Nigel didn't sit. He didn't blink or show any other signs of life—a thing that might have scared me a few months ago, but I knew better now. Men like us were a lot harder to kill than we looked. Long when the world passed on, when nothing was left but concrete and despair, we'd be here scrambling around like the nuclear cockroaches we were.

"And stop staring at me like that. I wouldn't ask if I wasn't desperate." A sharp, sudden pang clutched me by the heart. "And I *am* desperate, Nigel. She's going to leave. It took me thirty goddamn years to find her again, and she's leaving."

For the longest moment, he appeared to be on the cusp of leaving anyway. His breath hitched, his body arced toward the door, and his eyes took on a glimmer of panic that I recognized well. It was the panic of incoming sentiment, of being locked inside someone else's emotional pain with no hope of release.

But he sat. He hitched his slacks first, precise to a pin even under these circumstances, but he sat. That counted for something.

It counted for a lot.

"This is about the girl?" he asked.

I nodded. "Sloane. Sloane Parker. Up until a few months ago, she was the only friend I had in the world." I couldn't help smiling at how far I'd fallen since I'd, well, *fallen.* "As you already pointed out, I've got them coming out my ears now, but that's not the point. She gave them to me. She did this. Now it's my turn to return the favor."

"Where's she going?" he asked. With a show of sapience I could have done without, he added, "Or should I ask, *who* is she going with?"

Ah, old friends. A blessing and a curse, a boon and a bane. No one understood my pain as much as this man, and I hated him for it. But it also saved me a long-winded explanation I was in no mood to give.

You see, many years ago, when I'd been as young and naive as Sloane, I'd stood in the exact same spot, facing the exact same dilemma—and the exact same man. I could still feel the sharp agony of those days, when the love of my life, my own precious Genie, had packed up everything she'd owned and followed Nigel to New York to start their life together. There was no loneliness on earth quite like that of knowing that your life—your *soul*—was happily settled on the other side of the country, out of your reach but not even remotely out of your mind.

"She's leaving with a *chiropractor*," I said, the word a sneer.

"Oh dear." He chuckled. "As bad as all that?"

"Laugh all you want, but this is serious. He's taking her to Boston, the birthplace of American literature. How am I supposed to compete with that? What do I have to offer that can serve as counterpoint?"

Nigel sat back against the cushions of the couch, his gaze moving quickly back and forth across my face. He was a speed reader and always had been; even with so many years at his back, his extraocular muscles were in phenomenal shape.

"You love her?"

I waved an impatient hand. "Not like that—not the way you're thinking. This has nothing to do with romance and everything to do with…" I let the words trail off, unsure how to finish.

What I'd been about to say was that I'd died the same day that Genie had, that my heart had shriveled and shrunken until Sloane had brought it back to life again, but it wasn't true. I *hadn't* died when I'd buried Genie, even though I probably should have. Hannah would have been far better off as an orphan than living with a shell of a man filled with nothing but pain and rage. At least then she might have had a chance at happiness.

Nigel was waiting patiently for me to respond, so I drew a deep, painful breath and tried again.

"'Kindred spirits are not so scarce as I used to think,'" I quoted. It was pathetic for a fully grown man to struggle to say something that had been tripping off the tongues of little girls for over a century, but there was a reason Sloane had chosen *Anne of Green Gables* for our next book-club read. That girl had more wisdom than she knew.

So did Nigel. He nodded and finished it for me. "'It's splendid to find out there are so many of them in the world.'"

Silence descended for a long moment, broken only by the sound of the kitchen door slamming shut and the heavy tread of my grandson's footsteps. Nigel risked a quick peek at me, ready to take my cue at how to react, but all I felt was gratitude—gratitude for this strange young man who'd taken up residence in the corner of my living room, gratitude to my daughter for sending him to me just when I needed him most.

"Hey, Grandpa," he said, as if the familial term had been bandied between us for three decades instead of a few months. He blinked at the sight of Nigel, but that didn't stop him from nodding politely and acting as though there was nothing odd about me sitting around chatting with my sworn enemy. "And Nigel. Glad to see you're both upright and breathing."

I snorted on a laugh. The kid had a subtle way about him, that was for sure. Hannah had been the opposite, hot and full of fire—a lot like me, rising to every fly. We weren't the type to meekly show the other cheek; we bared our fangs and fought back, even if it meant we ended up in opposite corners licking our respective wounds.

I liked his approach better.

"I'll leave you two to your...chat." He ducked his head and turned back toward the kitchen.

"No. Don't." I lifted my hand and held it there, feeling its awkwardness but refusing to drop it back down again. "You might be able to help."

"Me?"

"Yes. It's about Sloane."

He hesitated. Sensing that it had to be now or never, I used that hesitation to make my case.

"She's leaving, Greg. Not tomorrow or anything, so you don't need to jump like that, but soon. In a few months. She's marrying that fiancé of hers and moving to the East Coast to live a long, happy life full of books and conversations about muscle tension."

Greg grunted. "Good for her."

"No, it's not good for her! It's terrible for her, and she knows it. Only she refuses to do anything about it—because she's scared and because she's lonely, because no one has ever given her a reason to stay."

"And you want...me to be that reason?" He rolled an uncomfortable shoulder. "Sorry, Grandpa, but—"

"Of course I don't want you to be the reason." Honestly, had these two never heard of such a thing as platonic love? "I want her to stay for me. And for Maisey. And for Mateo and maybe a little bit for you. But most of all, I want her to stay for *her*."

Nigel cleared his throat so gently that I had to steady my breathing just to hear him. But steady it I did—and none too easy it was, either. "I think you should tell him," he said.

"The devil I will."

Greg finally unbent enough to lower himself next to Nigel. Nigel winced at the sudden, unyielding dip of the couch, but that didn't stop him from speaking again. "He can't help you unless he knows the whole story, Arthur."

An ordinary man would have taken my silence for the strong, visceral negative it was, but Nigel was no ordinary anything.

"Your grandmother did the same thing once, and it almost broke your grandfather's heart. He's terrified of what will happen if he lets it happen a second time."

I stamped my foot on the floor. "Nigel! If you're going to tell the story, you can at least tell it right."

"I *am* telling it right. Did you or did you not stand by and watch as Genie accepted my proposal of marriage?"

"I wasn't in the room, no. In fact, I didn't hear about it until the next day—about how you went behind my back and lured away the woman I loved. Stole her out from underneath my very nose."

"As far as I can remember, she was happy to have me." He turned to Greg with a soft smile. "I gave her my mother's ring. It was too small for her ring finger, so she had to wear it on her pinkie—a pearl as sweet as she was."

Greg's interest was understandably starting to pick up, but for all the wrong reasons.

"Goddammit, Greg! Don't listen to him. She didn't want him, do you hear me? She didn't want anything to do with him. How could she? With all his airs and graces. More like a bag of wind than a living, breathing person!"

"Don't hold back on *my* account," Nigel murmured.

"What have I said that isn't the truth?" I snorted with all the contempt I could muster, with a little extra annoyance thrown in for good measure. "Greg, you should read his piece on James Joyce—the only author in the history of the world more full of himself than Nigel is."

"So you read that, did you?" Nigel asked. "I wasn't sure you would."

"Of course I read it. I've read all your so-called peer reviews and contributions." I started ticking off the ones that first sprang to my mind, although there were so many I doubted *he* could name them all. "*The Cambridge Quarterly. The Review of English Studies. Journal of the English Association.* Bah! When have you had a single opinion that you didn't steal from someone more original than you? You couldn't even fall in love with a woman of your own choosing. You had to go and fall in love with mine."

I thought for sure that one would get him, but all he did was nod and say, "I know."

"Wait," Greg said before I could catch my second wind. "So Grandma left to go be with Nigel?"

"Yes, but don't blame her for it. She'd had no other choice. I was too stupid and stubborn to—"

Nigel coughed. "I think you're forgetting one."

If there was a way to bring a man to ruin using only the power of a stare, I'd have ended all three of us on the spot. As it was, the only thing I could do was agree.

"Fine," I said. "I was too stupid and stubborn and—yes—scared to tell her the truth."

"The truth?" Greg echoed.

"That I loved her. That I wanted to spend the rest of my life with her. That even though I didn't have any money to my name or a fraction of Nigel's smarmy British charm, I could make her happy." I blamed my weakened lungs for the way my voice cracked, but they both knew. Greg because he was my blood, and Nigel because he'd *always* known. "I did it, too. I'm a terrible man and an even worse father, but Genie and I were happy together. That's the thing your mother probably never told you, Greg. I did a lot of things wrong where Hannah was concerned—so many things, each one stacking up on top of each other until she had no choice but to run away to avoid the crash—but once upon a time, we were a family."

I was almost panting by the time I was done, adrenaline pumping my heart much faster than Mateo would have been happy with, but at least I'd lived to tell the tale.

Until Greg replied.

"She told me," he said. "About the before...and about the after. She always used to say that you used up every ounce of your love on Grandma so that when she died, there was none left for my mom."

Something wild may have broken out of me then, but Nigel pressed his hand on top of mine, holding it in. "Tell him the rest, Arthur. About how you won Genie back, about the way you finally opened up your heart to her so that she had a real choice in the matter."

I didn't see what good that would do. The burden of the past was already becoming too much to bear, weighing down on my soul until if felt as flat as my heart.

"I don't see how it will help," I grumbled. "It's not like I can just give Sloane my entire library and tell her to skim the pages. She's already seen them. She already knows. That trick pony doesn't have any legs left to stand on."

Greg bolted up from his seat, once again jolting poor Nigel to the point of wincing. One of the worst things about all these blasted young people was that they had no sympathy for joints that had worn down every bit of elasticity they had.

"Do you mean the highlighted passages?" Greg asked as he pulled a book at random from the shelf above his bed. It was on the tip of my tongue to direct him to literally any other bookshelf in the house, since Sloane had cleared that one to make way for his belongings, but the volume he held out wasn't one of mine. It was his copy of *The Joy Luck Club*. I could tell because I'd have been caught dead before I'd buy a movie poster tie-in of any piece of literature. As he handed the book to me, it fell open to a page with a highlight across the bottom.

I read it aloud before I realized what it was.

"'So that morning, while my mother was dying, I was dreaming.'"

I'd read about people's faces draining of color more times than I could count, but it wasn't until that moment that I actually *felt* it happen.

"Greg." The book trembled in my hand, but I didn't know what else to say. Only "*Greg.*"

He smiled ruefully and took the book from me. "Until I got here, I never realized it was a family trait. I should've known. Mom always encouraged it, though she never told me why. She just said that when I couldn't find the words to say what was in my heart—when my throat got too tight and all I wanted to do was boil over—I could always find myself in a book."

"That was how your grandfather did it, too," Nigel said. "Won your grandmother back, I should say. I didn't even realize what was happening until I saw a copy of *Anne of Green Gables* clutched in her hand. Your *grandfather's* copy, crisscrossed and colored through like a children's Bible."

I still had that copy, though time hadn't treated it well. I'd gone back through those pages so many times that they almost disintegrated to the touch.

"I sent it by overnight mail. Fifty bucks, it cost me. Back then, that was a pretty penny." These words weren't the right ones—I never could find them, even after all this time—so I took a deep breath and tried again. "As soon as Genie got the book, she understood what I was trying to say. That she had a place with me, a *home* with me. After that, she never asked me for any kind of declaration of love. She knew that if she needed to understand what was in my heart, all she had to do was pick up whatever I was reading at the time, and she'd see it."

She was in every book I'd ever read, every tale that had ever touched my heart. Fiction and nonfiction, memoir and short story—no matter what I read, I always found her. It was why I resorted so often to thrillers and German philosophy in my declining years, even though Sloane did her best to steer me away from them.

Some days, I needed her to be near. Most days, I couldn't bear the pain.

"Well, that's it, then." Greg lifted *The Joy Luck Club* from my hands with a reverence that needed no explanation. If that was the book where his mother—my daughter—dwelled, then I understood exactly how important it was to him. "You know what you have to do."

"I'm not giving her my copy of *Anne of Green Gables*," I said. "I'm sorry, Greg, but I can't. It's too valuable."

"We'll buy her a new one," he promised, and in a tone of authority I didn't recognize. "And you and I will go through it, line by line, to pick out the ones that say what you need them to. Once you explain what they mean, she'll know what you're saying. She's too smart of a person not to."

"But what if doesn't work?" I asked. "What if she leaves anyway?"

I was careful not to look at Nigel. He didn't know it, but the three days it had taken for my book to be delivered to Genie and for Genie to be delivered back to me had been the longest of my life. In an age without cell phones and social media, all I'd been able to do was wait. And hope.

I hadn't hoped for anything like that in a long time.

Greg's hand crashed down and gripped me by the shoulder so hard that I almost cried out—not in pain, but with the sudden, comforting pressure of it. "Then we'll figure it out, Grandpa. I know she means a lot to you, but she's not all you have in this world."

His smile grew tremulous. I could tell he wanted to add more, but there was no need. Not in words and not in the lines of a book.

Not anymore.

32

—

I DON'T CARE WHICH LINES YOU PICK out, just as long as you don't include the one about Octobers," I said. "I *hate* the one about Octobers."

Greg sat at the end of the dining room table, a blue highlighter in his hand and a brand-new hardback copy of *Anne of Green Gables* in front of him. He also had a rapidly dwindling glass of scotch that Nigel kept discreetly topping up. *To boost morale*, he'd said.

"What's wrong with the October one?" Greg asked.

"October is a wet, cold, miserable month, and anyone who pretends that a few rotting leaves make up for it is an idiot."

Nigel laughed. "Isn't that rather the point? Beauty in decay? The last fiery burn of life before it goes dormant?"

I waved him off. The man was seriously starting to get on my nerves. Neither Greg nor I had invited him to participate in this, my last-ditch effort to hold on to the *one* thing of true beauty I had in this world, but he'd showed up like Rumpelstiltskin leaping about on a bed of straw.

"Seasonal changes have nothing to do with how I feel about Sloane." I set my jaw. "So keep looking."

"There's always 'My life is a perfect graveyard of buried hopes,'" Nigel suggested.

"Or 'It is ever so much easier to be good if your clothes are fashionable,'" Greg offered, grinning. "We're *kidding*, Grandpa. Don't forget to breathe."

I had no idea what would have happened if Maisey hadn't burst through the front door at that moment, carrying with her an energy that exceeded her usual maximum limit. For what was probably the first time since she'd started showing up at my doorstep, there wasn't a scrap of food anywhere.

"Guess what just happened to me," she said, not blinking at the tableau in front of her. She accepted Nigel with the same ease that everyone in this godforsaken group had—with neither question nor care for the wrongs of the past. I found more hope in that than they could possibly know. "Never mind. You'll never guess. I got a phone call."

"Alert the authorities," I said. "This is a matter of national security. Or maybe we should call the *Enquirer*. Take out a full-page ad in—"

Maisey clasped her hands to her chest and beamed, ignoring every word from my lips. "It was from Bella. She got into a huge fight with her father and wants to come home."

I clamped my mouth shut again before capping my highlighter and setting it aside. The woman might drive me batty nine days out of ten, but she'd been waiting for this for weeks. I wasn't about to rob her of it.

"Maisey, that's fantastic." Greg was up out of his chair and lifting her in a bear hug faster than most people blinked. "I mean, the part about her fighting with your ex isn't good, obviously, but the fact that she turned to you. Do you need help buying her plane ticket?"

She shook her head. "No, and I told you a million times to stop trying to buy me off. She's not coming back."

"Wait." Greg blinked. "Why not? You just said—"

"That she *wanted* to come back, not that I was going to let her. We talked for half an hour. Thirty whole minutes, Greg. I can't remember the last time we had a conversation that long."

She turned to me with simple pride. For once, I didn't mean that as an insult. Maisey would never be a complex woman, and if you handed her Schrödinger's box, she'd immediately open the lid so she could slip a can of tuna inside, but I was coming to appreciate that about her. *Someone* had to remember to feed the damn cat.

"She said she could see why people paid me $3.99," Maisey added. "Because I was helpful. Because I was wise."

Greg and I both nodded, though he was the only one to speak. "I bet you knew exactly what to say to her."

"I did." Maisey fell to one of the dining room chairs without waiting to be invited. "It was the hardest thing I've ever done in my life, but I've had a lot of practice. I just had to pretend she was one of my clients. I'm always fighting with myself not to tell them what I really think—and believe me, some of them *desperately* need to hear it. But they don't call because they want the truth. They call because they need someone to listen."

"So that's what you did?" Nigel's brows were lifted in genuine interest. "You listened?"

She beamed like a golden retriever who'd just been praised for excellent showmanship. "Yep. I let her get it all out—apparently, they've been fighting over curfews—but that was only one piece of a much bigger problem. She's not making friends as quickly as she'd hoped. She's lonely, poor love. She misses her old life."

We all grew quiet. Loneliness was something that hit a little too close to home for everyone here.

"She's going to join a few clubs to see if that helps. I suggested volleyball and drama. She'll give them a two-week trial and call back to update me on her progress." She tapped the side of her nose and winked at Greg. "See? I can learn. Keep her on the hook. Give her an opening so she has no choice but to come back for more."

"Greg said that?" I demanded.

"I'm more than just a pretty face, Gramps."

I grunted to show what I thought of his new term of endearment, but I didn't argue the point. Instead, I did something that had needed to be done for a while now. If I was going to fight for Sloane, then I needed to fight for the rest of this group, too.

After all, they'd been fighting for me from the start.

I cleared my throat. "I'm sorry for what I said the other day, Maisey."

She grew perfectly still, her hand upraised like a statue about to pour water out of a pitcher. "For which part?"

"Yeah, Grandpa," Greg drawled. "There are an awful lot of potential apologies to choose from."

"There has been the need for at least a dozen in my hearing alone," Nigel agreed.

I might have reached a breakthrough in my personal life lately, but not so much that I was willing to take *this* much cheek. "You know very well which one I mean, so don't give me that. Any of you."

I'd have preferred to do this without an audience, but I'd been cruel to Maisey in front of one, so it was no more than I deserved. Justice always demanded payment in full, and as had been pointed out to me so many times as of late, I was falling behind on my bills.

"You're a good mom to that child," I said. "Better than she deserves, that's for sure."

Greg coughed in warning, so I swallowed and took a different tack. Even though I was right.

"I know you think I've been shut up in this house like a hermit all these years, but it's not true. You can't live on a street like this one and not see what's going on around you. I watched you bring that baby home. I saw the way you built lopsided snowmen together and heard you clang pots and pans *well* past midnight every New Year's. I drove by the day you took the training wheels off her bike, and I was even ready to call the ambulance when she crashed into that mailbox, which any fool could have seen she was about to do."

Maisey blanched white before going pink all over. "Arthur."

"Let me finish," I barked.

She made the motion of a zipper over her lips, but I could see it was costing her.

"Raising kids is tough. Raising kids when you're doing it on your own is even tougher." I could feel the weight of Greg's gaze and knew exactly what was going through his mind. I hadn't raised one scrap of the woman who'd become his mother. Anything good she turned out to be was due to Genie's influence and Genie's influence alone. "Believe me, if anyone knows what it looks like to fail, it's me. I drove my daughter out because I didn't love her enough. You drove yours out because you love her too much."

"Arthur," she said again, softer this time.

"There's not a doubt in my mind that she'll be the better for it in the end," I said, ignoring her. If I didn't, there was a good chance I'd never get this out. "She's testing her boundaries right now, and I know it hurts, but she'll be fine. More than anything, kids need to know they have a soft spot to land. Your Bella? She knows. She'll know it until the day she dies."

I should have known what was coming next. *Of course* Maisey was a woman who hugged, and who hugged with all the bodily strength God had given an elephant. I felt the air being crushed from my body, but it wasn't as if I could collapse. Not when I was literally being propped up.

"Thank you, Arthur," she said. "That means a lot coming from you."

And then, of all blessed events, she let me go. Oh, I could see her eyes getting all misty, and I knew she wanted to say more, but she seemed to sense that I'd reached my limit. I guess there was something to that *wise old soul* stuff of Sloane's, after all.

Maisey swept her wise, expert eyes around the room and

immediately changed the subject. "Wait. Are you guys having a secret book club meeting? Without me?"

Since I could hardly kick the woman to the curb after we'd shared what could only be called *a moment*, I gestured for her to join us.

"Not exactly," Greg said. "It's a…project for Grandpa."

"A project?" Maisey's eyes fairly goggled from her head. "Like arts and crafts time? I don't believe you."

Nigel chuckled and showed her the copy of *Anne of Green Gables*. "It's true. We're finding quotes in the book that capture everything inside Arthur's heart."

She blinked. "Well, that's easy. I already know that one." She took the book and flipped through the pages, her shiny silver fingernail running over the lines until she found what she was looking for. "'I can't cheer up—I don't *want* to cheer up. It's nicer to be miserable!'"

I did my valiant best not to smile, but my valiant best was no match for the laughter that resounded throughout that room. From the way they all carried on, you'd think I'd never been the butt of a joke before.

"Fine," I grumbled, feeling my ears grow hot. They'd always done that, though I thought I'd outgrown the need for blushing decades ago. "You can have that one, but this is serious. We're doing this for Sloane. I imagine you know that fiancé of hers is planning to take her across the country after their wedding?"

Maisey grew so instantly somber that I knew she'd already heard—and that she felt the same way I did about it. "Yeah. She told me."

"Well?" I demanded.

"Well, what? I already tried reading her palm. You saw how well that worked." She smiled at me in such a sad, knowing way that I had no choice but to take the hand she offered me. Her fingers squeezed mine. "We might just have to let her go, Arthur. If that's the life she wants for herself, then it's not really our business, no matter how much we want it to be."

"I know," I said. "But there's one thing I want—no, need—to do first. And I'd like you to help."

Maisey's surprise at hearing the plan I outlined was secondary only to her outrage that I hadn't included her from the start. "I love her just as much as you do, you miserable old goat. Why shouldn't I be allowed to help?"

"Does that mean you're in?" Greg asked eagerly.

"Yes, but only on one condition."

"Fine." I heaved a sigh and reached for the phone. "I'll order a pizza, but only if you let me have anchovies on it this time."

She took the phone from me before I could dial a single number. "I wasn't talking about a pizza. If we want to do this thing right, what we need is Mateo."

———

As soon as Mateo joined in, the party gathered around my dining room table became, well, a party.

The last party this house had seen was a feeble attempt at a birthday celebration for Hannah when she'd turned thirteen. When Genie had been alive, birthdays under this roof were always a big deal, weeklong galas full of sugary treats and staying up well past bedtime, two things I never condoned under any other conditions. But Genie and Hannah had worn me down—they always could back in those days, when my voice was just one among three, my natural severity offset by everything good and joyful they had to offer.

The store-bought cake and stack of VHS videos I'd rented to emulate the experience hadn't gone over well. Not enough time had passed since Genie's death, our wounds still seeping and raw. It would have been better to make no effort at all than to draw the focus on the stark differences that had bisected our lives.

It was exactly as Greg had said. There was the before…and then there was the after. The light and then the darkness. The mother and then the none.

"Okay, so we've got the kindred spirits covered, and that bit about laughter making life worth living," Mateo said, his hands turning the pages of the book faster than the rest of us could keep up. For a man who claimed to have never read the book before, he seemed to have made considerable progress over the past week. "I also like this one here. 'She makes me love her and I like people who make me love them. It saves me so much trouble in making myself love them.'"

"That's a good one, but…" Maisey wrinkled her nose as she examined the pages. "At this rate, we're pretty much highlighting the whole book. Doesn't that defeat the purpose?"

Mateo snorted. "Maisey, she's been wearing a replica of that hideous amethyst brooch every single day. She won't mind. I'm pretty sure she's a fan."

Greg glanced up from the appetizers he was arranging on a platter. He was no Maisey when it came to the kitchen, but he'd insisted on doing it himself. Since no one would take his money, he felt it was the least he could do.

"It was her sister's," he said gently. "That's why she wears it."

"Wait. What?" Mateo twisted to stare up at Greg. "What are you talking about? Sloane doesn't have a sister. I've known her for years, and she's never once mentioned one to me. It's not possible."

Not only was it possible, but it made perfect sense. I could have cursed myself for not realizing it sooner. In fact, I *did* curse myself for it, though I kept the outburst quiet for once. I remembered her mentioning a sister to me one time—the Elinor to her Marianne—and I also remembered the reply I'd made in response to this. It had been caustic and unfeeling, just as *all* my responses to her were.

"She died when they were kids," Greg said, thus confirming me as the worst kind of man. "I think they used to read *Anne of Green Gables* together. That's why she wanted to pick it for our next book club. It's probably the last chance she'll have before she leaves."

Greg didn't elaborate beyond that, but we could all sense the shift in the air. Even Nigel, who'd only met Sloane once, seemed to know that this thing we were doing wasn't just about begging our friend to stay. Although I might not have known until this exact moment what had happened in that girl's past to close her off to everything except books, I'd understood it all along.

Oh, how I understood it.

This world was a terrible place. It gave you people to love and then took them away before you stopped loving them. It made you mean and angry and cruel to those who needed you most. It ground you down until it was all you could do to get through the day.

But most of all, it tried to convince you that you were alone in your suffering.

Everyone in this room had fallen for that lie, but I wasn't having it anymore. Not one goddamn second longer.

"Mateo!" I barked. "Come with me. Now."

"Geez, old man, you just about gave me a heart attack," he said, but he got up and followed me into the hallway. I could feel everyone watching us go and didn't doubt for a second that they'd rush forward and eavesdrop as soon as the coast was clear. "I'm sorry I didn't know about Sloane's sister, if that's what you want to yell at me about. She's not exactly a Chatty Cathy when it comes to her personal life."

"This has nothing to do with Sloane. This has to do with the things I said to you the other day."

His eyes lit up, a look of unholy glee on his face. "Is it my turn for an apology? Like the one you gave Maisey? Because Greg told me about it, and I have some ideas—"

I held up a hand, something warm bubbling up in the pit of my stomach. The sensation wasn't, as it had been for the past three decades, the hot burn of an anger that had no outlet. Unless I was very much mistaken, it was laughter.

"God save me from a pack of irreverent millennials," I muttered before launching into what I had to say. "Yes, it's your turn, and no, your apology isn't like the one I gave Maisey."

"That's not fair. You were just as mean to me as you were to her. I deserve one that's equally grovelly."

"Well, too bad." I reached into my pocket and pulled out the application from the home health services company. "Yours is coming in the form of a gift. I picked that up for you. They're looking for nurses."

He took the paper and scanned it, his face falling comically with every line. "You're apologizing to me with a *job application*?" He tried shoving it back at me. "Yeah…no. Apology not accepted."

"For the love of Pete, just take it! Fill it out, don't fill it out. Find a new job, don't find a new job. Leave that boyfriend of yours, don't leave him. I don't care."

At the mention of his boyfriend, all his irreverence fled. "What does Lincoln have to do with anything?"

"How should I know?" I asked. "Your personal life doesn't interest me in the slightest. What *does* interest me is that you're the best performer I've seen in a long time. Possibly ever. I'm not ready to pass a final verdict."

"Um. Then why did you give me a nursing application?"

"Because you're a perfectly adequate nurse, and because the lady at the agency said they offer flexible hours. Do I have to do *everything* for you?"

"Arthur, this isn't how apologies work. Are you sure you don't want to start over?"

I pinched the bridge of my nose and called on all the power of Genie's benevolent influence over me. I could it feel it strengthening with each day Greg stayed under this roof.

"Your problem—other than a tendency to levity—is that you refuse to let anything that's good in your life become *great*," I said. "And don't give me that look of outrage. You're not fooling anyone. The other day, I said your problem is that you're afraid of failure, and even though I could have phrased it better, I wasn't wrong. You *are* afraid of it. Or rather, you're afraid of what happens if you don't fail. You're afraid of success."

"Arthur," he said again, slower this time. "Is that a compliment?"

"Of course it's a compliment." I could see that I was going to have to spell it out for him. "You've spent your whole adult life—and I'm guessing a hefty chunk of your youth—doing everything you can to separate yourself from your mother. The thing I can't figure out is *why*. Althea Sharpe is a fantastic lounge singer, there's no doubt about that. But if you think that's the greatest accomplishment in her life, then you're as muttonheaded as you pretend to be. Anyone with eyes in his head can see how proud she is of you when she pulls you up onto that stage. Not because you're a great double act—even though you are—but because she's happy to have you there next to her. From the look of things, that boyfriend of yours feels that way, too."

He stood gawping at me like a landed fish.

"For God's sake, Mateo. Stop hiding and let people love you. Take it from a man who learned that the hard way—life's a hell of a lot better when you do."

I felt slightly winded after a speech that went on for much longer than I'd intended, but I was starting to see a ray of hope. At least he'd stopped gawping.

"Does this mean you'll take it?" I asked.

"Take what?" Mateo glanced down at the slip of paper in his hand. "Oh. You mean your so-called gift?"

I nodded. I hadn't been lying before—I really didn't care whether or not Mateo became a lounge singer like his mother—but he needed to at least give himself permission to try. He glanced back and forth between the application and me for much longer than the situation warranted—so long, in fact, that *I* was the one who started to feel a little lost.

"You want me to take this because you think I'm a perfectly adequate nurse?" he asked.

Had he not heard a word I just said? "I want you to take it because you should give yourself options."

"Because I'm adequate at this nursing thing?" he persisted. "You're satisfied with my level of care?"

Honestly, the younger generation's need for external validation was going to be their undoing. "Yes, Mateo, because I'm satisfied with your level of care. There. I said it. Does that make you happy, or do you want me to put it in writing?"

"I don't need it in writing." He hesitated. "I just needed to hear that you respect my medical opinion before I say this next part."

I was starting to feel uncomfortable at the direction this conversation was taking. "Why? Are you about to tell me that you've been lying all this time and I'm about to die? Because if that's the case, you can keep it to yourself. I have no intention of popping off that easily. Not when I'm just starting to—"

I cut myself off before I could finish, though my meaning was obvious. *When I'm just starting to get to know Greg. When I'm just starting to take an interest in life again.* Not only was it unnecessary to say these aloud, but something about Mateo's sympathetic flicker made me think that what he was about to say had nothing to do with me.

"I have no confirmation of this, and I wouldn't say it if you hadn't…" He took a deep breath, his eyes growing watery again. "If you hadn't said those nice things about letting myself be loved. But you're right. I *do* need to stop hiding from the things that matter. And I'm not the only one."

"Don't—" I pleaded, but it was too late. Already, his words were starting to reach me as if from the end of a long tunnel.

If I'd had the capacity to run away, I'd have done it in a heartbeat. I wanted to throw my hands over my ears, dig my head in the sand, turn the proverbial blind eye. But I'd given Mateo the truth without any varnish, and he was determined to take his revenge.

"Unless I'm very much mistaken, your friend Nigel isn't doing well."

"What are you talking about?" I croaked. "He's fine."

Mateo shook his head, his expression so somber it was like looking in a mirror. "I don't think he came all this way to chat about books and rile you up about the past, Arthur. I think he's here to say goodbye."

A soft cough sounded from behind me, and that was when I knew I was in real trouble. Not because Nigel was a nosy, eavesdropping bastard, but because he didn't offer a word in protest. He *always* had words in protest. It was his stock in trade.

"That's not how I'd have broken the news, but it'll have to do. He was always going to find out one way or another."

"Nigel." With a struggle, I lifted my gaze to his. I saw it then, the hand of death pressing his shoulder, the resignation in a pair of eyes that had once looked on me with kindness and—yes—even friendship. "Tell him it isn't true. Tell him you're only here to make my life miserable."

"It's very much the truth," he said with a sad smile. "But if you still want me to make your life miserable, all you have to do is say the word. I'm amenable if you are."

I didn't say the word—not that word or any other. I *wanted* to, but I couldn't. As my head spun and my knees started to give way, I once again felt the world close in around me.

And this time, Lord help me, I let it.

SLOANE

33

"YOU'RE GOING TO LOVE THE PLACE I found for us in Cambridge."
Brett turned the screen of his laptop to face me. "Look. It has
built-in bookcases on either side of the fireplace. One for your stuff,
and one for mine. According to this website, it's only a few blocks from
the place where Henry Wadsworth Longfellow used to live."

I glanced up from where I sat quietly scrolling through my own
laptop. Like Brett, I was researching places to land in the Boston
area—only instead of homes, I was looking at libraries. Twenty-four
separate branches, and that wasn't even including the collegiate ones.
There were so many employment openings that I got dizzy just looking
at them all.

"You researching fireside poets for me?" I asked, oddly touched.

He ignored this and cast a sweeping look around my apartment.
We rarely spent time here together, since he vastly preferred his own
clean, uncluttered condo downtown, but my place was closer to
Arthur's. I needed the quick access.

"You'll have to seriously pare down your books before we start
boxing things up, though," Brett said. "Or better yet—I'll buy you an
e-reader. If we start converting everything to digital now, we might be
able to just toss the whole collection out."

I wrinkled my nose. "You want to throw all my books away?"

He laughed in a way that felt like a personal attack. "We can donate them to the library if that makes you feel better. Or we can have my sisters come in and do it. Didn't you say you had to sneak some of Arthur McLachlan's books out when he wasn't looking or he'd have never parted with them? Just think of me as your own personal librarian."

"That's different," I protested, but I don't think he heard me. His attention was already back on his computer.

"Actually, if we go fully digital, we might even be able to skip the bookcase apartment and get this one with a river view. It's really nice. I'm going to email the guy and see if it's still available."

He started typing happily away, so intent on his task that he almost—*almost*—forgot I was there. Right before he pushed Send, he remembered to glance up and smile at me. "You don't mind, do you? This one's a lot closer to my work. We could sell your car and just take the Tesla."

What else could I say? He was so boyish and full of plans, fully in his element as he clicked all the pieces of our future into place.

"That sounds—"

My phone buzzed before I could finish what I was going to say. I glanced down at the screen to find that it was from an unknown number. "Hello?"

"Yes, hello." The voice on the other end was terse but professional. "Is this Sloane Parker?"

"Um. Yes. Can I help you with something?"

"I'm calling from Kootenai Health. You're listed as the emergency contact for a man named Arthur McLachlan."

My heart jumped to my throat, and I almost dropped the phone in my haste to keep it in my slick-palmed grip. "I am? What's wrong? When did he put me on his form? What does he need?"

Instead of being confused by my jumbled questions, the woman only clucked a soothing sound. "I just wanted to let you know that he's stable for now."

"For *now*?" I echoed. I glanced up to find Brett watching me with his finger still hovering over the keypad. "What's the matter with him?"

"I'm not authorized to provide any details over the phone. Just that he's been admitted and is currently accepting treatment."

She hung up before I could ask any more questions. Not that it mattered. I was already halfway to the door, my whole body shaking with the sudden pulse of adrenaline. I'd have made it all the way out, only I was stopped by a pair of hands clamping down on both shoulders.

"Calm down, Sloane. Breathe." Brett's low voice started working immediately to subdue the pounding of my heart. "What's going on?"

"It's Arthur," I said. "He's at the hospital. I have to go."

Instead of releasing me and whisking immediately to Arthur's rescue, Brett started leading me to the couch. *Away* from the door.

"What are you doing?" I shook him off with a force I'd never used before. "Did you hear a word I just said? Something's wrong. He had me listed as his emergency contact. Why would he do that unless he was desperate?"

"I'm sure it's just an administrative error," Brett soothed. He still held his hands up in midair, as if unsure where they should go now that I'd thrown them off. "Did he ask for you specifically?"

"No, but—"

"Don't forget that he has Greg to look after him now—not to mention Mateo as his private nurse. He's going to have to learn to make do without you eventually. He might as well start now."

"Yes, but—"

"If he's in the hospital, that means someone either drove him in or called an ambulance. Someone is probably already there with him. There's no need to get hysterical." Brett's voice didn't waver, not even when I groaned with frustration at the sound of that word—*hysterical.* I'd always hated it. "Let's sit down and talk about this before we go rushing over."

"There's nothing to talk about," I said. "He's my friend and he's hurt. I'm going."

Brett blinked. I thought I'd been speaking moderately, but I guess I might have yelled a little of that last part.

"Sloane?" he said, looking puzzled. I didn't know why but that slight furrowing of his brow, that pucker that seemed so surprised by my reaction snapped what was left of my restraint.

"I wasn't asking for your permission, Brett. I was informing you of my intentions." I was pretty sure I was yelling again, but I couldn't seem to stop myself. I wondered if this was what had happened to my parents, a sloughing off of all restraint, a determination to say what needed to be said no matter what the cost. Maybe, after a while, you just got used to it.

Maybe, after a while, you started to like being heard.

"You're more than welcome to come with me if you want, but this is happening. When your friend is in the hospital, you go. When the people you care about are hurting, you take care of them. You don't stand by the side of the river waiting to make sure they're drowning before you jump in."

I started heading for the door again. This time, Brett didn't try to stop me. He was too busy staring at me with a look I'd never seen him wear before. It was as if a curtain had fallen away between us, and he was seeing me—really seeing me—for the first time.

"Sure thing, Sloane," he said, his voice sounding as if from far away. "If it's what you want, we'll head over right now. But we're taking my car. You're in no state to drive."

34

HOSPITALS WERE ONE OF THE WORST places in the world.

As soon as Brett pulled up in front of the squat, white building surrounded by strip malls and retail outlets, I could feel myself starting to sink. Mind and body and most of all soul started to quaver at the sight of it.

Another one of literature's great lies was that the dangers of quicksand were something I needed to look out for. Sherlock Holmes had warned me not to traverse the Grimpen Mire without a sidekick to pull me to safety; Nancy Drew had taught me to look out for them in the forests of Blackwood Hall. In this moment, I could only wish for such a fate. When it came to getting sucked in and trapped, hospitals seemed a much more likely place to fall.

"Are you sure about this, Sloane?" Brett asked as we sat out in front of the main hospital entrance, his Tesla idling like the sleek, silent mass it was.

"I'm sure." Since I didn't make a motion to exit the car, my words didn't carry much weight. The whole drive over, I'd been willing Brett to go faster, take more risks, do *something* to take the edge off my worry. Now that I was here, however, the old familiar doubts were starting to creep in. "I know Arthur probably doesn't want me here, but I didn't let that stop me from barging in on him before. I can't very well abandon him now. You know how he feels about hospitals.

I keep expecting to see him running out that door with an IV drip dangling from his arm."

Brett didn't laugh at my attempt at a joke, but that was no surprise. What *was* a surprise was the way he turned to me and took both my hands in his. His thumb grazed the top of my enormous engagement ring. It was too big and grand for a hand like mine, but so was he.

"No, my love," he said, his voice as serious as it ever was. "Are you sure about *this*?"

With a start, I tried to yank my grip away, but a chiropractor's hands were necessarily strong. They could probably pull me from quicksand in a pinch, so they could certainly hold onto me in my sudden, weightless fright.

"What are you talking about?" I demanded in a tone that sounded a lot like more like an irascible Arthur McLachlan than the quiet and temperate woman Brett was accustomed to.

"You know what I'm talking about," he replied, still somber, still grave, still so *kind* that I thought my heart might break. Ever since I'd run out of that dinner at his family's house, fleeing his generous affection and my realization that I could never live up to it, my heart had been on this cusp.

The words he'd spoken to me that night haunted me the way the ghosts of my past never could: *You know how I feel about you.*

You know. You know.

It was true. I did know. I also knew that to accept the gift he was offering me was unforgivable. Not when I couldn't repay it, not when the only thing I had to give in return was half of the life he'd been promised. That half of a life wasn't fair to anyone, least of all someone I cared about as much as I cared about Brett. I understood that now. There was more than one way to break a heart.

And there was more than one way to heal it.

My hands went limp in his, and I used his suddenly slack grip to make my escape. That was a trick Greg had taught me and Maisey—part of an impromptu course on self-defense we'd demanded after he and Mateo made that big show of learning how to physically subdue a man. In all my wildest imaginings, I never thought a book club could transform willy-nilly into a fight club...or that I'd happily participate in the exchange.

Then again, there was a lot about this particular book club that I hadn't been expecting. Including a conversation like *this*.

"I know I'm not a very exciting companion," Brett said as he tucked his hands in his lap, his gaze fixed on the glittering extravagance of my ring. "No, don't say anything, Sloane, please. I'm not an idiot. I've seen what's been happening to you these past few months."

"What do you mean?" I asked. "I wasn't aware that I was any different with you."

A soft, wry smile touched his lips. "You aren't. That's the whole point. When you're with me, you're the same Sloane Parker I first fell in love with. Quiet and reserved. Uncertain of herself. Predictable."

None of those were particularly complimentary, but I wasn't about to take offense. I was all those things with him because that was how I *wanted* to be with him. Since the moment we'd met, I'd balanced myself on a tightrope and done everything in my power to keep from falling.

"You think I'm predictable?" I asked.

"No," he said. He lifted a finger to my cheek but didn't make contact. He hovered on the brink. More electricity passed through that non-touch than I could remember ever feeling in the rest of our relationship combined. "I think you *used* to be. Do you know my favorite thing about you?"

He shook his head before I could answer. "Never mind. Of course you don't. It's that whenever I walk into a room with you in it, I know exactly what I can expect. Everything in the world moves fast except for you. I don't want to use the word 'quaint' but…" He rolled his shoulder in an apologetic shrug. "It's the truth. I liked that about you. I *loved* it. You were the one thing I knew would stay the same no matter what chaos was happening around you."

The moment of electricity passed, leaving me alone in the car with nothing but the sensation I'd imagined the whole thing.

"Only you didn't, did you?" Brett said. "You changed. With Arthur. *For* Arthur."

I cast a quick, nervous glance up at the hospital, as if the mere seriousness of our conversation gave it legs to stand on and scale those walls. But that was fanciful, of course, and Brett hated fanciful things.

"Not me," I said, unaware until the words left my lips that I was speaking aloud. "I *like* fanciful things."

"Do you?" he asked, again with that wry smile. "I didn't know that. I'm beginning to think I don't know a lot of things about you."

My throat hurt from holding back the things I wanted to say to this man—not just in the moment, but in the many years leading up to it.

"If you go up there, he's going to yell at you and threaten to throw his bedpan, isn't he?" Brett asked.

"We're doing better with the threats of violence lately, but, yeah. Probably."

"And you want that, don't you? You'll yell back until you have him twisted around your little finger, and then you'll talk about books for hours and…what, exactly?"

"I don't know," I said. Such a vague answer wasn't fair to Brett, who was being open with me for what was probably the first time in our entire relationship, but it was the truth. I *didn't* know what was going to happen when I was with Arthur. Sometimes, I got to be exactly as soft as Brett liked, sitting for hours in one position without doing much of anything at all. Other times, we argued about classification systems or ate Maisey's reheated leftovers. There was always a chance that someone would pop by or that Arthur would need to be talked into doing something he was nonsensically against. And always, always, there were books.

It was the same thing I loved about working at the library. On the outside, it was a place of whispers and stillness. But inside—oh, what marvelous depths there were to explore.

"He reminds me a lot of my sister," I said. Brett knew only the bare bones of my past but he seemed to sense the importance of what I was about to say. "I know that seems weird considering he's a retired professor in his seventies and my sister died when she was twelve, but it's the only way I can explain it. Our life together—mine and Emily's—was a small one. It had to be. We never did anything exciting or grand, never went anywhere farther than a few blocks from home. In fact, we spent most of our time snuggled up inside a blanket fort. But I was more alive in the eight years I spent with her than in all my years since."

Brett was silent for a moment. "Because you loved her."

My eyes flooded with sharp, sudden tears. "Yes."

"And you love Arthur, too."

I nodded, not trusting myself to speak enough to say that one little syllable. I was afraid that if I punctured the thickness in my throat, everything that was bottled up inside me would come pouring out.

"But you don't love me."

"Brett," I gasped. "I'm sorry. I'm so sorry."

His hands clasped mine, a warm pocket closing over my fists as I sobbed all over him. I had no way of knowing what I was crying for—for his sake or for mine, for the little girl who was only just starting to realize what she'd lost—but it didn't matter. As he let the tears pour and my incoherent sobs wash over him, he gently tugged the ring from my finger. The moment I felt it slip off, it was as though a huge weight had been lifted from my shoulders and I could suddenly stand on my own two feet again.

"I think you'd better get up there," he said with a smile. For all that I was a sobbing, heaving mess, he looked remarkably in control of himself. "If only to relieve the poor nurses for a few hours. Take it from me—they work harder than anyone else in the medical field. They'll appreciate the intervention."

"But what are you going to do?" I asked as I pulled out my handkerchief and blew liberally into it. Maisey had picked the embroidered flower out of the corner, but the holes where the needle had gone through would always carry its shape. "About your family, I mean? And Boston and the wedding and—"

"I'll take care of it, Sloane. I might not be able to make you happy, but that much I can do." When he touched a finger to my cheek this time, he made full contact. He traced away the path of the tear and stared at the pad of his thumb, as if surprised to find it had come away wet. "And as for the rest, well…there isn't much, is there? I imagine you'll slip out of my life as easily as you slipped into it."

It was true. Other than a toothbrush and a few hair scrunchies, I kept very few of my belongings at his condo. I'd never wanted to intrude on a place—on a life—that had never really felt like mine to begin with.

I slid out of the car before Brett could say any more nice things to me. My heart and my newly unshackled shoulders wouldn't bear it. I had no doubt that he'd have sat there with me for hours if I asked him to, soothing me with his bland, no-nonsense approach until I could face my future with clear eyes and a clearer heart, but that was why I couldn't accept it. The smooth, unbroken path wasn't the one I wanted to tread anymore.

With a resolute breath, I turned my step in the opposite direction and headed into the hospital. In there, I'd find anger and passion, irritability and wrath. In there, I'd find my friend.

In there, I'd find myself again.

35

―

I COULD SENSE TROUBLE THE MOMENT I tiptoed up to the door of Room 418. None of the nurses had been able to tell me the exact nature of Arthur's illness, but I knew that he'd been admitted under observation for the next twenty-four hours. That was much longer than his last stint at the hospital had lasted, and I had no doubt he was taking it just as hard.

Which was why the unprecedented silence behind that door scared me.

"You can go on in, hon." A friendly nurse popped her head out of the nurses' station and waved for me to enter. "The rest of your party is already there. I'm sure they won't mind."

"My party?" I echoed, my hand flat against the wood-grain door. I couldn't hear anything, but vibrations seemed to indicate that *something* was going on in there.

"I've had to tell them to keep it down three times already. They say laughter is the best medicine, but this is still a hospital." She winked. "You look like you might be able to keep them in check."

Since inanely repeating everything she said wasn't going to get me any closer to answers, I gave the door a push. The scene that revealed itself on the other side wasn't, as I'd expected, Arthur in the middle of crafting a rope ladder. It was Arthur cackling on his bed as the entire book club sat around him, all of them holding copies of *Anne of Green Gables* in an animated discussion of its contents.

As terrible as it was to admit it, the shock of seeing them so happily occupied without me hurt more than the break of my engagement to one of the best men I'd ever known.

"Sloane?" Greg was the first to notice me. He jumped to his feet so quickly that his copy of the book slid to the floor. "What are you doing here?"

"Oh no," Maisey wailed. "She wasn't supposed to find out."

Mateo tipped his head back with a groan. "Ugh. Sloane, you're the worst. Aren't you supposed to be apartment shopping with Brett or something?"

Even Nigel, a man Arthur professed to hate, had been invited. He was gently folded in a chair near one corner. At the sight of me, he raised his eyebrows in mild surprise. "Oh dear. This isn't good. This isn't good at all."

I had strong words for each and every one of them, but it was Arthur I turned to, Arthur who was on the receiving end of my sudden, overwhelming wash of emotion. After everything we'd been through, all the breakthroughs we made together, this was how it ended? With me kicked out of my own book club, cut out as easily as Octavia had removed me from the library?

"Arthur, how could you?" I cried in a voice that I felt sure the nurse outside would be sure to admonish. "When I heard you were in the hospital again, I dropped everything to get here. And I mean *everything*."

"Now, Sloane—" he began, but I cut him off.

"I was determined that you wouldn't be alone this time around. Even if I had to use all my powers of coercion, I was going to sit here by your side until you were discharged. Because that's what friends do. They come running. They *care*." I glanced around at the shocked faces of my so-called friends and started to sag. "But you don't need me, do you? You called everyone to your bedside except me."

Greg had one large hand wrapped around my waist and was leading me to a chair before I'd finished. "Sloane, I think you should sit down. This isn't—"

"My business?" I asked, shaking myself out of his grip. I wasn't about to sit down for this. "My concern?"

"I know how it looks, but it isn't a regular book club meeting. We're working on a special project."

That was even worse. I liked special projects. I *loved* them. And if anyone in this room had cared about me even a little bit, they'd have known that

"I can't believe you'd do this to me after everything we've been through. You know how much I enjoy our book club. I love how little we get done every single meeting, and how mad Maisey gets if there's a movie version and we don't tell her. I love that we can get Mateo to read things against his will, even though he secretly enjoys every minute. I love that Greg spends most of the time fixing things around the house instead of participating in the discussion."

That word—*love*—came tripping off my tongue with an ease I'd never known before. For twenty years, I'd fought against every part of my nature to suppress it. Now that it was back, it was making up for lost time.

And so, it seemed, was I.

"Most of all, I love that you opened up enough to let your personal nemesis into the club—not because you wanted to, but because books are the most important thing to you. Nothing can stand in the way of that. You wouldn't deny a man a book any more than you'd deny him water. It's the one soft spot you've never been able to hide, the one place where all your feelings are allowed to thrive." I was getting worked up now, my voice rising to a pitch I didn't recognize, but I couldn't stop.

The floodgates had opened, and I was no longer in command of the tide. "I've seen the books around your house, Arthur. All of them. I know what they mean. I know what they're trying to say."

"And what's that?" he asked with infuriating coolness. This man practically *breathed* fire; for him to display reserve the one time I had something real to say to him was almost too much. "What do the books say?"

"What's in your heart. The things that your wife made you feel—the things she *still* makes you feel, even after all these years. You pretend to be angry and bored with life, but you're as full of wonder and joy as the rest of us. And don't you dare try to deny it, because I'll drag every book from your house into this hospital room to prove it. You love this world, and you love the people in it. I know you do."

Instead of looking guilty, Arthur smiled up at me. It was a soft, gentle smile that I'd never seen him wear before. Considering how may monitors he was hooked up to right now, I couldn't imagine the cause.

Until he spoke.

"*There* she is," he murmured. "I knew you had a big and bright life burning somewhere inside you."

Burning or not, all the fight fled out of me. I felt hollowed out as I finally allowed Greg to lead me to a chair. He lowered me onto it with so much tenderness—and with a smile so much like the one Arthur was currently wearing—that the last of my defenses were stripped away.

"I don't understand," I said with a bewildered look around me. "If this isn't a book club mutiny, what is it?"

"A book club intervention," Mateo said with a laugh. "But yours sounds much cooler."

Greg placed himself at my back, his presence so warm I could feel it pulsing through the frame of the chair. "I think you should give it to her, Grandpa."

"But we aren't done yet," Maisey protested.

"It doesn't matter," Arthur said as he lifted the book on his lap and extended it toward me. "This will have to be enough. And if it isn't...well. After an outburst like that, I think she's going to be okay no matter what."

The hand Arthur held out was hooked up to an IV, his veins a protuberant network on his skin. Even with all those needles and tape, his hand didn't waver.

"Go on," he urged. "This is from us—from *all* of us."

My own hand wavered plenty as I took the book and flipped the cover. It was a gorgeous copy of *Anne of Green Gables*, hardbound and embossed, the first page holding nothing but my name in one corner like a new family Bible waiting for the generational splendor to come.

"This is really nice, but—" I cut myself off as soon as I flipped the pages. The first two looked ordinary enough, but a stark yellow highlight stood out on the third. Since everyone in the room seemed to be holding their breath waiting for me, I read it aloud. "'Friendship existed and always had existed between Marilla Cuthbert and Mrs. Rachel, in spite of—or perhaps because of—their dissimilarity.'"

I glanced sharply up at Arthur, but he only smiled and nodded for me to continue. The highlights in this book occurred at a much more rapid pace than the other books in his collection, and in a variety of colors that seemed to indicate more than one reader.

"The pink ones are mine," Maisey said, confirming it.

Mateo nodded. "I got green, but only because the other colors were taken."

"Grandpa is yellow," Greg added, "and I'm blue."

Even Nigel felt compelled to add to this. "I'm orange, but as we're only just starting to get to know each other, there aren't as many as I'd like. I hope that's all right."

My head swam as I scoured the pages, the colors and the words blurring together so much that it felt like wading through a neon rainbow.

Every highlighted passage spoke of friendship and affection, of hope and optimism. Alone, they were happy little sound bites that were pleasing to the eye. Stitched together, they became something else entirely.

They became a love letter of words and sentiment—and one that was addressed entirely to me.

"You guys did this?" I blinked back tears as I searched their faces for some sign of sarcasm, but there was none to be found. Everywhere I looked was honesty and love. Love most of all. "For me?"

"It was Arthur's idea," Maisey said as she pulled me to my feet. She put her arms around me and hugged me so tightly that I felt my bones might crack. It was the hug of a mother and a friend, and I felt like I could rest there for hours. "He wanted to make sure you knew how he felt before you took off and left us. And we do feel that way—all of us. Since the moment you showed up in front of my house in your little car and stakeout hat, my life has become everything I've dreamed of. My relationship with Bella is on its way to being mended, I've never had so many appreciative mouths to feed, and I can't wait to read whatever book we pick out next. Thank you for giving me that."

She let me go so abruptly that I thought I might cry out, but Mateo was right there to take her place.

"Lincoln gave me strict instructions to add his words to mine, so I'm speaking for both of us when I say that we're going to miss the crap out of you. The library hasn't been the same since you left, so it's probably for the best that I'm leaving."

"Wait. You are? What will you do?"

"Officially? Part-time nursing for Arthur's staffing company. Unofficially?" He grinned almost shyly at me. "My mom and I are staging a show together—just a small one. To see how we like it. I'm wearing a fedora. It was Arthur's idea."

"The devil it was. No man under the age of sixty should wear a fedora."

Mateo smiled. "You can't take it back now, old man. I already booked you a table in the front." He winked at me before pulling away. "Octavia is at her wit's end. If you want your job back, now's a good time to put in for it. She'd probably dedicate an entire wing to you at this point. Or at the very least give you complete control over the two vans she just bought at a sweet discount."

"No way," I breathed. "She actually bought them?"

"Yep. She said something about how great it would be to hand them over to a capable librarian, if only she knew where to find one. Someone who could pick what books to stock and which communities to reach out to, someone who knows this town and its reading habits like the back of her hand..."

There was no mistaking his meaning—or how badly I wanted to pick up the phone and call Octavia. Just when I felt as though the room was starting to spin in circles around me, Greg stepped up. He didn't hug me, but the quirk of that now-familiar smile made me feel just as comforted as a physical embrace. In fact, when he accompanied it with a slow, careful crinkle around his eyes, prickles stood up on the back of my neck.

"I know it took me a while to warm up to you, but I mean it when I say our house isn't going to be the same without you."

"Our house?" I echoed. "You mean—"

He nodded with a shy duck of his head. "Grandpa asked me to move in for a while. My boss is willing to let me try remote work for a while, and with Grandpa's health the way it is—"

"I'm fine," Arthur said. "It was a palpitation, that's all."

Mateo snorted. "Oh, sure. *Now* it's a palpitation."

"You heard what the doctor said. It was the shock that got me. Twenty-four hours, a few IV fluids, and I'll be as good as new." Arthur huffed but with a smile that robbed it of any malice. "The truth is, I *need* Greg at the house—not to look after me, but because I have a lot of apologizing left to do. Unfortunately, it's going to take more than a few speeches or highlights in a book to start repairing the wrongs I did his mother. He is being gracious enough to stick around long enough for me to try."

Greg's signature tinge of red crept up to his ears. "I think it'll be nice for us both to have some company right now."

"Wait. That's it?" The book was starting to feel heavy in my hand. All these beautiful speeches, all these beautiful goodbyes—and that was the end of it? Everyone got their happily ever after except me?

"Not quite." Nigel drew forward with a smile that looked as sad as I felt. "The thing they haven't said—the thing I think they're all too scared to put into words—is that they'd really like it if you stayed here with them."

"Dammit, Nigel. We were getting to that part."

"Too slow and too late, as usual," he said, tossing a challenging look over his shoulder. "Do you know what happened when Genie opened that copy of *Anne of Green Gables* you sent her all those years ago?"

"Of course I know what happened. She packed everything up and left you. She came home to me where she belonged."

Nigel winked at me before turning to face his friend—for friend I felt sure he was. "Not quite. The truth is, she looked as shell-shocked as this poor creature right here. Lost and on the brink of tears, unsure how to meet you halfway."

When Arthur could do nothing more than goggle angrily at him, Nigel laughed outright. "You fool. Who do you think bought her that plane ticket home? Who do you think packed up her things and explained to her what a lovesick idiot you were?"

"Nigel!" The monitors attached to Arthur started an erratic cacophony of beats. "You didn't. She came home to me because she saw those quotes. She understood how I felt about her and forgave me for failing to speak up earlier."

"Well, yes," he admitted, chuckling softly to himself. "But I think she was afraid of hurting my feelings. Of the three of us, she always did have the best heart."

Arthur groaned and sank back on his pillow. "You can't torment a man in a hospital bed, Nigel. It's not sportsmanlike."

Nigel sighed with mock heaviness. "I know. That's why I'm about to make it up to you." He turned to me with a look that promised mischief and hope and so much more to come. "Stay, Sloane. Don't marry the man that none of these people seem to like. Take it from one who picked the path of success and lived long enough to regret it. You'll never find anything better than what—or who—is in this room right now. That's the one thing I can guarantee."

"I know," I said as I flashed my empty left hand. "That's why I broke it off with Brett before I came up here."

No sooner had my meaning settled than the entire book club cried out in shouts of incredulity and delight—delight so powerful it shook me, delight so full I felt as if I might burst. I hoped the news of it would never reach Brett's ears. He didn't deserve their antipathy, but in that moment, with the nurse determinedly shooing us from the room, I finally felt I deserved their joy.

"That's enough out of you lot," the nurse said as she ushered us down the hall and away from the rooms where the business of life and death was carrying on without us. "I'm happy to hear you all so excited, but you can go be excited somewhere people aren't trying to sleep."

Mateo and Maisey took this admonishment in good form, but I dug my heels in before they could drag me down the hallway with them.

"Shouldn't we pull Nigel out of there with us?" I asked with a nervous glance behind me. Something about the scene we'd just walked out of didn't sit right, like an alternate ending we were never meant to see. "We can't leave him alone in there with Arthur. He'll eat that poor man alive."

Greg chuckled. "I think it's best to leave them to fight it out. Nigel prefers it that way. He'd rather be eaten alive in an embittered battle with his oldest friend than endure the quiet peace of his former life." He paused. "To be honest, I can't say I blame him. Fighting with Grandpa will be one heck of an entertaining way to go."

"To go?" I echoed. Suddenly, our earlier hilarity was starting to feel misplaced. "What do you mean?"

"Exactly what it sounds like," Mateo said. "I suspected it from the start. The yellowing in his eyes, how thin he looks, the fact that he's throwing massive amounts of cash around—it's end-stage liver disease. He only has a few months left. He confirmed it on the way over here."

My mouth fell open in a soundless O. "That's why Grandpa's in the hospital again," Greg added. "The shock of hearing about Nigel's diagnosis sent his heart rate off the charts."

"No," I whispered. So many of us had lost important people in our lives; for this one to leave us before we even got to know him felt like the height of cruelty. "You must be mistaken. He can't possibly be terminal. That's not how any of this is supposed to end."

Every part of me yearned to turn back the page, to start over and smooth out the epilogue, but I didn't. Instead, I flipped open the book they'd given me—this great, heavy gift that I'd never be able to repay. I'd read through the story so many times that I found the section I was looking for within seconds.

Chapter 37, The Reaper Whose Name Is Death. The ending that turned out to be a beginning.

There, in bright orange, stood the words I'd never before taken the time to appreciate—the ones promising that life would go on, that joy was still to be had in the world. They were the words my sister had tried so hard to instill in me all those years ago, the words I'd been too young and too heartbroken to understand. It had taken twenty years and a stranger with an orange highlighter to finally break through.

She felt something like shame and remorse when she discovered that the sunrises behind the firs and the pale pink buds opening in the garden gave her the old inrush of gladness when she saw them—that Diana's visits were pleasant to her and that Diana's merry words and ways moved her to laughter and smiles—that, in brief, the beautiful world of blossom and love and friendship had lost none of its power to please her fancy and thrill her heart, that life still called to her with many insistent voices.

I clutched the book to my chest in sudden, heart-wrenching sadness. Not because of the people we'd lost and would continue to lose, but because even with that loss on every horizon, life still called to me.

Its voice took the form of an irascible old library patron who refused to let life quieten his passion, even when that passion burned hot to the touch. It spoke as a friendly neighbor across the street, who always had a smile and a cookie waiting. It was the sound of a coworker who'd been waiting patiently for me to notice his generous and never-wavering offer of friendship. It was even detectable in the low rumble of an angry-looking young man who was quite possibly the least angry person I'd ever known.

Life was calling to me—it had been calling to me for years—but it had taken this random, beautiful collection of people for me to realize what I had to do.

It was time for me to answer.

READING GROUP GUIDE

1. Books help shape the characters in *The Lonely Hearts Book Club* in different ways. Which character's approach to reading matches your own?

2. The novels that the book club chooses to read mirror what's going on within the characters' lives. What book best captures your life and outlook?

3. Arthur once used highlighted passages in a book to express his secret feelings for the woman he loved. If you were to choose a book to represent your love for someone, which one would it be and why?

4. Does *The Lonely Hearts Book Club* have a villain? If so, who is it?

5. Sloane teases Arthur with a social media challenge intended to knit two titles together to create a unique sentence. (For example, the darkly humorous *A Time to Kill Pollyanna*.) What are some other great combinations?

6. Mothers and their relationships with their children are a strong central theme in the book. How is each character shaped by the parents and/or children in their life?

7. Sloane describes herself as quiet, meek, and fairly average in every way—until she meets Arthur. What do you think it is about Arthur that encourages a spark within her?

8. The relationship between Arthur and Sloane is the backbone of the book. What do you think is so special about inter-generational friendships? What are some of your favorite inter-generational friendships across books and film?

9. In your opinion, is the ending to the book more happy or sad? As a reader, what are you meant to take away from it?

ABOUT THE AUTHOR

Lucy Gilmore is a celebrated novelist in a wide range of genres, including literary fiction, contemporary romance, and cozy mystery. She began her reading (and writing) career as an English literature major and ended as a book lover without all those pesky academic papers attached.

She lives in Spokane, Washington, with her family.

Visit her online at LucyGilmore.com.